Praise for *First Grave on the Right*

"Jones's wickedly witty debut will delight aficionados of such humorous paranormals as Casey Daniels's Pepper Martin Mysteries and Dakota Cassidy's Accidental Friends series." —*Booklist* (starred review)

"Jones skillfully establishes the novel's setting and keeps up the pace with plenty of action. And let's be honest—the sex is pretty hot, too. Fans of Sherrilyn Kenyon and other authors of paranormal romance will love this series debut." —*Library Journal* (starred review)

"Fast-talking Charley's wicked exuberance and lust for life will appeal to fans of MaryJanice Davidson and Janet Evanovich." —*Publishers Weekly*

"It's a fun, sexy, exciting read." —*Suspense Magazine*

"The best debut novel I've read in years! Hilarious and heartfelt, sexy and surprising . . . I'm begging for the next one!"
—J. R. Ward, *New York Times* bestselling author of *Lover Unleashed*

"This book is full of surprises and fun to be had for all. I barely finished this book and already can't wait to visit with Charley Davidson again in the next novel . . . deserves nothing less than a 'Five Angel, Recommend Read' status." —*Fallen Angel Reviews*

"A smashing, award-winning debut novel." —*Goodreads*

Praise for *Second Grave on the Left*

"Jones perfectly balances humor and suspense in her tight second paranormal thriller featuring grim reaper, PI, and 'all-around badass' Charley Davidson. . . . The fiery relationship between Charley and Reyes will satisfy paranormal romance fans, but it's the distinctive characters, dead and alive, and the almost constant laughs that will leave readers eager for the next installment."
—*Publishers Weekly* (starred review)

"Snarky, sassy Charley is back and taking no guff in Jones's funny, action-packed new offering. This time it's her traditional PI skills, rather than her grim reaper credentials, that are essential to solving two urgent cases. There is murder and mystery aplenty as Jones's fun read."
—*RT Book Reviews*

"In this follow-up novel to *First Grave on the Right* author Darynda Jones dives right in and delivers the readers into a very dangerous, crazy, and twisted life. I found the novel to be very interesting. I love that Jones has this interpretation of the grim reaper and Charley is written with a lot of wit and sarcasm, but not over the top."
—*Suspense Magazine*

"This is an amazing book and a fantastic series! I fell in love with this series from the cover of *First Grave* with the awesome skull shoes. When *Second Grave* arrived, I started doling out the chapters to make it last! Darynda Jones has an amazing talent. . . . In a lot of ways it is similar to Janet Evanovich's Stephanie Plum series only ten times better!"
—*Night Owl Reviews*

Praise for *Third Grave Dead Ahead*

"Smart, wickedly hilarious." —*Publishers Weekly* (starred review)

"If you enjoy Janet Evanovich's Stephanie Plum, you will certainly enjoy Charley Davidson! . . . you might want to invite a friend over to help disperse all the extra heat this book is likely to create!"

—*Suspense Magazine*

"Charlie continues to fascinate. Readers will be dying to know where the fourth grave is." —*Booklist*

"If you're game, Charley's sass and the suspenseful plot will keep you coming back for more." —*New Mexico Magazine*

Also by Darynda Jones

Second Grave on the Left

First Grave on the Right

Third Grave Dead Ahead

Darynda Jones

St. Martin's Griffin
New York

This is a work of fiction. All of the characters, organizations, and events portrayed in this novel are either products of the author's imagination or are used fictitiously.

 For information, address St. Martin's Press, 175 Fifth Avenue, New York, N.Y. 10010.

www.stmartins.com

The Library of Congress has cataloged the hardcover edition as follows:

Jones, Darynda.
Third grave dead ahead / Darynda Jones.
p. cm.
ISBN 978-1-250-00154-2 (hardback)
I. Title.
PS3610.O6236T48 2012
813'.6—dc23

2011033806

ISBN 978-1-250-00828-2 (trade paperback)

First St. Martin's Griffin Edition: July 2012

10 9 8 7 6 5 4 3 2 1

For Carol and Melvin,
aka the crazy people next door.

Love you, love you, love you.

Acknowledgments

As always, my deepest and most heartfelt thank-you to Jen and Alexandra, for making the sun shine and the moon glow. You have my heart forever. And to everyone at Macmillan and Janklow & Nesbit. I'd point fingers, but I'm sure I'd miss some deserving unsung hero in the process. You all rock so hard.

To my family, including but not limited to spouse, parents, grandparents, sisters, brothers, sons, daughters, first cousins, second cousins, first cousins once removed (I have no idea what that means), nieces, nephews, and my wonderful, wonderful family of friends. I have to thank especially my sister Annette, who is demanding royalties because I keep publishing tidbits of her life, my brother Luther for letting me use his name even though I didn't actually ask beforehand, and my brother Quentin for being the bestest most pimpin'-est pimp ever!

Thank-yous must go out to my critique goddess, Tammy, the incomparable Celeste Bradley, the beautiful Dan Dan, and the knockout Kit, who read this book at the speed of light to give me much-needed feedback. And, of course, thank you to the goddesses of LERA and the

Dorothys of the Ruby Slippered Sisterhood. Where would I be without you? Especially Liz. Thanks for naming my book!

And thank you so much to all the readers and reviewers who love Charley and Reyes's story as much as I do. May their adventures be many and their love everlasting. After, of course, I put them through the wringer.

A special thank-you to Mike Davidson for Garrett's list and for doing his darnedest to get me on *Oprah*. I'm sure my absence was an oversight. Thanks for giving it your all.

1

Death comes to those who wait.
And to those who don't. So either way . . .
—CHARLOTTE JEAN DAVIDSON, GRIM REAPER

There was a dead clown sitting in my living room. Since I wasn't particularly fond of clowns, and it was way too early for anything coherent to come out of my mouth, I pretended not to notice him. Instead, I let a loud yawn overtake me as I headed toward my kitchen. That was when a jolt of panic rushed through me. I glanced down to make sure my girl parts hadn't been compromised and sighed in relief. I had on a white tank and pair of plaid bottoms. My girls, also known as Danger and Will Robinson, were safe.

Mentally making the sign of the cross, I padded through my humble abode. Trying not to draw attention. Wondering if the dead clown, with his gaze following my every move, had noticed me. My apartment was a comfy cross between a storage room full of pillows and a broom closet, so it wasn't a long journey. Nor an especially enlightening one. Though I did come to a rather morbid conclusion in those few fleeting seconds: Better a dead clown in my apartment than a live one.

My name is Charlotte Davidson. Charley to some, Charlotte the Harlot to others, but that was mostly in middle school. I came with a decent set of curves, a healthy respect for the male anatomy, and a slightly disturbing addiction to brown edibles. Other than that—and the fact that I'd also been born the grim reaper—I was about as normal as a surly girl with a private investigator's license could be.

I strode toward Mr. Coffee with lust in my eyes. We'd had a thing for quite some time now, Mr. Coffee and I, and there was just enough of him left for one more cup. No need to make a fresh pot, to get him all hot and bothered. I popped the cup into the microwave, set it to nuke anything unfortunate enough to be caught within its grasp for thirty seconds, then raided my fridge for sustenance. Eating would keep me awake for at least another five minutes, and my one goal in life for the past couple of weeks was to stay awake at all costs. The alternative was exhausting.

After an epic search, I finally found something neither green nor fuzzy. It was a hot sausage link. I named it Peter, mostly because I liked naming things and partly because it seemed like the right thing to do. As soon as my java was piping hot I popped him into the microwave. Hopefully the radioactive environment would sterilize Peter. No need to have little Peters running around, wreaking havoc.

As I stood contemplating world peace, the exorbitant price of designer underwear, and what life would be like without guacamole, Peter beeped. I wrapped him in stale bread and ate him whilst loading my coffee up with enough imitation product to make it a health hazard. After a long draw, I plodded to my overstuffed sofa, sank into it, and looked at the dead clown. He was sitting in the club chair that catty-cornered my sofa, waiting patiently for me to acknowledge him.

"You know, I'm not really fond of clowns," I said after taking another sip.

Seeing a dead person in my living room was hardly a surprise. Apparently, I was super-duper bright, like the glowing lens of a lighthouse in a storm. The departed who didn't cross when they died could see me from anywhere on Earth and, if they so chose, could cross through me to get to the other side. That was pretty much the grim reaper gig in a nutshell. No scythes. No collecting souls. No ferrying the departed across a lake day in and day out, which would probably get old.

"I get that a lot," the clown said. He seemed younger than I'd originally suspected, perhaps twenty-five, but his voice was rough from too many cigarettes and late nights. The image conflicted with the bright mural on his face and curly red hair on his head. His saving grace was the lack of a big red nose. I seriously hated those, especially the squeaky kind. The rest I could handle.

"So, you got a story?"

"Not really." He shrugged. "Just wanted to cross."

I blinked in surprise, absorbed his statement, then asked, "You just want to cross?"

"If that's okay."

"That's more than okay," I said with a snort. No messages to loved ones left behind. No solving his murder. No hunting down some memento he'd left for his children in a place where no one in his right mind would ever think to look. These situations had all the creamy goodness of *piece of cake* without the added calories.

He started toward me then. I didn't get up, didn't think I could manage it—the coffee had yet to kick in—but he didn't seem to mind. I noticed as he stepped forward that he wore a ragged pair of jeans and his sneakers had been painted with Magic Marker.

"Wait," he said, pausing midstride.

No.

He scratched his head, a completely unconscious act from his previous life. "Can you get messages to people?"

Damn. The bane of my existence. "Um, no. Sorry. Have you tried Western Union?"

"Seriously?" he asked, not buying it for a minute. And it was on sale, even.

I sighed and tossed an arm over my forehead to show how much I didn't want to be his messenger, then peeked out from under my lashes. He stood there, waiting, unimpressed.

"Fine," I said, giving in. "I'll type a note or something."

"You don't have to do that. Just go to Super Dog right down the street and talk to a girl named Jenny. Tell her Ronald said to bite me."

I scanned his clown getup, the reds and yellows of his hoodie. "Your name is Ronald?"

With a grin, he said, "The irony is not lost on me, I promise." He stepped through before I could question him on the *bite me* part of his comment.

When people crossed, I could see their lives. I could tell if they'd been happy, what their favorite color was, the names of their pets growing up. It was a ritual I'd learned to savor. I let my lids drift shut and waited. He smelled like grease paint and iodine and coconut shampoo. He'd been in the hospital, waiting for a heart transplant. While there, he decided to make himself useful, so he dressed up like a different clown every day and visited the kids in pediatrics. Each day he'd have a new name, something funny like Rodeo Ron or Captain Boxer Shorts, and each day they had to guess what it was from his voiceless clues. He couldn't talk well near the end, and while gesturing was difficult and left him exhausted, he felt it was better than freaking out the kids with his gravelly voice. He died just hours before a heart had been found. Despite my original assumption, he'd never smoked a day in his life.

And he loved a girl named Jenny who smelled like baby oil and sold hot dogs to put herself through college. Jenny would be the part of this whole grim reaper gig I hated most. The people-left-behind part. I could feel their hearts contract with grief. I could feel their lungs fight for air. I could feel the sting of tears behind their eyes at losing someone they loved, someone they were sure they couldn't live without.

I sucked in a sharp breath and pulled myself back to the present. Ronald was a cool guy. I'd have to look him up when my time was up, see how his eternity was going. I sank farther into the sofa cushions and took a long draw of coffee, absorbing the caffeine, letting it spark and reawaken my brain cells.

Glancing at my *Looney Tunes* wall clock, I bit back the despair I felt at finding it was only 3:35. I had hours to go before dawn. It was easier to stay awake during the day. Night was so calm and relaxing. But I couldn't let myself fall under. I'd managed to dodge sleep like it was an ex-boyfriend with herpes for almost two weeks straight. And when I didn't, I paid the price.

The mere thought of that price gave me unwanted butterflies in my nether regions. I pushed it from my mind as heat from the sultry night wafted around me like a heavy vapor, seeping into my skin, suffocating any thoughts of comfort. Utterly annoyed, I sat up, pushed a dampened strand of hair out of my face, and headed to the bathroom, hoping a splash of cool water would help and wondering how the heck the night got so sultry. It was freaking November. Maybe global warming had amped up its game. Or a solar flare had pushed through the magnetosphere and was cooking us all alive. That would suck.

Just as I reached for the light switch, wondering if I should buy sunscreen, a sharp stab of arousal sparked in my lower abdomen. I gasped in surprise and grabbed the doorjamb for balance.

This was so not happening. Not again.

I glanced at the faucet longingly. Water would set things right. Couple of splashes and I'd be back to my normal curmudgeonly self in no time. I flipped the switch, but the overhead just flickered as though gasping for air, then died out. I flipped again. And again, before giving up. Mostly because the definition of insanity came to mind.

The wiring in my apartment demoted the term *code violation* to an understatement. Thankfully, I had a night-light. It cast a soft glow in the bathroom, allowing just enough illumination for me to maneuver my way to the sink without stubbing anything vital. I stepped to the mirror and squinted, trying to siphon every last atom of light the universe had to offer out of the atmosphere. It didn't help. My image was nothing more than a shadow, a ghostlike apparition, barely existing.

I stood there contemplating that fact when a ripple of desire gripped me again, seizing me with fierce, delicious claws, trembling through me so hard, I had to clamp my jaw shut. I clutched the vanity as the fervor bathed me in a sensuous heat I couldn't fend off. It seeped inside me, lured me to the edge, led me to the dark side. Hungrily, I parted my lips and parted my legs and gave it room to grow. And grow it did. It built up strength and power, its tendrils pushing into me, swirling and pulsing in my abdomen.

My knees buckled, and I shifted my weight to my palms as the pressure grew more intense, forcing me to fight for every breath I took. Then the sound of another's breath mingled with my own, and I glanced up into the mirror.

Reyes Alexander Farrow—the part-human, part-supermodel son of Satan—materialized behind me, his powerful shoulders glistening as steam rose around him, giving the impression he'd just come from hell. He hadn't, of course. He'd escaped from hell centuries ago and was currently furious with me for binding his incorporeal body to his physical one. But that knowledge did little to lessen the effect.

I squinted to see him more clearly. "What are you doing here?"

He lowered his head, his dark eyes piercing me with an angry glare. The butthead. It was my bathroom.

But I'd bound him. I'd bound his incorporeal body to his physical one. How was he even there? How could he be?

"You summoned me," he said, his deep voice tight with animosity.

I shook my head. "That's impossible."

He reached an arm over my shoulder and braced his hand against the wall in front of me. To tower. To dominate. To make sure I knew I was trapped. His lean body pressed against my backside as he braced the other hand against the wall to my right, completely imprisoning me.

His hard gaze locked on to mine. "Is it impossible because you bound me like a dog to a chain?"

Oh, yeah. He was pissed. "You left me no choice," I said, my voice quivering, not nearly as confident as I'd hoped.

He lowered his head until his mouth was at my ear. "And you leave me none." His features darkened. His eyes narrowed as he stared at me in the mirror from underneath his thick lashes, hooded with passion.

I couldn't look away. He was so beautiful, so masculine. When he wrapped an arm around me, slid his hand down the front of my panties, I grabbed his wrist. "Wait," I said between ragged breaths. "I still don't understand how you're here."

"I told you, you summoned me." His fingers tunneled between my legs despite my best efforts, and I gasped aloud when they dipped inside. "You always summon me. You've always had the power to call me whenever you want or need me, Dutch. Or haven't you figured that out yet?"

I fought the delicious sensations spiking in my abdomen with each stroke of his fingers. Fought to grasp the meaning of his breathy words. "No, you've always come to me when I needed you. When I was in danger." And he had. Growing up, he'd always been there anytime my life was threatened.

His breath fanned across my cheek, the heat emanating off him scorching as his mouth sought the pulse point at my throat. "It's always been you."

He was wrong. He had to be. The idea that I could summon him, that I'd always summoned him, was unfathomable. I didn't even know what he was until very recently. I was afraid of him, in fact. He was a dark being made of smoke and shadows, and the last thing I wanted was to be in his presence. How could I have summoned him? What he proposed was impossible.

"But as long as I'm here . . ." He let that statement linger as he locked me against him and pushed down my bottoms and underwear in one smooth movement. Then he let the slightest grin lift one corner of his beautiful mouth, nudged my legs apart, and entered me in one long thrust. I gasped aloud, and the swirling that had begun only moments before grew to hurricane strength in an instant. I clamped one hand around his wrist at my throat, the other on to his steely buttocks, pulling him deeper, clawing for release.

I kept my eyes open, watching him in the mirror, studying his reaction. The slight parting of his lips. The furrowing of his brow. The fall of his lashes.

"Dutch," he said in his smooth, deep voice, as though helpless against what he was about to do. His jaw locked together as his climax neared. He lifted one of my legs onto the vanity and pushed into me, burying himself over and over, the act almost violent, coaxing me with each thrust, with each powerful stroke.

And with each stroke, the current inside me surged with more potency, his erection filling a need so deep, so visceral, it devoured every inch of my being. The raw yearning that lingered in the distance rushed forward to pool between my legs. It swelled like a tide, milking me, coaxing me ever closer.

My fingernails dug into his wrist, suddenly remembering he didn't want to be there. Not with me. Not after what I'd done. "Reyes, wait."

I felt it the moment it seized him, felt it quake and convulse through his body, and in an instant an explosion burst and shot through me, sending a sharp sting of pleasure ricocheting against my bones, coursing through my veins, searing my flesh with a scalding ecstasy.

And then the world came crashing in as the violence of an orgasm splitting me in two jolted me from a fitful sleep. The dying remnants of a scream echoed in the room, and I knew instantly it was my own reaction to the climax. I forced myself to pause, to catch my breath, to unclench my fists from around the coffee cup that had emptied its contents in my lap. Luckily, there wasn't much left. I put the cup on a side table, then I fell back onto the sofa and threw an arm over my forehead to wait out the familiar storm trembling through my body.

Three times in one week. Within seconds of closing my eyes, he'd be there, waiting, watching, angry and seductive.

I glanced at the clock again. The last time I'd looked, it really did say 3:35. Now it said 3:38. Three minutes. I'd closed my eyes three minutes ago.

With an exhausted sigh, I realized it was my own fault. I'd let myself drift.

Maybe this was Reyes's way of making me pay for what I'd done. He'd always been able to leave his body, to become incorporeal and wreak all kinds of havoc on humanity. Not that he actually wreaked havoc, but he could've had he wanted to. Now he was stuck in his body. A minor indiscretion if you asked me, and when I bound him, a necessary one.

But now he was back to haunting my dreams. At least when he'd entered my dreams before, I actually got some sleep between rounds of hide-and-seek and tug-of-war. Now, I close my eyes for a second and he's there in the most intense way possible. As long as I'm asleep, we're going at it like rabbits on a bunny farm.

And the worst part of the whole thing lay in the fact that he really was pissed as hell at me. As a result, he had no desire to be there. He was angry, consumed with rage, and yet oh so passionate, like he couldn't help himself. Like he couldn't control the heat coursing through him, the hunger in his veins. I couldn't exactly control myself either, so I knew how he felt.

But I'd summoned him? Impossible. How could I have summoned him growing up? Like that time I was four and I was almost kidnapped by a convicted child molester? I didn't even know what he was. I'd been scared of him.

Just then, I heard my front door crash open and decided it was time to clean up anyway. Coffee never felt as good on the outside.

"What? Where are you?" I heard my neighbor who moonlighted as my receptionist and best friend say as she stumbled into my apartment. Cookie's short black hair stuck out in all kinds of socially unacceptable directions. And she wore wrinkled pajamas, striped in alternating blues and yellows that fit tight around her robust middle half with long red socks that bunched around her ankles. She was such a challenge.

"I'm here," I said, hoisting myself off the sofa. "Everything's okay."

"But you screamed." Alarmed, she scanned the area.

"We really need to soundproof these walls." She lived right across the hall and could apparently hear a feather drop in my kitchen.

After taking a moment to catch her breath, she leveled a cold stare at me. "Charley, damn it."

"You know, I get called that a lot," I said, padding toward the bathroom, "but Charley Damn It's not really my name."

She stepped toward my bookcase and braced herself with one hand while the other tried to still her beating heart. Then she glared. It was funny. Just as she opened her mouth to say something, she noticed the plethora of empty coffee cups scattered about the place. Then she glared again. It was still funny.

"Have you been drinking all night?"

I disappeared into the bathroom, came back with a toothbrush in my mouth, then pointed toward the front door with raised brows. "Break and enter much?"

She stepped around me and closed the door. "We need to talk."

Uh-oh. Scolding time. She'd been scolding me every day for a week. At first, I could lie about my lack of sleep and she'd fall for it, but she started suspecting insomnia when I began seeing purple elephants in the air vents at the office. I knew I shouldn't have asked her about them. I thought maybe she'd redecorated.

I went to my bedroom and changed into a fresh pair of pj's, then asked, "Want coffee?" as I headed that way.

"It's three thirty in the morning."

"Okay. Want coffee?"

"No. Sit down." When I paused midstride and raised my brows in questions, she set a stubborn tilt to her jaw. "I told you, we need to talk."

"Does this have anything to do with that mustache I drew on you while you were sleeping the other night?" I lowered myself slowly onto the sofa, keeping a wary eye on her, just in case.

"No. This has to do with drugs."

My jaw fell open. I almost lost my toothbrush. "You're on drugs?"

She pressed her mouth together. "No. You are."

"I'm on drugs?" I asked, stunned. I had no idea.

"Charley," Cookie said, her voice sympathetic, "how long has it been since you've slept?"

With a loud sigh that bordered on a whine, I counted on my fingers. "Around thirteen days, give or take."

Her eyes widened with shock. After she let that sink in, she asked, "And you're not on anything?"

I took the toothbrush out of my mouth. "Besides Crest?"

"Then how are you doing it?" She leaned forward, her brows glued together in concern. "How are you not sleeping for days at a time?"

"I don't know. I just don't close my eyes."

"Charley, that's impossible. And probably dangerous."

"Not at all," I assured her. "I'm drinking lots of coffee. And I hardly ever fall asleep while driving."

"Oh, my gosh." She let her head drop into her palm.

I popped the toothbrush back into my mouth with a smile. People like Cookie were hard to come by. Stalwart. Loyal. Easy to punk. "Hon, I'm not like you, remember?"

She focused on me again. "You're still human. Just because you heal really fast and can see the departed and you have this uncanny ability to convince the most mundane of persons to try to kill you—"

"But he's so mad at me, Cook." I lowered my head, the sadness of my situation creeping up on me.

She stopped and absorbed my statement before commenting. "Tell me exactly what's going on."

"'Kay. Need coffee first."

"It's three thirty in the morning."

Ten minutes later, we both had a cup of coffee à la fresco, and I was in the middle of describing my dreams—if one could call them that—to a starry-eyed divorcée with lust in her loins. She already knew about my binding Reyes to his physical body, but she didn't know about the dreams.

Not entirely. I'd just told her about my most recent encounter with God Reyes, a being forged in the fires of hell, created from beauty and sin and fused together with the blistering heat of sensuality.

I fanned myself and refocused on her.

"He was actually—"

"Yep," I said.

"And he put your leg—?"

"Yep. I think for ease of access."

"Oh, my." A hand floated up to cover her heart.

"Yep again. But that's the cool part. The orgasmic part. The part where he touches me and kisses me and strokes me in the most amazing places."

"He kissed you?"

"Well, no, not this morning," I said, shaking my head. "But sometimes he does. Strange thing is, he doesn't want to be there. He doesn't *want* to be with me. And yet, the minute I close my eyes, there he is. Fierce. Sexy. Pissed as hell."

"But he actually lifted your leg—?"

"Cookie," I said, grabbing her arm and forcing her to focus, "you have to get past that part."

"Right." She blinked and shook her head. "Right, sorry. Well, I can certainly see why you don't want to experience *that* kind of trauma night after night."

"But I don't get any actual rest. I swear I'm more exhausted when I wake up, like, three minutes later. And he's just so mad at me."

"Well, you did bind him for all eternity."

I sighed. "Surely it's not for all eternity. I mean, I can fix this." I decided to leave out the part where I'd already tried to unbind him and failed miserably. "I'll figure out how to unbind him, don't you think?"

"You're asking me?" she asked, balking at the very idea. "This is your world, hon. I'm just an innocent bystander." She looked at my *Looney Tunes* clock.

As usual, my selfless concern for my fellow man amazed me. "You need to get back to bed," I said, taking her cup and heading for the kitchen. "You can get in a good two hours before you have to get Amber up for school." Amber was Cookie's twelve-going-on-thirty-year-old daughter.

"I just drank a cup of coffee."

"Like that ever stopped you."

"True." She stood and headed for the door. "Oh, I meant to tell you, Garrett called. He might have a case for you. Said he'd get in touch this morning."

Garrett Swopes was a bond enforcement agent whose dark skin made the silver in his eyes glisten every time he smiled, a feature most women found attractive. I just found him annoying. We'd weathered some rough times, he and I, like when he accidently found out about my otherworldly status and decided to have me committed.

For the most part, he was okay. For the rest, he could bite me. But as a skiptracer, he was phenomenal and came in super-duper handy at times.

"A case, huh?" That sounded intriguing. And slightly more profitable than sitting around twiddling my thumbs. "Maybe I'll just run over there and talk to him about it in person."

She stopped halfway out the door and looked back at me. "It's a quarter past four."

A huge smile slid across my face.

Her own expression turned dreamy again. "Can I come?"

"No." I pushed her out the door. "You have to get some sleep. Somebody has to be sane during regular office hours, and it's not going to be me, missy."

A little over fifteen minutes later, as I stood knocking on Garrett Swopes's door in my Juicy Couture pajamas and pink bunny slippers, I realized I may have died on the way over. I was so tired, I could no longer feel life flowing through me. My fingers were numb. My lips were swollen. And my eyelids had dried to the consistency of sandpaper, their sole purpose to irritate and drive the will to survive right out of me.

Yep, I was most likely dead.

I knocked again as a shiver rippled down my spine, hoping somewhere in the back of my mind that my probable deadness wouldn't keep me from performing my supernatural duty, which was basically to stand there while dead people who hadn't crossed immediately after their deaths crossed through me. But as the only grim reaper this side of forever, I provided an invaluable service for society. For humanity. *For the world!*

The door swung open and a grumpy skiptracer named Garrett stood glowering at me with a fury I found difficult to describe, which meant I probably hadn't died after all. He looked like he had a hangover. When hungover, Garrett could barely see elephants, much less the departed. He managed to growl a question from between his clenched teeth. "What?"

"I need ibuprofen," I said, my voice distant and unattractive.

"You need therapy." It was amazing how easily I could understand him, considering he had yet to unclench his teeth.

"I need ibuprofen," I said with a frown, in case he didn't hear me the first time. "I'm not kidding."

"I'm not either."

"But I wasn't kidding first."

With a loud sigh, he stood back and motioned me inside the bat cave. I looked down at my bunny slippers, silently begging them to hop forward, when Garrett curled his fingers into my Juicies and eased me inside.

It helped. With the momentum I'd gained, I crossed his carpet straight to his kitchen cabinets, flipping light switches along the way.

"Do you have any idea what time it is?" he asked.

"Not especially. Where are your over-the-counter drugs?" I'd recently developed a headache. Possibly when I hit that telephone pole on the way over.

Garrett's bachelor pad was much tidier than I'd expected. Lots of tans and blacks. I rummaged through cabinet after cabinet in search of his drug stash. Instead I found glasses. Plates. Bowls. Okay.

He stopped short behind me. "What are you looking for again?"

I paused long enough to glower. “You can’t be this slow.”

He did that thing where he pinched the bridge of his nose with his thumb and forefinger. It gave me a chance to size him up. Mussed dark hair in need of a trim. Thick stubble along his jaw also in need of a trim. Manly chest hair also in need—

“Oh, my god!” I said, throwing my hands over my eyes and hurtling my body against the counter.

“What?”

“You’re naked.”

“I’m not naked.”

“I’m blind.”

“You’re not blind. I’m wearing pants.”

“Oh.” That was embarrassing.

He shifted his stance in impatience. “Would you like me to put on a shirt?”

“Too late. Scarred for life.” I had to tease him a little. He was so grouchy at four thirty in the morning. I went back to scouring his cabinets.

“Seriously, what are you looking for?”

“Painkillers,” I said, feeling my way past a military-issue canteen and a package of Oreos. Oreos just happen to fall under the category of brown edibles. I popped one in my mouth and continued my noble quest.

“You came all the way over here for painkillers?”

I gave him a second once-over while crunching. Other than the bullet wounds he now sported on his chest and shoulder from when I almost got him killed a couple weeks ago, he had good skin, healthy eyelashes, six-pack abs. Cookie may have been on to something. “No, I came over here to talk to you,” I said, swallowing hard. “I just happen to need painkillers at this moment in time. They in the bathroom?” I headed that way.

“I ran out,” he said, blocking my path, clearly hiding something.

“But you’re a bond enforcement agent.”

His brows snapped together. “What the hell does that mean?”

“Come on, Swopes,” I said, my voice sharp with accusation, “I know you track down drug dealers when you're not watching *Debbie Does Dallas*. You have access to all kinds of drugs. You can't tell me you don't pocket a little crack here, a few prescription-strength Motrin there."

After scrubbing his face with his fingers, he strolled to a small dining room table, pulled out a chair, and sat down. "Isn't your sister a psychiatrist?"

I stepped into his bedroom and switched on the light. Besides the rumpled bed and clothes strewn about the room, it wasn't bad. I hit the dresser first.

"Actually, I'm glad you're here," Garrett called out. "I might have a case for you."

That was exactly why I'd come over, but he didn't need to know that. "I'm not cleaning out your truck in search of some mysteriously lost object again, Swopes. I caught on."

"No, a real case," he said, a smile in his voice, "through a friend of a friend. Seems this guy's wife went missing about a week ago and he's looking for a good PI."

"So why send him to me?" I asked, stumped.

"Are you finished in there?"

I'd just gone through his nightstands and was headed for the medicine cabinet in his bathroom. "Just about. Your choice of porn is more eclectic than I thought it would be."

"He's a doctor."

"Who's a doctor?" Nothing of use in his medicine cabinet. Absolutely nothing. Unless nondrowsy allergy medication could be considered a painkiller.

"The guy whose wife is missing."

"Oh, right."

Who on planet Earth didn't have aspirin in the house? My head ached, for heaven's sake. I'd nodded off on the way over to Garrett's place and veered into oncoming traffic. The honking horns and flashing lights had me believing I'd been abducted by aliens. Thank goodness a well-placed telephone pole put a stop to that nonsense. I needed stronger coffee to keep me awake. Or maybe something else entirely. Something industrial.

I peeked around the door and asked, "Do you keep syringes of adrenaline on hand?"

"There are special programs for people like you."

In a moment of sheer terror, I realized I couldn't feel my brain. It was just there a minute ago. Maybe I really was dead. "Do I look dead to you?"

"Does your sister have an after-hours emergency number?"

"You're not helping," I said, making sure the disgust in my voice was unmistakable. "You would suck as a customer service representative."

He unfolded himself from the chair and headed for the fridge. "Want a beer?"

I shuffled to the table and stole his seat. "Seriously?"

A brow arched into a shrug as he twisted the cap off a bottle.

"No, thank you. Alcohol is a depressant. I need these lids to stay open for days." I pointed to them for visual confirmation.

"Why?" he asked after a long swig.

"Because when they're closed, *he's* there."

"God?" Garrett guessed.

"Reyes."

Garrett's jaw pressed shut. Probably because he wasn't horridly fond of Reyes or our unconventional relationship. Then again, nobody ever said consorting with the son of Satan would be easy. He set the beer on the counter and strode to his room, his movements suddenly sharp, exact. I watched him disappear—he had a nice tapering thing going on—and reappear almost instantly with shirt and boots in hand. "Come on, I'll drive you home."

"I came in Misery."

"Exactly, and I think you've caused enough."

"No, my Jeep. Misery? Remember her?" Sometimes people found it odd that I'd named my cherry red Jeep Wrangler Misery, but Gertie just didn't seem to fit. "She'll be upset if I just leave her here on a strange side street. Alone. Injured."

He looked back at me, startled. "You wrecked your Jeep?"

I had to think about that one. "I can't be entirely certain. There was a telephone pole, screeching tires, the strong possibility of alien life. It all happened so fast."

"Seriously. I need your sister's number." He shrugged into the shirt as he hunted down his keys.

"Desperate much? Besides, you're not my sister's type."

After Garrett escorted me to his truck none-too-gently, he climbed into the driver's side and brought the vehicle to life with a roar. The engine sounded pretty good, too. I gazed out the window as we swam through Albuquerque, the night thick with an almost impenetrable darkness. The tranquil serenity didn't help my current predicament. My scratchy lids were like lead and grew heavier and heavier with every minute that passed. Every second. Despite the discomfort, I fought with all my strength to keep them open, because this was better than the alternative: Reyes Farrow being drawn into my dreams against either of our wills, like an invisible force pulled him toward me every time I closed my eyes. And once inside my head, all our anger and inhibitions washed away into a sea of sensuality where mouths scorched and hands explored. Which sucked because we were both quite annoyed with each other.

But for him to say that I'd summoned him just didn't make sense. I'd have to look into that one.

"How long have you been awake?"

I snapped back to Garrett and looked at my watch. Or, well, my wrist where my watch would have been had I remembered it. "Um, about thirteen days."

He seemed to still beside me. I couldn't be sure, though. I was drifting in and out of reality, if the little girl with the kitchen knife on his hood was any indication. I suppose she could have been a departed, but they rarely rode on hoods.

"Look, I realize you're different than the average human," Garrett said, his tone guarded, "but thirteen days without sleep can't be good for anyone, not even you."

"Probably not. Did you buy a new hood ornament?"

He glanced at his hood. "No."

"This doctor have a name?"

He reached across my lap into the glove box and pulled out a card. "Here's his info. He's supposed to go to your office this morning if you make it in."

Dr. Nathan Yost. "I'll make it in. Is he a friend of yours?"

"Nope. He's an asshole. But everyone else on planet Earth seems to worship him."

"All righty, then." I tried to stuff the card into a pocket, then realized I didn't have any. "Hey, I left my bag in Misery."

Garrett shook his head. "The things you say, Charles. Oh, I keep meaning to tell you, I've been working on a special list of things one should never say to the grim reaper."

I chuckled. "I have so many comebacks to that, I don't think I can pick just one."

"I'll start at the bottom," he said with a grin. "Are you ready?"

I shrugged my right eyebrow. "As I'll ever be."

"Okay, number five, *I'm dead tired*."

"So, it's not a particularly long list."

"Do you want to hear the list or not?" he asked as we pulled into the parking lot of my apartment building.

"I'm weighing my options. This list could either be a revelation of apocalyptic proportions or a complete waste of my limited brain fuel. I'm leaning toward the latter."

"Fine, I'll tell you the rest when you're in a better mood. It'll make it more suspenseful."

"Good idea," I said with a thumbs-up. Suspenseful, my ass.

"Nobody recognizes true talent anymore." He escorted me upstairs.

"Are you going to get some sleep?" he asked as I inched the door closed between us, leaving him in the hallway.

"Not if I can help it." At least he'd been of some use to me. I'd made it through another hour without sleep.

Just as I closed the door and turned toward the coffeepot, he reopened it, muttered, "Lock this," then closed it again.

I trudged back and locked the door only to hear keys jiggling in the lock about two seconds later. Either that, or I'd fallen asleep standing up again. Since Reyes hadn't appeared to offer me an earth-shattering climax, probably not.

Cookie burst in, walked right past me, and headed straight for the coffeepot. "Did you talk to Garrett?"

I followed her. "Yep. I think there was a clown in my apartment this morning."

"Are my pajamas that bad?" she asked, surveying the pj's she still wore.

"No." I blinked back to her. "A dead clown."

"Oh. Like a departed?"

"Yes."

"Is he gone?" she asked, glancing around in concern.

"Yes. He crossed."

"Well, that explains the clown comment. I just thought you were being a smart-ass."

That trip made me super sleepy. Maybe I really did need a shot of adrenaline. "Hey, I thought you were going back to bed."

"I was, but visions of sugarplums kept dancing through my head. Sugarplums of the male variety, if you know what I mean. Speaking of which," she said, taking a long draw on her java, "was Garrett naked?"

"Why would Garrett be naked?" I asked, carefully placing a frown on my face to camouflage the giggle bubbling up inside.

"I was just wondering if he sleeps naked."

"I have no idea if he sleeps naked. He would hardly answer the door that way."

She nodded in thought. "That's a good point. Oh, crap, I have to get Amber up for school."

"Okay, I need a shower anyway. I still smell like coffee. And I need to run by Super Dog sometime today. Don't let me forget." I headed for the bathroom.

"You got it. Oh," Cookie said, pausing at the door, "I meant to tell you, I borrowed a can of coffee from the office."

I stopped and hit her with my best glower of astonished disappointment. "You stole a can of coffee from the office?"

"I *borrowed* a can of coffee from the office. I'll buy another with my next paycheck."

"I can't believe this."

"Charley . . ."

"Just kidding. Don't worry about it," I said with a wave of my hand. "It's not like I pay for the stuff."

She had started out the door but stopped again. "What?"

"The coffee. I don't actually pay for it."

"Where do you get it?"

"I swipe it from Dad's storeroom." When she flashed me a look of shock and disapproval, mostly disapproval, I held up my hands and did the time-out gesture. "Hold up there, missy. I solved cases for that man for years. The least he can do is provide me with a cup o' joe every now and then."

My dad had been a detective with the Albuquerque Police Department, and I'd been helping him solve crimes since I was five. For some reason, it's a lot easier to solve crimes when you can ask the victim who did it. While my dad retired a few years ago, I still did the same for my uncle Bob, also a detective with APD.

"You steal our coffee from your dad?"

"Yep."

"I drink stolen coffee?"

"On a daily basis. Do you remember that morning about a month ago when we were out of coffee and then that guy came in with a gun and tried to kill me, and Reyes materialized out of nowhere and sliced his spine in half with that ginormous sword he keeps tucked under his robe, and Uncle Bob came with all those cops, and my dad started questioning the whole spinal cord thing?"

After a long moment, she said, "Barely," her voice dripping with sarcasm.

"Well, I needed a cup of coffee after that near-death experience like you would not believe, and we didn't have any. So I took a can out of Dad's storeroom."

"Charley," she said, looking around as if someone were listening, "you can't just steal your dad's coffee."

"Cook, at that moment in time, I would have sold my body for a mocha latte."

She nodded in understanding. "I can certainly see why you did it that one time, but you can't keep doing it."

"Oh, so it's okay for you to steal, but not me?"

"I wasn't stealing. I was borrowing."

"Whatever helps you sleep at night, *Bonnie.* Say hey to Clyde for me."

With a loud sigh, she headed out the door again. Just before I closed the bathroom door, I called out to her, "By the way, he answered the door shirtless."

After a loud gasp, she said, "Thank you."

2

There is a great need for a sarcasm font.

—T-SHIRT

I took a quick shower, pulled my hair into a ragged ponytail, and dressed in a pair of comfortable jeans, a loose black sweater, and a pair of killer boots I got off a biker for a lap dance. He was pretty darned good, too, after I got past my aversion to back hair.

"I'm leaving the whole shebang in your hands, Mr. Wong!" I shouted as I gathered up my paraphernalia. Mr. Wong had come with the apartment and acted as part roommate and part creepy dead guy hovering in the corner. I'd never actually seen his face. It was difficult to see with his nose buried in the corner day after day, year after year. But his plain, gray clothing suggested he'd likely been an immigrant from the 1800s or even a Chinese prisoner of war. Either way, I liked him. I just wish I knew his real name. I called him Mr. Wong because he looked more like a Mr. Wong than a Mr. Zielinski. "Don't do anything I wouldn't do."

Cookie had taken her daughter, Amber, to school then walked the thirty-something feet to work earlier. Our business was on the second floor of Calamity's, my dad's bar, which sat right in front of our apartment building. The short commute was nice and rarely involved rabid raccoons.

I strolled to the office, my thoughts wandering, as they always did, to Reyes Farrow. The moment I closed my eyes, he was there, and it seemed like neither of us had any control over that fact whatsoever.

I was smack-dab in the middle of reviewing our last encounter in my mind, my girl parts tingling at the mere thought of him, when a wave of sadness drew me out of my musings. As a reaper, I could feel emotion radiate off people, but normally the emotions of the everyday person didn't interfere with my thoughts. I'd learned long ago to block them out, like white noise, unless I purposely wanted to read them, to study the aura of someone I was investigating. Today, however, the heart-wrenching emotions emanating from a car across the street caught my attention. Oddly, they seemed to be directed my way. I glanced over. An older-model Buick sat idling half-obscured by a delivery truck, and I could just make out a woman with dark hair and large sunglasses as she watched me cross the parking lot. The reflection of the early morning sun made it impossible to gather any specifics.

While I normally entered through the back entrance of the bar and took the interior set of stairs to my office, today I decided to go around to the front in hopes of a better look at her.

I was doing my best nonchalance, glancing to the side as much as the next person would, when the woman shifted into drive and took off. The sadness and fear she'd left in her wake saturated the air around me, and I couldn't help but breathe it in.

I paused on the sidewalk and felt inside my pocket for a pen to write down her license plate number on my palm. Alas, I had no pen. And I'd already forgotten several of the six digits. There was an *L,* I think. And a 7. Damn my short-term memory.

Without giving it another thought, I hiked up the stairs to the office. The front door led directly into the reception area, fondly referred to as Cookie's God Danged Office so Keep Your Dirty Feet off the Stinkin' Furniture. Or CGDOSKYDFOTSF for short.

"Hey, hon," she said without looking up from her computer.

I hoofed it to the coffeepot that resided in my own little slice of official heaven. The offices of Davidson Investigations were a tad dark and dated, but I had high hopes wood paneling would come back into style eventually. "The oddest thing just happened to me."

"You remembered the night you lost your virginity?"

"I wish. There was a woman parked in the street watching me."

"Hmmm," she hmmed, only slightly interested.

"And she reeked of sadness. It just consumed her."

Cookie looked up at last. "Do you know why?"

"No, she took off before I could talk to her." I scooped enough coffee grinds into the filter to give it the taste and texture of unrefined motor oil.

"That is strange. You know your dad's going to figure out you're stealing his coffee. He was a detective for over twenty years."

"See this?" I asked, showing her my pinkie between the doorways. "I have that man wound tight around this baby. So don't sweat it, *chiquita*."

"Don't expect me to visit you in prison." A tinkling bell sounded as the front door opened. "Can I help you?" Cookie asked as I walked into the reception area for a look-see.

"Yes, I need to talk to Charley Davidson." A nice-looking man with light hair and pale blue eyes walked up. He wore a white doctor's lab coat with a sky blue shirt and navy tie and had an expensive briefcase in one hand. With my super-sleuth powers of deduction, I decided he could be the very doctor Garrett had told me about.

"I'm Charley," I said, but I didn't smile in case I was wrong and he was really there to sell me magazine subscriptions. I didn't want to encourage him.

He reached out his hand. "I'm Dr. Nathan Yost. I got your name from Garrett Swopes." For a man with a missing wife, his innards were oddly panic-free. His emotions were in turmoil, just not the kind of turmoil one would expect from a man with a missing wife. A missing dog maybe. Or a missing eyebrow after a night of debauchery, but not a missing wife. Still, his hair was mussed and unkempt and his eyes were lined with fatigue and worry, so he fit all the grieving-husband criteria at first glance.

"Please, come in." I showed him into my office. "The coffee'll be ready in a minute, or I can offer you a bottled water," I said after he sat down.

"No, nothing for me, but thank you very much."

"Not at all." I sat behind my desk. "Garrett told me you'd be coming in. Can you tell me what happened?"

He straightened his tie and glanced around at the artwork covering my walls. I had three paintings that my friend Pari had done. Two were very old school detective—the detectives female, naturally, with fedoras, trench coats, and smoking guns to go along with their sultry gazes. And the one right behind my desk was a little more goth, with a young girl washing blood from her sleeves. It was just enough of an abstract to make it difficult to see exactly what she was doing, an inside joke between Pari and me. Mostly because laundry day ranked right up there with paper cuts and stubbed toes.

"Absolutely," he said after taking a deep breath. "My wife has been missing for a little over a week."

"I'm terribly sorry," I said, fishing out a notepad and pen from my desk. "Can you explain what happened?"

"Of course." His expression turned mournful. "My wife was out late with some friends, so I wasn't worried when I woke up around midnight and she wasn't home yet."

"What day was this?" I asked, taking notes.

He raised his eyes and thought back. "Last Friday night. So, I woke up Saturday morning and she still wasn't home."

"And you tried her cell?"

"Yes, and then I called the friends she'd been out with."

"And was her cell on?"

"Her cell?"

I paused and looked up at him. "Her cell phone, when you called it, was it on or did it go straight to voice mail?"

"I'm not sure," he said, his brows sliding together. "Um, voice mail, I think. I was very upset by that point."

Wrong answer. "Naturally. What time did she leave her friends?"

"Around two."

"I'll need their names and contact information."

"Of course." He combed through his briefcase and handed me a piece of paper from a leather portfolio he'd retrieved. "This is a list of most of her friends. The ones she was out with that night are starred."

"Great, thank you. And what about family?"

"Her parents died a few years ago, but she has a sister here in Albuquerque and a brother in Santa Fe. He owns a construction company. You know"—he scooted closer to my desk—"they weren't really close. It's not something she liked to talk about, but I wanted you to know in case they seem uncooperative."

Interesting. "I understand. Little of that in my family, too." While my sister and I had recently reconnected after years of borderline apathy, my stepmother and I had barely spoken in decades. Since most things out of her mouth were rude and self-centered, I'd always considered our cool relationship a good thing.

I took down the names of her siblings and the places his wife had done volunteer work, just to make it all official looking. He'd stumbled a little with the verb tense, but I let it go for now.

"Has there been a ransom demand?"

"No, that's what the FBI's waiting for. I mean, that's what this has to be about, right? I'm well off. They just want money."

"I can't say, but it's certainly a motive. I think I have enough to get started. I just have one more question." I fixed an Alex Trebek gaze on him, sympathetic with a trace of arrogance, mostly because Alex clearly has the answer to Final Jeopardy! ahead of time. Kind of like me now. "Sometimes, we have a feeling, Dr. Yost, a gut instinct. Do you ever get those?"

Pain flashed across his face and he lowered his head. "Yes, I do."

"Do you have one now? Do you feel like your wife is still out there, waiting for you to find her?"

With his stare still locked on the floor, he shook his head. "I would like to believe she is, but I just don't know anymore."

Wrong answer again. He would totally suck at Final Jeopardy! The slip in verb tense, the fact that he didn't know if his wife's phone had been on or not—had he actually been looking for her, he would have known—and the fact that he hadn't used his wife's name throughout the entire conversation all added up to a wealthy doctor with blood on his hands. The omission of his wife's name meant that he no longer saw her as a living, breathing person. While that didn't necessarily mean Mrs. Yost was dead, it was a strong indicator. Either that or he was purposely trying not to see her as a person, trying to put her out of his mind.

But the final nail was the fact that people with missing spouses or children clutched on to the belief that their loved ones were still alive with every ounce of strength they could squeeze out of their bodies, especially after only a week. Sometimes even seeing a loved one's remains didn't help. They simply couldn't let go. But someone who had killed his spouse would never know to cling on to that hope, no matter how false it might be. Which meant Mrs. Yost was most likely dead. But I wasn't about to tip him off to the fact I knew he was as guilty as sin on Sunday, just in case I was wrong. If she were alive, I'd need time to find her before he finished the job.

"I understand," I said. "But I want you to hold on to the belief that she's okay, Dr. Yost."

He looked at me, his eyes filled with fabricated grief. "So, you'll take the case?" he asked, his face brightening. After all, a grieving husband doing anything possible to find his missing wife would look less suspicious.

"Well, I have to be honest, Dr. Yost, with the FBI already on it, I'm not sure what more I can do."

"But, you can do something, right? I can write you a check right now if it's about the money." He pulled out a checkbook from the portfolio and patted his shirt pocket for a pen.

"No, it's not about the money," I said, shaking my head. "I just don't want to take yours if there's nothing I can do."

He nodded in understanding.

"Let me look into this for a couple of days. If I think I can be of any help to your wife, I'll give you a call."

"All right," he said, a spark of hope resurfacing. "So, you'll call me?"

"Absolutely."

I led him to the door and placed a hand on his shoulder. "I promise, I'll do everything I can for her."

A sad smile slid across his face. "I'll pay anything."

I saw the good doctor out, waited a hot second, then turned to Cookie with a roll of my eyes. "That man is as guilty as my accountant."

Cookie gasped. "He's guilty? He doesn't look guilty."

"Neither does my accountant," I said, sifting through the papers on her desk.

She reached across and slapped my hand. "What's your accountant guilty of?"

I sucked on the back of my hand before answering. "Fudging numbers."

"Your accountant fudges numbers?"

"Why else would I pay someone to do my taxes? Anywho"—I hitched a thumb over my shoulder—"guilty. And we have another missing wife. They must be in season."

We'd just solved a missing wife case a couple of weeks ago. In the process, I was kidnapped, tortured, shot at, and I came pretty darned close to getting Garrett, Cookie, and our client killed. Not a bad week, if I did say so myself.

"So, he's guilty. Does that mean his wife is dead?"

I knew the statistics, and there was about a 95 percent chance of a resounding yes, but I refused to work under that assumption. "That part's a little fuzzy, but this guy is good. He only let his verb tense slip twice, letting me know he believes she's already dead. And he never once said her name."

"That's not good," Cookie said, her face lined with worry.

"If I hadn't felt the guilt radiating out of every pore in his body, I would've been completely fooled."

"I was fooled."

With an appreciative grin, I said, "You're always fooled. You always think the best of people. That's why we get along so well. You can't see past my charm and stunning beauty to the real me."

"Oh, no, I see the real you. I just feel sorry for the mentally challenged. I think you guys deserve just as much of a chance at a normal life as the next guy."

"That's so sweet," I said like a cheerleader on meth.

She shrugged. "I try to be a positive influence on the less fortunate."

Then a thought occurred to me. "Crap."

"What?"

"I just realized something."

"Did you forget to put on underwear again?"

I glanced at her point-blank. "Since the good doctor is guilty, he'll probably try to kill me soon. You might want to take precautions."

"Got it. Where should we start?"

"A Kevlar vest, maybe. Pepper spray at the very least."

"I meant on the case." Cookie looked past me into my office. "Oh, hi, Mr. Davidson."

I turned as Dad walked in. He'd come up from the bar by way of the inside stairs, which was fine, since he owned it and all. His tall, thin frame seemed to sag just a bit. His blond hair looked barely combed, and his bloodshot eyes were lined with a purplish hue. And not a pretty purple either. It was that dark grayish purple that depressed people wear.

Things hadn't quite been the same between us since he tried to have me murdered a while back. One of his collars from his former life as a detective had been released from prison and decided to get even with Dad by going after his family. So, by deftly placing a target on my back to save my sister and stepmother from the guy's dastardly plan, he'd almost gotten me killed. That part wasn't the problem. The problem lay in the fact that, believing they would catch the guy before any harm could be done, he neglected to tell me that he'd sent a killer my way. Thus leaving me vulnerable. He'd put Garrett Swopes on my tail, which would normally have been enough protection for the president making an anti-gun speech at the NRA, but the new guy Garrett had assigned to me decided to go for coffee right when the parolee decided to go on a killing spree. And I had a nasty scar across my chest to prove it. Or I would have had I not healed so fast. A grim reaper thing, apparently.

Those kinds of family indiscretions were hard to get past. Nevertheless, I was willing to let bygones be bygones, but the guilt that wafted off him like bargain-brand cologne acted as a constant reminder and seemed to keep him just out of arm's reach. He seemed unable to forgive himself. And that guilt was taking its toll, as guilt is wont to do.

So I couldn't tell if the powerful emotion pouring out of him now was a by-product of that incident or if this was something new and improved with no preservatives, fillers, or artificial colors. He was definitely frowning. Maybe he had heartburn. More likely, he'd heard the pepper spray comment.

"Hey, Dad." I bounced up and kissed him on his grumpy bear cheek.

"Hon, can I talk to you?"

"Abso-freaking-lutely. I'll be right back," I said to Cookie.

Dad nodded to her, then closed the door between our offices, not that it would help. That door made cardstock look indestructible.

"Is this about the coffee?" I asked, suddenly nervous.

"Coffee?"

"Oh"—*whew*—"um, want a cup?"

"No, you go ahead."

I made a quick cup of contraband coffee, then sat behind my desk as he folded himself into the chair across from me. "What's up?" I asked.

His gaze flitted toward me, paused, then veered off again, never quite touching mine. Not a good sign.

With a heavy sigh, he said what was on his mind in all its psychotic glory. "I want you to quit the investigations business."

Though his statement was only slightly less welcome than chlamydia, I had to give him kudos for using the direct approach. For a former detective who'd retired with honors, he could be the most evasive man in my immediate gene pool, so this was a nice change.

But give up my business? The same business I'd built from the ground up with my own two hands and designer Louis Vuittons? The same business for which I'd sacrificed blood, sweat, and tears? Well, maybe not sweat and tears, but there was blood. Lots of blood.

Give it up? Not likely. Besides, what else would I do? I totally should've gone to Hogwarts when I had the chance.

I shifted in my chair as Dad waited for a response. He seemed determined, his resolve unwavering. This would take tact. Prudence. Possibly Milk Duds.

"Are you psychotic?" I asked, realizing my plan to charm and bribe him if need be flew out the window the minute I opened my mouth.

"Charley—"

"Dad, no. I can't believe you're even asking this of me."

"I'm not asking." His sharp tone brought me up short, and all the huffing and puffing that had built beneath the surface slammed into me, knocking my breath away. Was he serious? "You can tend bar for me full-time until you find something else."

Apparently.

"Unless, of course, you want to stay on. I could use someone to do my books, keep inventory, and do the ordering."

What the hell?

"But I'll understand if you don't want to. I can help you get on somewhere else. Or you could go back to school, get your master's." He looked hopeful. "I'll pay for it. Every cent."

"Dad—"

"Noni Bachicha is looking for a new office manager."

"Dad, re—"

"He'd hire you in a heartbeat."

"Dad, stop." I bolted out of my chair to get his attention. When I had it, I placed both my palms on the desk, leaned forward, and said as nicely as I could, "No."

"Why not?"

"Why not?" I threw my hands into the air, flabbergasted. "For one thing, this isn't just about me. I have employees."

"You have Cookie."

"Exactly, and I hire other investigators when the situation warrants, as well."

"Cookie can get a job anywhere. She's overqualified and you know it."

He was right. I didn't pay her nearly what she was worth, but she liked it here. And I liked her here. "And I have a case. I can't just pack up and call it a day."

"You didn't accept his money. I heard you. You don't have a case."

"There's a woman missing."

He stood as well. "And that man did it," he said, pointing toward the front door. "Just tell your uncle Bob and stay out of it."

I let the frustration I felt slip past my lips. "I have resources they don't. You know that better than anyone. I can help."

"Yes, by passing along anything you get to your uncle." He leaned forward. "And staying out of it."

"I can't do that."

His shoulders deflated, anger and regret churning inside him. "Will you please just think about it?"

I stood dumbfounded by the whole idea. My own father asking me to give up my livelihood. My calling. I should've known something was up when he tried to have me killed.

He turned to leave, so I cornered the desk and clutched his arm much more desperately than I'd have liked. "Dad, what brought this on?"

"You can't guess?" He seemed surprised that I'd asked.

I fought to pinpoint his exact meaning. This was my dad. My best friend growing up. The only person I could turn to, who believed me, in what I could do, without looking at me like I was a sideshow freak. "Dad, why?" I tried to squelch the hurt in my voice. It didn't work.

"Because," he said, his voice harsh, "I can no longer sit idly by and watch as you're beaten, kidnapped, shot at . . . hell, you name it, and it's happened since you started this business." He raised his hands, indicating my office—his second floor—as though the building were somehow at fault.

I stepped back and plopped back into my chair. "Dad, I've been solving crimes since I was five, remember? For you."

"But I never put you in the thick of things. I kept you out of it."

I couldn't help the harsh bark of laughter that escaped me. Of all the asinine things to say. "Two weeks ago, Dad. Or have you already forgotten the target you painted on my back?" It was a cheap shot, but so was his coming in here and basically demanding I quit my job.

The guilt that seemed to swallow him whole bit into my resolve. I fought it. No matter what his intentions had been when that ex-con came after us, he'd handled it poorly, and now he was taking it out on me.

"Fine," he said, his voice soft, "I deserve that, but what about the others? The time that angry husband came after you with a gun. The time those men kidnapped you and beat you to a pulp before Swopes showed up. The time that kid hit you and sent you crashing through the thirty-foot roof of a warehouse."

"Dad—"

"I could go on. For quite a while, in fact."

I knew he could, but he didn't understand. Those were all very explainable. I lowered my head, feeling oddly like a pouting child, amazed that my father could make me feel so small. Amazed that he would. "So, your answer is to ask me to give up everything I've worked for?"

He exhaled slowly. "Yes, I guess it is," he said as he turned and started for the door. "And stop taking my coffee."

"Do you really believe my leaving this business will alleviate your guilt?"

He didn't even slow his stride, but I'd stung him. I felt it in one quick burst before he disappeared around the corner.

After stewing a few minutes—only partly because of the coffee thing—I gathered myself up and walked back into Cookie's office.

"We're so busted. He knows about the coffee."

"He's wrong," she said without looking up from her computer, almost as though her feelings were hurt.

"No, I've really been taking his coffee." I sat in the chair across from her.

"I'm not overqualified."

"Yes, hon, you are," I said, hating that whole honesty-is-the-best-policy business.

She stopped typing and focused on me. "No. I love this job. Nobody does what we do. Nobody saves lives like we do. How could anyone ask for more?" Her passion surprised me. I'd never realized how she felt about what we did.

I forced a smile across my face. "He's just upset. He'll calm down. Well, maybe not about the coffee."

Cookie thought a moment, then said, "Maybe . . . maybe if you told him."

"Told him what?"

"I mean, he knows you can see the departed, Charley. He would understand. Really he would. Even your sister knows you're the grim reaper."

I shook my head. "I can't tell him something like that. What would it to do him? To know that his daughter was born the grim reaper?" The death-incarnate gig had such a bad rap.

"Give me your hand."

I glanced down at my hands, then eyed her warily. "Did you get into palm reading again? You know how I feel about that stuff."

She chuckled. "I'm not going to read your palm. Give me your hand."

I did, reluctantly.

She took it into both of hers and leaned toward me. "If Amber were capable of what you're capable of, I would be so proud of her. I would love and support her no matter how creepy her job title."

"But you aren't like my dad."

"I disagree." She squeezed lovingly. "Your dad has always supported you. All of this negativity, this pent-up aggression and self-loathing—"

"I hardly loathe myself. Have you seen my ass?"

"—all of it is because of your stepmother, the way she's treated you. Not your father."

"My stepmother *is* a bitch," I said, semi-agreeing. "But I don't know if I can tell Dad. Not that. Not the grim reaper thing." I pulled my hand back.

She let me. "I just think it might make him feel better about all of this, if he knew you had more on your side than just your ability to talk to the departed."

"Maybe."

"So, seriously, your accountant is crooked?"

"As a do-it-yourself haircut," I said, grateful for the change in subject. "It took me forever to find an accountant with *flexible* morals." I added a double wink to get my meaning across. "Apparently there's this whole code-of-ethics thing they have to get past."

My cell rang. I fished it out of my front pocket and checked the caller ID. It was Neil Gossett, a friend I'd gone to high school with who was now a deputy warden at the prison in Santa Fe.

"Hello?" I said, because Charley's House of Pasties seemed wrong.

"Reyes wants to talk."

3

Damn it, Jim!

—T-SHIRT

"A long time ago, in a galaxy pretty much exactly like this one, a little girl was born to a set of wonderful parents named Mom and Dad."

"I already know this part."

"She had a head of dark hair," I said into my phone, ignoring Gemma, my slightly OCD sister, as I steered Misery onto the interstate toward Santa Fe. Hopefully, there were no cops around, because I really didn't need another ticket for talking on the phone while driving.

Garrett had dropped off Misery after he checked for any mechanical damage from the fender bender, and Misery seemed to have forgiven me, so we were good to go. I set Cookie on the mundane task of checking out the good doctor's background, then tore out of the office so fast, papers went flying behind me.

"And she had shimmering gold eyes that the nurses cooed over for days," I continued.

"The nurses cooed? That's what you're telling people?"

"The mom so loved her daughter, she sacrificed her life to give the little girl a chance at one."

"I don't think it was really a choice."

"On the day her daughter was born, the mom died and crossed through the infant, as the girl was made of magic and light, but this saddened her father. Not the light thing. He didn't know about that. But the mom passing thing."

"Yeah, I got that."

I charged past a trucker who clearly didn't get that ninety was the new seventy-five. "And the little girl lay in the nursery for three long days."

"Three days? Are you sure?" Gemma asked, doubtful.

Gemma and I had been sisters my whole life, and she'd always known that I could see the departed, that I'd been born the one and only grim reaper this side of the Milky Way, which resulted in my assisting Dad and now my uncle Bob with their cases. But we'd never been particularly close. I figured my whole status as death incarnate had put her off, and I'd only found out recently that it wasn't my job title that kept her at a distance, but my insistence that she stay far, far away. I never dreamed she'd take me seriously.

"Yes, stop interrupting," I said, swerving to miss a tire in the road. Of all the places to leave a tire. "Where was I? Oh, right. No one came to get her. No one came to see her, except for a plethora of dead people who'd gathered around, standing vigil until her father could fight through his grief long enough to come back and take the little girl home."

"I don't think it was three days."

"The infant remembered all of this because she had really good short-term memory for a newborn."

"Obviously," Gemma said. "Get to the good part."

Gemma was a psychiatrist, which meant she could take care of everybody's problems but her own, just one of a dozen ways we were alike. But our looks was not one of them. While I had dark hair and gold eyes, she was the classic blond-haired, blue-eyed beauty that set men's hearts aflutter. I could set men's hearts aflutter, too, but I owed my success to mad skill. The things I could do with my mouth.

"So, you already know I remember the day I was born?"

"Duh, you told me a thousand times when we were little."

Wow, I didn't remember that. "So, I told you about the huge scary being enshrouded in an undulating black robe that filled the entire delivery room, like ocean waves crashing against the walls, and how he hovered in a corner, stayed with me for three days, promised me Dad would be there soon, though I never actually heard his voice? And how I was deathly afraid of him because his mere presence seemed to sap my strength and steal my breath?"

After a long pause that had me wondering if she'd fallen asleep again, she said, "No, you didn't mention that part."

"Oh, okay, then." I thrummed the fingers of one hand on the steering wheel to the classic rock playing in the background, happy I could get back to my story. "So, that happened, then on the third day, when the little girl's father finally showed up to take her home, she really wanted to ask him, 'Where the fuck you been, Dad?' but she lacked the motor skills necessary to speak. A year passed and the little girl was a happy camper. She hadn't seen the big scary creature again, and her dad seemed to genuinely like her. Except when she ate pureed peas, but that was his own fault. Then he brought home a woman named Denise, and camping pretty much sucked from then on."

"Okay," Gemma said, "I get the whole stepmother thing. Go back to the powerful-being thing."

Reyes was probably the one and only mind-blowing part of my life Gemma didn't know about, besides that night with the 122nd Fighter Attack Squadron. They'd been celebrating the promotion of one of their comrades. I helped. Damn wine coolers. I learned a lot about evasive maneuvers that night. And my boundless will to survive even the most voracious of hangovers.

"Okay, I'm going to give you the *Schoolhouse Rock* version."

"Are you driving?"

". . . No."

"Are you sure? I hear road noise."

". . . Yes."

"Okay, I'll have to settle for that version. I have a nine o'clock."

"Got it," I said, glancing at my watch. "So, I'm born and this massive being is there, cloaked in black and such. And he's just amazing but scary. And he called me Dutch."

"Wait a minute."

"You have a client in like five seconds. Can you hold your questions until the end?"

"He called you Dutch? When you were born?"

Wow, I was a little surprised Gemma picked up on that. "You remember, don't you?"

"That night, when you stopped that man from abusing that kid. The boy we saved called you Dutch."

She was good. When Gemma and I were in high school, I was helping her with a school project late one night on the seedier side of town. She'd wanted to capture life on the streets for a video about the harsher side of Albuquerque. We were huddled in the corner of an abandoned school, basically freezing our asses off, when we noticed movement in the window of a small apartment. We realized in horror that a man was beating a teenaged boy, and my immediate and only thought was to save him. Out of desperation, I threw a brick through the man's window. Miraculously, it worked. He stopped hitting the boy and came after us. We ran down a dark alley and were searching for an opening along a fence that blocked our path to freedom when we realized the boy had escaped as well. He was doubled over on the frozen ground, coughing and trying to breathe past the pain.

We stumbled back to him, and when he looked up at us, blood streaked down his face and dripped from his incredible mouth. We tried to help, but he refused our offer, even going so far as to threaten us if we didn't leave.

We had no choice. We left him there, injured and bleeding, but I'd gone back the next day and found out from the landlady the family had slipped out in the middle of the night and stiffed her for two months' rent. She also told me his name. Reyes. That was all I had—for years that one name sustained me. When I finally found him over a decade later, I wasn't completely surprised to find that Reyes had spent the last ten years in prison for killing that very man.

And that night, the night we'd tried to save him, he called me Dutch.

"I can't believe you put that together," I said. "It took me years to do that."

"Well, I'm smarter. So, is there a connection?"

"Yes. That being and Reyes Farrow are one and the same."

After taking a moment to absorb that nugget, she asked, "How is that even possible?"

"Well, you'd have to know a little more about Reyes." While I rarely told the truth, the whole truth, and nothing but the truth about Reyes to anyone but a select few individuals whom I'd probably placed in mortal danger by doing so, Gemma already knew so much and I'd kept her at arm's length for so long. I wanted our relationship to be what it once was. I wanted to be close to her again. Our stepmother Denise had driven a wedge between us that I was no longer willing to leave wedged. No more wedgies. Period.

"Before I tell you, I have to know three things," I said.

"Okay."

"One, are you sitting down?"

"Yes."

"Two, are you mentally stable?"

"More than you'll ever be."

Well, that was uncalled for. "And three, how do you spell *schizophrenia*?"

"What does that have to do with anything?"

"Nothing. I just wanted to see if you'd tell me."

She exhaled loudly. "You were saying?"

"Okay, but just remember, I warned you."

"Wait, no you didn't. There was no warning."

"Right, I know, that was my warning. 'Just remember, I warned you,' was my warning."

"Oh, sorry."

"Are you finished?"

"Yes."

"Can I continue?"

"Charley."

"Okay, here goes. Reyes Farrow is the son of Satan." Whew. I'd said it. I'd laid it out there. Bared my soul. Spilled my guts. And then I waited. And waited. I checked my phone. Still connected. "Gemma?"

"As in, *the* Satan?"

"Yes."

"Because I had a client who'd changed his name to Satan once. Are you sure that's not Reyes's dad?"

I tried not to laugh. "No, Reyes Farrow is the gorgeous and stubborn and unpredictable son of Satan, and many centuries ago, he escaped from hell to be with me. He waited for me to be born, then chose a family and was born on Earth himself. Only to later be kidnapped and traded off to the man who raised him, Earl Walker. But he sacrificed everything to be with me, Gemma, knowing that when he was born, he wouldn't remember who he was or who I was. And the memories of his past have been coming back to him over the last few years, kind of like things are revealed to me. Slow as molasses in January." I passed a truck hauling cows, their big sad eyes looking on as I drove by. Poor little guys. "Did you hang up on me?"

"Okay, I have an opening Tuesday at four. I'm going to pencil in a two-hour session, just in case."

"I'm not crazy, Gem. You know that."

With a reluctant sigh, she agreed. "I know you're not, but I've never even believed in Satan and you're telling me he's not only real, but he has a son? And that son has been stalking you since you were born?"

"Yes. Well, basically. And he's been in prison for the last ten years for killing the man who raised him, the man from that night."

"Holy cow, he killed him? That doesn't happen often."

"I know. It's rare for an abused child to turn against his abuser, but it happens."

"So, Reyes was the being who used to follow you?"

"Yes. From what I've found out, he used to have seizures as a kid, and it was during those seizures he would leave his body and become that being, or the Big Bad, as I used to call him. He was this huge, larger-than-life entity that would save my life whenever I was in danger."

"That was him? When you were, what, four or five?"

"I can't believe you remember that. He was there over and over. When that convicted sex offender tried to play house with me, the Big Bad was there. When a classmate tried to run me down with his dad's SUV in high school, the Big Bad was there."

"Oh, I remember that. Owen Vaughn tried to kill you."

"Right, and the Big Bad stopped him."

"Owen seemed so normal. Did you ever figure that out?"

"No. He hates me to this day."

"Bummer."

"Yeah, and one time this man was stalking me in college and decided to get to know me better one night while he held a knife to my throat and the Big Bad was there."

"You didn't tell me that," she said, her tone scolding.

"You weren't talking to me anymore."

"I wasn't talking to you, because you told me not to."

"I know. Sorry."

"Any more life-threatening situations you've been in?"

"Oh, yeah, tons. The abusive husband of a client felt the need to end my life with a chrome-plated .38 once, and Big Bad was there. And the list goes on. So, for the life of me, I was never really certain why he scared the bejesus out of me. Nothing scared me growing up. I've been playing with dead people since the day I was born, so it's good thing, yet the Big Bad scared me. Which brings me to the reason I called."

"Which was to give me nightmares for the rest of my life?"

"Oh, no, that's just a plus. Why was I so scared of him?"

"Hon, for one thing he was this powerful, massive, black smokelike being."

"So, you're saying I'm a racist?"

"No, Charley, I'm saying you have the instinct to preserve your life just like the rest of us. And you couldn't help but see him as a threat. You are too driving. Where are you going?"

"Will you think on it and get back to me?" I asked, completely unsatisfied with her answer. Absolutely no Freudian theories in there whatsoever. No Jung or Erikson. Not even a hint of Oprah. "Which brings me to the second reason I called. I'm headed to Santa Fe to see him. And remember how he was injured in the basement of my apartment building a couple of weeks ago?" She knew that Reyes had been injured. She didn't know why.

"Yes."

"Well, a funny thing happened on the way to eternity. Demons escaped from hell—several hundred, actually—and they were torturing his physical body to try to lure me to them."

"Demons."

"Demons."

"As in—"

"Yes. Hellfire and brimstone."

"And why would they try to lure you to them?" she asked after a long moment, her voice a bit shaky.

"Because, as the grim reaper, I'm the portal to heaven, and they want it."

" 'Kay."

"But, you have to understand, Reyes is the portal out of hell, and they want that, too."

"Mm-hmm."

"I know, right? Thanks for telling me, Rey-Rey. And remember his tattoo from that night? It's a map to the gates of hell, but that's another story. So, he's all, 'I'm too vulnerable like this. I'm going to let my physical body die,' and I'm all, 'No, you're not,' and he's all, 'Yes, I am,' and I'm all—"

"Charley," she said, totally interrupting. "None of this is possible. What you're saying—"

"Stay with me here." I could hear the breathless panic rising in her voice. But really, she was part sister and part therapist. No one was more qualified for me to talk to about this stuff. I had discovered this really cool ability that night and ended up vanquishing all the demons, but the things they did to Reyes. I could hardly think of it without growing light-headed. She probably didn't need to know that part.

"I'm trying."

"So anyway," I said, charging ahead before I lost her, "to keep him from basically committing suicide, I bound his incorporeal self to his physical body."

"You did what?"

"I know. But I was desperate. He was going to kill himself. If you saw what he can do with that blade. Oh, did I mention his ginormous sword? And, no, I'm not speaking metaphorically. Though, I gotta say—"

"Charley, wait," she said, interrupting again. "You bound him? What exactly does that entail?"

"You're not usually this slow."

"You're freaking me out!" she literally screamed at me, and I realized we should have had this conversation face-to-face. I could hardly read her emotions over the phone. She really should take that into consideration.

"I know, sorry." Maybe I needed to explain myself better. "Well, in other words, he can't leave his physical body. He's bound to it. And now Reyes Farrow, one of the most powerful beings in the universe, wants to talk." My stomach clenched every time I thought about it. "And!" I added, almost forgetting the best part. "Dad comes into the office this morning and wants me to quit."

"Seeing the son of Satan?"

"No, my investigations business."

"Oh, right."

"So what do you think?"

"About Dad?"

"No, I'll deal with Dad." Though, maybe I should worry. The last time he was behaving strangely, a man attacked me with a butcher's knife. A sharp one. The knife, not the man. "About Reyes. I'm on my way to see him as we speak."

"Charley, I can barely wrap my head around this, and my nine o'clock is here."

"Seriously? You're going to leave me now?"

"For the time being, I'd say run. But that's just me. Call me in an hour."

"Not likely," I said, but she'd already hung up. Geez. I was totally counting on her.

It was a lot to take in. I understood that. Heck, Reyes Farrow was a lot to take in. And right now, I needed to be concentrating on Dr. Yost's missing wife instead of traipsing about the country, hoping for an audience with the prince of the underworld. He was so angry after I bound him that he'd refused to see me. Thus my surprise when Neil Gossett called.

And now, everything was coming to the surface. All the emotion surrounding Reyes bubbled and simmered inside me. I had searched for him for so long, kept him in my prayers every night, only to find that he'd been in prison for over ten years for murder. I was disappointed, but for purely selfish reasons. I'd wanted to be with him. I'd wanted to save him that night when Gem and I were in high school, to take him away from that horrible situation, that horrible man. But he'd refused our offer of help. When I learned that he'd killed the very man who'd beaten him so badly that night, I felt like I'd failed. And I didn't even know who he was at the time, that he was literally the son of Satan. I'd only recently found out.

"Being raised in hell had to suck," I said aloud.

"Are you talking to yourself again?"

I looked over at the thirteen-year-old departed gangbanger who'd popped into the passenger's seat. "Hey, Angel. How're things on the other side?"

I'd met Angel the same night I met Reyes. He died over a decade ago when his best friend decided to do a drive-by without consulting him first. Since he was the driver, he was a tad surprised when his friend started firing out the window of his mother's stolen car. In an effort to stop him, Angel paid the ultimate price. But the way I saw it, the price I paid on a daily basis was much heavier. No idea what I did to deserve the little shit. Not that I'd trade a single minute.

"Pretty cool," he said with a shrug of his shoulders. He wore a dirty T-shirt and a red bandanna to frame a face caught between childhood innocence and teenage hellion. "My mom's getting all kinds of new clients. She got this review or something in the paper, and they said she was the best cosmetologist in the city when it came to the pixie, whatever that is."

"Wow, that's awesome." I socked him on the shoulder and he grinned in sheepish agreement.

"I guess," he said. "So we got a case?"

"We do indeed. There's a doctor near the university who tried to off his wife."

"Seriously?"

"Seriously."

"A rich guy?"

"Yep."

"And he committed a crime? Get outta here."

I nodded and let Angel gloat. Nothing pleased him more than rich people doing stupid things. "Are you done?" I asked after he went into all the reasons rich people should get harsher sentences than poor ones instead of vice versa.

"There should be a scale. The richer you are, the more you risk."

"Are you finished *now*?"

"I guess."

"Do you feel better?"

"I would if you'd let me see you naked."

"So this doctor," I said, interrupting before he got too carried away, "he did something to his wife, then reported her missing. We don't have a body, so I need you to follow him."

"Did he get the job done?"

"That's what I need you to find out. I'm hoping he'll lead us right to her. You know, like revisit the crime scene or something." I gave him all the info on Dr. Nathan Yost, including a physical description and his home address.

"Okay, but if he did it, why not just arrest him?"

"I don't arrest people."

"Then what are you good for?" he asked teasingly.

I offered him my best smile. The award-winning one, not that abominable runner-up. "That is a topic of great debate, handsome man."

"Well, I don't think this is a good idea." He was playing with the air-conditioning vent, the sprinkling of potential along his chin and above his upper lip giving him that almost-a-man look. He had rich brown eyes with thick eyelashes and a square jaw any cholo would be proud of.

"You might be right," I said, turning back to a motorcyclist with a death wish, if his swerving in and out of traffic was any indication. "He might not lead us anywhere, but it's all I've got at the moment and I really want to jump on this."

"No, *you*. Going to see *him*."

Angel had never taken to Reyes. He didn't seem able to see past the whole son-of-Satan thing. "Why do you say that?"

He sighed in annoyance, as if he'd already told me a thousand times. "I've already told you a thousand times. Rey'aziel is not what you think he is."

The mere mention of Reyes's otherworldly name sent a tingle over my skin. "Hon, I know what he is, remember?"

He looked out the window for almost a mile before saying, "He's really mad."

I nodded. "I know."

"No, you don't." He turned back, his huge brown eyes narrowing seriously. "He's angry. As in disrupting-the-universe angry."

I wasn't sure what he meant, but okay. "He's that mad, huh?"

"I didn't even know he could do that shit, that he was that powerful. I just don't think now is a good time to go see him."

"I did bind him, Angel."

He looked at me pleadingly then, worry drawing his brows together. "And you can't undo it now. Please, Charley. If you set him free . . . there's no telling what he'll do. He's so pissed."

I chewed my bottom lip a moment, guilt assaulting me. "I don't know how to anyway," I admitted.

"What?" he asked, surprised. "You can't unbind him?"

"No. I've tried."

"No! No, don't." He waved a hand as though erasing the notion. "Just leave him. He's already causing all kinds of crap all over the world. Who knows what he'll do if you unbind him?"

"What do you mean? What crap is he causing?"

"You know, the usual. Earthquakes. Hurricanes. Tornadoes."

I tried to smile but couldn't quite manage it. "Angel, those things are happening all on their own. Reyes has nothing—"

"You really don't know?" He looked at me like I was part blithering and part idiot.

"Angel, how can Reyes affect the weather?" I'd never taken Angel for a conspiracy theorist. Who knew?

"His anger is throwing everything off balance, like that ride at the fair that spins and turns at the same time. Haven't you noticed?"

Ah, yes, many a child had lost his lunch to that ride. "Honey—"

"Did you know there was an earthquake in Santa Fe? Santa Fe!" When I started to argue again, he held up a hand and said, "Just don't unbind him, whatever you do. I'll go follow this *pendejo* doctor."

He was gone before I could say anything else. I couldn't possibly give credence to his claims. What he suggested was impossible. Reyes's anger causing natural disasters? I'd made a few people angry in the past, but not enough to cause an earthquake.

I picked up my phone just in case and called Cookie.

"What's up, boss?"

"Question, was there an earthquake in Santa Fe?"

"You didn't hear about that?"

"Holy cow. Where the hell was I?"

"You totally need to watch the news."

"Can't."

"Why?"

"It's too depressing."

"Right, because hanging with dead people isn't."

Well, that was just rude. "So, really?" I asked. "An earthquake?"

"The first one of that magnitude in over a hundred years."

Crap.

4

Lead me not into temptation.
I can find it myself.
—T-SHIRT

I flashed my ID at the guard standing duty at gatehouse of the Penitentiary of New Mexico. He waved me through and I parked in visitor parking, close to level five, the maximum-security unit of the prison. The minute I stepped inside the turquoise-trimmed building, Neil Gossett walked up to me, took the coffee out of my hands, and threw it in a wastebasket. Right. Bad idea.

"Hey," I said breathlessly, butterflies dive-bombing the lining of my stomach, "what's up?"

Neil and I went to high school together, but we didn't hang in the same social circles and we certainly weren't friends. He'd been an athlete, which only partially explained his asinine behavior toward me throughout our high school careers. Not that it was entirely his fault, but blaming him was healthier for my self-image.

I had trusted my best friend Jessica Guinn when I was a sophomore with my most prized secrets, not the least of which involved the words *reaper* and *grim,* and not necessarily in that order. I should have known better. It shouldn't have been such a surprise when she blabbed it to the whole world and dropped me like a hot potato—when I was clearly much more the couch potato variety—and branded me a freak. I didn't argue that point, but neither did I appreciate my sudden reputation as a leper. And Neil had been right in the middle of it all, joining in on the harassing and name-calling and eventual shunning.

While Neil had never believed in what I could do back then, he'd since changed his mind when our paths crossed again. As he was the deputy warden of the prison where Reyes Farrow had spent the last decade, I'd had no choice but to look him up in my quest to find the man most likely to win the Sexiest Son of Satan on the Planet award. And because of an incident that happened when Reyes first arrived here ten years ago that involved the downfall of three of the deadliest gang members the prison population had to offer in about fifteen seconds flat, Neil was beginning to believe there really were things that went bump in the night. Whatever Neil saw left an impression. And he knew just enough about me to believe I knew what I was talking about. Poor schmuck.

He turned and started walking away, which I thought was really rude. But I followed nonetheless.

"He just wants to talk?" I asked, hurrying to catch up. "Did he ask you to call me? Did he tell you why?"

He led the way past the security posts before answering. "He asked for a one-on-one with me," he said, glancing around to make sure no one was listening. "So I went to the floor, you know, fully expecting to die since he was so angry at being bound by a mutual acquaintance of ours." He cast a quick glower over his shoulder. "So I get to his cell and he says he wants to talk to you."

"Just out of the blue?"

"Just out of the blue." He led me through a couple more checkpoints, then into a windowless interview room with a table and two chairs, like the kind they used for meetings with lawyers. It was tiny, but the bright white cinder block walls made it seem less so. It looked like the only form of visible monitoring from the guards would be through a postage stamp window in the door.

"Wow."

"Exactly. Are you sure you want to do this, Charley?"

"Of course. Why wouldn't I be?" I sat at the table and laid a file folder I'd brought on top, surprised he'd let me keep it.

"Well, let me think." Neil was agitated, started pacing back and forth. He still had a fairly nice physique despite the tragic onset of male pattern baldness. From what I'd gathered, he'd never married, which came as quite the shocker. He'd always had hordes of girls after him in high school. He glanced at me as he made another pass. "Reyes Farrow is the son of Satan," he said, starting the count off with his thumb. "He is the most powerful man I've ever met." Index finger. "He moves at the speed of light." Middle finger. "Oh, and he's pissed." Fist at side.

"I know he's pissed."

"He's pissed as hell, Charley. At you."

"Pfft. How do you know he's mad at me? Maybe he's mad at you."

"I've seen what he does to people he's angry with," he continued, ignoring me. "It's one of those images that haunts you forever, if you know what I mean."

"I do. Damn it." I pulled my bottom lip between my teeth.

"I've never seen him like this." He paused and placed his palms on the table in thought. "He's been different since he got back."

"Different how?" I asked, alarmed.

He started pacing again. "I don't know. He's distant, more distant than usual. And he isn't sleeping. He just paces like a caged animal."

"Like you're doing now?" I asked.

He turned to me, not amused. "Remember what I saw when he first got here?"

I nodded. "Of course."

The first time I'd visited, Neil told me the story of how he became aware of what Reyes was capable of. He'd just started working at the prison and was on the floor in the cafeteria when he saw three gang members heading toward Reyes, a twenty-year-old kid at the time who'd just been released into gen-pop from Reception and Diagnostics. Fresh fish. Neil had panicked and grabbed for his radio, but before he could even call for backup, Reyes had taken down three of the deadliest men in the state without breaking a sweat. Neil said he moved so fast, his eyes couldn't follow. Like an animal. Or a ghost.

"That's why I'll be watching through that camera," he said, pointing to the device in the corner, "and I'll have a team just outside this door, waiting for the word."

"Neil," I said, leveling a warning gaze on him, "you can't send them in and you know it. If you care anything about your men."

He shook his head. "Maybe if something happens, they can at least stop him long enough to get you out."

I stood and stepped next to him. "You know they can't."

"Then what am I supposed to do?" he asked, a hard edge to his voice.

"Nothing," I said pleadingly. "He won't do anything to me. But I can't make the same promise for your men if you send them in with batons and pepper spray. He might get a bit miffed."

"I have to take precautions. The only reason I'm letting this happen is—" He lowered his head again. "—you know why."

I did know why. Reyes had saved his life. Out in the real world, that was saying a lot. In prison, the weight of that statement multiplied exponentially. "Neil, you never even liked me in high school."

He scoffed humorously and raised his brows in question.

"I'm a little flattered you're worried, but—"

"Don't be." He grinned. "Do you know how much paperwork is involved when people get killed in prison?"

"Thanks," I said, patting his arm, really hard.

He pulled out my chair. "You sit tight. I'm going to help bring him in. I don't want any incidents along the way."

"Okay. I'll sit tight."

And I did. My stomach churned with excitement and adrenaline, fear and too much coffee. It was hard to believe I was finally going to see him.

In the flesh. Conscious. I'd seen him in the flesh before, but he was either in a coma or unconscious from being tortured. Torture sucked so bad.

A few minutes later, the door opened and I scrambled to my feet as a man in handcuffs stepped halfway in, then turned back toward the burly corrections officer who'd followed. It was Reyes, and his presence took my breath away. He had the same dark hair in desperate need of a trim, the same wide shoulders straining against the orange fabric of his prison uniform, the sleeves rolled up and the sharp, crisp lines of his tattoos visible, curling up his corded biceps to disappear under the faded material. He was so real, so powerful. And his heat, like a signature, snaked toward me the minute the door opened.

The corrections officer looked at Reyes's cuffed hands then at his face and shrugged. "Sorry, Farrow. Those stay on. Orders."

Neil walked up then. Reyes was only slightly taller yet seemed to tower over him.

He lifted his cuffed hands. They were attached to a chain that clasped on to a belt around his waist and led down to lock to another set of cuffs at his feet. "You know these won't make a difference," he said to Neil, his deep voice washing over me like warm water.

Neil glanced past him toward me. "It'll buy me a few seconds should I need them."

Then Reyes looked over his shoulder. For the first time in over a decade, I was looking into the eyes of the real, in-the-flesh Reyes Farrow, and I thought my knees would give beneath me. I'd seen him several times in a much more spiritual sense, when he could come to me incorporeally, but this in-the-flesh thing was fairly new. And the last time I'd seen his corporeal body, he was being ripped apart by a hundred spidery demons with razor-sharp claws. He seemed to have healed nicely, if the surge of sensual adrenaline that now coursed through his veins was any indication.

While I could feel his reluctance to break eye contact, I was sure he could feel the lust that crept up my legs and seeped into my abdomen, a Pavlovian response to his nearness, and somewhere deep inside, I was embarrassed. But I could also feel his desire to tear off the cuffs, partly to spite Neil and partly to remove the table that stood between us. And he could have done it, too. He could have removed the cuffs like papier-mâché. But I could also feel his unabated anger, and I was suddenly glad for the camera, for that extra sense of protection, as ridiculous and noneffective as it would be should it come to that.

He stepped to the table, and the light illuminating his face sent my pulse into double time.

His features had hardened since high school, matured, but those mahogany eyes were unmistakable. He'd definitely grown up, in some places more than others. He was still lean, but his shoulders were broad. Their width seemed to make wearing the cuffs even more uncomfortable.

His dark hair and unshaven jaw framed the most handsome face I had ever seen. His mouth was full, sensual, and his eyes were exactly as I remembered. Like chocolate accented with gold and green flecks and lined with impossibly thick lashes. They shimmered even in the unnatural light above us.

Ten years in prison. In this place. My chest tightened at the thought, and a bizarre sense of protection swept over me.

Unfortunately he felt it. He offered a frigid stare. "Tell him we're fine," he said, and only then did I realize Neil was still in the room.

I took in a deep breath to gather myself. "We're fine, Neil. Thank you."

Neil hesitated, pointed at the camera to remind me, then left, closing the door behind him.

"That's sweet," he said as he folded himself into the chair, taking note of the file I had on the table. His chains rattled against the metal when he placed his hands on top of it.

I sat, too. "What?"

He gestured toward the door with a nod. "Gossett." Then, with an expression of disapproval, he added, "You." A trace of a humorless grin lifted one side of his beautiful mouth.

I knew what that mouth was capable of, from my dreams, from our encounters, but never in the flesh. "What about Neil and me?" I asked, pretending to be offended. I was too taken aback by him to be much of anything but stunned. "We went to high school together."

He arched a brow as though impressed. "Well, that's convenient."

"I suppose."

Just then I felt my chair being pulled forward and gasped. He'd wrapped his foot around a leg and was easing me closer to the table.

When I started to protest, he placed a finger from his cuffed hands over his mouth. "Shhh," he whispered, mischief sparkling in his eyes. After he pulled me to the table, he dropped his gaze to my chest.

The table had stretched my sweater tight, defining Danger and Will Robinson more fully.

"That's better," he said, appreciation shimmering in his eyes. Just as I was about to chastise him, he asked, "How long has he known?"

His inquiry threw me. "Who? Known what?"

"Gossett," he said, glancing back at my face. "How long has he known what I am?"

His question knocked the air out of my lungs. I stuttered as I tried to come up with an answer that wouldn't get Neil killed. "I . . . he doesn't know anything."

"Don't." It was a quiet warning, yet I flinched as though he'd yelled at me.

"How did you—?"

"Dutch." He tsked and tilted his head, waiting, and I realized there was no getting around the truth.

"He doesn't know, not everything. He's not a threat to you," I said, trying to convince both of us. When I'd blurted out the fact that Reyes was the son of Satan to Neil on my last visit, I had put the deputy warden's life in danger. I knew it the moment the words left my mouth. This was different from my telling Cookie or Gemma. Neil was locked in the same place with him day in and day out. It was honestly one of the stupidest things I'd ever done.

"You're probably right," he said, and I almost breathed a sigh of relief. "Who would believe him?" He glanced up and looked right into the camera, the smile he still wore dripping with a silent threat.

I felt as though I hardly knew him, which in truth was the case. Our encounters were always brief and to the point. We rarely had heart-to-hearts, and when we did, they always ended the same way. Though to say I regretted for a moment having sex with a being forged from the fires of sin would be a bald-faced lie. His body—both corporeally and incorporeally—was like molten steel, his passion insatiable. And when he touched me, when his mouth pressed against mine and his body pushed into me, everything else fell away.

The mere thought caused a visceral tightening between my legs, and I sucked in a soft breath.

He watched me close as though trying to read my thoughts, and I wrapped my fingers around the file I'd brought, tried to calm myself. The file held the transcripts from his trial, a copy of his arrest record, and the contents of his prison jacket, the parts Neil could share with me anyway. The psychological profile had been off-limits. And I know they'd tested his intelligence. What'd they call it? Immeasurable?

I decided to get my questions out of the way before we got to the real reason I was there. Reyes had been physically and mentally abused by the man he'd gone to prison for killing, yet none of that history was brought out during the trial. I wanted to know why. I straightened my shoulders and asked, "Why weren't the issues of your abuse at the hands of Earl Walker addressed during your trial?"

He stilled. The easy smile disappeared, and a wall of distrust forced its way between us. His posture shifted ever so slightly, turned defensive, the set of his shoulders hostile, and a wary tension thickened the air.

My fingers tightened around the file folder. I needed to know why he'd just sat back and let them send him to prison without so much as lifting a finger in his own defense, in defense of his actions. "They weren't brought up at all," I said after a quick gulp of air, charging forward.

He glanced at the file, a malevolent glint in his eyes. "So you know everything about me now?" The idea alone seemed to chafe him.

"Not hardly," I assured.

He thought a long moment before responding. "But everything you want to know is in that file. All neat. Orderly. Small."

The power of his gaze siphoned the breath from my lungs, and I had to fight for air under the weight of it. "I think you're underestimating yourself."

"The only one in this room underestimating me is you."

The hair on the back of my neck stood up with that statement. "I don't think so."

"Gossett didn't want to leave you alone with me. At least he's got the sense God gave a walnut."

I chose not to address his insult. He was angry and taking it out on me. Hadn't my own father done that very thing only an hour earlier? Men and their inability to cope with their own emotions astounded me. My gaze dropped to his hands, fatigue and stress taking their toll.

He planted an inquisitive stare on me. "You're not sleeping."

I blinked in surprise. "I can't. You're . . . there."

The tension in his shoulders eased ever so slightly and his chin lowered as though ashamed. "I don't mean to be."

"I can tell." His confession stunned me. Though I hid the pain of that statement from my voice, he had to have felt the emotion churning inside me.

"What do you mean?"

"You're just . . . you're angry." I bit back a surge of humiliation and admitted, "You don't want to be there, to be with me."

He looked to the side, annoyed. It gave me a chance to study his profile, fierce and noble at once. Even in a prison uniform, he was the most powerful being I'd ever seen, like a beast who lived on strength and instinct alone.

"I'm not angry because I don't want to be there, Dutch," he said, his voice soft, hesitant. He pinned me to the spot with the seriousness of his gaze. "I'm angry because I do."

Before my heart could soar too high with that tidbit, I decided to address his earlier claims. "This morning when you came to me," I began, my cheeks suddenly burning in embarrassment, "you said that it was all me. That I'm summoning you. That I've always summoned you, but that's impossible."

After a long pause that had me almost squirming in my chair, he said, "Someday you'll figure out what you're capable of. We'll talk about it then." Before I could question him on that front, he spoke again. This time his voice was little more than a harsh whisper. "Unbind me."

I cringed in reaction. I knew it would come to this. I knew it was the reason he wanted to talk in the first place. Why else? Like he would actually just want to see me. I lowered my head. "I can't unbind you. I don't know how."

"Actually, you do," he said, watching me with a practiced eye.

I shook my head. "I've tried. I just don't know how."

The chains rattled against the table as he leaned in. "I won't—" He glanced at the camera self-consciously. "—I won't try what I attempted to do the last time you saw me." Meaning, he wouldn't try to rid himself of his corporeal body by essentially committing suicide. "You need to know that. You can't undo what you did unless you trust me."

"I told you, I tried. I don't think trust has anything to do with it."

"Trust has everything to do with it." He rose from the table, knocking his chair back, and fought visibly to control his emotions.

I raised a hand toward the camera, letting Neil know it was okay; then I stood as well. "I'll try again," I said, forcing my voice to stay calm.

"You have to unbind me," he whispered, his voice laced with desperation.

It occurred to me that this was about more than his being set free. He had a goal, a purpose; I could see it shimmering in his eyes. "Why?"

The heat that forever radiated off him seeped into my clothes and skin, causing a flush of unwanted desire to wash through me. Clearly Reyes had better things to contemplate than me and my pathetic crush.

He stared hard and spoke through clenched teeth. "I have unfinished business. And if you think these chains will keep me from it, you're gravely mistaken, Dutch."

Though the table was still between us, I stepped back warily. "Neil will be in here in two seconds."

He lowered his head, watched me from underneath his dark lashes as though I were a meal. "Do you have any idea what I can do in two seconds?"

The door to the interview room burst open and three guards rushed in, batons in hand. Neil stepped past them and looked from me to Reyes, then back again. "This is over."

Reyes didn't lift his head. He just turned it and offered Neil an incredulous stare. The blood drained from Neil's face, but he stood his ground, impressing everyone in the room who knew what Reyes was. The guards stood oblivious, ready for a fight. They were clearly new.

I'd barely taken a step when Reyes's attention snapped toward me again. He stood there, so still, my mind conjured a cobra ready to strike.

"I think we're finished, Neil. Thank you." My words were breathy with a combination of fear and adrenaline.

Two of the guards stepped forward and took Reyes by the arms to lead him out. To my utter astonishment, he let them, but just before he crossed the threshold, he turned back to me and said, "You leave me no choice." After a quick glance at Neil, he stepped out and let the men escort him down the hall.

Neil turned an ashen expression on me. "So, it went well?"

5

I know karate, and like two other
Japanese words.
—T-SHIRT

I careened onto the interstate and set Misery to medium-high, my head still reeling. Reyes was nothing short of an enigma. So primal and ethereal. So fierce and, well, pissed. But damn those biceps.

My cell started singing out the chorus to "Da Ya Think I'm Sexy?" I flipped it open. "What's up, Cookie?"

"So?"

"So?"

"So?"

"Cookie, seriously."

"Charley Davidson," she said in her best motherly voice, "don't think for a minute you're going to keep even the smallest details from me."

I cracked up, then thought about Reyes again and my breath hitched in my chest. "Oh, my god, Cook, he's so . . . he's just so . . ."

"Stunning? Gorgeous? Magnetic?"

"Add *really, really angry* to that, and you've nailed him with a sledgehammer."

She sucked in air through her teeth. "I was afraid of that. You have to tell me everything. Wait, where are you?"

"On the interstate, heading out of Santa Fe."

"Well, stop."

"Here?"

"Yes."

"Okay, but if I die, I'm coming back to haunt you." It was only fair. I took the next exit and headed back toward town.

"Deal. From what I've found out, Dr. Feelgood has no priors, but he was arrested in college. A death threat, or something. The charges were dropped, so there's nothing really juicy in the database."

"Interesting."

"I thought so. I'm working on the hows and whys. In the meantime, I've been trying to get ahold of our missing wife's sister to no avail, but I did get ahold of her brother in Santa Fe."

"Ah, hence the near negligent homicide to get me back to town."

"Exactly. I take it you survived?"

"As always."

"Her brother's name is Luther Dean."

"I remember. Big, strong name." It made me conjure a white supremacist. Or a sausage.

"Yeah, he sounded big and strong over the phone."

"Wonderful." This could be interesting. "Did he give you any info on the case?"

"Nope. Won't talk to me."

Uh-oh. "Will he talk to me?"

"Nope."

"So, I'm going to see him because?"

"You're a charmer. If anyone can get him to talk, it's you."

"Aw, thanks. And I repeat, if I die, I'm coming back to haunt you."

She thought about that a moment. "You do have a tendency to almost get murdered in the most unlikely places."

She was right. I did. I'd considered therapy, but the never-ending search for mental stability would cut into my couch potato time. That couch was not going to sprout roots itself.

"Wait," she said, excited. "You don't have to worry. He's a contractor. You're going to a construction site. Getting killed at a construction site with all those tools and equipment about is very likely, so surely nothing will happen."

"Oh, good thinking." She was so smart. "What's the address?" I wrote down the address amidst honking horns and a couple of flying birds, then said, "And get me the name of the woman who pressed charges against the good doctor in college. I'd love to hear that one."

"You got it, boss. So, everything's okay, right?"

"Absolutely. The minute my knees stop shaking from being in the presence of God Reyes, I'll be fine."

"Man," she said, her tone more nasally than usual, "I want a god. Just one. I'm not selfish."

"Well, if mine kills me, he's all yours."

"You're so sweet." I could hear her nails clicking on the keyboard in the background.

"What are bestest friends for?"

"Oh, and that Mistress Marigold keeps emailing. She's practically begging you to email her back."

I pulled up to a stop sign and watched as a group of Deaf kids shuffled past, all of them laughing at a story one of the boys was telling. Something about a hearing counselor jumping on his desk to get away from a Chihuahua.

"It's a good thing you set up that fake email address," I said, chuckling at the boy's story. "She's a nut."

Mistress Marigold hosted a website on angels and demons. I'd been doing research on it one night when Reyes was being tortured by the latter and I was trying to learn more about them. On a page buried deep within the site, I'd come across a peculiar line that read, *If you're the grim reaper, please contact me immediately.*

It was so strange and we were so curious, Cookie emailed her the next day, asking what she wanted with the grim reaper. She'd written back with *That's between me and the grim reaper.* Which, naturally, sent Cookie on a mission. She had Garrett email her saying he was the grim reaper, and Mistress Marigold had written back; this time she said, *If you're the grim reaper, I'm the son of Satan*. It was enough to stun me a good thirty seconds. How did she know about Reyes? It couldn't have been a coincidence. Next, Cookie had set up an alternate email address for me to use. So, in the interest of all things scientific and creepy, I emailed her, again asking what she wanted with the grim reaper. I'd fully expected another brush off. Instead, she wrote back with, *I've been waiting a long time to hear from you*.

I figured she was either clairvoyant or just a really good guesser. Either way, I decided to leave well enough alone.

"I think you should email her back," Cookie said. "I feel sorry for her now. She seems a little desperate."

"Really? What'd she say?"

" 'I'm a little desperate.' "

"Oh. Well, I don't have time to play games at the moment. Speaking of which, we should play Scrabble tonight."

"I'm not going to play games with you all night so you won't fall asleep."

"Chicken."

"I'm not chicken."

"Bock, bock."

"Charley—"

"Bk, bk, bk—"

"Charley, really—"

"Bk-*kaw*!"

"I'm not scared you'll beat me at Scrabble. I just want you to get some shut-eye."

"Keep telling yourself that, *chiquita*."

Twenty minutes later, I pulled into the construction site of a sparkling new shopping center on the eastern outskirts of the city. Santa Fe was growing and had the traffic congestion to prove it. But it was still a pretty town, the only one in the country with a city ordinance requiring that all construction adhere to a Spanish Territorial or Pueblo style of architecture. As a result, the City Different was simply that, different, stunning, and one of my favorite places on earth.

I stepped out of Misery to examine the half-finished shopping center. It had adobe walls with terra-cotta tile and thick wooden archways.

"Can I help you?"

I looked over as a kid carrying a two-by-four walked past, unadulterated interest glistening in his eyes. Damn Danger and Will's perky disposition. "Absolutely, I'm looking for Luther Dean."

"Oh, sure." He scanned the area, then pointed through the openings that would one day have glass panes. A man stood inside. "The duke's in there."

"The duke?" Impressive title. And the owner of it was impressive as well. He looked part professional football player and part brick wall with crisp sable hair peeking out from underneath his hard hat. "Can I go in?"

"Not without one of these." He knocked on his hard hat while dropping his load, then jogged over to the portable office that sported a DEAN CONSTRUCTION sign. After rummaging through a plastic bin, he hurried back with a bright yellow hard hat. "Now you can," he said, handing it over, a boyish grin flashing across his face.

"Thank you." Normally I would have offered a wink or something equally flirty, but he looked too young, even for me. I didn't want to get his pubescent hopes up.

"Not at all, ma'am." He tipped his hard hat before hefting the board onto his shoulder again.

I stepped carefully over castoffs and debris and walked through the opening where the doors would someday stand. "Mr. Dean?"

A ginormous man stood studying a pile of architectural plans, his shoulders so wide, they actually looked uncomfortable. I knew bank vault doors less intimidating. He glanced up, his cerulean blue eyes only slightly curious. "Yes."

"Hi." I walked toward him and held out my hand, hoping he wouldn't crush it. "My name is Charlotte Davidson. I'm a private investigator working on your sister's case."

His face darkened instantly, so I dropped my hand, my instincts for self-preservation being what they were.

"I've already told your assistant, I have nothing to say to you."

The emotional weight behind his response—one full of anger, worry, and resentment—hit me head-on. The force of it stole the air from my lungs, and I had to take a moment to recover as he rolled up the plans and barked orders to a group of men in another room. They jumped to do his bidding. Literally.

"Mr. Dean, I assure you, I'm on your sister's side."

The scowl he hit me with could have convinced a seasoned assassin to empty his bladder. "What's your name again?" The paper in his hand surrendered to the pressure he was placing on it and crumpled as he squeezed his fist closed.

"Jane," I said, swallowing hard. "Jane Smith."

He narrowed his eyes. "I thought you said it was Charlotte or Sherry or something."

"It was. I very recently changed it."

"Do you know what I do to people who mess with my family?"

"And I'm moving to South America."

"I hurt them."

"And possibly getting a sex-change operation. You'd never recognize me, you know, if you ever came looking."

"Are we finished?"

Damn. Trick question. He turned and headed toward his office. I should've said yes, I really should've, but I couldn't leave him with such a bad impression of me. A shaking mass of spineless jellylike stuff. Cookie was wrong. I was going to die at a construction site. I was so coming back to haunt her.

"Look, asshole," I said. Out loud.

He stopped short of his destination and turned to gape at me. So did pretty much everyone else, but this was between me and the duke.

I stepped closer and lowered my voice. "I get it. You think I'm working for Dr. Feelgood, so you don't trust me."

He tilted his head, suddenly interested.

"I'm not. He hasn't paid me a dime. I'm looking for your sister, and if you don't want to help me, that's on you. But if anyone can find her, it's me." I fished a card out of my jacket and pushed it inside his shirt pocket. The shirt pocket that covered a really fit pec. Amazed that I was still conscious, I added, "Call me if you'd like to know where she is."

Then I turned and walked back to Misery before I blacked out.

"You said what?" Cookie asked, her voice rising an octave in three words flat.

I grinned and repositioned the phone as I downshifted, and said, " 'Look, asshole.' "

"Oh, my goodness. Wait, you said that to Luther Dean or are you saying that to me right now?"

She was funny. "I wanted to go to Rocket's and check on Teresa Yost's mortal status, but the Rottweiler was out."

Rocket was a departed savant who lived in an abandoned mental asylum I had to break into just to see him. He knew the names of every person who'd ever been born and their status in the grand scheme of things. He could tell me if Teresa Yost was alive or if the doctor had already done the deed, a bit of information that would really help about now. But the biker gang who now owned the mental asylum also owned a slew of Rottweilers, and I preferred my limbs attached, thank you very much.

"Ugh, damn that Rottweiler. So do you think he's married?"

"Well, I don't know, Cookie, but I'm sure he'd prefer something in four legs."

"Not the Rottweiler. Teresa's brother. Oh, your uncle called. He said he needs you to unclog his drain or something. Have you already found a new profession?"

I snorted, then mentally repossessed that snort and replaced it with an epiphany. "You know what? That's not a bad idea. How would you feel about us becoming plumbers? I have a nice crack."

"I'll take a rain check."

"Are you sure? They have wrenches."

"Positive. So, how are you doing?" she asked. I could tell by the tone in her voice she'd switched back to our earlier conversation about Reyes.

"I'm okay. That meeting left me with enough fodder to fuel a thousand lonely sleepless nights."

"Damn it, Charley, will you never learn to document these things? I need visuals, flowcharts."

"Hey, I'm going to Super Dog for a quick bite and to pass along a message from a dead guy to his girlfriend. You should come with me."

"I can't go with you."

"Is it because of my questionable morals?"

"No, it's because it's three o'clock in the afternoon and I have to pick up Amber from school."

"Oh, right. So the morals thing doesn't bother you?"

She laughed and hung up.

I called Ubie, my hemorrhoidal, hypertensed uncle and a detective for the Albuquerque Police Department, wondering about his message. Thanks to him, I'd been hired by APD as a consultant and helped him with cases on a semi-regular basis. The pay wasn't bad. The access to their databases was better.

"What is this about your drains?" I asked when he picked up. "'Cause that sounds almost incestuous."

"Oh, that was code for call me ay-sap."

"Really?" I squinted in thought. "You couldn't just say call me ay-sap?"

"I suppose I could've. I was trying to be cool."

Suppressing an inappropriate giggle, I said, "Uncle Bob, why don't you just ask her out?"

"Who?"

"You know who." He'd recently developed a crush on Cookie. Disturbing? Absolutely. On several levels. But he was a good guy. He deserved a nice girl. Unfortunately, he might just have to settle for Cookie.

"What are you working on?" he asked.

"I have a missing wife."

"I didn't even know you were married."

"Smart-ass. What do you know about this Dr. Nathan Yost?" I asked as I scanned the signs along Central for a giant hot dog. I could never remember if Super Dog was by the adult toy store or the Doggie Style pet grooming boutique. I just remembered it was something sexual.

"I know his wife is missing," he offered.

"That's it?"

"In a nutshell."

"Well, bummer, because he did it."

"Holy shit, are you positive?"

"As a pregnancy test a month after prom."

"This is big. Who are you working with on it?"

"Cookie."

He blew out a heavy sigh. "Well, I'm about seventeen months behind on my paperwork, but I can look into this for you, see if we have anything on the guy."

"Thanks, Ubie. Can you get a copy of the statements for me, as well?"

"Sure, why not."

There it was, next to the law offices of Sexton and Hoare. "You should come eat with me at Super Dog."

"No."

"Is it because of my questionable morals?"

"No, it's because I'd have heartburn all night if I ate a Super Dog this late in the day."

"So the morals thing doesn't bother you?"

"Not as much as my heartburn."

That was good to know. At least the people in my life weren't completely appalled by me.

I pulled up to Super Dog and walked inside, keeping a weather eye for a name tag with JENNY on it. As luck would have it, she was my cashier. I ordered my food first, knowing that once I gave Jenny the message from Ron, the departed clown I'd found in my living room that morning, I'd be bombarded with questions and my dreams of eating a chili dog would die a sad and lonely death.

In the interest of all things romantic, I decided not to repeat Ron's message word for word. Jenny was a pretty girl with dark blond hair and supermodel eyebrows and probably deserved better than a quick *bite me,* the message from Ron.

After she handed over my chili dog and fries, I said, "Jenny, my name is Charlotte Davidson. I have a message for you from a friend."

She refocused on me. Grief had moved in and set up shop, seeping into every nook and cranny of her being. "For me?" she asked, not the slightest bit interested.

I could hardly blame her. "Yes. This is going to sound really odd, but I just need you to work with me a minute." She laced her long, thin fingers together and waited. "Ronald said that he loved you very much."

She swallowed as my words sank in, slowly, methodically. Then her eyes filled with tears that pushed past her lashes and streamed down her cheeks like the floodgates of a damn opening, only her expression didn't change. "You're lying," she said, her voice suddenly edged with bitterness. "He would never say that to me. Never."

She turned and walked to the back room as I stood there dumbfounded. All in all, the experience rated somewhere between the Bedouin woman who crossed when I was twelve and wanted me to take care of her father's camels and the wannabe porn star who'd refused to cross until I called him Dr. Love. So not too out there, but not too in there either. I walked around the counter and headed for the back room.

Someone yelled, "You can't be back here!" just as I spotted the break room. Jenny sat huddled in a plastic chair, staring at a cat poster encouraging its readers to hang in there, her cheeks wet with grief.

"Jenny, I'm so sorry," I said.

She wiped her face on a sleeve and looked up at me. "He would never have said that."

Damn, I hated to be caught in a lie. I much preferred my lies to go unnoticed, like a movie star's career who'd been arrested and sent to rehab. "He didn't." I lowered my head in shame and vowed to self-flagellate later.

Her mouth opened as if to ask me something, her expression suddenly filled with hope.

"He said, and I mean this in the nicest way possible, 'Bite me.' "

Her face transformed just as slowly, just as methodically as before, and she threw her arms around me. "I knew it!" she yelled as a couple of coworkers came into the cramped room to see what was going on. "I knew that's what he said." She leaned back and tried to explain past the lump in her throat. "He couldn't speak well at the end, and I could barely understand him, he was just so weak." She stopped and leaned back for a better look at me. "Wait, you're the light," she said, realization dawning in her eyes.

"The light?" I asked, all innocence and myrrh.

"Of course. When he was . . . right before he died, he said he saw a light, only it was coming from a woman with brown hair, gold eyes, and—" She cast a quick glance at my feet. "—motorcycle boots."

"Really?" I asked, stunned. "He saw me? I mean, he should've gone into the other light. You know, the main one, the direct route. I'm mostly reserved for those who've passed and didn't go up immediately." I glanced down at myself, annoyed that I couldn't see what the departed saw. My brilliant, come-hither beacon. "I totally need to check my wattage."

"He said bite me?" she asked, already over the fact that I was a light the departed went into. It would hit her later.

"Yes," I said with a wary grin. "What did he mean?"

A smile that resembled those searchlights on cop cars flashed across her face. "He meant he wanted to marry me. It was kind of our code." Her long fingers picked at a thread on her Super Dog shirt. "We never liked to argue in front of people, so we made up codes for everything, even the good stuff."

"Ah," I said, understanding her earlier outburst, "and 'I love you very much' was code for—?"

With a sheepish smile, she said, "I would rather suffer the sting of a thousand fire ants on my eyeballs than look at your face another minute."

"Oh, wow, so you came up with a code for that, huh?"

She giggled, but soon the grief caught up with her again and her smile faltered. She caught it and pushed it back up for my benefit.

"No," I told her, placing a hand on her shoulder, "you don't have to pretend for me." In an instant the tears reappeared and she hugged me again. We sat like that a long time as boys and men alike passed by the room to look in, mostly for a glimpse of the girl-on-girl action.

6

Ask me about my complete lack of interest.

—T-SHIRT

The minute Jenny started putting two and two together and asking me questions about how I got the message from Ronald and could I communicate with the other side, I suddenly had to be somewhere. Thankfully, she understood and offered to buy me another chili dog before I left, as mine had literally become chilly, but by then, I was out of the chili dog mood and had careened into hankering for a guacamole burger from Macho Taco. Plus Macho Taco had excellent coffee. Which would explain my presence there.

I decided to call the FBI agent who'd been assigned to the Yost case, see what I could dig up. "Yes, is this Agent Carson?" I asked as I sat at a booth and piled jalapeños onto my guacamole burger.

"This is her," the woman on the other end of the phone said.

"Oh, awesome." I plopped the bun back on, licked my fingertips, then groped through my handbag for a notepad. Instead, I came up with a napkin that had some long-forgotten phone number on it. It would have to do. I flipped it over and clicked my pen. "My name is Charlotte Davidson and I've been hired by Teresa Yost's family to look into her disappearance," I said, lying a little.

"Well, then, you must be in contact with them. You probably know everything we do." Her tone was sharp and brooked no argument, but there were few things I liked better than brooking arguments. I'd dealt with the FBI before, and not just those annoying Female Body Inspectors. I'd dealt with the real FBI on several occasions. Apparently, one of the prerequisites to becoming a federal agent was the inability to play well with others.

"Oh, I'm sure I do, about the case. I was actually wondering about Dr. Yost."

"Really?" Her interest piqued. "Didn't he hire you?"

"Well, yes and no. Let's just say I haven't accepted any money from him. I'm out to find Teresa Yost, not to make friends."

"That's good to hear," she said, a smile in her voice. "But I'm still not sure—"

"Nathan Yost was arrested in college. While going to medical school, in fact. Surely, you've checked into that."

After a long silence where I tried really hard not to ogle a transvestite in the most beautiful ruby stilettos I'd ever seen, she said, "It's nothing you can't find out on your own."

"True, but this is faster. I'll make a deal with you."

"This should be good." I heard the squeak of a chair as if she'd leaned back in it, possibly to put up her feet. "So?"

"I'll call you the minute I find her."

It was odd. She didn't scoff, bark with laughter, grind her teeth in annoyance, at least not that I could hear. She just said, "And I get partial credit?"

"Of course."

"Deal."

Wow.

"The arrest in college was due to a complaint by an ex-girlfriend."

Okay, way too easy.

"She said Yost became agitated when she tried to break up with him, told her one stick was all it would take. Her heart would stop in seconds, and no one would be able to trace it back to him. She got scared and moved in with her parents the next day."

"I can see why."

"They convinced her to press charges, but it was all hearsay. No concrete evidence, no other reports of abnormal behavior on file, so the DA's hands were tied."

"That's really interesting. One stick and her heart would stop, huh?"

"Yeah, he probably learned something in medical school and decided to use it for evil instead of good."

"Have you questioned her in light of the more recent developments?"

"Nope. But she still lives here, as far as I know. Guess I could give her a shout."

"Do you mind if I talk to her?"

"Knock yourself out."

Marveling at how smooth this whole conversation was going, I asked, "Can I get a name?"

After some rifling of papers, she said, "Yolanda Pope."

"Wait, seriously?" I asked. "I went to school with a Yolanda Pope."

"This particular Yolanda Pope is . . . Oh, here it is. She'd be twenty-nine now."

"That's about right. Yolanda was a couple grades ahead of me."

"Then you two should have a lot to talk about. Saves me from swallowing a hefty dose of wasted time and energy."

Okay, I really liked her, but I couldn't help myself. FBI agents just weren't this into sharing. "Can I ask what's going on here?"

"Excuse me?"

"Why share?"

She chuckled. "You think I haven't heard of you? About how you helped your father solve crimes when he was a detective? How you're helping your uncle now?"

"You've heard of me?"

"I'll take success where I can get it, Ms. Davidson. I didn't fall off the turnip truck yesterday."

"I'm famous?"

"Though I did actually fall off a turnip truck when I was nine. Just make sure you put me on speed dial," she said before hanging up.

Score! I had an in with the local FBI. This day was getting better and better. And the guacamole burger didn't hurt either.

Cookie had yet to track down Teresa Yost's sister. She lived in Albuquerque but apparently traveled a lot. Still, with Teresa missing, I couldn't imagine she'd be out of town. I gave Cookie the name of Yolanda Pope with instructions to get whatever she could on her, then spent the rest of the afternoon interviewing friends of both the good doctor and his missing wife. And according to every single person I talked to, he was a saint. They loved him, said he and Teresa were perfect together. In fact, he was a little too perfect. Like he'd used some kind of glamour, cast a spell.

Maybe he was magic. Maybe he was supernatural. Reyes was the son of Satan. Maybe Nathan Yost was the son of Pancake, a three-legged pigmy goat Jimmy Hochhalter used to worship in the sixth grade. Pancake was a lesser known and often misunderstood deity. Most likely because he stank to high heaven. Jimmy didn't smell too hot either, which didn't help the goat's rep.

I stopped off at Della's Beauty Salon and stepped inside to the sound of an electronic bell. Either that or the ringing in my ears was back. Della was a friend of Teresa's and one of the last people to see her the night she disappeared.

A woman with spiky hair and fantastic nails asked if she could help me.

"Absolutely, is Della in?"

"She's in the back, honey. You have an appointment?" She glanced up at my hair and made a sympathetic face.

I ran a hand over my ponytail, suddenly self-conscious. "No, I'm a private investigator. I was wondering if I could ask her a few questions."

She stammered in surprise. "Of-of course. Go on back," she said, pointing a zebra-striped nail toward the back room.

"Thanks." After another glance at her hair—I could do spikes—I stepped to the back and into a room lined with cabinets on one wall and shampoo sinks on another. A portly woman with a messy bob stood leaning over a sink, washing a client's hair. I'd always loved the distinct smell of hair salons. The way the chemicals mingled with the scents of shampoos and perfume and the pounds of hair spray applied each day to clientele. I breathed it in, then walked forward.

"Are you Della?" I asked.

She turned a half smile on me. I could feel the weight of depression on her chest as she said, "I sure am. Did you bring the perm solution?"

"No, sorry," I said, patting my pockets. "Must have left it at home. I'm a private investigator." I pulled out my PI license to make it look official. "I was wondering if I could ask you a few questions about Teresa."

My statement surprised her and she nearly drowned the woman beneath the spray. "Oh, my goodness," she said, turning off the water. "I'm so sorry, Mrs. Romero. Are you okay?"

The woman sputtered and turned bright eyes on her. "What?"

"Are you okay?" she asked, really loudly.

"I can't hear you. You got water in my ears, *mi' ja*."

Della turned a patient smile on me. "She can't hear me anyway. I've told the police everything I know."

"I'll get your statement from them as soon as I can. I was just wondering if you noticed any unusual behavior. Did Teresa seem preoccupied lately? Worried about anything?"

She shrugged as she towel-dried Mrs. Romero's hair. The elderly woman had been swallowed by a massive turquoise cape, and only her shoes peeked out from underneath it. "We don't go out that much anymore. Not like we used to. But she did seem a bit off that night," Della said, helping Mrs.

Romero to her feet, "nostalgic. Said if anything should happen to her, she would love us always."

Sounded like Teresa knew her husband was up to something. "Did she give you any specifics?"

"No." She shook her head. "She wouldn't elaborate, but she seemed sad. I was surprised she'd called us. It had been so long, and then for her to be so depressed." Her eyes glistened with sadness. "If we hadn't gone out, none of this would have happened."

"Why do you say that?" I followed her as she led Mrs. Romero to a salon chair.

"Because she never made it back to the house."

That surprised me. "How do you know?"

"Nathan told me. He said the security system had never been disarmed. If she'd come in the front door, there would have been a record."

"You mean, every time someone goes in and out, it's recorded?" I took out my memo pad and made a note to check on that.

"From what I understand, yes, if the security system is armed."

"What?" Mrs. Romero yelled.

"Do you want the usual?" Della yelled back.

The woman nodded and closed her eyes, apparently her naptime.

I dragged as much information out of Della as I could before heading out. She agreed with everyone else. Nathan was a saint. A pillar of the community. And oddly enough, as much as she cared for Teresa, she seemed to think Teresa was the reason their marriage was in trouble. Obviously, the doctor could do no wrong, so it had to be Teresa's fault.

With my list whittling down to almost nothing, I decided to hit the doctor's office just before closing, when everyone was tired and wanted nothing more than to go home. People in that position talked less and got to the point faster. Because the doctor always left early to do his rounds at the hospital, I figured he'd already be gone when I walked into his offices. He was apparently an otolaryngologist. I couldn't begin to guess what that meant.

The receptionist was just packing up and had to hurry out to pick up her daughter from daycare. Luckily, one of the doctor's assistants, an audiologist by the name of Jillian, was still in, finishing up some paperwork.

"So, have you worked for Dr. Yost long?" I asked her. Jillian was a big-boned girl with curly blond hair and one-too-many chins to be considered traditionally pretty. But her features were pleasant, her eyes warm. I could see her working with kids. The waiting room had toys and games scattered throughout.

We sat in the receptionist's area on padded chairs that rolled. It took every ounce of strength I had not to take advantage of that.

"I've been with Dr. Yost for twelve years," she said, her eyes filling with sadness. "He's such a good person. I just can't believe this is happening to him."

Wow. Fooling friends and family, I could see, but fooling someone you worked with day in and day out for twelve years? Who was this guy? "Did he seem different lately? Upset about anything? Or possibly mention someone following him or calling and hanging up?"

At this point, I was trying to figure out how premeditated the doctor's actions were, if he'd set up an alibi beforehand. Had he been planning to harm his wife or was it a spur-of-the-moment thing?

"No, not until that morning."

"Can you describe what happened?"

"Well, I don't know really," she said, shaking her head. "He just called my house Saturday morning, frantic, said he couldn't get in to do his rounds at the hospital that day and to see if Dr. Finely could cover for him."

"Did he tell you his wife was missing?"

After grabbing a pen from her lab coat, she nodded and said, "He even asked if she'd called me. He said the police were at his house and would probably be over to talk to me." She transferred some numbers onto a chart, signed it, then closed the file.

"And did they come?"

"Yes. An FBI agent came to my house late that afternoon."

"Agent Carson?"

"Yes. Are you working with her?"

"In a way," I said, trying not to stretch the truth too far. "So, there were no noticeable changes in his behavior in the days prior to his wife's disappearance?"

"No, I'm sorry. I wish I could be of more help."

Well, whatever happened, it didn't sound premeditated. Then again, the guy was obviously good.

"After everything he went through before . . ."

I froze. "Before?"

"Yes, with his first wife."

Those bells that ding between boxing rounds? Yeah, in my head. "Right, his first wife. Tragic."

A tear that had been shimmering against her eyelashes finally pushed past them and slid down her cheek. She turned to get a tissue, embarrassed. "I'm so sorry. It's just . . . I mean, for her to have died so suddenly."

"Oh, no, I completely understand." I tried not to notice how her curls vibrated when she blew her nose.

"For her heart to just stop, and while on vacation, no less. He was just so alone after that."

Now we were getting somewhere. Didn't Agent Carson mention something to that effect? One stick and her heart would stop? "I can't believe it myself."

I had to look into this ay-sap. And Jillian seemed more taken with the guy than I'd originally assumed. I wondered how much of her ignorance was him and how much of it was her. Puppy love was a powerful elixir. I should know. The things I did for Tim La Croix, my senior-year crush. Unfortunately, I'd been in kindergarten at the time, otherwise he might have taken note.

Before heading home, I hit the Chocolate Coffee Café for a mocha latte, Macho Taco for a chicken burrito with extra salsa, and a twenty-four-hour convenience store for a couple packages of microwave popcorn and some chocolate to tide me over for the night. I wasn't sure how much longer I could stay awake, though. I'd have to watch action movies, or horror, something bloody. Even then, I figured I had a 50/50 chance.

What had Reyes said? He wasn't angry because he didn't want to be there, but because he did? I didn't know how to take that. My innards were in turmoil, but leaning toward happy, as desperate and pathetic as my innards were. Mostly 'cause Reyes did things to them. Delicious, devilish, heart-stoppingly decadent things. Damn him.

Before I could ponder myself into an orgasm, I opened my phone and called Cookie.

"Hey, boss. Where are you?" she asked.

"I just picked up something to eat. What about professional belly dancers?"

"Um, I don't know, maybe with horseradish."

"No, our new careers. We have to look to the future now, and I've always wanted to learn how to do the wave with my stomach. Not to mention the fact that my belly button could use the exposure. Almost no one knows about it."

"You're right," she said, playing along. "I don't even know its name."

I gasped and glanced down. "I don't think Stella heard you, but you need to be more careful. Oh, I meant to tell you, I think that server at Macho Taco with the short hair and strange eyebrows is Batman."

"I've wondered about her. Did you want to discuss anything that actually pertains to a case?"

"You mean besides the fact that our Dr. Yost was married before?"

"You're not going to believe this, but I was just about to call and tell you the same thing. It's like we're connected or something, like we have ESP."

"Or extrasensory perception."

"Exactly. I got a number on Yolanda Pope and left a message on her cell."

"Most excellent. I'm dying to get the story behind those charges she filed on one Mr. Nathan Yost. In the meantime, I want you to get everything you can on Yost's first wife."

"Got it. I'll put everything I've found so far on your counter. You're on your way home, right?"

"I am indeed," I said, turning onto Central.

"See. I didn't even need to ask."

"I know. It's weird."

"How many cups of coffee have you had today?"

I counted on my fingers before remembering they should remain on the steering wheel at all times while driving. "Seven," I said, swerving to narrowly miss a horrified pedestrian.

"Just seven?"

"And twelve-halves."

"Oh, well, that's not bad. For you. Maybe now that you've talked to Reyes, you can get some sleep. Maybe, you know, he'll stop."

"Maybe. Sleep sounds really nice about now," I said, the mere mention of it weighing me down, coaxing my lids closed before remembering they should remain open at all times while driving. So many rules. "I'm not sure, though. I get the feeling he doesn't have any more choice in the matter than I do."

"It's all so cosmic," she said, a wistful sigh in her voice.

"It's definitely something. Okay, I'm almost home. Be there in a jiff."

At exactly 8:23ish I stumbled across the threshold of my apartment, food, coffee, and DVDs in hand, while fishing through my bag for my phone. I had a text from Garrett. He was probably going to bitch me out for waking him before the sun shone that morning. I flipped it open. It read,

Four: You're killing me.

I texted back.

Clearly I need to try harder.

"Hey, Mr. Wong," I said after dumping the contents of my arms on the kitchen counter.

While Garrett's list of the top five things you never want to say to the grim reaper was interesting, I had a better list for him. A to-do list. Vacuum. Clean out my fridge. Do the dishes in his underwear. Though why he would have dishes in his underwear was beyond me.

Just as I began perusing the research Cookie had put by Mr. Coffee—she knew me so well—someone knocked on my door. I found the prospect appealing. Maybe I'd won a million dollars. Or maybe someone was going to try to sell me a vacuum cleaner and would offer a free demonstration. Either way, it was a win–win.

I put down my chicken burrito and opened the door to my good fortune, realizing I would do anything I could think of to stay awake.

Cookie's daughter, Amber, stood on the other side. Well, not *the* other side, just the other side of the door. She would have been tall for a twenty-year-old, but she was only twelve, which made her really tall. I could've sworn she was much shorter that morning. Fresh out of the shower, her long black hair smelled like strawberry shampoo and hung in wet tangles over her shoulders. She wore pink tank-topped pajamas with capri-styled bottoms covering the longest, skinniest legs I'd ever seen. Dancer's legs. She was like a butterfly on the verge of bursting out of her cocoon.

"Are you going to watch TV on your TV?" she asked, her huge blue eyes completely serious.

"As opposed to on my toaster?" When she pressed her mouth together and blinked, waiting for a response, I caved. "No, I'm not going to watch TV on my TV."

"Good." She grinned and bounced past me.

"But I am going to take a shower in my shower."

"Okay." She picked up the remote, plopped onto my sofa, and draped her bare feet over the side. "Mom canceled our cable prescription."

"She didn't," I said, fighting back a giggle.

Cookie came out her door and into mine just then, also wearing pajamas. I glowered at her in horror.

She rolled her eyes. "Has she convinced you to call child services yet?"

"Mom," Amber said, flipping onto her stomach, "it's just wrong. Why should I have to pay because you want to be all healthy?"

I cast her another horrified glare. "You don't," I said, the contempt in my voice undeniable.

She sighed and handed me another printout after she closed the door. "My doctor says I need to lose weight."

"Dr. Yost?" I asked. The paper she handed me had our would-be client's name on top. Why would an otolaryngologist tell her to lose weight? Especially if she wasn't going to him?

"No, not Dr. Yost." She padded over to the bar and climbed onto a stool. "Why would I go to Dr. Yost?"

"Oh, this is his arrest record." I scanned it while taking another bite of burrito, then asked, "So, what does your losing weight have to do with cable?"

"Not much, besides the fact that it's much more expensive to eat healthy than it is to eat junk food."

"Exactly why I don't eat healthy." I shook my chicken burrito at her. "There's a lesson to be learned here."

"You don't count. Skinny chicks are dumb."

"I beg your pardon. You think I'm skinny?"

"The doctor's right. I have to cut back." Her shoulders deflated. "Do you know how hard it is to diet with a name like Cookie?"

"That's so weird." I stared off into space, marveling at the similarities of our situation. "It's hard to diet with a name like Charley, too. Maybe we should just change our names?" I said, refocusing on her.

"I would do it in a heartbeat if I thought it would help. What do you think?" She gestured to the file she'd left while reaching over the snack bar and pouring herself a cup of coffee.

"You have all the movie channels!" Amber squealed. "How did I not know that?"

"Seriously?" I asked. "No wonder that bill is so friggin' high." I zeroed in on a newspaper article about Yost's previous wife. "Dr. Yost's wife was found dead in her hotel room of an apparent heart attack." I looked up at Cook. "She couldn't have been more than twenty-seven. A heart attack?"

"Keep reading," Cookie said.

"According to sources," I said, reading aloud, "Ingrid Yost, who was on vacation alone in the Cayman Islands, called and left a message on her husband's answering machine only minutes before her heart stopped, so despite the strange chain of events surrounding Mrs. Yost's death, police say there will be no follow-up investigation." I glanced up at Cookie. "The strange chain of events?"

"Keep reading," she said, tearing off a bite of my chicken burrito.

I took a bite as I read, then put the article down. "Okay," I said, swallowing hard, "so Ingrid Yost files a police report stating her husband was threatening her two days before she files for divorce. Two days after that, she flies to the Cayman Islands packed with little more than her toothbrush, calls and leaves a message on the doctor's home answering machine about how she was sorry she wasn't a better wife and how she no longer wants a divorce, then she dies five minutes later?"

"Yep."

"With no previous history of heart problems?" I picked up the phone and speed-dialed FBI Agent Carson. Cookie's brows raised in curiosity as she tore off another bite.

"So, what's wrong with this picture?" I asked when Agent Carson answered.

"Hold on, let me get to another room." After a moment, she asked, "Did you find Teresa Yost already?"

"Where are you?"

"At the Yosts' house. My partner still thinks there'll be a ransom demand."

"Over a week later?"

"He's new. What's up?"

"His first wife had filed charges against him two days before she filed for divorce, two days before she flew to the Cayman Islands and died of a heart attack? Really?"

"So, you haven't found her."

"A divorce in which he stood to lose a small fortune?"

"And your point is?"

"Um, maybe it's all connected?"

"Of course it's connected, but try proving that. We checked the doctor's passport and flights. He didn't go to the Cayman Islands. Says he went hunting to try to work things out in his head."

"That doesn't mean he didn't do it. The doctor's loaded. He could have paid someone to dispose of her. He had more than enough knowledge on what drugs to use to induce a heart attack. And don't you think the message on the answering machine was a little much?"

"In what way?"

"I'll give you two ways. One, according to the police report, she was hysterical. Who's to say she wasn't being coaxed or threatened to leave that message?"

"True, but to what end?"

"To allay suspicion. If they were making up, no one would suspect the doctor of any wrongdoing. It would cast sympathy on him and the whole situation."

"That's possible. And two?" she asked.

"Since when do doctors have answering machines at home? Don't they have answering services for that? Voice mail at work? It just seems really convenient."

She was quiet a long time, but I heard footsteps as if she were moving in and out of several rooms. "You're right. And he doesn't have one now. Let me check that out, find out when he got the answering machine and how long he had it."

"Sounds good. And can you get a copy of the message she left?"

"Mmm, I doubt that. Since there was no investigation, I can't imagine anyone would have kept a copy, but I'll find out."

"Thanks. And can you check on the security system as well? Della Peters from the beauty salon said Yost knew Teresa never made it inside that night, because the security system would have recorded her entering."

"It would have, had it been armed. That was one of the first things we checked. Yost said he forgot to arm it."

"Then he's a liar, liar, pants on fire." I made a mental sticky note to that effect, in case I forgot later. "Thanks for the info."

"You're welcome. And, no offense, but shouldn't you have found her by now? I mean, isn't that what you do?"

"I'm working on it. Don't push me."

She sniffed. "Okay, just don't forget about this."

"Never." I knew what was at stake for anyone in law enforcement. Making a name for oneself got you noticed. Took you places. And I wasn't just talking about the Sizzler.

Cookie and I made plans for the next day as I drank two huge glasses of water. The natural tears I'd been using to moisturize my eyes were losing their efficacy and my mouth was full of cotton. Too much coffee, too little sleep. I needed to rehydrate.

"So, I'll keep on the Yost case," she said, writing down some ideas, "and you're going to try to see Rocket."

"That's the plan. At least we can find out if Teresa Yost is still with us."

She took the cup of coffee I'd just made out of my hands. "You need to get some sleep."

"I need to soak in a hot bath, hydrate myself from the outside in."

"That's a good idea. Maybe it'll relax you so much, you'll fall asleep whether you want to or not."

"Are you on my side, or what?"

An evil grin spread across her face as she called out to Amber. "Come on, hon."

"Mom!" Amber said without ungluing her eyes from the TV screen. "This movie just started."

"It's almost your bedtime."

"It's okay," I said. "She can stay." I leaned in and whispered, "She'll be asleep in no time."

"True. But are you sure?"

"Of course," I said, shooing her out the door. "I'm just going to soak a bit, then join her."

Amber was watching one of the horror movies I'd rented. Come to think of it, that movie might keep her awake. At least it would keep one of us awake.

"I'm going to take a quick bath, kiddo," I said, leaning over the sofa and kissing her forehead.

"Don't make the water too hot. My teacher says it gives you old-timers."

After squelching a snicker, I said, "I don't think hot baths have anything to do with Alzheimer's, but I'll take that under advisement."

"Okay, but my teacher says," she warned. I could see why Cookie threatened repeatedly to sell her to the gypsies if she weren't so cute.

7

I totally take back all those times
I didn't want to nap when I was younger.
—T-SHIRT

I stripped down and sank into the tub, cringing when the scalding water slid up my legs and torso. A sultry heat settled around me, the steam seeping into my skin, and my lids started to drift shut almost immediately. My mind wandered aimlessly to greener pastures. Pastures with a four-poster bed perched in a field of grass with fluffy down pillows that just begged to be slept on. And baby ducks. For some reason, there were baby ducks. I rubbed my eyes, forcing myself back to the present, and led a dampened strand of hair behind an ear. Maybe this wasn't such a good idea after all. If I was going to make it another night without sleep, the last thing I needed was a hot, relaxing bath.

I washed quickly and immersed myself fully in the water to rinse off, looking from beneath it at the glint of light before resurfacing. Reluctantly, I pushed the stopper with my toes to let the water drain and stood to get a towel, which I draped over my head to wring the water from my hair.

The drain gurgled as the water stirred at my feet. I felt something solid there and slowly lowered the towel. A telltale heat rose like steam around my legs, and Reyes materialized in front of me, his powerful shoulders glistening as water sheeted off them. He locked a hand around my throat and leaned me back against the cool tile wall, so at odds with the blistering heat that radiated off him. His expression was hard and unforgiving.

And before I could say anything, that familiar need gripped me. I steeled myself, fought it, but it was like fighting a tsunami with a spork. He stepped closer as his gaze locked on to mine, his deep brown eyes almost inquisitive under his spiked lashes.

I felt him nudge my legs apart with his knee. "What are you doing?" I asked, gasping as the heat penetrated my core.

Without answering, he pulled the towel out of my hands and tossed it aside.

"Reyes, wait. You don't want to be here." My palms rested on his rib cage. "You don't want to do this."

He leaned in until his full mouth was almost on mine. "No more than you want me to," he said, daring me to argue, his breath like velvet over my lips. He smelled like a lightning storm, like earth and ozone and electricity. His hand rose to hold my chin captive as the other slid between my legs. My stomach lurched with the contact, the center of my being so sensitive to his touch, I almost came right then and there.

A knock sounded at the bathroom door and I looked over with furrowed brows.

"Not yet," he said in warning, his fingers diving inside me, drawing me back to him.

I gasped and clutched on to his wrist to push him away. Instead I pulled him deeper, clawed at him, begging for release.

He pressed his steely body against mine and leaned in until his mouth was at my ear. "Stay with me," he said, his deep voice rich and smooth. He released my chin, took hold of one of my hands, and led it down the solid wall of his abdomen.

The knock sounded again and I felt myself being ripped away from him.

"Dutch," he said as my hand encircled his erection, but water rushed up and around us like a flash flood until I was literally fighting for air.

I bolted upright, sending bathwater splashing over the edge of the tub as I remembered where I was.

"Okay?" I heard a voice say. Amber.

"What, sweetheart?" I said, wiping water from my face. "I didn't hear you."

"I'm going home. My cell's about to die and I have to call Samantha. Her boyfriend broke up with her, and the world is apparently going to end."

I struggled to catch my breath. "Okay, hon. See you tomorrow," I said, my voice too airy.

"'Kay."

I forced myself to calm, to get a grip on reality, to unclench my fists and free the sopping towel I'd dragged into the bathtub at some point. Then I eased up and perched my chin on my knees as I waited out the storm trembling through me.

This was getting ridiculous. If I'd bound him, how was he still entering my dreams? What the hell was that about? Not to mention the fact that I'd fallen asleep in a bathtub. I could've drowned.

Freaking son of Satan.

My phone chimed, letting me know I'd missed something. I reached over with a shaking hand and grabbed it off the vanity. My sister, Gemma, had sent me a text. Three, in fact. She was having car trouble, couldn't get a hold of Dad, and wanted me to pick her up at a convenience store just outside of Santa Fe. I tried to call her as I stepped out of the tub, but an annoying voice cut in, saying her phone was either off or she was out of the calling area. Wonderful. She did say her battery was low. Maybe it died.

Having no choice, I patted dry, dragged on a pair of jeans, a Blue Öyster Cult sweatshirt, and my hard-won biker boots, and stepped out of the bathroom. The television sat silent, the living room dark.

I didn't bother drying my hair before I left the apartment, advising Mr. Wong not to let strangers in as I did so. A freezing rain pelted me when I rushed outside to Misery, swearing on all things holy if Gemma wasn't at the convenience store when I got there, I would begin my illustrious career as a soul collector for real, starting with hers. I supposed I'd have to pick up a jar first.

I drove to Santa Fe for the second time that day as sheets of icy rain cascaded down my windshield. My hair, frozen to my head, was slowly thawing. At least it was easier to stay awake in Popsicle mode. Misery was doing her best to warm me, and I had to admit, my toes were pretty toasty. I should have brought a towel or a blanket. What if something happened? What if Misery died and I froze to death? That would suck.

I wondered if Reyes ever got cold. He was so hot, as though his body generated heat from its own source inside him. He should've come with a HIGHLY COMBUSTIBLE warning label.

When I was finally warm, I realized the shaking I'd been experiencing was not due to the temperature but to Reyes's latest visit. Figures. I forced my mind away from him and onto the case at hand. My first order of business would be to use my supernatural connections to find out if Teresa Yost was still alive. The odds were certainly against it, but with any luck, she'd survived whatever the good doctor had in store for her. I needed more information on him as well.

The rain continued to fall in a procession of thick angry droplets that sounded more like hail against Misery than raindrops. It forced me to slow, to take the turns more cautiously than I wanted to. But its aggressive disposition matched my own. The slapping of the windshield wipers lulled me into serenity, and no matter how hard I tried, I couldn't stop my thoughts from traveling back to Reyes.

Why did he come to me? He was so angry, so reluctant to be with me, yet there he was, enjoying it each and every time as much as I.

Then again, he was a man. Why men did anything they did was beyond me. And they have the nerve to complain about women.

I took the exit that would lead to the convenience store outside of Santa Fe. It sat in a fairly remote area, and I couldn't help but wonder what in the name of jelly beans Gemma had been doing out here. As far as I knew, she rarely went spotlighting for jackrabbits. A delivery truck ahead of me caused me to slow even more, but since the rain made it impossible to see beyond twenty feet, I actually felt safer behind it. I focused on its taillights to stay on the road. Rain in the parched deserts of New Mexico was always a good thing, but driving in it was becoming dangerous. Thankfully, the heavily lit convenience store came into view. The truck continued on as I coasted into the parking lot, then stopped short. Only one car sat off to the side, probably the night clerk's. I scanned the area for Gemma's Volvo, a realization coming to light along with a stunned kind of anger. She wasn't there.

Clamping my jaw together to keep from cursing aloud, I tried her cell again, to no avail. Then I checked the texts again to make sure I had the right place. I did. Maybe she was lost, had told me the wrong convenience store. Before I could make a decision on what to do, my passenger's-side door opened. Thank goodness. I figured her car was stuck somewhere out in this tempest and she'd had to hoof it to the store on foot. But instead of my sister's blond hair and slight frame climbing in, a large wet man crawled inside and closed the door behind him. After an initial period of astonishment, a jolt of adrenaline rushed through me in a delayed reaction I would later shake my head at in befuddlement.

Cookie was right. I almost get killed in the most unlikely places.

I jumped to open my door, but long fingers that could easily be mistaken for a Vise-Grip locked around my arm. The fact that I knew the survival rate of abducted women spurred me into action. I fought him with a few well-placed punches while groping for the door handle. When he jerked me toward him, I raised my feet over the center console and kicked. But he bound my legs within a steel-like arm and pulled me underneath him.

A large hand muffled the screams I'd let rip as he pushed himself onto me. His weight caused the console to grind into my back painfully, but I still kicked and squirmed and used everything I'd learned in the two weeks I'd lasted in jujitsu. No way was I going to make this easy for him.

"Stop fighting me and I'll let you up," he said with a growl.

Oh, *now* he wants to negotiate. I began my struggles anew, clawing at him and kicking. A primal instinct had taken hold, and I no longer controlled my actions. He forced my head back, leaned into me, and the sickening feel of a cold sharp object against my throat stilled me instantly. My senses came rushing back at a dizzying speed, along with the chilling reality of my predicament.

"Don't stop fighting me," he added in a husky voice, "and I'll slice your throat right here and now."

For an endless minute the only thing I heard was my own labored breathing. The flood of adrenaline coursing through my veins shook me from head to toe. The man was soaking wet. Cold rain beaded off him and dripped onto my face.

Then something familiar registered in the back of my mind. The heat. Though his clothes and hair were soaking wet and bitterly cold, a heat radiated toward me and I blinked in utter astonishment.

He rested his forehead against mine as if catching his breath. Then he moved his hand from my mouth to the back of my neck and lifted me to a sitting position. My legs were still draped over the console when he straddled my hips—an amazing feat in the cramped space—and placed the weapon against my throat again.

Looming over me, he seemed larger than life. I recognized the prison uniform underneath a pair of work coveralls, filthy and torn.

"I won't hurt you, Dutch."

The sound of my name, the name he'd given me, sent an electric charge rushing through every molecule in my body.

I stared at him as a flash of lightning illuminated the confining space, and looked into the deep brown eyes of Reyes Farrow. The realization stunned me. He had escaped from a maximum-security prison. Things didn't get much more surreal than that.

He was shaking with the cold, answering a question I'd asked myself of him earlier. Though his gaze was laced with desperation, his actions screamed otherwise. He seemed very much in control, and something other than desperation was driving him. A fierce determination fueled his every move. I didn't doubt for a moment his willingness to kill me if need be. He was super pissed at me for binding him anyway.

"Take the Jeep," I said, unable to believe I was actually scared of him. Of course, he'd always been the only thing I was afraid of growing up. I just didn't know it was him until recently.

His eyes narrowed. He hovered over me, allowed his gaze to roam over my face. I wanted to turn away but found it impossible. The things we had done over the past few weeks. The things he was capable of. And now I was sitting here with a knife at my throat, placed there by the very man who could make me scream out his name in my sleep. "It's yours," I said. "Take it. I won't call the police."

"I have every intention of doing just that."

Somehow, this was so different from any other encounter I'd had with him. Different because it was him, Reyes Alexander Farrow, Rey'aziel, the son of Satan in the flesh. Aside from that morning, I didn't have experience with this part of him, with a beast capable of ripping a man to shreds between commercial breaks, if the stories Neil Gossett told me were any indication.

When a burst of lightning illuminated our surroundings again, he glanced at his watch. Only then did I realize his muscles were tense as if in pain. "We're late," he said tightly, the barest hint of a grin lifting one corner of his mouth. "What took you so long?"

I drew my brows together. "Late?"

His smile faltered and he ground his teeth, leaned forward, and placed his forehead against mine again. I realized he was hurt. He went limp against me for half a second, as though he'd lost consciousness. With a jerk, he forced himself to attention. He grabbed the steering wheel for balance, then refocused on me.

In my mind, history was repeating itself. That night so long ago, a teenage boy went limp from a violent blow. He raised his arms in a futile effort to fend off the attack. The image brought back feelings of empathy, of a blinding need to help him.

I fought it. This was no teenage boy. This was a man, a supernatural being, holding a knife to my throat. A man who had sat in prison for more than a decade, being molded, tempered, and hardened by the hatred and anger that procreated in such places. As if growing up in hell hadn't fueled such malevolence enough. If he wasn't incorrigible before going in, he was sure to be now. I couldn't allow compassion to intervene, no matter our history. Nice boys didn't use knives to get girls. Maybe he really was his father's son.

I glanced to the side. The hand with the makeshift knife gripped the steering wheel as if his life depended on it. The fact that he was hurt reminded me of a line he'd told me a while back: Beware the wounded animal.

"Why are you doing this?" I asked.

He opened his eyes to me and said, matter-of-fact, "Because you'll run if I don't."

"No, I mean, why did you escape?"

He frowned. "They wouldn't let me out otherwise." Another pained expression flashed across his face.

I glanced down. The dark coveralls were drenched in blood, and a gasp escaped before I could stop it. "Reyes—"

An aggressive knock on my door made us both jump. The knife was at my throat instantly. The wounded animal indeed.

"If you try anything—"

I ground my teeth. "Seriously?"

"Dutch," he said, a warning in his voice.

"I won't." Even if I'd been brave enough to fight him, the knife was simply too close, too menacing for me to do anything foolhardy. Not that foolhardy wasn't my middle name.

"I don't want to hurt you, Dutch."

"I don't want you to."

"Then don't make me."

The persistent knock sounded again.

I reached over to unzip the plastic window, and he pressed the knife deeper into my skin.

Leveling a steady gaze on him, I explained, "He's not just going to go away. I have to talk to him."

When he didn't respond, I reached over and unzipped the window, but just a little. It was still pouring out. That's when I felt Reyes's thumb across my lips and looked back, startled. He lowered his intent look to my mouth, let it linger for half a second, then bent his head and kissed me. I knew instantly what he was doing. Who would question two lovers taking advantage of the weather?

The kiss was amazingly gentle. Liquid and warm. His tongue slid across my lips and I opened them, giving him access, permission to deepen the kiss. And he did. He tilted his head and dived inside, his mouth scalding against mine. Irony at its finest. This was the first kiss we'd actually shared in the flesh, the real deal.

Without thought, I raised my hands to his chest, solid and blisteringly hot. A steely arm snaked around my neck and pulled me into him. Despite the unhurried tenderness of his actions, his muscles were rigid, poised to strike should the need arise.

I could not mistake this for more than what it was. As heavenly as it felt to be wrapped in the arms of Reyes Farrow, to feel his mouth on mine, the courts had declared him a murderer. More than that, he was desperate. And desperate men did desperate things.

"Guess you two have things under control."

Startled, I broke the kiss off and glanced over to see an elderly man in a bright yellow slicker chuckling at us.

"Personally, I'd have gone for the backseat, but that's just me."

I turned to the face framed within the window opening, and felt the pressure of a blade at my throat, angled so the man couldn't see it. As I flashed my best smile to the man practically drowning outside my window, I felt another wave of pain wash over Reyes and the knife tip pierced my skin. I flinched when it drew blood. He immediately eased up.

"I'm sorry," I said to raincoat man, my voice unsteady. "We were just taking advantage of the storm."

"I understand," he said with a huge grin. "You might want to pull over a little farther. Never can tell in a storm like this what other drivers'll do."

"Thank you. We will."

He looked at Reyes, studied him a moment, then turned back to me. "But everything's okay?"

"Oh, sure," I said as Reyes sank down into the passenger's seat. He probably realized he was hovering over me like an escaped convict might hover over a hostage. But that could just be me projecting. Lowering the knife to my rib cage, he pressed it into my jacket to let me know it was still there. He was so thoughtful.

"Everything's fine," I continued. "Thank you so much for checking. Not many people would brave such a storm." I glanced up at the rumbling sky.

"Well," he said, smiling sheepishly, "I'm at the store over there. Saw you pull over and thought maybe something was wrong."

"Not a thing," I said as if I were not being held against my will by a convicted murderer who also happened to be the son of the most evil being in the universe.

"Glad to hear it. If you need anything, come on in."

"We will, thank you so much."

I zipped the window closed as raincoat man trudged back to the convenience store with a wave. I smiled and waved back. What a nice guy.

As soon as he was inside, I turned to Reyes. Aware of his pain now, I could feel it assault him in hot waves, and again I fought the empathy that threatened to overcome my generally annoyed mood. I pointed to the blood. "What happened?"

"You."

"Me?" I asked, surprised.

Lowering the weapon, he settled farther down into the passenger's seat. "You fell asleep."

Oh, damn, I did. "But what does that have to do with—?"

"It seems every time you fall asleep, you draw me to you."

"So, it's my fault? I do it?"

He focused pain-filled eyes on me. "I'm bound. I can't go to you now without you summoning me."

"But I'm not doing it on purpose." I was suddenly very embarrassed. "Wait, what does that have to do with your being wounded?"

"When you summon me, it's like before. I go into a seizurelike state."

"Oh."

"A word of advice. Never have a seizure when you're trying to escape the crushing jaws of a garbage truck."

"Oh. Oh! Oh, my god. I'm so . . . wait, why am I apologizing? You escaped. From a maximum-security prison. In a garbage truck?"

"I told you. They wouldn't let me out otherwise." He laid his head back against the headrest and closed his eyes. The pain coursing through his body was wearing on him. "Let's get out of here."

After a long moment, I asked, "Why don't you just take my Jeep?"

A mischievous smile slid across his face. "I am."

"Without me in it."

"So you can run to the clerk? I think not."

"I won't tell anyone, Reyes. I promise. Not a soul."

With a sigh, he opened his eyes to me. He was so beautiful. So vulnerable. "Do you know what I would have done had that man figured out the truth?"

I lowered my head and didn't answer. Maybe not so vulnerable.

"I don't want to hurt anyone."

"But you will if you have to."

"Exactly."

I turned the ignition and swerved onto the highway. "Where are we going?"

"Albuquerque."

That surprised me. Not Mexico? Not Iceland? "What's in Albuquerque?"

He closed his eyes again. "Salvation."

8

When everything is coming your way,
you're in the wrong lane.
—T-SHIRT

A light drizzle misted the atmosphere, making the headlights of oncoming vehicles blossom into a spectrum of colors like dozens of mini-rainbows. The rain had let up, but the stars were hidden by dense clouds. As we drove, Reyes seemed to be sleeping. Still, I wasn't about to risk my life by trying an escape, no matter how much I'd always wanted to execute one of those dive rolls out of a speeding vehicle like in the movies. With my luck, I'd just be plowed under by the next car on the interstate. Wait a minute. That gave me an idea: Cookie and I could be stuntwomen.

I practiced a little evasive maneuver, mostly because movie directors loved that stuff, and Reyes jolted in the seat. He grabbed his side with a sharp intake of breath, clearly hurting. And from the amount of blood that had saturated the coveralls, the wound was significant. We healed faster, much faster, than everyone else. Hopefully that would be enough to keep him alive until I could get him help.

I let the air escape from my lungs slowly, wondering how I could be so utterly scared of someone and yet so consumed with his well-being at the same time. Reality took hold again. I had actually been abducted by an escaped convict. On a scale of one to surreal, this one rocketed into the double digits. The optimistic part of me that saw the cup half full was—disturbingly—a little elated. After all, this wasn't just any escaped convict. This was Reyes Farrow, the man who haunted my dreams with far more sensuality than should've been legal to carry in public.

Playing chauffeur to a convicted felon with a homemade knife who insisted on poking me in the ribs every time I hit a bump in the road had not been part of my plans for the evening. I had a case. I had places to be and people to see. And two horror movies just waiting to wreak havoc on my nervous system.

"Take the San Mateo exit."

He startled me. I turned to him, a tad braver than an hour ago. "Where are we going?"

"My best friend's house. He was my cell mate for over four years."

"Amador Sanchez?" I asked, the surprise in my voice undeniable.

Amador Sanchez had gone to high school with Reyes and seemed to be Reyes's only connection to the outside world before he was arrested as well for assault with a deadly weapon resulting in great bodily harm. Against a police officer, no less. Never a wise decision. What neither Neil Gossett nor I could figure out was how Amador and Reyes had ended up cell mates for four years. And Neil was the deputy warden. If he didn't know how that happened, nobody did. Clearly Reyes's résumé included more than just *general in hell*.

Reyes opened his eyes and turned to me. "You know him?"

"We've met, yes. When I was trying to find your body before." I couldn't help a quick glance at that very thing. Demons had attacked him by the hundreds, had practically ripped him to shreds, yet here he was, two weeks later, almost completely healed. From that event, anyway.

His mouth widened into a grin. "I take it he was a lot of help?"

"Please. You must have something on him."

He laughed softly. "It's called friendship."

"It's called blackmail and is, in fact, illegal in most countries." I glanced over at him as oncoming headlights illuminated the gold and green flecks in his eyes. He was smiling, his eyes warm, soothing. They made my insides gooey.

I blinked and turned away.

"What time is it?" he asked after continuing to stare a long moment.

I looked at the clock on my dashboard. "Almost eleven."

"We're late."

"Sorry," I said, both syllables dripping with sarcasm, "I didn't realize we were on a schedule."

We pulled up to the Sanchezes' house, a stunning trilevel Spanish-tiled adobe in the Heights with a stained glass entryway. It hardly fit the image of an ex-convict who'd done time for assault. It was much more of a tax-evasion rap, an embezzlement kind of stretch.

Maybe he stole it.

"Drive up to the garage and flash your lights."

A little surprised by the level of thought he'd put into his escape, I did what he asked. The garage door opened immediately.

"Pull in and turn off the engine."

I'd met Amador and his wife, and they were actually quite lovely. Nonetheless, the situation didn't sit well, like Suzy Dervish in Girl Scouts before she got on Ritalin. "I don't think I like this plan."

"Dutch."

I turned to him. His eyes were glassed over and he had paled. He'd obviously lost a lot of blood. I might could outrun him now.

"I won't let anything happen to you," he said.

"You're in no condition to be playing the white knight. Just let me go."

Regret flashed across his face. "I'm sorry. I can't do that." He reached over and took hold of my arm as if afraid I would bolt.

I'd been considering that very thing. How far could he chase me with his pallor?

"Pull in," he said.

After taking a deep breath, I drove into the double-car garage and turned off the engine, not happy at all about having done so. The garage door closed—effectively locking me in with a band of criminals. The lights came on, and an entire family of them came out the side door toward us.

Reyes sat up straighter with only a slight wince and flashed a genuine smile at the man opening his door for him, Amador Sanchez. Amador's wife, Bianca, stood back in anticipation, holding a small boy in her arms and the hand of a little girl. She waved at me through the windshield.

I waved back—apparently Stockholm syndrome worked fast—then watched as Amador leaned in and grasped Reyes in a burly hug.

"*Hola,* my friend," he said, patting Reyes's back aggressively.

Reyes's jaw clamped shut as he bit back a curse.

"You're late." Amador Sanchez was a good-looking man in his early thirties with short black hair, hazel eyes, and the confidence that seemed to be bred into the Chicano culture.

"Blame the driver," he said from between gritted teeth. "She kept trying to escape."

Amador glanced at me and winked. "I can understand that, Ms. Davidson. I tried to escape his company for four years."

Reyes laughed. He laughed. It was the first real laugh I'd ever heard from him. An odd sense of happiness emerged despite my inner turmoil.

"You're hurt." The man stepped back to get a look at him.

"Move, Daddy! Let me see."

The little girl, gorgeous with long black curls, pushed past her father to get a better look. Her tiny brows snapped together. "Uncle Reyes, what happened?"

Reyes grinned at her. "I'm going to tell you something very important, Ashlee. Are you ready?"

Her nod sent curls bouncing around her head.

"Never, ever, ever crawl into the back of a garbage truck."

"I told you it was a stupid idea." Amador stood clicking his tongue at him.

"It was your freaking idea in the first place."

Bianca pushed forward. "Then it was more than stupid." She leaned over him and tried to peel the blood-soaked coveralls back from the wound, worry lining her lovely face. "I can't believe you listened to him."

"I can't believe you married him."

She narrowed her eyes on Reyes, though her expression held more humor than admonition. And love. Genuine, unadulterated love, and an unusual streak of jealousy slashed through me. They knew him better than I did, possibly better than I ever would. I'd never been jealous in my life, but lately it seemed to be the only emotion I could conjure when it came to the people in Reyes's life.

"When you gonna come to your senses and divorce him?" he asked her.

I lowered my gaze. Bianca was nothing if not stunning. Like her daughter, she had huge sparkling eyes and long dark hair that hung in thick curls over her shoulders.

"She's in love with me, *pendejo,*" her husband said with a shrug. "Go figure."

"I'll marry you, Uncle Reyes."

He laughed again and smiled lovingly at the girl. "Then I will be the luckiest man alive."

Ashlee jumped into his lap as her mother screeched in surprise. "Baby, no!"

Reyes reassured her with a wink and gingerly hugged the young girl to him, trying not to get blood on her. He seemed to cherish the feel of it, as if he'd been waiting a long time to be able to hug her. Tears leapt into Bianca's eyes as she leaned in and kissed his cheek. He reached for her and hugged them both.

When I looked up, Amador stood smiling in earnest appreciation, and I realized I was intruding on a long-awaited family reunion. I shouldn't have been there. In a thousand ways, I shouldn't have been there.

Reyes looked down at the young boy now standing beside his mother and offered a smile. "Hello there, Mr. Sanchez."

"Hello," the boy said as a set of bashful dimples peeked out from the corners of his mouth. "Are you gonna live with us now?"

Bianca chuckled and picked him up for Reyes's inspection.

"I don't think your dad would appreciate that, Stephen." He took his pint-sized hand in a very official-looking handshake. "You've grown enough for the both of us. Guess I can stop now."

The boy laughed.

"Okay, okay," Amador said from behind. "Let Uncle Reyes breathe."

Stephen turned to his father. "Can he live with us, Dad?"

"Pretty please," Ashlee chimed in.

"You've clearly never lived with Uncle Reyes. Uncle Reyes is scary. And he snores. *Vete!*" He shooed the kids inside and paused to take a good look at Uncle Reyes. His expression turned grave. "Can you walk?"

"I think so."

Amador stood up slowly with Reyes's arm draped over him. "I don't remember this being part of the plan."

"It's her fault," Reyes said, nodding toward me as I climbed out of Misery.

With a laugh, Bianca said, "I think he's going to blame everything on you, Charley."

"Figures." I walked around the car. "Can I help?"

Reyes paused and looked at me as if surprised by the question. The lopsided grin he wore stopped my heart in my chest. I didn't miss the appreciation shimmering in his eyes. Nor did I miss the silent exchange between Bianca and Amador, the hint of a smile on Bianca's lovely mouth.

"Mamá, Mamá!" Ashlee bolted into the garage so fast, she almost knocked over Reyes and her father.

"Careful, *mi' ja.*" Bianca caught the excited child in her arms.

"There's a policeman at the door."

"Can I hold your gun?"

I thought I would pass out when I heard Stephen's heartfelt plea. Reyes and I had been stashed in the laundry room in the hopes that the local officers were just collecting for the annual food drive. A night-light lit the small space, and the room smelled like wildflowers in spring.

"Mi' jo," Amador said in a loving voice, "you know you can't play with guns."

"I just wanna hold it. I won't play with it. I promise."

A soft laugh penetrated the air. I could imagine Bianca's nurturing smile. "Stephen," she said softly, "the officer is trying to talk."

The man cleared his throat. "As I was saying, we're checking all known associates of Reyes Farrow."

This was it. The kids would give away our position in a heartbeat. Like taking candy from a baby.

And here I stood, surrounded by piles of freshly washed laundry with an escaped felon for company. If the officer found us, I would look more like an accomplice than a hostage, cowering in the dark.

What in the supernatural afterlife was I doing? This was my chance. My big break. I could put an end to all this right here and now.

My hand took hold of the doorknob just as a long arm reached over my shoulder. Reyes braced his palm against the door and leaned over me from behind.

His breath fanned across my cheek as he spoke. "Forty-eight hours." He whispered the words as the warmth from his body enveloped me. "That's all I need," he added.

The fact that I believed Reyes didn't get anywhere near a fair trial pushed to the forefront of my thoughts. Maybe he deserved to escape, to live free. No one really knew what happened. Earl Walker's death could have been an accident, or more likely, Reyes was defending himself against that monster. What was his escape to me?

And then the reason for my hesitation dawned, washing over me like a bucket of ice water. If he escaped from prison, if he was a fugitive, he would have to leave. He would have to go to Mexico or Canada or Nepal and live completely under the radar.

I would never see him again.

I took a deep breath and released it slowly. He was waiting for an answer. “What do you mean?” I asked, pretending not to realize why he needed the time. Surely it took a while to get fake papers. Forged IDs weren’t easy to come by. “What can you possibly do in forty-eight hours?”

He leaned in closer, like he didn’t want anyone else to hear. “I can find my father.”

That got my attention. I turned to face him as quietly as I could. It wasn’t easy. He stood his ground, forced me to look up into his eyes. “I can find your father in about fifteen minutes.”

Raising his brows in interest, he questioned me with a tilt of his head.

“Sunset Cemetery—” I hitched a thumb over my shoulder in that general direction. “—and I doubt he’s going anywhere.”

A hint of a smile tipped the corners of his mouth. “If Dad’s at the cemetery,” he said in a teasing tone, “he’s visiting his late aunt Vera. Which is highly unlikely, because he really didn’t like her.”

I frowned, suddenly wishing I’d been granted access to his psych profile. “I don’t understand.”

He lowered his gaze to the floor, then closed his eyes with a sigh. “Earl Walker is alive,” he said almost reluctantly. After a long pause, he opened his eyes, a worried expression lining his face. “I went to prison for killing someone who is still alive, Dutch.”

That was impossible. As much as I wanted to, I couldn’t quite bring myself to believe him. The medical examiner had identified the body. Because it had been burned, they had to use dental records. But there was a positive match. In the transcripts, Reyes himself had identified his father’s class ring, which had been found on the body’s charred ring finger.

Reyes had to be mistaken . . . or . . . or what? Crazy?

The doubt must have shown in my eyes. With a sigh of resignation, he lowered his head and stepped back. Was he letting me go? Could it be that simple?

Then he looked up, the dark determination back in his expression, and I realized the answer to my questions would be a resounding no. If he hadn't convinced me of the lengths he was willing to go to get what he wanted yet, his next statement certainly did.

"Fifty-five forty-seven Malaguena northeast."

I stood deathly still and absorbed his words, his meaning. My heart stopped in my chest as an utter disbelief and an odd sense of betrayal washed over me. It wasn't every day that an escaped convict recited my parents' home address. Every nuance of Reyes's demeanor confirmed the sincerity of his threat. He stared at me, waiting as the realization that he was giving me no choice but to cooperate sank in.

"And my reach," he added with a knowing tilt of his head, "goes far beyond those prison walls."

Visions of my dad emerged, of his warm smile. Even though he was trying to force me out of my own business, I would do anything for him, including aiding and abetting. Hot tears burned the backs of my eyes as I glared at Reyes. Our relationship had just dropped to a new low, one filled with contempt and distrust. How could I have felt so much for him?

I stood a long while, refusing to comment, letting the anger churning inside me take root, lead me, harden my heart. I had been a fool. No more. Never again.

"We understand each other, then?" he asked. He hadn't moved a muscle. He just stood there and eyed me as if allowing me to soak in his words, to contemplate the consequences of any action I might take against him.

I eyed him right back. "You're an asshole."

His smile held no humor. "Then we understand each other."

The door opened and I stepped to the side without averting my gaze. If he wanted a war, a war he would have.

We were shown into a spacious kitchen with commercial appliances and the coolest toaster oven I'd ever seen as Bianca put the kids to bed. They'd apparently been waiting up to see their uncle Reyes. Poor kids. They had no idea how dysfunctional even their pretend family members were.

Amador closed all the blinds, then started peeling Reyes's clothes off as Bianca hurried in with what medical supplies they had on hand. I couldn't help but let my eyes wander when the coveralls came off, then the prison uniform. He was completely naked underneath and I tried to look away, but even injured, he resembled a Greek god. His perfect skin tight around the hills and valleys of his muscles. Bianca wrapped a towel around his lower half as Amador inspected the wound.

"I need a shower," Reyes said as he downed three of whatever pain-killer Amador handed him.

Amador shook his head. "I don't know, bro. If this gets infected."

"It'll heal long before it has a chance. Just give me that peroxide," he said, gesturing toward the table, "and I'll be good."

As he spoke, I stepped around for a better look, and my head spun at the sight. His entire left side looked shredded, deep gashes exposing muscle and bone. He couldn't have weathered those injuries without at least one or two broken ribs, possibly more. Dark bruises were already spreading over his abdomen and up his chest. "Oh, my goodness," I said, reaching for a chair.

"Charley!" Startled, Bianca scrambled to help me into one. "Are you okay?"

"Yes," I said, fanning my face. "No." I stood again and faced Reyes with a new fury. "Why are you doing this? Why risk your life?"

"Dutch," he said in warning.

"No, this is crazy. Why would you do this? You'll get nowhere."

"Thanks for the vote of confidence."

"You know what I mean." I stepped closer, forcing my eyes to stay locked on his face. "They'll find you. They always do."

"Dutch," he said, reaching out and taking hold of my chin, "I do actually have a plan." He glanced back at Amador before I could say anything else. "Speaking of which, I'll also need some duct tape and a pair of handcuffs."

Amador grinned. Bianca sighed, a blissful expression softening her face.

9

What would MacGyver do?
—T-SHIRT

"Is this really necessary?" I asked, jiggling the handcuffs.

The animosity I felt at having my father threatened had waned ever so slightly in the wake of one constant reality. Reyes had threatened me before, more than once. Truly like a cornered animal, he lashed out until he got what he wanted, and yet he'd never hurt me, or anyone I care about, for that matter.

There had been police officers in the next room and he didn't want to be taken back to prison, so he did what he always does, he went for the jugular, knowing how I would react, knowing I would do anything for my dad. Despite my rationalizing the situation, it was hard to get past the fact that an escaped murderer could recite my parents' home address on cue.

"It's either that," Reyes said, gesturing toward the handcuffs with a nod, "or I tie you up and lock you in the basement. I'm good either way." The most devilish grin I'd ever seen crept across his face. Damn his evil dad.

Bianca brought in more towels and a fresh change of clothes for Reyes and set them on the closed toilet seat. Which made sense, since we were now in a freaking bathroom and I was handcuffed to the towel rack. Handcuffed! This was too much.

She giggled, raised her brows in a gesture that was nowhere near subtle, then closed the door behind her. It was a conspiracy.

Though he had yet to turn on the water, Reyes dropped the towel and stepped into the shower. The bleeding had stopped. With his back to me—not that that fact helped my weak knees in the least—he poured the peroxide over the open wound. I heard it bubble and him hiss, but my eyes were glued to his lovely backside. Immaculate shoulders covered in the smooth lines and sharp angles of his tattoo tapered down to a slim waist and quite possibly the most beautiful ass I'd ever seen. His legs were next, solid and built for battle. Then my gaze wandered back up to his arms, like corded steel and—

"Are you finished?"

I jumped, the handcuffs scraping loudly on the metal bar, and glanced up at him. "What? I was examining your wound."

He grinned. "With your X-ray vision?"

True, I couldn't actually see it from that angle, but his back was bruising on his left side all the way to his spine. That was bad enough. "You're lucky to be alive."

"Right." He turned toward me and with the will of a recovering alcoholic resisting a much needed drink, I forced my gaze to stay locked on his face. "I've been hearing that a lot lately." He leaned out to put the brown peroxide bottle on the vanity and brushed past me, the heat of him grazing over my cheeks and mouth. Then he ducked back in and turned the shower valves.

"You know, you should probably put more peroxide on after you shower."

"Worried about me?" he asked just before he closed the shower door.

"Not especially." Watching him through the wavy glass was like studying an abstract painting and knowing the model the artist used for his masterpiece was utterly perfect. I forced my gaze away. He had threatened my parents. I had to remember that. Still, it was really hard to stay mad at a wounded naked man.

A soft knock sounded at the door and Bianca peeked around the doorjamb. "Coast clear?" she asked.

"Yep. Dr. Richard Kimble is in the shower."

She stepped in quickly and put a pair of boots on the floor.

"You're risking a lot for him," I said under my breath.

Bianca offered a sympathetic smile. "He gave me everything, Charley," she said, her voice almost begging me to understand. "I would have nothing without him. Besides the fact that I would be a waitress or cashier, barely scraping by, he gave me Amador. My husband wouldn't be alive right now if not for Reyes. The only thing I'm risking is what he gave me. Who better to risk everything for?" She smiled, then closed the door behind her as she left.

The smell of a woodsy shampoo drifted toward me and I shifted my weight to the other foot, took hold of the towel rack with my other hand, perused the array of soaps in the soap dish, sighed in annoyance really loudly, then let my gaze wander back to where it most wanted to be, as though he were made of gravity. Soap bubbles drifted down the glass door, making it oddly clear. I leaned closer. He wasn't moving. He stood there with one arm braced on the wall, the other holding his side. It reminded me of our earlier encounter, making him seem almost vulnerable.

"Reyes?"

His head turned toward me, but I couldn't make out his features. "You fall for my threats too easily," he said, his voice echoing against the tiled walls.

I leaned back. "Are you saying I shouldn't?"

"No." He turned off the water, opened the door, and wrapped a towel around his waist without drying off first, then offered me his full attention. "That would make the entire effort pointless."

"You do make a mean bluff stew," I said, glancing away. "Your threats are rarely without merit. But I'll remember that in the future."

"I wish you wouldn't."

Remembering who he'd threatened, I offered him my best glower. "Even if you weren't serious, you shouldn't have threatened my parents like that."

"I was desperate," he said, shrugging an eyebrow.

"I understand you didn't want to be taken back to prison, but—"

The expression on his face stopped me. He seemed almost disappointed. "No, Dutch, not because I didn't want to go back to prison. Because I *wasn't* going back to prison."

I blinked, my mind stumbling to grasp his meaning.

"Do you know what could have happened to those officers had they found me? To Bianca and the kids had they seen . . . that? What I'm capable of?"

His meaning dawned. "You were protecting them. Protecting the officers." I suddenly felt like the village idiot. Of course he wouldn't have been taken back. He would have died—or horridly maimed someone—first. And there I stood in that laundry room, thinking of no one but myself. Even looking at it from a different perspective, what would it have done to the kids had they seen Reyes handcuffed and taken away? He didn't hurt me. He'd never hurt me. He'd literally saved my life on several occasions, and I pay him back over and over with doubt and distrust.

Then again, he had held a knife to my throat.

"I was keeping you quiet," he said, inching closer. Water dripped down his face, his hair hanging in wet tangles over his forehead. He watched me like a predator watches his prey, his eyes unblinking, his lashes spiked with moisture. He raised a long arm and braced it over my head.

"Would you really hurt my parents?" I asked.

His lashes lowered as his gaze rested on my mouth. "I'd probably go after your sister first."

Why did I bother? "You're such an ass." I would have pushed him away had my hands been free.

He shrugged. "Gotta keep up the illusion. Someday you're going to figure out exactly what you're capable of—" He leaned in close. "—then where will I be?"

He removed the towel and began drying off. I turned toward the wall, both hands clutching the bar amidst his deep chuckle. He scrubbed his hair with the towel, then dressed in the loose-fitted jeans and T-shirt Bianca had laid out for him.

"Can I borrow a finger?" he asked.

I turned back. He was holding up the T-shirt and trying to wrap gauze around his waist at the same time. "I thought you had a genius IQ."

His head whipped up, all traces of humor gone. "Where did you hear that?"

"Just, I—I don't know, it was in your file, I think."

He turned from me as if disgusted. "Of course, the file."

Wow, he really hated that thing. "Uncuff me and I'll help."

"That's okay, I got it."

"Reyes, don't be ridiculous." When he headed for the sink, I lifted my leg and braced my booted foot against it, blocking his path.

He stopped and looked down at it for a long moment. Then he was in front of me, one hand wound in my hair, the other pulling me into him. But he took it no further. He just watched, studied, then said, "Do you know how dangerous that is?"

A loud pounding sounded at the door, and I jumped about three feet into the air. "*Pendejo,* we gotta fly. They're already watching the house. This is going to be tricky enough as it is, without you suffering from exhaustion and dehydration from too much strenuous exercise, if you know what I mean."

As if it took every ounce of strength he had, Reyes dropped his arms and stepped back, his jaw flexing in frustration. "One minute," he said as he bent down and pulled on the socks and boots Bianca had supplied.

He stood and inserted a key into the handcuffs, the fingers of one hand lacing into mine as he unlocked the restraint with the other. Then we started down the hall, the current that arced through us becoming stronger with each breath, each heartbeat. Amador checked the backyard before waving us forward while he ran to the side of the house.

"Uncle Reyes, are you leaving?"

Reyes turned. Ashlee was peeking out her bedroom window through the storm screen.

"Just for a little while, smidgen," he said, walking up to her. "Why aren't you asleep?"

"I can't sleep. I want you to stay." She placed her small hand on the screen. He did the same, and my head fought to wrap itself around how fiercely animalistic Reyes could be one minute, then how amazingly tender the next.

She puckered her lips and pressed them to the screen. He leaned forward and offered her an adoring peck on the nose, and all I could think about was the fact that I never have a camera when I need one. Freaking Kodak moments sucked when you didn't actually have a Kodak.

"When we're married," Ashlee said, resting her forehead against the mesh, "we can kiss without a screen between us, huh?"

He laughed softly. "We sure can. Now go to sleep before your mom sees you."

"Okay." She yawned, her tiny mouth forming a perfect O, then disappeared.

"Dude, did you just make out with my daughter?"

Reyes turned to Amador with a grin. "We're in love."

"Okay, but you can't have her until she's eighteen." He put a duffel bag on the ground. "No, I know you. Make that twenty-one."

Bianca rushed out and handed her husband another bag. "For the road," she said as she rushed over to Reyes and hugged him gingerly, kissing his cheek as they parted. "Be careful, handsome man."

"For you, anything."

"Twenty-five," Amador said when Reyes wriggled his brows at him.

Amador, Reyes, and I raced through the backyard, scaled a fence, and darted through a neighbor's yard to the next street, where an old Chevy two-door truck sat waiting. All the while, I seemed to be the only one amazed at Reyes's recovery, and I was the only other person present who could tote a supernatural badge if I wanted to. Amador didn't seem the slightest bit surprised.

He threw the bags into the bed and tossed Reyes the keys. "Two minutes," he said, tapping his watch. "Don't be late this time." He strode up to Reyes and embraced him hard. *"Vaya con Dios."* Go with God. What an ironical thing to say.

"Let's hope so. I'm probably going to need His help," Reyes said.

Amador glanced at his watch again. "One minute thirty."

Reyes grinned. "I would run if I were you."

And Amador took off the way we had come.

"What's going on?" I asked.

Reyes climbed into the truck, and I saw the grimace he tried to hide. He certainly wasn't 100 percent, but he was getting there fast. "A diversion," he said when I got in.

About one minute later, cop sirens began wailing through the quiet neighborhood as two muscle cars raced down a side street.

"That's our cue," Reyes said. He started the truck and drove to the freeway with nary a cop in sight.

"Who was driving the other car?"

He smiled. "Amador's cousin who owes him about a million dollars. Don't worry, they'll get away. Amador has a plan."

"You guys are big on plans. How long has it been since you've driven?" I asked him, realizing he'd been in jail a long time.

"Worried?" he asked.

Was it even possible for him to just answer a question? "You're more evasive than a Navy SEAL."

We drove to a shoddy hotel in the southern war zone and walked into the office hand in hand. Actually, Reyes wasn't about to let me go in alone. He didn't trust me. It was giving me a complex. Or it would've if I'd cared.

"This place is a health violation," I said. "You want to stay here?"

He just grinned and waited for me to pay the clerk, a middle-aged woman who looked like she frequented bingo parlors.

"Wonderful."

I paid and we gathered our bags and strolled to room 201.

"You know, *you* could take a shower this time, if you were so inclined." Reyes wore a mischievous grin as he went around pulling on pipes and fixtures before he seemed to settle on the bed frame.

"I'm pretty clean, thanks."

He shrugged. "It was a thought." Without warning, he lifted the mattress and box springs off to the side, exposing the frame, and motioned me toward him.

"What?"

"I can't have you escaping when I least expect it."

"Seriously? Look," I said as he motioned me to sit, led my hands behind my back, and cuffed them to the freaking frame, "let's say Earl Walker is still alive."

"Want to, really?"

I sighed to express my annoyance nonverbally and shifted to get more comfortable. "I'm an investigator. I can, you know, look for him. And I can investigate a lot better without an escaped convict handcuffing me to anything metal within arm's reach."

He paused and eyed me. "So, what you're saying is you can do your job better without me around?"

"Yes." I was already getting uncomfortable in the awkward position.

He leaned into me and whispered into my ear. "I'm counting on it."

"Wait, you're going to let me go?"

"Of course. How else are you going to find Walker?"

"Then why did you handcuff me to this bed?"

A grin as smooth as glass spread across his face. "Because I need a head start." Before I could comment, he raised a paper in front of my face. "These are the names of Earl Walker's last known associates."

I tilted my head and read. "He only had three friends?"

"He wasn't real popular. I promise you, one of these men knows where he is." He sat beside me, his dark eyes sparkling even in the low light, and it hit me again that Reyes Farrow was in my presence, a man I'd been infatuated with for over a decade, a supernatural being who radiated sensuality like other people radiated insecurity. He pushed the small piece of paper into one of my pockets and let his hand linger on my hip.

"Reyes, uncuff me."

He bit down and turned away. "I couldn't be responsible for my actions if I did."

"I'm not asking you to be."

"But they'll be here any second," he said, regret edging his voice.

"What?" I asked, surprised. "Who?"

He stood and rummaged around in the bag before he kneeled down next to me again. "I apparently made the ten o'clock news. The clerk recognized me, probably called the cops the minute we walked out."

My mouth fell open. "Why didn't you tell me?"

"Because this has to look good."

"I can't believe I didn't pick up on that." Then I found out why he needed the duct tape. "Wait!" I said as he readied the tape. "How did you text me from my sister's number?"

"I didn't," he said with a grin, and before I could say anything else, I had duct tape covering part of my face.

Reyes grabbed the duffel bag, then took my chin into his palm and planted a kiss right on the tape. When he was finished—and I was breathless—he looked into my eyes apologetically. "This is going to hurt."

What? I thought, half a second before I saw stars and the world darkened around me.

10

The police never find it as funny as you do.

—T-SHIRT

Moments after I'd been clocked by the man voted Most Likely to Be Killed by an Angry White Chick, the world came spinning back with a nauseating vengeance. A SWAT team crashed through the door, rifles at their shoulders as they swept the room. One of them knelt beside me and I moaned, partly to make it look good and partly because that was all I could do.

Reyes hit me! He'd actually hit me! It didn't matter that hitting me wasn't really like hitting a regular girl and I'd be completely healed in a matter of hours. I was still a freaking girl, and he damned well knew it. I'd just have to hit him back. With a lead pipe. Or an eighteen-wheeler.

"Are you okay?" SWAT guy asked, studying my eye.

Damn, I loved it when men in uniform studied my eyes. Or my ass. Either way. I nodded as he slowly peeled the tape off. He secured it onto a piece of plastic and sealed it in an evidence bag as a detective and two patrolmen strolled in to talk to the sergeant in charge. With the help of one of the patrolmen, the officer unlocked the cuffs and helped me onto the bed after they righted it.

"Would you like some water?" he asked.

"No, I'm good, thank you."

"I think we should arrest her."

Startled, I looked up at the patrolman. It was Owen Vaughn. *The* Owen Vaughn. The guy who tried to kill-and-or-horribly-maim me in high school with his dad's SUV. Well, this sucked ass. He hated my guts. And everything about my guts. He even hated the cavity encapsulating my guts. What was that thing called?

"I don't think that'll be necessary, Officer," the detective said. "Wait a minute." He stepped closer. "You're Davidson's niece."

"Yes, sir, I am," I said, testing my eye with my finger. It stung. Not my finger, but my eye.

After releasing a long breath, he looked at Vaughn and said, "Okay, arrest her."

"What?"

A satisfied smirk spread across Vaughn's face and an evil grin spread across the detective's. "Just kidding," he said.

Vaughn scowled in disappointment and stalked off as the detective sat beside me.

"What's going on here?" he asked.

"I was carjacked." Obviously, my telling the cops was the plan. Otherwise, Reyes wouldn't have hit me. Or I hoped not. "And handcuffed to this bed frame with handcuffs."

"I see." The detective took out his notepad and jotted down a few notes right as a U.S. Marshal came through the door. "Does he still have your car?"

With a mental sigh, I realized this could take a while.

Annnnnnnnnnd it did.

Two hours later, I sat in the back of Owen Vaughn's patrol car waiting for Uncle Bob to pick me up. I'd been checked out by an EMT and harassed by a rascally officer named Bud. After that, I figured it was time to get the heck outta Dodge, so I called for backup in the form of my favorite uncle to convince Albuquerque's finest to let me go. The black eye helped. Holy cow, Reyes packed a punch. And I doubted he was even trying. Which, thank God.

I looked into the rearview mirror at Vaughn. He was sitting in the driver's seat, which was cool, since it was his car. "Are you ever going to tell me what I did?" I asked, hoping he wouldn't pop a cap in my ass for the asking.

"Are you ever going to die screaming?"

That would be a big fat *hopefully not*. Man, he hated me, and I'd never found out why. I decided to try to humanize myself so he'd be less likely to kill me if ever the opportunity arose. I'd read that if you say a victim's name repeatedly to, say, a kidnapper, then the kidnapper forms a mental attachment to the person they're holding hostage.

"Charley Davidson is a fair person. I'm sure if you just told Charley what she did, she'd be more than willing to fix it."

He stilled, then eased around to me, slowly, as though I'd mortified him. "If you ever talk about yourself in third person again, I'll kill you where you stand."

Okay, he was clearly sensitive about narrative forms. I wasn't sure it was legal for a police officer to threaten a civilian like that, but since he had a gun and I didn't, I decided not to question him on it.

I learned two things about Owen Vaughn as we sat there waiting for Ubie: First, he had the uncanny ability to stare a person down in a rearview mirror without blinking for like five minutes. I wished I'd had eye drops to offer him. And second, he had some kind of nasal deformity that made him squeak a little when he breathed.

Not long after my nerve-racking stretch in hell—otherwise known as Owen Vaughn's patrol car—a very grumpy man named Uncle Bob gave me a ride to my apartment.

"So, Farrow carjacked you?" Ubie asked as we pulled into the parking lot, unconcerned with his bed head.

"Yes, he carjacked me."

"And why were you at a convenience store in the middle of nowhere in the middle of the night in the middle of a flash flood warning?"

"Because I got a text from . . . Oh! Gemma!"

I dug my phone out of my bag, which Reyes was nice enough to leave on the nightstand, and called hers. Still off. So I tried her home phone.

"Gemma Davidson," she answered, her voice as groggy as I felt.

"Where are you?" I asked.

"Who is this?"

"Elvis."

"What time is it?"

"Hammer time?"

"Charley."

"Did you text me? Did your car break down?"

"No and no. Why are you doing this to me?" She was funny.

"Check your cell."

I heard a loud, sleepy sigh, some rustling of sheets, then, "It won't come on."

"Not at all?"

"No. What did you do to it?"

"I ate it for breakfast. Check the battery compartment."

"Where the hell is that?"

"Um, behind the battery door."

"Are you punking me?" I heard her fumbling with the phone.

"Gem, if I was going to punk you, I wouldn't simply turn off your phone. I would pour honey in your hair while you slept. Or, you know, something like that."

"That was you?" she asked, appalled.

She'd totally fallen for the open-window technique of throwing the victim off the trail of the true assailant. She thought Cindy Verdean did it for years. I was going to tell her the truth eventually, but after what she did to Cindy in retaliation, I changed my mind. Cindy's eyelashes were never the same.

"Wait," she said, "my battery's gone. Did you take it?"

"Yes. Did you go out this evening?"

After another loud sigh, she said, "No. Yes. I went out for drinks with a colleague."

"Did anyone bump into you? Drop something in front of—"

"Yes! Oh, my gosh, this man bumped into me, apologized, then about five minutes later, personally brought over a bottle of wine to make up for it. It was nothing. I mean, he barely touched me."

"He took your phone, texted me from it, stole the battery, then put it back when he brought the wine over." With Reyes's circle of friends, I was hardly surprised a pickpocket was among them.

"I feel so violated."

"About the phone or the honey?"

"You know that whole payback's-a-bitch thing. Hey, you never called me back after your meeting with Reyes. How'd it go?"

"Oh, it went super." I looked over at Uncle Bob, who sat waiting for a report. "Well, that explains that," I said as I closed my phone midsentence.

"Charley, I've said this before, but I'm going to say it again. The man is a convicted murderer. If you'd seen what he did to his father . . ." He trailed off, shaking his bed head.

I decided to confide in him despite the state of his hair. "Uncle Bob, is it possible that the man in that trunk wasn't Earl Walker?"

His brows slid together. "Is that what Farrow told you?"

"Is it possible?" I asked again.

Ubie lowered his head and turned the engine off to his SUV. "He's like you, isn't he?"

His question surprised me, and I wasn't sure what to say, but I should have been expecting it. He'd seen Reyes's body after the demons got a hold of him. He'd seen how fast he healed. The doctors were calling the fact that Reyes survived at all a miracle. And two weeks later, he's walking around in gen-pop at the prison like nothing happened. I would have bet a large mocha Frappuccino Ubie was keeping tabs on Reyes. I would've been after what I saw.

"You have this uncanny ability to live through the most impossible situations," he continued. "You heal faster than anyone I've ever seen. You move differently sometimes, almost like you're not human."

He'd been keeping track.

"I have to ask you something, and I want you to be totally honest."

"Okay," I said, a little worried. I was not at my best. I hadn't had caffeine in like three hours. And he was definitely putting two and two together.

"Are you an angel?"

And coming up with twelve. "No," I said with a chuckle. "Let's just say, if I ended up in the lost-and-found bin at the airport, I don't think the Big Guy upstairs would come down to claim me."

"But you *are* different," he said, his tone matter-of-fact.

"I am. And . . . yes, so is Reyes."

A long sigh slipped through his lips. "He didn't kill his father, did he?"

"First, Earl Walker is not his real father."

Ubie acknowledged that with a nod. That fact had come out in the trial.

"Second, I'm beginning to believe the man isn't even dead."

After staring out the window for a long moment, he said, "It's possible. Not likely, certainly not probable, but possible. There are ways."

"Like switching the dental records?" I asked.

He nodded.

"And the fact that Earl Walker's girlfriend at the time was a dental assistant at the very office the authorities obtained those records from didn't strike anyone as odd?"

I knew Ubie had been the lead detective on the case, so to say I was skating on thin ice would have been more than appropriate. And I sucked at ice skating.

His lips thinned under his thick mustache. "Are you helping him?"

"Yes." There was no reason to lie. Uncle Bob wasn't an idiot.

I felt a spike of adrenaline emanate from him when I answered, the surprise he felt, but I think he was more surprised that I was being honest. So he tried again. "Do you know where he is?"

"No." When his brows slid together with a hint of doubt, I added, "That's why he handcuffed me, to get a head start. He didn't want to put me in that position."

"And he hit you because?"

"I called his sister a doody head."

He fixed an exasperated gaze on me.

"He's very sensitive."

"Charley—"

"He wanted it to look good, you know, for the cops."

"Aw. Did you have anything to do with his escape?"

"Besides getting carjacked? No."

"Are you going to fill in the details that you so conveniently left out for the sergeant on duty?"

"No." I couldn't tell him about Amador and Bianca or the super-spy plan they'd concocted to get him out of there.

"Do you think Cookie is up?"

I refrained from rolling my eyes and glanced over at Misery. Apparently, Amador had her delivered sometime during the night. Thoughtful of him.

Maybe the unholy union of Cookie and Uncle Bob wasn't such a bad idea. They'd started flirting recently, and as much as it caused this burning sensation in my stomach, they were both healthy, responsible adults, capable of making their own bad decisions that resulted in years of couple's therapy and, eventually, court fees.

It would be disturbing to watch, though. I could just pack up all my worldly possessions and live in Misery. The Jeep, not the emotion.

I glanced back at Uncle Bob, at his pathetically hopeful expression, and decided to negotiate. "You gonna get that tail off my ass?" I gestured toward the car parked across the street with a nod.

His face fell. "No. It's good for your ass."

"So is taking the stairs, but I take the elevator every chance I get." When he shrugged, I added, "Cookie's asleep," right before exiting the vehicle.

11

Mistakes were made.
Others were blamed.
—T-SHIRT

Since I still had a couple more hours before we opened up shop, I decided to read some more of the research on my missing-wife case before hitting the showers. Uncle Bob had totally scored with the statements, but I mainly focused on Teresa Yost herself. Besides tons of volunteer work and sitting on a couple of boards, Teresa Yost had graduated magna cum laude from the University of New Mexico with a degree in linguistics. Which meant she was freaking smart. And she probably knew another language or two. She'd worked a lot with disabled kids and had been instrumental in starting a horse ranch that catered specifically to children in wheelchairs.

"And she didn't deserve to die," I said to Mr. Wong, who continued to stare into his corner.

Two hours later, I sat drinking coffee with a towel on my head, placating a very disappointed-that-I-hadn't-called-her Cookie. "He was naked?"

"He was in the shower, so . . . yes."

"And you didn't get a picture?" She sighed in frustration.

"I was in handcuffs."

"Did he . . . did you . . . ?"

"No. Oddly enough, the actual act doesn't seem to matter where he's concerned. Just looking at him causes these sharp waves of ecstasy to flood my girl parts, so it's almost the same thing."

"That's so unfair. I'm going on a killing spree."

"Can I drop you somewhere?"

"No, I have to get Amber to school. At least let me help with Reyes's case."

"No."

"Why not?" She frowned in disappointment. "I can research shit. It's what I do."

"I have names. I'll look them up while you check into the good doctor's finances."

"Oh, well, okay. Isn't he like a billionaire?"

I smiled. "That's exactly what I want to know."

After covering my black eye with enough concealer to make the late Tammy Faye Bakker proud, I trudged across the parking lot, my feet getting heavier with every step. This whole lack-of-sleep thing seemed to be wearing on me if the little girl following me with the knife was any indication. "Weren't you a hood ornament yesterday?" I asked.

She didn't look at me. Which was horridly rude. She wore a charcoal gray dress with black patent leather boots, an outfit that could have doubled as a Russian school uniform, and she had shoulder-length black hair. Her only accessory was the knife, which didn't really match. Apparently accessorizing was not her thing.

I walked over to the tail parked across the street and knocked on the window. The guy in it jumped with a start. "I'm going to work now!" I yelled through the glass as he squinted at me. "Pay attention."

He rubbed his eyes and waved. I recognized him as one of Garrett Swopes's men. *Garrett Swopes,* I thought with a snort. What a freaking traitor. My uncle Bob says, *Follow Charley,* and he does it. Like, just does it. Like our friendship means nothing to him. Of course, it doesn't, but still. Punk ass.

"Are you Charley Davidson?"

I turned to see a woman in a worn brown coat and penny loafers. Practical but hardly appealing. "Depends on who's asking."

She walked up to me, scanning the area as she went. She had long black hair that could've used a good brushing and huge sunglasses covering half her face. I recognized her from the Buick in the street yesterday morning. The same hair. The same sunglasses. The same sadness percolating beneath the surface. But her aura was warm, its light like the soft glow of a candle, as though afraid to shine too brightly.

"Ms. Davidson." She held out her hand. "My name is Monica Dean. I'm Teresa Yost's sister."

"Ms. Dean." I took her hand. All the emotions of a woman with a missing sister were present and accounted for. She was scared and grief-stricken and sick with worry. "I've been looking for you."

"I'm sorry." She pushed her sunglasses up nervously. "My brother said not to talk to you."

"Yeah, I don't think he appreciated my visit yesterday. Can you come in?" I gestured toward the back of Dad's bar. The wind bit through my jacket, nipping at me like an elderly Chihuahua.

"Of course," she said, pulling her coat tighter. "And my brother doesn't know what to think of your visit. He was quite taken with you."

"Really?" I started for the bar. "I got the feeling he wanted to put me in a choke hold and insist I say *uncle* repeatedly." *That's it! A professional wrestler!* "I'm so sorry about your sister," I added, steering my thoughts back around. But seriously, I would rock as a wrestler. I'd have to get a tan, though. And maybe veiny muscles.

"Thank you."

Health insurance would be good, too.

I turned on lights as we entered the back of Dad's establishment, though the illuminated kitchen told me Sammy was already in prepping for the dinner crowd. My dad's bar was a cross between an Irish pub and a Victorian brothel. The main room had a cathedral ceiling with dark woods and hundred-year-old ironwork that crested the walls like ancient crown molding. It spiraled around and lured the eye to the west wall, where a glorious wrought-iron elevator loomed tall and proud. The kind you see only in movies and very old hotels. The kind with all its mechanisms and pulleys open for its audience to enjoy. The kind that took from here to eternity to get its occupants to the second floor. Framed pictures, medals, and banners from various law enforcement events covered every available surface with the original mahogany bar to the right of us.

"Want some coffee?" I asked, gesturing for her to sit at one of the corner booths. Monica looked half-starved, her hands shaking with grief and fatigue. I figured if we sat down here, we could get Sammy to whip us up something. "I was just about to have breakfast if you'd like to join me."

The back door crashed open, and a very unhappy man named Luther Dean stormed inside. "You can't be serious," he said, glaring at his sister.

She took a seat and blew out a long breath, expelling such a deep, abysmal sadness when she did so that I felt consumed by it. I filled my lungs to ease the weight and ducked behind the bar for coffee.

"I've done my research," she said to her brother. "She's very good at her job."

He glanced over a massive shoulder toward me. "She doesn't look very good at it. She has a black eye."

"I beg your pardon," I said, feigning offense. He was funny.

"Luther, sit down." Monica took off her sunglasses and offered him a glower of annoyance when he didn't comply. "I told you, she can help us. So, either behave yourself or leave. It's your decision."

He jerked a chair out from a nearby table and sat down. "She called me an asshole."

"You *are* an asshole."

I grinned and brought over three coffee cups, realizing how much fun this conversation was going to be. Thirty minutes later, we were polishing off an amazing rendition of huevos rancheros with green chile enchiladas on the side. God I loved Sammy. I'd considered marrying him, but his wife got upset when I asked for his hand.

"What makes you so trustworthy?" Luther asked, his icy-blue glare particularly brutal. He took skeptic to a whole new level. "I mean, you're working for Nathan. Why should we believe anything you have to say?"

"Actually, I'm not," I said, hoping they'd believe anything I had so say, "and why don't you trust your sister's husband?" We had yet to actually talk about the case. I decided to lull them into a false sense of security, which would have gone over better had I not stolen the last bite off Luther's plate. He was very touchy about his food.

Still, I could tell he was coming around. They exchanged glances.

With a sigh of resignation, Monica admitted, "No reason whatsoever." She shrugged. "He's perfect. The perfect husband. The perfect brother-in-law. He's just . . ."

"Too perfect?" I offered.

"Exactly," Luther said. "And there were things, instances, that just didn't quite make sense."

"Like?"

He glanced at his sister, getting her approval before explaining. "Teresa invited us out to eat one night a couple of months ago when Nathan was out of town, just the three of us."

"She seemed concerned about something," Monica said, and I could've sworn I felt a pang of guilt assault her. "She told us she took out a huge life insurance policy on both her and Nathan, and that if anything were to happen to her, anything at all, we would get it all."

"So *she* took it out?" I asked. "Not Nathan?"

I felt it again. A quiver, a tremble of guilt emanating from Monica as she replied, "Exactly. I'm not even sure Nathan knows about it."

"She wanted us to know where the policy was," Luther added. "She made sure of it."

Monica produced a key. "She even put us down as her beneficiaries on her bank account so we would have access to her safety deposit box where she kept it."

"That does sound odd," I said, fighting to ignore the bells going off in my head. Was she afraid of her husband? Did she think her life was in danger? "How big was the policy?"

"Two million dollars," Luther said. "Each."

"Holy mother of crap." I was ever the wordsmith. "Is that even possible?"

"Apparently," Monica said.

Luther crossed his arms over his chest. "The policy was his idea. It had to be. Why would Teresa take out such a big policy? He had her do it to make himself look good."

"We don't know that," Monica said.

"Please." He scooted back in his chair, irritated. "Everything that man does is to make himself look good. That's what he's all about. Looking good. Presenting the perfect picture for his hordes of fans."

I had to agree with him, from what I'd seen so far anyway. "Anything else?" I asked.

"Nothing I can think of." Monica wiped the wetness from her eyes, and that was when I noticed the odd coloring around them, the unnatural puffiness and the yellowish tint lining her mouth. The mystery of her sister's whereabouts was overwhelming for her, the not knowing, and . . . the guilt. "She did mention that Nathan was spending more and more time at home with her, refusing to go to conferences and getting furious if he was called to the hospital in the evenings. I think she felt smothered."

"Did she say that to you?"

"Not in so many words," she said, shaking her head. "But she said he did strange things."

"Like what?" Luther asked. "She never told me that."

"Because she couldn't." Monica offered him a frown. "You fly off the handle for the most ridiculous reasons, we can't tell you anything."

Luther's jaw muscles flexed in reaction, and I could feel guilt assault him as well, but his stemmed from shame. Monica's was deeper and full of regret. And she said *we*. *We* can't tell you anything.

He seemed to force himself to calm down, then asked, "What did she say?"

Monica appraised her coffee cup as she thought back. "She said he would do strange things like wake her up in the middle of the night, scaring her on purpose, and then just laugh. And one time he said her dog got run over by a car. She cried for two days. Then, out of the blue, he showed up with it. Said he'd been picked up by the pound. But she'd checked the pound. They never picked him up." She looked at me and shrugged. "He just did odd stuff like that all the time."

Everything he did was a form of manipulation. Simply put, he was an extreme control freak, a very unhealthy habit. Still, I needed to get Monica alone. Clearly there were things she couldn't say in front of her brother. I freshened their coffees, mentally calculating how much java his bladder could hold. He was a big guy, but hopefully he'd need a potty break soon.

"Nathan never was the sharpest scalpel on the instrument tray," he said. "He passed medical school with a C average. Would you want a surgeon who scraped by medical school with a C average?"

"Not hardly." Though I doubted the legitimacy of such a claim, the thought was admittedly terrifying. I turned to Monica. "Can I ask why you were here yesterday morning? I hadn't even talked to Nathan yet."

She lowered her head, embarrassed. "I didn't realize you saw me." She drew in a ragged breath. "I've been following him. He was in front of the bar, talking on the phone when you walked past."

"So you didn't know who I was?"

"No, not at first. When he told me he'd hired a private detective, I looked you up."

Luther tapped an index finger on the table. "And he hired you to make himself look good, I'm telling you."

The guy was clearly smarter than he appeared. "He told me you two don't really get along with Teresa."

Monica's jaw fell open. "He said that?" She was appalled.

"See," Luther said. "See what he's doing?"

I watched as tears shimmered in Monica's eyes again, but now she was angry. She leaned into me, the spitfire in her surfacing. "He's tried to keep us apart for the last two years. He's so jealous of us, it's unreal. We're sisters, for God's sake."

Luther nodded. "Chalk that up to one of those strange things Monica told you about. He says things, makes up shit, does everything in his power to keep us away from Teresa."

"He's so controlling," Monica agreed. "That fact alone raised a red flag when they began dating, but Teresa just wouldn't listen."

"The more we talked, the less she listened."

"I can imagine," I said. "I have a sister, too."

"And then," Monica said, her head tilting to the side in befuddlement, "he'll be so sweet to her. He buys her gifts all the time, brings her flowers, makes sure her favorite sparkling water is on hand at all times. Citrus flavored."

"In other words, he smothers her," I said, coming back around to Monica's original assessment.

"Exactly." She nodded. "I think it all really bothers Teresa. She doesn't even drink the water anymore. Hasn't for months. But she doesn't tell him, because I drink it." She grinned then, her smile soft and sincere. "He gets so jealous of our time together, so we meet secretly every weekday and walk through the mountains, supposedly exercising. But really we just talk." She chuckled to herself then. "And drink his stupid flavored water."

"So, she doesn't work?" I asked.

"Oh, no," she answered as though what I'd asked was ludicrous. "He wouldn't have it."

"See?" Luther's hands curled into fists. "Nuts. I promise, if he did anything to her, he's a dead man."

Between the insurance and the bizarre behavior, I was surprised the good doctor was still alive with a brother-in-law like Luther. And Yost knew that. He would know better than to implicate himself in any way. He would've known he'd never make it to trial if there was any suspicion of his guilt, so whatever he did, he did it well. He'd have to make it look like an accident, but Teresa's car was still at the house. And a kidnapping was only as good as the ransom it demanded. With no demand, an abduction would be only slightly less suspicious than a knife in her chest and blood on his hands.

But right now, I needed both Luther and Monica off his back. If he knew they were watching, he would never revisit the crime scene. "Give me a dollar," I said to him.

He wrinkled his brows. "Why?"

I rethought my demand. "That's a good question. You're loaded. Give me a twenty."

He exhaled, then fished a twenty out of his wallet.

"Now I'm working for you."

"You're cheap."

"This is a retainer," I said, showing him the twenty he just handed me. "Add a few zeros, and you have my daily rate. You'll get a bill. It will be large." I had to pay for my wrestling career somehow.

"I already have a guy on Yost. He won't leave his side, and I promise you, Yost won't know." I wasn't about to tell them he was a departed teenage gangbanger. "If the doctor does anything suspicious, my guy will let me know. And I have my assistant looking into his background as we speak. If there's anything that doesn't fit, we'll find it."

"So, you were already investigating him?" Luther asked, surprised.

"I told you, I'm out to find your sister, and since spouses are almost always the main suspects in disappearances, then yes, I'm already investigating him." I leaned in and added, "Like I would be you if you were a suspect."

Monica asked, "Are the cops looking in the same direction you are? Does the FBI consider him a suspect?"

"Hon, the FBI considers everyone a suspect," I said, answering her question without actually giving her any information. I had to admit, with a brother-in-law like Luther Dean, I was a little surprised the doctor would pull something like this. Maybe, for some reason, he was desperate. And again, desperate men did desperate things. Which did not bode well for Teresa Yost.

The spark of hope that ignited inside Monica humbled me. She seemed to have a lot of faith in my abilities.

"There a restroom in this place?" Luther asked at last, glancing around the bar.

"Right through there." I pointed to the men's room and watched as he strolled in that direction. A little because I wanted to make sure he was out of hearing range when I asked Monica my next question, but mostly because he had a nice ass.

When he pushed past the door, I turned to her. "Okay, we only have a few seconds. What are you not telling me?"

Her eyes widened in surprise. "I don't understand."

"Tick-tock," I said, glancing back at the men's room. With any luck, Luther practiced basic hygiene, but one just never knew with guys. Offering Monica a sympathetic gaze, I said, "I can see the burden of guilt you carry." When she blinked and lowered her head, I added, "I won't say a word, Monica. Whatever it is. I just need to know all the angles of this case."

Her mouth thinned into a sad line, and she said reluctantly, "Luther doesn't know this, but I'm sick."

I thought she might be. Her skin had a yellowish, unhealthy tint as did her nails with the exception of the white lines spanning them in horizontal rows. But I wasn't sure why that would conjure the guilt I'd been picking up on. "I'm sorry, but—"

She shook her head. "No, Luther doesn't know for a reason. When our mother died . . ." She stopped to touch a tissue to her eyes before planting her gaze back on me. "He took it very hard, Charley. She was sick for a long time, and when she passed . . ."

After a moment, I placed a hand over hers, encouraging her to continue.

She turned it over and laced her fingers into mine gratefully, then leaned into me and whispered, "He tried to kill himself."

To say I was shocked would be an understatement of the highest form. My jaw dropped before I could catch it, and Monica saw.

"I know. We were all surprised. He just took her death so hard."

I glanced once again toward the bathroom. With the coast clear, I asked, "Is he getting help?"

"Yes. Well, he was. He's doing so much better."

"I'm so glad. May I ask what you have?"

"You can ask all you want," she said, a sad smile sliding across her face. "The doctors don't know. I've been diagnosed with everything from chronic fatigue syndrome to Hutchinson's disease, and nothing ever pans out. I just keep getting sicker and nobody knows why."

Luther was headed back toward us when I asked one more question, "Monica, why would your being sick make you feel guilty about Teresa's disappearance?"

She pressed her mouth together as guilt washed over her again. "The insurance. There was a clinic in Sweden Teresa was looking into, lots of breakthroughs. I think she took out the insurance for me, so I could go to Sweden." As Luther neared, she leaned into me and said quickly, "He can't know that I'm sick."

I gave her hand a quick squeeze before we broke apart. As Luther sat back down, my dad strolled in through the front door, and I had to hustle to put my sunglasses back on.

"Hey, Dad," I said with a big smile. "These are my clients, Monica and Luther."

"Nice to meet you." His voice and posture were nice enough, but his innards were not the happy camper type. They were more like a disgruntled bear who tried to eat the happy camper only to find the happy camper was a champion sprinter. He bent down to kiss my cheek. "Have you given any thought to what we talked about earlier?"

"Do elephants glow in the dark?"

"You can take off your glasses," he said, a look of disappointment lining his weathered face. "Your uncle Bob already told me."

I gasped. "Uncle Bob ratted me out?"

"I'd like to talk to you later, if you have a minute."

"I'm pretty booked today," I said, sunglasses still on my smiling face, "but I can try to come down in a bit."

"I'd appreciate that. I'll leave you to your business." He nodded to Luther and Monica, then strode away to his office.

After questioning the Deans a little while longer, I said good-bye and took the stairs up to the office two at a time, excited to share the latest with Cookie. Was this an insurance scam? Surely Dr. Yost found out about the policy his wife took out. Maybe he saw it as an opportunity. I needed his financial records. But for that I needed a subpoena. No, I needed Agent Carson.

I started across the balcony that looked down into the bar. My office was just past the elaborate iron elevator, but the little girl with the knife stood blocking the way. I stepped around her and inside my office.

"Oh, I'll get you some coffee," Cookie said really loudly. She rushed into my office where the coffeepot was and waved at me, her eyes wide.

I smiled and waved back.

She rolled her eyes, hurried to the coffeepot, and gestured toward her office with a nod. "Do either of you U.S. Marshals take cream?"

Oh. Close call. I backed out the way I came in and inched the door closed. Whew. The little slasher girl was gone. Our encounters were fleeting yet meaningful. I was certain of it.

Not really in the mood to talk to Dad either, I snuck past his office and out the back door. Uncle Bob called my cell phone as I booked it to Misery.

"You ratted me out," I said, skipping the pleasantries.

"I did no such thing." He seemed really offended, then said, "Well, okay, I probably did. To whom did I rat you out?"

"Dad. Duh."

"What? The Reyes thing?"

"Did you know he wants me to quit?" I dug my keys out of my bag because Misery lacked the technology to sense my DNA and open the door when I approached.

"Quit what? Your gym membership?" He laughed out loud.

I slid the key into the lock. "That was so amazingly offensive."

"What?" He sobered. "Don't tell me you actually have a gym membership."

"Of course I don't have a gym membership. He wants me to quit work. My job. The investigations business."

"Get outta here."

"No, I'm telling you." I threw my bag in the passenger's side floorboard and climbed in one-handed. "He's lost it. He really wants me to quit. So I'm thinking either professional wrestling or belly dancing." Nor did Misery say things like, *Hello, Charley. Shall I arm the missiles for you?*

"I'll talk to him. In the meantime, I got a flag on the doctor."

"Like, an American flag?"

"In the database. Nothing ever came of it, but his name was mentioned in some kind of a forgery investigation. I can give you the detective's name who was in charge. He retired last year. I know him. Plays a lot of golf now."

"Cool. He probably deserves it. I've got two U.S. Marshals in my office," I said as Misery purred to life. No voice recognition software or retinal scanning required.

"What do they want?"

"No idea. I already talked to a marshal last night, so I snuck out the back way."

"In true Davidson style."

"Hey, can you check on Dr. Yost's financial situation? I've already got Cookie on it, but I need official stuff that I can't get without a warrant." I steered Misery onto Central. Steered her. Like with my two hands.

"Don't have to. He's rich. Have you seen his house? His monthly water bill would feed a small country for a month."

"Well, how do you know he's rich if you haven't checked his bank accounts?"

"You really want me to check into his finances?"

"Is the pope Catholic?"

"Did I mention how behind I am on my paperwork?"

"Did I mention how much you owe me?"

"Finances, it is."

12

Nothing sucks more than that moment during
an argument when you realize you're wrong.
—T-SHIRT

I'd parked Misery on a side street half a block away from the abandoned mental asylum and did a crouch run to the nearest Dumpster, where I dived for cover behind a group of evergreen bushes. Then I waved my arms about wildly and spit a few times when I realized the bushes were covered in spiderwebs. After a shiver of revulsion, I gathered myself, summoned my *Mission: Impossible* chi, and scaled a chain-link fence to the top of a dilapidated shed. Once there, I curled into an embryonic ball and whimpered. Chi or no chi, scaling fences sucked, mostly 'cause it hurt.

I pried open my throbbing fingers and scanned the area. Nary a Rottweiler in sight, so I jumped down and booked it to the basement window I used to sneak into the place. I turned the latch I'd rigged to unlock the window and pulled. Normally, the window opened out and I could do a drop-and-roll kind of thing into the basement, which was kind of like a duck-and-cover thing with less concern over radiation poisoning resulting in permanent hair loss, but the window was stuck. I pulled harder and it gave. For about half a second before it slammed shut again. What in the name of Zeus's testicles?

Before I could try again, Rocket appeared, his nose pressed against the glass like a giant kid in a nightmare version of peekaboo. He grinned. "Miss Charlotte!" he yelled, as though I were a thousand miles away.

"Rocket," I whispered, jamming an index finger over my mouth, "shh-hhh." I glanced around, waiting for the pitter-pat of Rottweiler paws. I had no idea if canines could hear the departed but figured this was not an ideal situation to find out. "Rocket, let me in."

He giggled again. "Miss Charlotte, I can see you through the glass!" he yelled louder, pointing to it over and over in case I missed it. "Can you hear me?"

Oh, for the love of Godsmack. I crawled onto my stomach and inched the window open. "Rocket," I said through the open slit, "you have to let me in."

"You can't come in. I have company."

"Company? Seriously?" Rocket had died sometime in the fifties. How many people could he know? "There are huge dogs out here, and I have to give you some names."

He brightened. Like literally. It was weird. He pushed open the window another inch and poked his nose and mouth out. "Names?" he whispered.

"Yes, names of people. I need to know if they've passed or not." I could lose him any second. Keeping Rocket's attention for more than several seconds was similar to winning the lottery, minus the monetary gain.

He pushed the window frame against his face to scrunch it and was making fish faces at me. "Hellllllloooooo, Miss Charlotte."

I drew in a deep, calming breath. "Rocket, where are Strawberry and Blue?" Blue Bell was his sister who died in the thirties from dust pneumonia. I'd never met her. Apparently, she didn't want to be introduced to the grim reaper. Strawberry was the departed little sister of a local police officer who worked with my uncle. She was a pain in the ass.

With his face still scrunched, he smiled. "They're hiding from you."

"Oh, great, now they're both going to avoid me?" At first I got a little irked under the collar; then I remembered I disliked children, so this was actually quite nice. I had no choice. I had to give him the names. He would probably bolt through the asylum and I'd lose him entirely, but that was better than having a leg gnawed off. "Teresa Dean Yost."

He stepped back and froze, his lids fluttering as he flipped through his mental registry. Then, as quick as that, he refocused on me. "No. Not her time."

His answer stunned me. Really? She was still alive? What the hell? I was positive Doc Holliday killed her. Two million smackeroos was a lot of smackeroos. But she was alive. I still had time. "Rocket, I love you."

He laughed, then slammed the window shut again.

"Rocket, wait." I pulled and jerked to no avail. The guy was like a boulder. Rocks were digging into my ribs and elbows, and I'd have to go home and change before I could do anything else. After a herculean yank, it budged, but only a little. "One more name, sweetheart," I whispered into the slit.

"Can you say the magic word?"

"Please?" I said, after exhaling loudly.

"Please is the magic word? I thought it was abracadabra."

"Oh, right, sorry. Okay, are you ready?"

He nodded, his eyes glistening in anticipation.

This was going to be trickier. Earl Walker had several aliases, and who's to say what his real name was, but it was worth a shot. "Earl James Walker."

"Dead," he said, matter-of-fact.

I blinked in surprise again. "Wait, are you sure?"

Rocket closed the window and latched it with an evil laugh.

"Rocket, damn it." I pulled and fought, unlatching it over and over only to have him latch it back. "Rocket!" I rasped.

He finally stopped laughing long enough to look at me.

Hoping he could hear me through the window, I said, "Earl James Walker. You're sure he's dead?"

He opened the window again, just enough to talk through it, refusing to give up the game, then shrugged. "Most of them are."

"Most of what? Earl James Walkers?"

"Yessiree." He counted on his fingers. "Seven dead since the black storms. Who knows how many before that?"

I had no idea what the black storms were, but Rocket had grown up during the Dust Bowl era. Maybe that's what he meant. "But, are there any alive?"

He counted again. "Two."

Wow, that meant maybe Reyes wasn't crazy. Clearly these Walkers weren't the most creative lot, naming all their kids Earl James. "Can you tell me where they are?" I asked, knowing the answer.

"Not where, only if. Alive or dead. That's what I know."

Well, crap, this was not helping. Maybe if I explained some things about this particular Earl Walker, we could narrow it down. "Rocket, let me in."

"Why?" he asked, as if thoroughly confused.

"Because I need to talk to you, and I don't want to be eaten by a freaking Rottweiler."

A huge grin spread across his face. "Like that one?"

He pointed over my head as a massive dollop of saliva dripped onto my jacket sleeve. Then it breathed, its hot breath fanning across my cheek, and I tried not to wet my pants.

A rush of adrenaline flooded my body, making it difficult to lie still, but lie still I did. Running only made them happy. As though defusing a bomb, I eased a hand into my jacket pocket and took out a rawhide strip in the shape of a bone. I had barely pulled my hand out of my pocket when a huge set of jaws clamped down on it and rolled over on top of me with a bark, likely breaking several ribs in the process.

I grunted and looked to my side as the Rottweiler spread out beside me and started gnawing, thankfully on the bone. He nudged me as if begging me to try to take it. And my heart was lost.

"Aren't you a sweetheart?" I asked, and he—correction, she—rolled onto her stomach, bone locked between jaws, stubby tail wagging hard enough to cause a hurricane in China. I rubbed her stomach. "You're just a doll. Yes, you are." She nudged my hands with her nose, and I looked at her collar. "Artemis? Your name is Artemis?"

Figuring it would be good practice for my new career, we wrestled for a while. "Are you a goddess? You look like a goddess. What a pretty name for a pretty pupp—" I stopped talking baby talk and froze when a large set of boots stepped into my line of sight.

My gaze wandered up chap-covered legs, a skull-shaped belt buckle, and a T-shirt framed within a leather vest that said KILL THEM ALL, LET GOD SORT THEM OUT. I continued my journey up to a scruffy jaw, a pair of black wraparound sunglasses, and hair so dark, it didn't reflect, but absorbed the sunlight.

"You're lucky your jugular is still intact," he said, the tenor of his voice deep and soothing despite its message. "Artemis doesn't like people much."

Completely covered in dirt, I rose into a sitting position with my arms braced behind me and gazed up. "She's a sweet dog."

Two more men walked up, looking just as scruffy as the first. One was young and looked like a Greek prince. The other looked more Italian Mafia than biker gang.

The first man turned to them. "She said Artemis is sweet."

The prince shrugged. "She is sweet." After receiving a jolting punch to the shoulder, he rubbed it and said, "She is. It's not my fault."

"It's entirely your fault, bitch." He seemed angry enough, but I found it difficult to pinpoint his exact emotion. "This chick should be missing half her face."

Tony Soprano nodded in agreement. I shook my head, disagreeing wholeheartedly.

"She's not even a good guard dog anymore. What the fuck am I supposed to do with that?"

Artemis jumped on his chest, as if to show him her new toy.

"Yeah, yeah. I know. You got a present." He rubbed her ears playfully and pretended he was going to eat it as he led her back to the ground and had her sit. She tried to jump again, but he kept a hand on her until she gave up and placed her full attention on the bone.

"Me, huh?" the prince said. "You old softy."

After another loud thud echoed against the building, one that had my own arm aching in response, I looked up at the guy who was apparently the leader of this here motorcycle club. "You're probably wondering what I'm doing here."

They glanced at one another and chuckled. "Are you kidding?" Mafioso asked.

"You can see them, can't you?"

I refocused on the leader. "Them?" I was still on the ground and started to get up when he placed a boot on my stomach. Not hard, just enough to keep me down. Apparently, that's how he liked his women. Despite the fact that I was already dirty, I glared up at him. "Do you mind?"

"You're trespassing, remember? I can do whatever I want to you."

And just when I was starting to like him.

"Who are they?" he asked.

"I don't know what you're talking about."

The prince kneeled beside me, leaned in until his mouth was almost on mine, then reached into my back pocket and pulled out my PI license. He stayed there a full ten seconds longer than need be, then glanced at my ID. "She's a private investigator."

He stood and handed it to the leader.

"Charlotte Davidson, PI," Fearless Leader said, taking his boot off my stomach. "You any good?"

"You'd have to define good. Where are the other dogs? You guys usually have three."

A silence fell over them. "Gone," he said quietly. "Poisoned. Artemis barely made it."

I gasped and climbed to my feet. "Who did it?" I couldn't help but be outraged.

Mafioso shrugged. "We're looking into it." Then he eyed me suspiciously.

I chose to ignore the accusation. As if.

"So who are they?"

Turning back to the leader, I lifted my brows in question while swiping at my clothes. Artemis took my movement as a sign and darned near tackled me through the wall of the asylum. "Who are who?" I asked, falling back and hugging her to me.

"The ghosts in the asylum."

I paused in surprise as the leader took Artemis's collar and sat her down again. I realized how gentle he was being with her. Perhaps she was still sick. "You don't look like the kind of guy who believes in ghosts."

"Didn't. Do now."

"'Kay. What makes you think I know who they are?"

The prince spoke up. "Because you're the only one who visits regularly to talk to them. Everyone else who breaks in here just wants to party, or take video of the *haunted asylum*." He wiggled his fingers for effect. "Freaking ghost hunters. Of course, sometimes guys bring girls here just to scare them. It's fun when they jump in your arms." He smiled. "I've used that a couple of times myself."

I couldn't help but grin. "And what makes you think this place is really haunted?"

"We see the walls," Mafioso said, "names there one day, new names the next. The ghosts scratch name after name, over and over into those walls." He glanced up at the dilapidated building. "This thing's going to fall down someday."

I was worried about that, too. "Actually, it's a he. Well, a Rocket, to be more exact. He's the one who carves the names into the walls. His sister's here, too, but I've never met her."

Their belief stilled them. The underlings looked back at the leader to see what he would say. He wanted to ask me questions, but I really didn't have time to go into it. I decided to shoot for the *Reader's Digest* version.

"Look," I said, drawing a deep breath, "Rocket died sometime in the fifties. He has this . . . I don't know, ability. He knows the names of every person ever born and knows if they've died or not. I use that to my advantage when investigating rather often. He's a savant. He's—" The thought of Rocket's personality made me smile. "—he's like a kid. Like a big, burly kid with a really bad case of ADD."

They glanced at one another.

"Can I go?" I asked, hitching a thumb over my shoulder and inching that way. "I kind of have a missing woman to find."

"Can you talk to him for us?" Fearless Leader asked.

"Sure can, any day but today."

The prince's head tilted as he watched my lower half appreciatively.

"You can go out the front," the leader said, taking hold of Artemis's collar. She was panting with her tongue hanging out, clearly wanting to play.

"Really? The front?" This was great. Scaling fences was not my forte.

"When you coming back?" one of them asked.

I was busy hightailing it to the front gate. "Soon!" I promised. I'd really wanted to talk to Rocket more, but now was not the time to get chummy with a biker gang. They always wanted lap dances, for some reason. As I rushed to Misery, I stopped dead in the middle of the street and looked back behind me. A large black truck sat about half a block away. The window slid down, and Garrett leaned out with a huge smile before saluting.

My jaw clamped shut. It was apparently his shift. My uncle had put him on my tail again. Reyes had escaped, and I was the obvious path of least resistance to find him.

I offered Garrett the best death stare I could conjure, hopefully blinding him for all eternity.

He chuckled and yelled, "Three! *I'm dying to try that!*"

Oh, my god, with the list already. I turned and stalked away, refusing to look back when he laughed out loud. Damn him. He could tell Uncle Bob no once in a while.

I hopped in Misery and started to dial Cookie's number on my cell when Rocket popped in beside me. Just popped in and sat in the passenger's seat. I'd never seen Rocket out of his element, so it took me a moment to adjust. And, well, to recognize him. He obviously needed a moment as well. He blinked, glanced around like he didn't know where he was, then turned his childlike face toward me.

"You left."

"Rocket, what are you doing here?"

A huge grin spread across his face; then he grew serious again. "You left."

"Yes, I know, I'm sorry. Is everything okay?"

"Oh, yeah," he said, jumping when he remembered what he had to tell me. "Teresa Dean Yost."

Startled, I asked, "What about her?" Surely her vital statistics hadn't changed in the last few minutes.

He turned a concerned face toward me. "Hurry."

Before I could say his name again, he was gone. Damn it. Hurry. I would if I knew where she was. What on planet Earth could the doctor have done with her?

I dialed Cookie.

"Do you think red and pink go well together?" she asked in lieu of a greeting.

"Only if you're a cupcake. Teresa Yost is alive," I said, turning the ignition and swerving onto the street.

"What? Really? A cupcake?"

Forty minutes later, I was driving a golf cart on the Isleta Golf Course. Uncle Bob had called. He'd gotten in touch with the detective who had been in charge of the forgery case, the one who'd flagged one Dr. Nathan Yost. I wanted to know why.

I picked up my phone and called Cook again. "Dude, we have to get a golf cart to go back and forth to work in."

"It's like a thirty-second walk."

"Exactly! This will shave minutes off our commute every year."

"Have you slept yet?"

"Sure. I took a power nap on the way over."

"Didn't you drive there?"

"Yeah. Other drivers kept waking me up. Car horns should be illegal."

Before she could get too into scolding me—she was clearly still upset about the cupcake remark—I closed the phone and hung a left at the sand pit by the junipers. A small gathering of men stood on a grassy knoll, gazing at the long fairway before them. Or, possibly at me as I was practicing my evasive maneuvers in case I was ever shot at while driving a golf cart. This thing was just cool. But it needed flames. Possibly a lift kit.

I screeched to a halt in front of the men. Metaphorically. "Are any of you named Paul Ulibarri?"

One man stepped forward, an older gentleman with a nasty-looking club in his hand. "I'm Paul," he said, slightly curious.

"Hi." I stepped out and offered my hand. "I'm Charley Davidson."

"Oh, of course, I just talked to your uncle. I wasn't expecting you so soon."

"Well, we have a missing woman, and I need to find her as fast as humanly possible."

"Of course. Howard," he said, turning and handing the club to a man nearby, "I'll be right back."

They all smiled and nodded graciously, almost too graciously, as we walked a distance away. Only one seemed a little annoyed at having the game interrupted, a younger man with a goatee, a flashy watch, and a frown lining his face.

"I'm sorry to interrupt your game."

"Oh, don't be. We're purposely taking our time. It seems we old farts don't play fast enough, and young Caleb there has places to be and people to see."

I laughed. "So, he's in a hurry?"

"Yep. He promised his father a game of golf and has regretted it ever since."

I looked back at them. "Who's his father?"

"I am." He grinned, a mischievous sparkle in his eyes. "So, your uncle mentioned the case, and I do remember it quite well. I called Hannah—she's still at the department in records—and had her pull the file. She's got it if you want a look."

"Thank you." I was a little surprised at the cooperation I was getting.

"I really wanted to nail that guy," he said, working his jaw.

"Dr. Yost?" I asked.

"What? Oh, no." He shook his head, refocusing on me. "Eli Quintero. Best damned forger I've ever seen. He printed more paper than Xerox."

"Paper?" I asked, surprised. "You mean like forged papers? Like IDs and stuff?"

"Yes, ma'am."

"Wow, I wasn't really expecting that. So, why did you have the doctor's name flagged in the case?"

"Because he was on the list." When I shrugged my brows in question, he elaborated. "When we raided Quintero's place, he'd already fled the scene—went to Minnesota or Mississippi, some place with an *M,* last I heard—but he left behind a book, a ledger that had fallen behind a table in his haste to vacate the premises. It had dozens of names, including that of your doctor."

"Really?" I was more than a little surprised.

"Unfortunately, that's all we got. Not enough evidence to prosecute, and I'd spent months on that case."

"That sucks."

He nodded lazily in agreement. "It does indeed."

"Do you know about when Dr. Yost went to see Quintero?"

"Well, if I remember correctly, the doc was one of the last names on the list, so it had to have been around the time we raided his place. That would put it—"

"Really, Dad?" Caleb whined from behind us. Apparently, it was his father's turn.

He turned slowly, and offered a huge smile. "Really, Caleb. Really." He turned back to me as Caleb threw down a club and stalked off. "My wife spoiled that boy rotten. About three years ago, I'd say."

She spoiled him three years ago? 'Cause that kind of behavior took decades to cultivate.

"Yeah, that's right. It was one of my last cases, so I'd say almost three years to the day."

"Wow, well, okay. Thank you so much for your time, and I'll get in touch with Hannah for the case file if you don't mind."

"Don't mind a bit." He handed me his card and had written her number on the back. Then he glanced at his pacing son and turned back to me. "Sure you don't need anything else? Stock tips? Legal advice? To hear the Gettysburg Address recited verbatim?"

I laughed and headed for my sweet ride. "I'm good. Thank you so much."

"Tell your uncle he's an ass," he called out to me.

"Will do." I liked that man. As I drove off, his son was in the throes of a full-blown rant about how time was money.

"Let me express how much I don't care on a scale of one to bite me," the former detective said.

I called Hannah, the files clerk, about the case on the way back to the clubhouse and drilled her with a few questions. Apparently, right beside the doctor's name in the ledger was the name Keith Jacoby. I got an exact date from the ledger and asked Hannah if she could hold on to the file for a while in case I needed to come in and take a look. I might need to find the forger Eli

Quintero for more information. According to the detectives' report, they believed Eli had absconded to Mississippi and set up shop there.

"No problem," she'd said. "Anything for Bobby."

Bobby? Did she mean Uncle Bob? Ew.

I flipped Garrett off, climbed into Misery, and called Cook. "Forget the comings and goings on the islands of Dr. Yost," I said when she picked up.

"Good, because I'm not getting a whole lot of cooperation."

"Do people never watch *Sesame Street* anymore?" I asked, pulling onto 47. Garrett followed.

"You got me. What's up?"

"I want you to do exactly what you were doing, only look for the name Keith Jacoby."

"Did I tell you how much cooperation I'm not getting?"

"You sure did, and I appreciate the update."

"Where are you?"

I merged onto I-40, narrowly missing a semi. "On my way back, why?"

"You sound distracted."

"Well, I am. Garrett is freaking following me."

"Really? What's he wearing?"

"Cook, this is serious."

"Wait, what are you doing?"

She could apparently hear the strain in my voice as I craned my neck from side to side. "I'm trying to see past a little girl on my hood."

"Oh. Isn't that dangerous?"

"Normally. But she has a knife."

"Oh, well, then, I guess it's okay."

13

A Nun's Life: Chastity, poverty and obedience. Wait, chastity?
—BUMPER STICKER

As soon as I pulled up to the office, I ran up the stairs to tell Cookie the most incredible thing I'd just heard on the radio. I flew through the door and skidded to a halt in front of her desk. "Have you heard about Milton Berle's penis?"

Cookie's eyes widened and she gestured behind me with a nod.

I turned to see a young nun stand up. She'd apparently been waiting for me.

Awkward.

I smiled. "Sorry about that," I said, offering her my hand. She wore a navy skirt and sweater that just matched the habit on her head, her hair brown underneath it. "I'm Charlotte Davidson."

"I know." She took my hand into both of hers, an awestruck glow in her green eyes, as if she were meeting a rock star. Or she was stoned. "I've heard it was huge."

"Excuse me?" I asked, thrown by the admiration in her eyes.

"Milton Berle's penis."

"Oh, right. Weird, huh? So, what can I help you with?"

"Well . . ." She glanced from me to Cookie and back again. "You won't answer my emails, so I decided to come see you myself."

I frowned. "Your emails? Have we met?"

"No," she said, a soft giggle floating toward me, "but I know who you are. I just wanted to meet you."

"Who I am?" I asked warily.

She leaned in and whispered with a conspiratorial smile, "The grim reaper."

Besides the fact that I almost fell over, I handled her statement pretty well. I glanced at a wide-eyed Cookie, who was too busy gawking to notice she'd knocked over her coffee cup. I cleared my throat and gestured toward the cup. Fortunately, she'd downed most of its contents. She grabbed a tissue to see to the small spill as I led the sister into my office.

"Can I get you some coffee?" I asked, heading in that general direction. It'd been minutes since my last cup.

She shook her head.

"Well, God knows I need some," I said as I poured.

"He probably does," she said, and with an inward cringe I realized what I'd said. "I like your paintings."

Cookie took another cup as well and sat beside my desk while the nun sat across from it.

"Thank you. So, can I ask your name?"

"Of course," she said with another giggle. "I'm Sister Mary Elizabeth. But you know me as Mistress Marigold."

I paused in the middle of sitting, looked her over again, then continued to sit. "You're Mistress Marigold?"

She offered a patient smile and a nod.

"You're not what I was expecting," I said after taking a long sip. I was expecting a New Age kind of woman with love beads, tarot cards, and scented oils. Mistress Marigold was the woman with the angels and demons website. Quite frankly, it surprised me she knew how to build a website in the first place.

"I'm sure. I'm sorry for the illusion. I just don't want the others to know I've actually found you. Not yet," she said, holding up her palms. "I wanted to make sure it was you before I told them."

"Them?" I asked. This could get ugly. Only a handful of people on the planet knew what I was.

"The Sisters of the Immaculate Cross. We're right down the street."

"Of course." I examined her a long moment. She let me. "Look, it's not that I don't believe in the Big Kahuna, it's just, how the hell do you know what I am?"

"Well—"

"And how did you find me?"

"Oh—"

"And how do you know about the son of Satan?" I asked, remembering that when Garrett had emailed her pretending to be the grim reaper, she'd written back, *If you are the grim reaper, I'm the son of Satan.*

Cookie nodded as she sipped from her cup, her eyes large with curiosity.

She smiled patiently, waiting for me to finish, then started again. "Okay, well, before we get too far into this, you might want to know a couple of things about me."

"Fair enough." I leaned back and took another sip.

She sat up straight, her knees pressed together, her hands folded in her lap. "I hear angels."

I blinked, waiting for the punch line. When none seemed forthcoming, I asked, "And?"

"Oh, well, that's pretty much it. I hear angels."

"Okay, well, that explains everything."

She blew out a breath of air in relief. "Thank goodness. I was worried—"

"Seriously?"

"I'm sorry?"

"That doesn't explain a freaking thing," I put my coffee down and leaned forward. "I was being sarcastic."

"Oh, I see." She frowned and shook her head. "I miss that sometimes."

"So, that whole website, that How to Detect Demons, that's yours?"

She nodded, her smile genuine. "It's not a sin, strictly speaking."

"You're Mistress Marigold for real?"

Another nod. I think she was giving me time to let it sink in. Time I apparently needed.

"Okay, let's go over this."

Nod.

"Cookie emailed you, and you knew it wasn't her. Then Garrett emailed you saying he was the grim reaper, and you knew it wasn't him. Then, and let me make this clear," I said, holding up an index finger, "I email you, under a fake name Cookie set up for me, ask what you want with the grim reaper, and you knew it was me."

Nod.

"How—? What—?"

She took pity on me and spoke. "It was the name she picked." She glanced at Cookie, who was just as boggled as I. "Jason Voorhees."

I rolled my eyes. "I told you not to pick the guy from *Friday the Thirteenth*."

"It was either that or Michael Myers," she said defensively.

"No, I was the one who wanted the guy from *Halloween*. You wanted to call me Freddy Krueger at first." I looked at Sister Mary Elizabeth. "Really? Freddy? Have you seen his skin condition?"

"It wouldn't have mattered," she said with a confident shake of her head. "The angels would have known eons before she chose a name which one she'd go with. That's the name they said you'd use."

"The angels. They really talk to you."

She snorted and her hands covered her mouth self-consciously. "I apologize. Sometimes my manners are not what they should be."

"Not at all."

"Actually, the angels don't talk to me. I'm not even sure they know I can hear them." When I raised my brows in question, she said, "What I do is more like eavesdropping."

"On angels?" I asked.

"I've just always been able to hear them. Ever since I can remember."

"Wow, that's really interesting. You know, my friend Pari did something similar when she had been pronounced legally dead for a few minutes. On her way back to Earth, she heard the angels talking."

Mary Elizabeth giggled. "That happens. It's the same thing, only I hear them constantly." She leaned in as if to trust us with some sacred secret. "It's actually quite annoying at times. They never shut up."

"Yeah, I guess it would be," I said with a grin. "So, you knew what name I'd use, but how did you find me from there?"

"Um, connections." She scooted back in her chair, a guilty expression on her face.

"Are those connections, mayhap, illegal?"

She gasped. "No! Well, okay, I'm not entirely certain. I know a guy who knows a guy."

Coming from anyone else . . . "So, he . . . ?"

"Traced your IP address."

"Wow." I was a little impressed. "And you built that website with the database about angels and demons?"

She nodded.

"And you heard Charley's fake name from the angels?" Cookie asked.

"Yes, I hear all kinds of things. You would not believe what is going to happen next week if something isn't done." She rolled her eyes. "Which it won't be. It never is. Nobody ever listens."

"You're a prophet," I said, a little floored.

"Oh, pfft." She waved away the notion with a hand. "Not really. Not in the traditional sense. I mean, I don't prophesy. I just listen to those who do. It's rather naughty, if you think about it."

I couldn't help but laugh. "I am just so floored."

"Me, too," Cookie said. "I mean, you're just not what we were expecting."

"Yeah, I get that a lot. But the sisters want to know all about you. Oh, and Reyes, of course."

Uh-oh. "So, how much do you know about Reyes?"

"Well, let me think. He is the son of Satan who was born on Earth to be with you, the grim reaper, though the sisters don't really like that label. They feel it limits you. Anyway, his name is really Rey'aziel, which means 'the beautiful one.' He is also a portal, like you. Oh!" She bounced back to us. "And he is powerful enough to bring about the apocalypse."

"You're very informed."

"Yeah, like I said, blah, blah, blah." She opened and closed her hand like someone talking nonstop. It was too funny. "So you know he can end the world?" she asked.

"Yeah, I got the memo."

"But . . . I don't understand." Her brows cinched together. "You saved his life when the demons were going to kill him, and again when he was going to take his own life. Then you bound him to this plane, locked him on to it."

"Yeah, I did, huh?" After I'd vanquished the demons torturing Reyes by tapping into my inner floodlight—apparently demons are allergic—Reyes decided to take his own life to make himself less vulnerable. I stopped him, then bound him inside his physical body. But the fact that Sister Mary Elizabeth knew what I'd done, knew anything about me or Reyes, was a tad unsettling.

"I mean, the reasons are all there," she continued. "I'm just still a little surprised that you'd save his life knowing what you know."

"What reasons?"

"You two. You and Rey'aziel. You're magnets. Literally." She held up two index fingers to demonstrate. "You're drawn together by sheer force of will."

"Oh, that."

"I mean, it was written. It's not like I didn't know you would do it. It's just, if the demons get ahold of you . . ."

"Yes, I've heard. Very bad," I said, ignoring the tightening in my stomach.

"Very bad indeed, but don't worry, they're going to send you a guardian right after a time of great suffering for you."

"Suffering?"

"Yes," she said with a nod.

"I'm not really that into suffering. Will it be bad?"

"Suffering usually is. Especially when the angels prophesy about it."

"That sounds horridly unpleasant. And they're going to send me a guardian? But, I thought Reyes was my guardian."

She snorted. "Rey'aziel? Your guardian?"

"Yes," I said, a little taken aback. "He's always been there for me. He's watched over me and saved my life several times."

"Well, that's true, but he's not your guardian. He's . . . I don't think you understand the situation."

"What situation?" I asked, wary.

"He's, well, he's very powerful."

"Yeah, got that memo as well."

"And he's . . . I'm just not sure how to say this."

"Sister Mary Elizabeth, there aren't many things you could say that will offend me, if that's what you're worried about."

"Oh, good, then I'll just say it. He's kind of like your Achilles' heel."

"My what?"

"You know, your kryptonite."

"So, Reyes is my weakness?" I asked, more confused than offended.

"Exactly. You're in love with him. You can't make sound decisions when he's around."

"She does have a point," Cookie said, nodding in agreement.

"Pfft. Please. I make sound decisions all day. With my eyes closed. And my hands tied behind my back."

"Exactly," she said, her mouth a grim line, "which happens often when he's around."

The fact that she knew that was oddly embarrassing.

"So who is it, then? This guardian?" I took a long draw on my java. I'd need all the spunk I could get if I was scheduled for a time of great suffering. Suffering, great or otherwise, tended to leech the spunk right out of me.

"I don't know his name, but I do know he'll bring a balance. Oh, and he hasn't died yet."

"Okay." I leaned back in thought. "So he's going to be a departed?"

"Yes." She glanced at her watch. "He's going to die in two days, eleven hours, and twenty-seven minutes."

"Wow, that's pretty specific. I don't actually kill this guy, do I?" I laughed nervously. I would hate to kill my very own guardian angel. He might take it personally.

"Of course not," she said, chuckling along with me. "Not directly."

"Well, good." I took another shot of coffee before her words sank in. "Wait, what does that mean?"

"What?"

"Not directly."

"Hmmm," she hummed, glancing at the ceiling in thought, "I'm not really sure. That's all I got. I hadn't had my tea yet. Sometimes I miss things before tea."

"Holy cow." I put both feet on the floor and sat up straight. "I'm going to be indirectly responsible for someone dying?"

"Yep."

"Well, that sucks ass."

"Yes, it does."

"Can you ask them who it is?"

"Who what is?"

"This guardian I'm going to murder indirectly."

"Oh, of course." She laughed softly. "But, ask who?"

Perhaps her decision to remain chaste was for the best. "The angels."

"Oh, right. No."

"Why not?" I asked, glowering a little.

"I told you. I don't talk to angels. I just sort of hear them." She turned to Cookie. "Is she still not sleeping?"

Cookie shook her head.

"How did you—?" I stopped myself. "The angels? Really? They gossip that much?"

"You have no idea."

I showed Sister Mary Elizabeth to the door, then turned back to Cookie. "Is it just me, or was that weird?"

"Both." She eyed me with a wary suspicion. "So, you're going to off someone."

"Not directly," I said defensively. "I mean, who knows how many people I've killed indirectly. You, too, for that matter."

"Me?" she asked, appalled. "Okay, I'm going to find out if a man named Keith Jacoby was in the Cayman Islands around the time of the doctor's first wife's death."

"Perfect. I'll do a little research on Reyes's case and the names he gave me."

"That's so wild what she said." Cookie sat behind her desk. "How she actually hears angels."

But was that really the most important part? "Did you catch the time-of-great-suffering thing?"

Her expression softened. "Can you just make sure I'm not around when it happens?"

"No can do," I said, strolling back to my office with a negating wave of my hand. "If I have to suffer, then so does everyone else within a ten-mile radius."

She pursed her lips. "What ever happened to taking one for the team?"

"Was never much of a team player."

"Sacrificing yourself for the greater good?"

"Not that into human sacrifice."

"Suffering in silence?"

I stopped and turned back to her, my eyes narrowing accusingly. "If I have to suffer, I'll be screaming your name at the top of my lungs the whole time. You'll be able to hear me all the way to Jersey, mark my words."

"You're very testy today."

Fifteen minutes later, I stabbed the intercom thingy on my desk. "Remember that dental assistant at Reyes's trial? She said Earl Walker was scared of Reyes, and she just happened to work for the same dentist who identified Earl through his dental records?"

"Sure, I remember. Sarah something," she said.

"Sarah Hadley. And guess where Sarah Hadley is now."

"Jamaica?"

"Why would she be in Jamaica?"

"You told me to guess."

"Listen to this—"

"You realize I can hear you without the annoying intercom."

Cookie and I both leaned forward and looked at each other through the doorway.

"But this is more fun," I said. "More *Star Trek*kie."

"More annoying?" she asked.

When I pressed my lips together and waited, she caved.

"So where is she?"

"Okay, check this out." I brought up the article. "Sarah Hadley was found dead in her apartment Monday morning by her landlady while responding to complaints that Hadley's television was too loud." I looked back at her.

"No way," she said, leaning forward again.

"Way."

"Like, this Monday?"

"No, that's just it. Reyes's trial ended over ten years ago on a Thursday, right?"

"Right."

"She was found dead the following Monday right after his trial."

"Walker killed her. He was tying up loose ends."

"It would seem so. Not only that, he was a hairsbreadth away from going to prison himself for scamming elderly women out of their money—winner—and was facing a fifteen-year prison sentence."

"Then he's conveniently murdered?"

"About five minutes before his case went to trial."

"Lucky guy."

"Yeah. Or a conniving one."

"So, Sarah Hadley switches the dental records, thus proving the man Earl Walker chose to take his place in the afterlife was actually Earl Walker—"

"What? I can't hear you." I waved my hand and pointed to my ear and then at the intercom. "You need to speak into the intercom."

After a loud sigh, she pressed the button. "—then she testifies against Reyes at his trial, and good ole Earl repays her by—"

"Beating her to death with a bookend."

"I think Earl has issues."

"And I think he has about a gazillion years of jail time waiting for him." I jumped up, walked into Cookie's office to grab my coat, as that was where I'd left it, walked back into my office, then pushed the intercom button again. "Okay, I have addresses on the names Reyes gave me. I'm heading out. And hopefully I won't kill anyone."

"You still have days before that happens. Don't worry about it."

"True, and thankfully one of the men on the list is already dead, so there's no killing him again."

"And the others?"

"One is here in Albuquerque, and one is in Corona."

"The beer?"

"Sadly, no. The town."

"We have a town named Corona?"

"I know, right? Who knew? I'm going to interview the guy here first. Wish me luck."

"Wait!" she said as I walked past her desk.

I turned to her, but her finger was still on the button and she was giving me this impatient glare.

Oh fine. I'd started this. I once again walked into my office and pushed the intercom button.

"So, you're saying I look like a cupcake?"

14

Time to make today my bitch.
—T-SHIRT

I steered Misery in the general direction of south until we came to a crumbling group of apartments behind another crumbling group of apartments behind an abandoned group of apartments that made the first two look like the Ritz.

"Charley's House of Cards," I said into my phone while pulling in to the lot of the worst of the apartment buildings.

"Yost's first wife was cremated," Cookie said.

"What?" I turned the ignition to off. "But her death was suspicious. And they let him cremate her?"

"Apparently. He had it done on the islands before he brought her back to the States."

"Why do these people not check with me first?"

"No hit on the alias yet. Still looking."

"Okay, let me know. Soon, because the odds of me getting out of this neighborhood alive are nowhere near good."

"I knew it. I should have come with you."

"So we could die together?"

"True. Well, good luck."

I kept the phone to my face even after we'd hung up. A phone made the perfect excuse not to notice the people ogling me as I strode to apartment three. It didn't actually have a *3* on the door, but I was pretty good at counting in the single digits.

I rapped on the door of one Mr. Virgil Gibbs, and a thin man, hunched over with age and abuse, answered. He had dark hair and a graying beard.

"Hi," I said when I got his attention. He was busy looking at a group of men looking at me. "My name is Charlotte Davidson, and I'm a private in—"

"Maybe you should come inside, sweetheart."

He stood back but kept a wary eye around us.

"Okay." I was so going to die. I stepped inside nonetheless. He didn't look super agile. Surely I could outrun him.

His apartment wasn't bad, considering. A couple empty beer bottles on an end table. A television complete with foil-laced antenna sticking out. No dirty ashtrays, which surprised me. Or underwear on the couch.

"You want a beer?" he asked, the fact that he was missing a few teeth becoming evident with the question.

"No, thank you."

He stepped to the fridge to get one for himself. "What did you say your name was?"

"Charlotte Davidson. I'm a private in—"

"Davidson?" he asked, twisting off the cap and eyeing me with a squint of blue.

"Yes, I'm a—"

"Well, if you don't want a beer, what do you want?"

If he'd let me finish a freaking sentence, we'd get through this much faster. "Wait," I said, walking to the window. "Is my Jeep safe out there?"

"Honey, I could put a cup of gold out there and it'd be safe. They know not to mess with what's mine."

"You seemed pretty worried about me," I countered.

He smiled, showing his disastrous collection of teeth. "You ain't mine, unfortunately. But you're in my house. They'll leave your Jeep be as long as you're out of here before dark."

With several hours left in the day, I had every intention of being just that.

"So, you ain't selling anything?"

"No, I'm a private investigator looking for someone you know."

"Really?" His interest piqued, but in an amused way. "You don't look like no dick."

"Well, I am. And I'm looking for—" I paused and flipped through my notepad to give him a minute to let his emotions level out. I needed a clean read. "—a Mr. Earl Walker."

He balked, both mentally and physically. "You about ten years too late, missy. You weren't exactly his type anyway."

I knew that. I knew Earl's type, and it was neither female nor grown. And he wasn't lying. He truly believed Earl Walker was dead. Hell, maybe he was.

With two scratched off the list, it looked like I was going to Corona.

"Well, thank you for your time, Mr. Gibbs."

"Ain't no problem. If you find him, tell him Virgil says hey." He laughed into the bottle as he took another swig.

"I'll do that."

I climbed into Misery with several sets of eyes watching, including Virgil's. He wasn't a monster like his friend Earl, but I doubted I'd hang with him anytime soon.

I called Cook to let her know where I was headed.

"Hey, boss."

"I struck out."

"Oh, was he good looking?"

"No. What does that have to do with anything?"

"Well, if you asked him out and he said no."

"Not that kind of struck out. With the guy from Reyes's list."

"Oh, bummer. What now?"

"I was going to head out to Corona, but I think I'll go talk to Kim Millar first."

"Reyes's sister?"

"That's the one."

Reyes had a pseudo-sister, a girl he'd grown up with, and he cared for her deeply. While Reyes had been kidnapped from his birth parents as a small child and sold to Earl Walker, Kim had been given to the man. When she was two, her drug-addicted mother dumped her on Earl Walker's doorstep, the man she suspected was Kim's father, then died days later. Had Kim's mother known what kind of monster Earl Walker was, I could only hope she would never have left her daughter with him. Walker didn't sexually abuse her, as I'd feared. He did the next best thing. He used her to control Reyes, literally starved her to get what he wanted out of him. And while we never discussed exactly what it was he wanted from Reyes, the implications of sexual abuse were all there.

"I'll head to Corona after I talk to her," I said.

"It's getting late, and it'll take you a couple of hours to get there."

"Yeah, but I need to get this done, and since I can't do anything about the doctor without more info, I'll do this." I could hear her pressing buttons on the fax machine, then rustling a paper or two.

After a moment, she said, "Holy cow, he was there."

"What? Who was where? The doctor?"

"Yep, just got it. A receipt from the Sand and Sun Hotel in the Cayman Islands. One Mr. Keith Jacoby checked in on the very day Ingrid Yost was found dead. Paid for one night with cash and never visited again."

"Oh, my god, Cook. We got him."

"You need to call your FBI agent."

"Okay, I'll try her in a bit. Keep digging."

"You got it. Don't do anything stupid," she said.

"I resent that remark."

"No, you don't."

"Well, I might. You don't know."

"Do, too."

"I'll call you when I get out to Corona."

" 'Kay. And tell me what Agent Carson says. And tell me how Reyes's sister is. And how much coffee have you had?"

"Seventeen thousand cups."

"Don't fall asleep at the wheel."

I glanced in the rearview to make sure my handy-dandy tail was doing his job. Yep. Right on my freaking ass. I hated being tailed. What if I wanted to run naked through a wheat field? Or pick up a male prostitute?

"This guy ain't moving."

Startled, I turned to Angel, who'd popped into the passenger's seat. "Angel, you little shit. What guy?"

He shrugged. "That doctor you sent me to watch. He's all boo-hooing over his wife. Are you sure he did it? I mean, he seems really upset."

Geez, the guy was good. "Of course he did it. He was drowning in guilt when he came in."

"Maybe he was guilty of something else, like cheating on his taxes."

"Dude, I'm not wrong. Tax guilt is completely different. And unless I'm gravely mistaken, he killed his first wife, too."

"Okay, but I'd rather hang with you."

"Fine, but just for a few minutes. He didn't give you any leads? Make a suspicious phone call? Go out to the shed? Down to the basement? Meet a woman in the alley and have hot animal sex? Maybe he's having an affair."

He tossed me an irritated glare. "I would have noticed."

"Just checking." I threw out a *talk to the hand* sign to block his 'tude.

"Besides, there are feds all over that place. He could have hot animal sex if he wanted to, but he'd have an audience."

"Did you check his property? Maybe there's some freshly turned dirt. Or a new garden. That's always popular with serial killers."

"Nothing. The man's clean. Who's that guy following you?"

"Uncle Bob put a tail on me."

Angel smiled. "I like Uncle Bob. He reminds me of my dad."

"Really? That's so sweet."

"Yeah, not really, but if I knew who my dad was, I think he'd be like Uncle Bob."

I couldn't help but grin. "I bet you're right."

We drove in silence a few miles before Angel tossed me a "See ya," and popped out again.

I stopped for coffee at a twenty-four-hour convenience store, then booked it over to Kim Millar's apartment complex, flashed my ID to the guard at the gate—then offered him a ten-spot if he refused entrance to the black pickup following me—and parked close to her door. I wasn't sure if I was doing the right thing. Admittedly, this was more curiosity than honest-to-goodness investigative work. Did she also believe Earl Walker was still alive? Did she know something Reyes didn't? According to Kim, she and Reyes were in a zero-contact agreement. For her own safety, Kim's existence was never brought up in any of the court documents. Because she had a different last name, it was easy for her to fade into the background, at Reyes's insistence.

From what I could tell, Kim worked from home as a medical transcriptionist. No idea what that entailed, but it sounded really important. However, I'd been to see her twice, and after getting a glimpse of her life, her pristine apartment, and neat-but-out-of-date attire, I was beginning to think she needed to get out more. She was beautiful. Slim with auburn hair and silvery green eyes.

I padded up the walk to her turquoise door. The complex was styled to look like authentic Pueblo with round-edged adobe walls, flat roofs, and stepped levels, each one with vigas along the roofline, heavy timber beams extending through the exterior walls. Every door was painted a different Southwest color, from bright blues, reds, and yellows to the more earthy tones of terra-cotta and rich umber.

The last time I visited Kim, Reyes got a little upset. I tried not to let that worry me. He was bound now. He'd never know. Still, I couldn't help but hesitate before I knocked. But knock, I did. A few moments later, the door opened. Kim stood there, pencil in hand. I flinched. Not because she was gripping the pencil like a switchblade and my sister had tried to stab me with one once—a pencil, not a switchblade, her grip quite similar—but because if I thought she'd looked fragile before, she looked ten times that now. I regretted my decision to come here instantly.

Her huge green gaze landed on me, worry and despair saturating the air. "Ms. Davidson," she said, her voice soft and surprised. She glanced around, and I could feel the hope carried in each glimpse, each hesitant blink of her eyes.

"He's not with me," I said. "I'm sorry."

"But you've seen him."

Her grip tightened on the pencil and I forced myself to stand my ground. This time, I glanced around, then looked back at her and offered the slightest hint of a nod. Her eyes widened. She pulled me inside and slammed the door shut.

"They've been here already," she said, closing curtains and leading me to her small living room.

"I figured they might come here." Those U.S. Marshals were nothing if not thorough.

She turned back to me after closing one last set of curtains. "Do you think they've bugged the place?" she asked, sitting next to me on the sofa.

Despite the fragility that seemed to encase her like a thin layer of crystal, she had a healthy glow, a soft blush on her porcelain skin. She seemed almost excited.

I couldn't help but smile. "I don't know, but I don't really want to say too much."

"I saw on the news where he escaped." She was way too happy when she said that.

"Yes," I said with a chuckle. "Do you think he'll come here?"

"Heavens no. Remember, no contact. Like it matters anymore. The authorities know all about me."

I'd wondered how the marshals had discovered her in the first place. There was nothing to connect Kim with Reyes. Then, a couple of weeks back, I found a reference to the possibility of a sister on one of those prisoner groupie sites and figured that's where they caught her scent. Of course, the fact that fan sites existed at all for prisoners stunned me to my toes. And when I found out there was not one, but several dedicated to one Mr. Reyes Alexander Farrow . . . to say I'd been taken aback would've been the understatement of the millennium.

Still, it was the only explanation I could think of to explain how the U.S. Marshal's office had become aware of Kim's relation to Reyes. Like I'd said, thorough.

I thought I should warn Kim about Reyes's attitude toward our friendship. "Kim, the last time I came to see you, Reyes was none too happy."

Startled, she asked. "Did he . . . did he threaten you?"

"Oh, no. Well, maybe a little." He'd actually threatened to slice me in two if I ever came to see her again, but I doubted he really meant it.

She rolled her eyes. "He won't do anything. He's all bark, that one."

Her newfound boldness floored me. She was so excited and open. "You seem really happy."

"I am." Glancing down at the hands in her lap, she said, "Now he can go to Mexico or Canada. And he can live." Her hopeful gaze landed on mine. "For the first time in his life, he can live. But I need to give you something." She was glancing around again and went for the pencil. I braced myself, but she also went for paper. Thankfully. She scribbled a note, then handed it to me. "Can you get this to Reyes? This is the account number and the password. It's all there. Every penny."

"The account number?" I asked, studying the line of digits.

"It's his money." When my brows slid together in question, she said, "Well, my money. But he gave it to me. I just live off the interest. And I take only a little bit of that. It's his. All of it. He could live like a king in

Mexico with this." She rethought her statement. "He could live like a king anywhere in the world with this."

I folded the paper and held it in my hands. "Where on earth did it come from? How—?" Shaking my head, I realized I would never understand how Reyes did the things he did, so I switched gears. "I'm assuming this is a bank account?"

She nodded, a huge smile on her face.

"How much is in there?"

She looked up in thought, pursing her lips. "Last I checked, a little over fifty million."

I stilled.

She giggled.

I slipped into a mild state of shock.

She patted my shoulder, said something about the account being in Switzerland.

I grew light-headed.

She waved a hand in front of my face, offered me a paper bag.

I knew Reyes was good at computers. He'd hacked into the NM Public Education Department's database and given himself a high school diploma so he could take online classes while in prison, and with it, he'd gotten a master's degree in computer information systems. And the first time I'd met Amador and Bianca Sanchez, Reyes's aiders and abettors, they'd explained how he'd helped them get their house, how he'd studied the market, told them when to buy stocks and when to sell. But $50 million?

I pressed the paper back into her palm. "Kim, if he did this for you, then this is your money. I know him. He won't take any of it from you. But more importantly, you can't trust anyone with this information, even me."

She pushed it back. "You're the *only* one I'd trust with it. You're the only other person on the planet he'd want to have it if anything should happen to me."

I stuffed the paper in my pocket reluctantly. "What do you mean by that?"

"Nothing," she said, a reassuring smile on her face. "Just in case. You know."

My brows slid together in concern. She wasn't lying so much as not telling me everything. "Hon, is everything okay?"

She blinked in surprise. "Absolutely, why?"

Okay, that wasn't a lie. "No reason. I just wanted to make sure. You seem to be cooped up a lot."

Glancing around her apartment, she said, "I get out. Probably not as much as I should. I go walking around the grounds every day. We have a pool."

Part of me wanted to comment on how many pools she could have with 50 million *dólares* in her bathing suit, but she seemed comfortable here. Who was I to suggest a house on a beach in Hawaii?

She was feeling so good, so calm, I almost didn't bring up the reason I'd come. But I needed to get her opinion on the matter. I just wasn't sure if Reyes was seeing things clearly.

"Can I ask you something?" I said, pulling her attention back to me.

"Of course." She'd pinned that smile back onto her pretty face.

I scooted closer and braced myself for any reaction she might have. "Do you think it's possible that Earl Walker is still alive?"

The smile on her face didn't waver. It didn't falter or fade in the least. But the smile in her eyes, the genuine part of a smile, vanished. Then, like a geyser erupting from her core, panic rose in her and hit me full force, but she sat perfectly still. Motionless. Frozen in the throes of her own fear.

I put a hand over hers instantly and leaned forward. "Kim, I'm so sorry. I didn't mean to frighten you."

She blinked, appearing like a mannequin with the emotion that had been painted on her face a little too garish. "You didn't frighten me," she said, the lie hanging thick in the air. "What you asked is absolutely impossible."

I backtracked as fast as I could. "You're right," I said, shaking my head. "I'm sorry I even brought it up. I just thought if Reyes was innocent."

The smile faltered at last. "He's innocent? Did he tell you that?"

"No!" I lied, literally jumping forward. "No, he didn't. I—I just wondered why he would escape. I just thought—"

"But you were with him," she said, putting the facts together. "When he first escaped. I saw it on the news. He carjacked you."

"Yes, he did. But . . . that's not what I meant. He never said—" The fragility that had been there on my first two visits, the crushing sadness, resurfaced, and I was afraid her bones would crumble to dust before my eyes.

She pulled back, her gaze wandering past me to another place and time. "He's alive, isn't he?"

"No, hon—"

"I should've known Reyes would do that." Her eyes suddenly shimmered with unspent tears. "Of course he would do that. He's always done that."

My thoughts shot from *How do I get out of this?* to *Come again?* "What do you mean? Kim, what did he do?"

She replaced the smile and turned back to me. "He told me he killed him."

Well, shit. What the hell was going on? Was Earl Freaking Walker alive or not?

"And he lied." An iridescent pool sat trembling on her lower lashes as she battled her lungs for air.

"Why would he lie about something like that?" I asked, struggling to understand.

After glancing at the hand covering hers, she clasped her fingers around it, then looked up at me as though she felt sorry for my lack of depth. "Because that's what he does. He protects me. He does anything for me. He always has. Do you know there are pictures everywhere?"

"Pictures?" I asked, fighting past the grief.

With an almost invisible nod, she said, "He kept pictures. Proof. Blackmail."

"Reyes?"

"Earl." She shook visibly as memory after memory washed over her. "In the walls."

I leaned forward, trying to get through to her. "Sweetheart, what pictures?"

She stood, walked to the door, and opened it for me. Reluctantly, I followed. "I'll get in touch with you the minute I know something," I promised.

Her breath hitched in her chest, and I realized it was taking all her strength to hold herself together. The kindest thing I could do would be to leave. So I did. She closed the door softly behind me as I walked to Misery. And everything she'd told me before about Reyes and her surfaced. How Earl Walker had used her to get what he wanted out of Reyes. He had abused him in the worst way possible. Had he taken pictures? Wouldn't that implicate himself?

Then understanding of what she meant about Reyes protecting her dawned. He had gone to prison partly for her. Cleary, she needed to believe Earl Walker was dead with every ounce of her being. And I had just planted a seed of doubt in her mind.

Reyes was going to kill me.

15

If at first you don't succeed,
skydiving is NOT *for you.*
—BUMPER STICKER

With a lingering sadness after my visit with Kim still tightening my chest, I walked up to a dilapidated mobile home and knocked on a rusted door. The village of Corona sat nestled in the picturesque mountains of southeastern New Mexico. With less than two hundred people in residence, it had a small-town charm all its own. And it was a good two-hour drive from Albuquerque, which explained why it took me a little over an hour to get there. A man whom I'd assumed to be the last name on Reyes's list, Farley Scanlon, opened the door, an annoyed scowl bunching his brows.

Well built with shoulder-length brown hair intermingled with a streak or two of gray, a long mustache and goatee, and a strip of leather around his neck with a silver pendant, Farley proved to be one of those men in his late fifties who only looked in his late fifties up close.

"Hello," I said when he settled his frown on me in question. I noted the hunting paraphernalia in the background of his decrepit trailer. "My name is Charlotte Davidson." I fished out my PI license because he didn't look like a man who trusted easily. "I'm a private investigator working on a missing persons case."

He eyed my ID a long moment before returning his steady gaze to me. "Well, I ain't killed no one, if you're asking." The barest trace of a smile slid across his scraggly face.

"That's good to know." I smiled back, waited another heartbeat to give him time to adjust, then said, "Unfortunately, there are plenty of other things a man of your reputation can go to prison for."

His breathing remained calm, his gaze steady. But the emotion that hit me with hurricane force was full of both anger and fear, and I wondered which part of that was directed at me. It was probably too much to hope he was afraid of me.

I took out my notepad and started checking off the itemized list I'd basically pulled out of my ass. "Okay, we have a few months for obstruction of justice. Three years for possession and distribution of a controlled substance. Ten years for conspiracy to commit murder." I leaned in and smiled. "And that's if the judge is in a good mood." He looked like the conspiracy-to-commit-murder type, so I'd taken a chance. He didn't argue the fact.

"What the fuck do you want?" he asked, shifting away from me.

"Wait," I said, holding up a finger and continuing to read, "I also have nine months for accessory after the fact, but a good lawyer can probably get that reduced to time served once the trial starts, because it could take a while, if you know what I mean." I snorted.

The anger quickly overtook the fear.

I closed the pad and eyed him a good twenty seconds. He waited, his jaw working hard.

"Here's what I can offer you," I said, and he shifted his weight again, itching to be rid of me. "I'll give you one chance to tell me where Earl Walker is before I call the police and have your ass arrested on all these charges right here and now." I couldn't really have his ass arrested, but he didn't know that. Hopefully.

The shock that hit me was so palpable, so visible, I felt as if I'd blindsided him with a left hook. Clearly, he was not expecting the name Earl Walker to enter into the conversation. But his reaction had nothing to do with thoughts of lunacy. He was wondering how I knew. Guilt was so easy to sense. It was like picking out the color red in a sea of yellow.

"I don't have time for this shit," he said, readying to walk past me.

I put both hands on the doorjamb to block his path.

He cast an incredulous stare at me. "Really, sweetheart? You want to do that?" When I shrugged, he just sighed and said, "Earl Walker died ten years ago. Look it up."

"Okay, two chances. But that's my final offer." I wagged my finger at him in warning. That'd teach him.

"Honey, he's dead. Ask his son," he said with a knowing smirk. "His kid's been sitting in prison ten years for killing him. Ain't nothing you or the law can do about that."

"Look, I'm not here to give you any trouble." I showed my palms in a gesture of peace, love, and goodwill toward men. "You and I both know he's no more dead than the cockroaches that scurry across your kitchen floor every night."

His eyebrows seemed glued together.

"This isn't your fault," I said with a lighthearted shrug. "No one needs to know your name. Just tell me where he is, and you'll never see me again." I was so going to hell for lying. I had every intention of watching the man rot in prison.

Farley's mouth formed a grim line as he took out a hunting knife that would have made Rambo proud and began cleaning his nails with the tip of the blade. Like Rambo might have had needed a manicure. The move was very effective. My first thought was how much it would hurt when the blade slid into my abdomen, pushing easily past the muscle tissue and through those ovaries with which I had no intention of procreating. Then Farley looked past me and stilled. With the reluctance of a man who forgot to take his Viagra before his weekly visit with his favorite prostitute, he slipped the blade back into its sheath.

He must have seen Garrett parked in the distance, not that I dared take my eyes off him to check. He reached over and grabbed a jacket.

"I don't have anything else to say."

"'Cause you're a big fat liar?" I asked. It was a fair question. That scum-of-the-universe Earl Walker was alive.

A wave of anger washed over him. He probably didn't like to be called fat. I giggled, but because I wasn't stupid, I did it on the inside. On the outside, I raised my brows, waiting for an answer.

"No, because Earl Walker is dead."

I nodded in understanding. "Possibly. Or it could be you're just a big fat liar."

His free hand curled into a white-knuckled fist, but his face remained neutral. All things considered, he was pretty good. Probably played a lot of poker. "I have a meeting."

He forced his way past me even though I was blocking the door, his shoulder hitting mine in a desperate act of machismo.

I called out to him as he stalked to his truck. "Is it the weekly Big Fat Liars Anonymous meeting?" Nothing. He climbed in and slammed the door, but his window was down, so I took another pot shot. Mostly because I could. "Big Fat Liars bridge club?"

He glared as his engine roared to life.

"A Big Fat Liars Tea and Recognition Ceremony?" When he pulled the gearshift into drive, I shouted, "Don't forget to stick out your pinkie!" Teas were so tedious.

After he drove off, I glanced over at Garrett. He'd exited his vehicle and was leaning against it, his legs crossed at the ankles. For once, I was glad he was there, but I refused to let him know that. I climbed into Misery and called Cook.

"Are you still alive?" she asked.

"Barely. This one liked big knives."

Her startled gasp sounded in the phone. "Like Rambo's?"

"Exactly." Either she was getting better at this, or we really did have ESPN. "And even though he wouldn't give me the time of day if my life depended on it, he knew one thing for certain."

"Big knives are scary?"

"Earl Walker is alive."

The phone was silent for a moment; then she said, "Wow, I'm not sure what to say. I mean, Reyes said he was, but—"

"I know. I don't know what to think either."

"So, Earl's girlfriend, the dental assistant, switches dental records so the cops think it's really him," she said, thinking out loud.

"Yes, and Earl picks someone with the same general facial structure and build, murders him, puts him in the trunk of his car and burns it."

"And he makes sure Reyes is arrested for his murder," she said.

"Then kills his girlfriend one week after Reyes is convicted."

"So, was this Farley Scanlon with the big knife an accessory?"

"That part's not quite as clear," I said, sliding my key into the ignition, "but he knows beyond a shadow of a doubt Earl Walker is still alive."

"Well, we have to find him. We have to get Reyes out of jail. Well, really out of jail. Not just escaped out of jail."

"I agree. I'm going to grab something to eat at this little café—"

"Oh, you love small-town cafés."

"I do. I'll be back in a couple."

"You know, I had a thought about that," she said, her voice hesitant.

"Yeah?" I pulled out of Farley's dirt drive. Circling back around, I missed dismembering Garrett by a hairsbreadth as he jumped back into his truck, then offered me a questioning glare in my rearview. It made me smile.

"Yeah. Why don't you ride with Garrett and we can pick up Misery tomorrow?"

"Why would I do that?" I asked, appalled.

"Because you haven't slept in fourteen days."

"I'm good, Cook. I just need a little coffee."

"Just make sure he stays close. And make sure Rambo doesn't come after you. They always come after you."

I tried to be offended, but just couldn't muster the energy. "Okay."

"How was your visit with Kim?"

After a long, labored sigh, I said, "She was really happy when I got there. I'm pretty sure she was suicidal when I left."

"You do have that effect on people."

I pulled into the lot of a small café with about two customers to its name. Garrett pulled into the other side of the lot, turned out his lights, and waited. He had to be hungry, but no way was I inviting him in. He could bite my sexy tailed ass.

"Sit wherever, honey," a round waitress in jeans and a country blouse said when I walked in.

A bell overhead sounded as I closed the door. The café had all the country charm I loved with none of the commercialism. Antique kitchen items together with farming equipment hung on the walls and sat perched on barn wood shelves. Vintage tins punctuated the décor, everything from saltine crackers to sewing oil, and the nostalgia brought back memories from my childhood. Or it would have, had I been born in the thirties.

It did bring back the memories I'd gleaned off a man who'd crossed through me when I was a child. He'd raised sheep in Scotland, and castrating sheep is a big part of that occupation. Unfortunately, once something is seen, it cannot be unseen.

After a few minutes, the bell sounded again and a tall bond enforcement agent with a fetish for midget porn strolled in like he owned the place.

"Hello, handsome," the woman said, making me grin. "Sit wherever you'd like."

Garrett nodded, strolled to a corner table at the opposite side of the diner, and sat facing me.

"What can I get you, hon?" the waitress asked, holding pen and pad at the ready.

"I would kill for a green chile cheeseburger and an iced tea."

"Green burger and tea it is. With fries?"

"And extra ketchup."

"I'll have the same but with chips," Garrett called out. He probably didn't want me getting my order first and finishing before he did.

The waitress looked over at him and chuckled. "He must be hungry."

"I can't take him anywhere," I said, shaking my head.

When she walked away to get our teas, I asked him, "Why didn't you come to my rescue when trailer park guy pulled a knife on me?"

His grin flashed bright in the low light. "I'm just tailing you. I can't let you know I'm here. If I had interfered, you would know."

The waitress paused a moment before heading toward me with my tea. "He has a point," I said to her. She offered a hesitant smile, obviously unsure of what to think. "Hey, can you make sure I get my burger first?"

"Your voice carries really well," he said, his voice carrying really well.

With narrowed eyes, I said, "Shush, you tailgater, you. This is between—" I glanced at the server's name tag. "—Peggy and me."

He shrugged defensively. "I would've come to your rescue eventually."

"Oh, yeah? When? After I'd been gutted and lay bleeding to death in a ditch somewhere?"

"Absolutely," he said, clasping his hands behind his head. "I mean, I wouldn't jump in the ditch and try to suppress the bleeding or anything, but, sure. I'd call for help or something."

Offering my best smile ever, I said, "You're a real saint, Swopes."

"My mom says the same thing."

The realization that Garrett actually had a mother kind of disturbed me. But only for about twelve seconds. I rarely held thoughts in my head any longer than twelve seconds. Damn my ADD.

We sat in silence awhile as I jotted down some notes. I glanced up from underneath my lashes a few times to check on Garrett. He obviously took his tailing duties seriously, considering he had yet to take his eyes off me. The smell of the burgers and green chile on the grill had my mouth watering. By the time Peggy brought our burgers, I was moments away from drooling uncontrollably. Either from the smell or the lack of sleep. I couldn't be sure which.

"So, why are we here?" Garrett asked between bites. The asshole slipped Peggy a five-spot to bring him his burger first. Never trust a man with a penis.

"The man Reyes went to prison for killing isn't dead," I said, salting my burger before I'd even tried it.

"Are you serious?"

That got Peggy's attention, too. She glanced over at me as she wiped down the next table.

"Can I get a coffee to go?" I asked her.

"Sure can." She headed to the pot as I took a bite of one of the best burgers I'd ever had. Or I was just really hungry. It was hard to tell.

"And you're going to find him?" Garrett asked after she strolled off, an annoying mixture of humor and doubt in his voice.

"Thanks for the vote," I said, swallowing hard and washing the bite down with an iced tea chaser.

He shook his head. "Instilling confidence isn't really my thing."

"No!" I said, shocked.

"You 'bout done?"

"Holy cow, are you finished?" Having barely taken two bites, I blinked in surprise.

"Yep. It's a man thing."

"That can't be good for the digestion."

"I'll keep that in mind," he said, a grin brightening his features that may have been attractive, had I found nice-looking men with amazing skill appealing. Good thing I didn't.

Ten minutes later, we paid simultaneously and walked out the same way.

That's when I saw it. My heart leapt into my throat. My hands covered my mouth in shock. I ran, stumbling forward. "Misery!" I yelled in my best melodramatic tone.

"Holy shit," Garrett said, walking up to us, Misery and me, as I wrapped my arms around her fender. At least I think that's what the thing on the side was called. "You get very Shakespearean sometimes."

Misery's tires had been slashed. All four of them, and probably the spare on the back as well. Brutally. Heartlessly. And quite annoyingly.

"How much you want to bet," Garrett said, kneeling to analyze the vandalism, "these slashes were made by a big-ass hunting knife."

"I'm fairly certain they were. Farley Scanlon is a big fat liar!" I yelled into the dark atmosphere. I opened my phone to call the police.

On the bright side, two hours later, Misery had some brand-spanking-new radials. She looked good. I filed a report with the police, explaining who I was and my encounter with Farley Scanlon. The big fat liar. Maybe he didn't like being called fat, but since he wasn't, I really didn't see the harm.

"Are you good to drive?"

I frowned at Garrett. "Why do people keep asking me that?"

"Because you haven't slept in two weeks?"

"I guess. I'm fine. Just, I don't know, stay close."

"Roger that." He walked to his truck and started it up, waiting while I paid for Misery's new rubber. She was so worth it.

16

There comes a moment when you know
you just aren't going to do anything else
productive for the rest of the day.
—T-SHIRT

When I finally got home to my slightly-bigger-than-a-bread-box apartment, I realized how untidy I'd been keeping it. Garrett's replacement had been outside the apartment building, waiting for us when we pulled up, and Garrett took off to catch some *Z*'s. Wuss.

But I was thankful he'd left when I stepped inside my humble abode. Either Mardi Gras had been celebrated really early and in my apartment, or my apartment had been ransacked. Big time. Apparently, the slashing of the tires was more than just a gut reaction to the *big fat liar* comment. It was meant to keep me busy while someone hightailed it to Albuquerque to check out my digs. And tear them apart. So uncalled for, in my opinion.

"Mr. Wong, what did I say about letting strangers in?" I glared at his bony shoulders, then glanced at the girl with the knife behind me and shook my head. "That man never listens."

I scanned my living room. Papers and books cluttered the floor. Drawers sat open in different states of undress. Cabinet doors stood ajar, as though they'd been trying to fly.

Armed and ready with coffee carafe in hand, I crept to each closet—I only had two in the whole place—and peeked in. I would've had my gun, but it was in one of the closets, making the point moot. They'd been hit as well, their belongings strewn across the floor to mingle with underwear and shoes and hair scrunchies. *People* magazine mixed with *The New Yorker.* A crystal chess set mixed with my SpongeBob SquarePants edition of Monopoly. Utter chaos.

Still, it wasn't vandalism for the sake of vandalism. It was more deliberate than it looked at first glance. Cabinets and drawers had been scoured for information, while anything inconsequential had been tossed aside, including my emergency stash of chocolate. Clearly my intruder had no taste.

My computer had been turned on as well, so unless Mr. Wong had discovered Internet porn, someone was trying to figure out what I'd been researching. And that someone seemed a tad nervous.

In a moment of horror, I realized my mouse was gone. Just . . . gone. Who would take a poor, defenseless mouse? I looked back at his wireless USB connector—he loved that connector—and let myself grieve the loss of the mouse I'd taken for granted far too often. Then I picked up my phone and called a semi-friend, a cop named Taft, to file a quick report. The cops can do nothing without reports, so I wanted them to have one on file.

"I can stop by if you need me to," he said.

"No, whoever did this—and I have a good idea who it was—is long gone." I gave Taft my statement over the phone.

"So, have you seen my sister?" Taft's sister had died when they were kids and had been following him around his whole life.

"I think she's playing with Rocket's little sister at the asylum."

I'd recently introduced the two girls, in a roundabout way, and they'd been inseparable ever since. A good thing, 'cause it got her out of my hair. But I suspected Taft missed her, even though he couldn't see her and didn't even know she'd existed until I told him a few weeks ago.

"Good," he said, putting up a brave front. "I'm glad she has a friend."

"Me, too. I'm going over to the office real quick to check on things there, just in case. I'll call you back if anything's askew."

"Alone?"

"I can dial a phone all by myself, Taft."

"No, are you going over alone? Maybe you should just call your dad and have him check it out."

I glanced toward the girl at my side. "I won't be alone. Not exactly. There's a tiny dead girl with a knife following me at the moment."

"TMI."

"And the bar's open. I doubt an intruder would go there with a dozen off-duty cops right below him."

"Okay. Can I call your uncle to let him know?"

"No, he already knows it's a cop hangout. And he's probably already snoring like a buzz saw. I'll call him tomorrow."

Avoiding another lecture from Dad, I trudged over to the office and took the outside stairs to the front entrance instead of cutting through the bar. After a quick scan of the area to make sure Big Fat Liar was nowhere about, I unlocked the door and peeked inside. Everything looked fine and dandy. Which meant I had nothing left to do but clean my apartment. The only thing I hated worse than cleaning my apartment was torture, though the two were a hairsbreadth away from neck-and-neck.

I walked along the sidewalk back to the Causeway, regret eating at me at not having bought the golf cart, when I realized I had company. I could feel someone to my left in the shadows, but before I could get a good look, a car slowed in the street behind me. It kept pace without passing. I slowed my stride as the car followed. Garrett's guy was parked across the street, but I couldn't tell if he was awake or not. Awake would have been nice. As I rounded the building and cut across the parking lot, the car eased to a stop next to me.

The streetlight cast a soft reflection on the tinted glass as I took in the blue Nissan hatchback. The window slid down, so I figured I'd give the driver a moment of my time. It was probably too much to hope he just wanted directions.

"Charley?" a woman said from the inside. "Charley Davidson?" A head with curly brown hair leaned into the light, a supermodel smile on her face.

"Yolanda?" I asked. I hadn't seen her since high school, and we'd never really been friends. I took a microstep closer as she nodded. She hadn't changed a bit. In high school, she was more the cheerleader type, hung out with my sister's crowd. I was more the annoying type that made fun of my sister's crowd from a safe distance and hung out with losers, being a loser myself. Proud to say.

"I got the message your assistant left and tried your office, but you were already gone. And then I saw you walk up the stairs and figured I'd just catch you here."

Two things struck me instantly: First, it was late to be visiting my office. Or any office, for that matter. Second, why not just call? Why drive all the way over at this hour? Her smile faltered for the barest instant, and a nuance of concern filtered its way toward me.

I plastered a smile on my face. "Thank you for coming. How have you been?" When her arms reached out the window toward me, I leaned in for a hug, awkward considering the limited space we had. "I'd invite you up to my place, but it's kind of a mess right now." I gestured over my shoulder with a nod.

"No problem. And I've been great. Three kids, two dogs, and one husband." She laughed and I joined her. She seemed happy enough.

"Sounds busy. I just wanted to ask you some questions about a case I'm working on."

"Your assistant told me." The concern spiked again as her gaze did a quick perimeter check. "Do you want to just hop in? We can talk in the car."

"Absolutely." I cast a quick glance over my shoulder. Whoever was in the shadows looked on with interest. I could feel it. Maybe it was Garrett's man. No one seemed to be in the car parked across the way. I headed around Yolanda's Nissan as she unlocked the doors and raised her window. After I let myself in, I asked, "So everything's been okay?"

"Wonderful," she said, lowering the radio. She had yet to turn off the car. The heater was nice. "You're working on a case that involves Nathan Yost?"

Right to the point. I liked that in an old acquaintance. "Yes. His wife is missing. You may have seen it on the news."

"Along with other things." She smiled sadly, and I realized she'd seen the report of the carjacking. "Are you okay?"

"Oh, that?" I waved a dismissive hand. "That was nothing. I've known the guy for ages. He was a perfect gentleman the whole time he held me at knife point."

Suddenly her eyes sparkled with curiosity. "Will you tell me every single thing that happened? Were you scared? Did he threaten you?"

After a soft chuckle, I asked, "Watch a lot of crime shows?"

She nodded guiltily. "Sorry. I don't get out much."

"Not at all. Can you tell me what happened with Dr. Yost in college?"

Taking a deep breath, she said, "We dated for about a year. We were young and it all got serious pretty fast, but my parents refused to let us get married until after I'd graduated. It infuriated Nathan." She shook her head, remembering back. "I mean *infuriated* him that they butted in to what he saw as none of their business. His reaction was so bizarre that it knocked me out of my trance. I started to open my eyes to what was really going on. In the year that we'd been dating, I'd lost almost all my friends, hardly ever saw my family, and rarely went anywhere without him. What I saw as charming at first became—" She struggled for the right word. "—well, suffocating."

"I hate to say this, but you aren't the first person to tell me that about him. Why did you press charges against him?"

"He used to tease me about what would happen to me if I ever left him. He would make it into a joke, and I would laugh."

“Can you give me an example?” I had a hard time seeing a threat like that as something either of them would find comical.

“Well, once he said something like, ‘You know if you ever leave me, they’ll find your lifeless body at the bottom of Otero Canyon.’ ”

I offered her my best horrified smile, trying really hard to see the humorous side of that statement.

“I know,” she said, nodding in agreement, “I know it sounds horrible, but the way he’d say it, it was just funny. Then after my parents refused to let us get married, everything changed. He started pressuring me to elope, asked me over and over how I could let them interfere. And then the jokes became outright threats. He became unstable, and it dawned on me that he’d always been unstable, I’d just learned what to say and what not to say around him.”

“Did he hurt you?”

“Me?” she asked, surprised. “No. Not me. That’s not how he does things.”

My brows knitted in question.

“It took a lot of counseling for me to be able to say this, to come to this conclusion, but he was controlling me by controlling my environment. Who I hung out with. When I hung out with them. What I could talk about and what I couldn’t. He even monitored my phone calls.”

Classic domination.

“He never hurt me directly. He controlled me by hurting those around me.”

I had to wonder how he did it all. How he could be so controlling with a career like his, with the hours he must have kept. “But he did eventually threaten you?”

The sad smile she gave me made me realize I was wrong about that, too. She bowed her head and continued her story. “After my parents had put their foot down on the wedding plans, his animosity seemed to grow daily. And when I wouldn’t give in to his requests, he grew more and more furious until one day he just snapped out of it. Like a light switch had been turned off. He just, I don't know, got happy again."

"Sounds suspicious. Or drug induced."

"It struck me that way as well, but I was just so relieved, that when he invited my parents to have dinner with us one evening, it never occurred to me that he could be up to something."

"Let me guess. He made the dinner."

"Yes. And it was wonderful until about halfway through, when my mother became violently ill. So much so, we had to take her to the emergency room."

"Your mother?" I asked, surprised.

She nodded knowingly. "My mother. And while we waited out in the lobby, he leaned over to me and said, 'It's amazing how fragile the human body is.' He looked at me then, practically confessing what he'd just done with a single, satisfied expression." Her gaze turned desperate. "I was scared, Charley."

I could imagine his face, his blue eyes cold and calculating. "Yolanda, anyone would have been scared."

"No, I was terrified," she said, shaking her head. "I could hardly breathe. When I got up to leave, he told me to sit back down. I refused, and he grabbed hold of my wrist, looked me square in the eye, and said, 'She'll be in the hospital all night. One stick is all it will take. Her heart will stop in seconds, and no one will be able to trace it back to me.' "

When Agent Carson had told me that over the phone, I'd just assumed he was talking about Yolanda. But he'd threatened her mother. "Yolanda, I'm so sorry."

Nathan was beginning to sound like Earl Walker, and I wondered if the two were related. Earl would control Reyes by hurting his sister, Kim. Nathan would control his girlfriends and wives by hurting those around them as well. But neither Luther nor Monica had implied that he'd threatened them. They said he was controlling, manipulative, but he hadn't harmed any of her family. Still, every sign did point in that direction. Teresa's social activities had dropped to near nonexistent. She had to see her own sister in secret. Maybe he'd threatened them, but Teresa never admitted it, especially considering what Luther might do.

Yolanda's fingers pressed to her mouth while she took control of her emotions. Sadness had permeated the interior of the car, saturating everything in it. "I sat back down and stayed by his side all night long, scared to death to leave him alone even for a minute. Then when they released my mother, I waited until he went to work, packed my stuff, moved back home, and filed charges against him." She looked back at me. "But I think, as a way of getting revenge, he tried to hurt my niece."

I blinked in surprise and angled to face her. "Why? What happened?"

She shook her head as though chastising herself. "It's silly. I shouldn't have said that."

I decided not to push her, but my gut told me her gut was not far off the mark.

"He's a monster, Charley," she said, her voice breathy with suspicion, "and I would bet my life he had something to do with his wife's disappearance." She frowned hard. "If he couldn't control her one way, he'd find another."

Maybe he'd found out about Teresa seeing her sister every day and realized he couldn't control her as well as he thought. Clearly, his answer to that was murder.

"Anyway," she said, shaking off the sadness, "I knew I had to come talk to you, to warn you about him."

"I appreciate this so much, Yolanda."

"I think it's so great what you're doing." She offered me an excited grin, apparently able to block pain and switch emotions in the blink of an eye. We were more alike than I'd ever imagined. "I mean, a private investigator? That's like the epitome of cool."

How sweet. Perhaps I shouldn't have thrown spaghetti sauce in her hair that one night she was out with my sister and a group of their friends. "Thanks," I said, all smiles.

"By the way, did you throw spaghetti sauce in my hair that one night I was out with your sister and a group of our friends?"

"What? No," I said, feigning offense.

She snorted. "You're not a very good liar."

"Yeah, sorry about that. It was meant for Gemma. She'd stolen my sweater."

"Then clearly she deserved a little marinara in her golden locks," she said with a giggle.

"I know, right?"

I left Yolanda with a hug and a promise that I'd do everything I could to bring Dr. Nathan Yost to justice. But first, I simply had to find Teresa. Whatever he'd done with her, to her, it couldn't be good.

As I walked back into the building, I looked again to my left, trying to figure out who had been in the shadows before. It couldn't have been the intruder. I felt no resentment or desire to slit my throat with a big-ass hunting knife. Normally, I might have tried to discover the shadowy spy's identity, but I was too tired and didn't much care.

By the time I walked back up to my apartment, Cookie was standing smack-dab in the middle of it, her pajamas askew, her eyes wide in astonishment. She'd probably come over to discuss what happened in Corona and walked right into the war zone. I had no choice but to accuse her.

"Seriously, Cookie," I said, walking up behind her. She jumped and turned toward me. "Was the cupcake remark really that offensive?"

"I didn't even hear an intruder," she said, gawking at the surroundings. "How did I miss this? What if Amber had come over to watch your TV?"

She had a point. "I'm sorry, Cookie." I started picking up papers off the floor. "Being close to me is sometimes a very dangerous place to be."

"What?" After my meaning sank in, she said, "Don't be silly."

I stood with an armful of notes and magazines. "Okay, but you're raining on my parade. Being silly is kind of what I do."

She bent to help me.

"Oh, no you don't," I said, scolding her. I took what she'd already gathered and led her out the door. "I'll do this. You get some sleep."

"Me?" she said, protesting. "You're the one who's taken up insomnia as a hobby."

Since my arms were full, I nudged her out the door with my shoulder. "It's not so much a hobby as a burning will to hold on to every ounce of self-respect I have left." When she frowned, I added, "Admittedly, that's not saying much. Oh, and tomorrow I want you to check out a Xander Pope."

"Xander Pope. Got it," she said without taking her eyes off the chaos. "Wait, why?"

"Because I think something very bad happened to his daughter, and I need to know what it was." Yolanda only had one brother, so the niece she spoke of must be his. I wanted to know what happened.

"Ah," she said, nodding. "Do you think Yost had something to do with it?"

"Yolanda does, and that's good enough for me."

17

Cleverly disguised as a responsible citizen.

—T-SHIRT

After convincing Cookie I was fine and that I had every intention of getting some sleep—not—I spent the rest of the night straightening and cleaning the war zone. I found a book I'd been looking for that I'd given up on finding and bought again. Then I found that copy, as I'd lost it as well and had to buy the book a third time. But I never found the third copy, apparently gone forever.

Mr. Wong was a mess as well. He still hovered in the corner with his back to me, saying nary a word, but he just seemed a bit shaken up by the whole ordeal. Either that or I was projecting.

Even though it seemed nothing was taken, unless the culprit took that third copy of *Sweet Savage Love,* I felt strangely violated, as if my apartment was no longer the safety zone I'd imagined it. Like when I found out Santa wasn't real or that candy was fattening once you got past the age of nineteen.

The little girl with the knife looked on as I cleaned. I'd never considered that she could have been the one who had slashed my tires. I might owe one Mr. Big Fat Liar an apology. Then again, could a spirit slash tires?

I tried to talk to her, but she'd have none of it. She watched what I did but never looked directly at me. I considered pushing my luck, trying to find out who she was and convince her to cross, but I felt the need to avoid a stab wound imperative.

Somewhere between three thirty and get-your-ass-to-bed, I slipped into the shower, wondering where Reyes was, what he was doing, where he was sleeping. It must be hard to be an escaped convict with your picture on every television set in three states.

My cell phone rang, and I reached around the curtain for it.

"Ms. Davidson?" a man asked.

I didn't recognize the number or the voice. "That's me."

"This is Deputy Meacham with the Corona Sheriff's Department. We spoke earlier."

"Right, my slashed tires."

"I'm sorry to wake you, but can you come in today?"

I took a mental step back. "If I have to. I actually needed new tires anyway, so it's not that big a deal."

"The man you had the altercation with, Farley Scanlon, was found dead in his home early this morning."

Holy crap. "Seriously?" Maybe Earl Walker was tying up loose ends again, and my poking around had gotten a man killed.

"I rarely joke about these things."

"Okay, yes, I can be there. But I'm not sure how I can help."

"We need to ask you a few questions," he said, his tone sharp.

"Wonderful. So I'm a suspect?"

"If you'll just come in, ma'am. Immediately."

I blew out a long breath. "Okay, fine. Wait," I said as a thought hit me, "do you have a time of death?"

"If you'll just come in."

"Deputy," I said, letting the frustration I felt edge into my voice, "my apartment was broken into last night while I was in Corona dealing with the whole tire mess. I thought it was Farley Scanlon, but maybe not."

He hesitated, but only for a moment. "The closest we have is sometime between eight and ten. The medical examiner will have a more exact time of death later this afternoon."

That couldn't be right. "Are you sure?" I asked. "Because that would mean he couldn't have broken into my apartment."

"We'll need the gentleman you were with to come in, too."

"Okay, I can be there in a couple of hours." Naturally, I'd call Uncle Bob first and fill him in, just in case. He came in so handy when accused of murder. "Was Farley, by chance, beaten to death with a bookend?"

That was how Earl Walker had killed his girlfriend Sarah Hadley, after all, but since he was reportedly dead at the time, he was never actually charged.

"No, ma'am."

"A baseball bat?"

"No."

"A lawn mower?" I was trying to get every last drop out of the guy. Knowledge was power, baby. "You know, investigator to investigator."

He cleared his throat, and I couldn't help but notice his voice was a little softer when he spoke. "His throat was cut."

"Oh. Okay, be there in a while."

We hung up, and I went back to rinsing my hair. Farley Scanlon's throat was cut. I didn't think the guy they found in Earl Walker's trunk, who was supposedly Earl Walker, had his throat cut. But he was also burned beyond recognition, so who was to say for sure? Murderers usually stuck to one MO. Earl Walker had beaten that man to death with a baseball bat and, months later after Reyes's trial, had beaten his girlfriend to death with a bookend. But there was never any mention of cut throats. Maybe the knife was just handy.

Wait a minute. I may have gotten a man killed. I was indirectly responsible for a man's death. Maybe Farley Scanlon was my guardian, the one Sister Mary Elizabeth was talking about. I hoped not, because he really didn't like me. Then again, it hadn't been two days, eleven hours, and twenty-seven minutes. I still had time to be indirectly responsible for someone else's death. Thank the gods of Olympia.

"I like what you've done with the place," I heard a deep voice say.

Startled, I swiped at the water on my face and glanced around the shower curtain. Reyes Farrow stood leaning against my vanity, arms crossed over his wide chest, his hair mussed, his jaw unshaven, quite possibly the sexiest thing in existence. My knees weakened as a slow grin spread across his face.

He scrutinized the curtain. "Didn't I get rid of that?"

He was referring to my last shower curtain, which he'd slashed through when he was still able to leave his body incorporeally and wreak havoc across the lands with his ginormous sword thingy, not to be taken metaphorically. I'd refused to come out from behind the shower curtain, and the shower curtain paid the price for my impudence.

"This one is new," I said, a warning in my voice. "And I like the length."

He smiled. "Thank you."

"I was talking about the curtain," I said, though my heart skipped a pertinent beat at the reminder.

He waited a long moment to answer, studying what he could see of me. "Right." He was wearing a green army jacket and camouflage fatigues, probably had hit a Salvation Army store, and he looked tired. There was a slight discoloration under his eyes, and I found myself wondering again where he'd been staying.

I turned off the water and reached for a towel. He wrapped a large hand around my wrist and stepped closer, his mahogany eyes glittering with interest. "You look good in wet."

I fought to cover myself and to control my racing pulse. His heat snaked up my arm as he opened my hand and kissed my palm. His stubble tickled against it.

"How's your wound?" I asked, mesmerized with his mouth and the incredible things it could do to a simple palm.

The intense look that landed on me was so powerful, it took my breath away. "Better than other parts." His voice, deep and rich, felt better than the warm water that had been rushing over me moments earlier.

Since I didn't have an ETA on the hand he'd taken captive, I dropped the shower curtain and grabbed a towel with the other. His head tilted to the side for a better look.

"One of the men on the list you gave me was found dead this morning. Murdered."

He thought a moment, then wrapped my hand into one of his and dropped his gaze to the floor.

"Farley Scanlon," I continued. "You might have warned me good ole Farley was psychotic."

"He was a friend of Earl Walker's. I'd have thought it apparent," he said with a shrug. "Besides, your faithful dog was on your ass the whole way, right?"

I pulled back my hand and wrapped the towel around me. "How did you know that?" I thought a moment, then stared in astonishment. "Are you following me?"

He stepped back to the vanity and crossed his arms over a wide chest. "I thought he was following you."

"He is, but it's not his fault. Garrett's following orders."

"Garrett's following *you,*" he said, casting me a glance from underneath his dark lashes. When I pressed my lips together, he acquiesced. "Fine, then whose fault is it?"

"Yours, actually. Why do you think he's on my ass? And you show up here? You're lucky you haven't been arrested yet."

"Your boyfriend's not out there," he said, gesturing with a nod of his head. "That other guy's hardly a threat. He's asleep in his car."

I rolled my eyes. Garrett really needed to screen his applicants better.

"And what the hell were you thinking, getting into that car?"

"That was you in the shadows?" I should've known. I really should've. "Are you just begging to get caught? Because I can call my uncle right now and we can be done with this whole thing in a blink."

"I have no intention of getting caught. How was he killed?" he asked, changing the subject midstream.

"Tragically." I grabbed another towel to dry my face.

"Was his throat cut?"

I froze. How did he know that? "Yes."

"With what?" he asked.

"Probably something really sharp." When he didn't respond, I asked, "Is that what he does?" I stepped out of the shower, and Reyes's gaze wandered to my lower extremities.

"That's what he does," he said without looking up.

"I thought Earl's MO was to bash people in the head."

"Only when he has an ulterior motive."

"He's tying up loose ends, isn't he?"

"Don't go back there," he said, lifting a corner of the towel.

After slapping his hand, I asked, "Where? Corona?"

He'd grinned when I slapped his hand. "Yes."

I took the towel and tried to sop up the dripping water from my hair. "I have to. The sheriff wants to talk to me."

He snagged the second towel from me, draped it over my head, and started to rub, his hands kneading, massaging. He moved closer, and I couldn't help but take hold of the jacket he was wearing. For stability purposes.

"Don't go," he said again, only this time it sounded more like an order.

"I'll take it under consideration."

"It's not a suggestion."

What was it with men and their belief they could order me around? I pushed back the towel and leveled a hard stare his way, trying to decide if I should clock him. I did owe him one, though I rarely had a steel pipe or an eighteen-wheeler on me when I needed one. "You don't get to tell me what to do." I poked his chest with an index finger to emphasize my point.

He paused, his jaw tensing visibly, but to his credit, he didn't say anything else. He probably knew payback was a cold hard bitch and ever so slightly overdue.

"You look tired," I said, grabbing the towel, "and you need a shower." I turned and left him standing in the bathroom, the disappointment in my loins palpable. Five minutes later, the shower came on.

I dressed in a pair of nice jeans, a caramel button-down, and a killer pair of wraparound Dolce & Gabbana pumps with a low heel that looked part boarding school rebel and part naughty librarian. It tickled me to know that Cookie salivated every time she saw them. I had a wicked cruel streak.

Reyes emerged from the bathroom in wrinkled yet clean clothes and a smooth jaw. His hair hung in wet clumps around his face.

"Better?" he asked, stuffing his dirty clothes in a knapsack.

"Yes, but you still look tired."

His brows rose playfully. "Have you looked in the mirror?"

He was right. I looked horrid. Self-induced insomnia was hardly attractive.

He laughed and surveyed every inch of me. After dropping the knapsack, he stood straight, his long arms at his side as he watched me unblinkingly. "You should come here," he said, his voice velvety smooth, beckoning.

It was an invitation that I felt deep in the pit of my stomach. He stood there, all noble and godlike and otherworldly, and before I could say no, I took a minuscule step toward him.

"Holy shit!"

We both turned to Cookie. She'd stopped short just inside the door.

Amber ran into her backside. "Mom," she complained, stepping around her only to be brought up short as well. She eyed Reyes as if he were a rock star. "Wow."

I concurred, but these were not the best circumstances for them to meet the escaped convict hiding out in my apartment. "Cookie, can we go back to your place a minute?"

She fought visibly to tear her gaze off Reyes. She lost. It stayed locked on to him like a laser-guided tracking system.

"Cookie?" I said, walking up to her and nudging her out the door.

She blinked and, realizing what she'd been doing, blushed prettily. "I'm so sorry," she said, nodding to Reyes and hurrying back to her apartment with Amber in tow.

"Mom, wait," Amber said, not ready to abandon the local attraction.

"Get your backpack, honey. I'll drive you to school."

"Can't I just stay?" she asked, craning her neck to see more.

Once we were back inside their apartment, Cookie sent Amber after her backpack, then rested a look of astonishment on me. "Holy shit, Charley," she said, her voice a quivering whisper, "that was Reyes Farrow."

"I know. I'm so sorry. He just sort of showed up."

"I think I had an orgasm."

A hiccup of laughter escaped before I could stop it. "You just looked at him."

"I know. Have you seen that man's shoulders?" she asked, and I chuckled again.

"Yes, I have. Don't worry, you'll get the feeling in your legs back soon."

"And his forearms. For the love of god, who knew forearms could be that sexy?"

"It happens to the best of us."

"He's just so—"

"I know."

"And, so—"

"I know that, too. It might be a 'son of Satan' thing."

"Yeah, maybe."

I helped her to a sitting position on her sofa.

Amber rushed back in. "Can I snap a picture of him on my phone before I go to school?"

"School." Cookie glanced up at me, a worried expression lining her face. "I'll talk to her on the way."

I felt so bad. This wasn't their fault, but I just couldn't have Amber talking about Reyes with her friends. Who knew who might be listening, who might make the connection? "I'm so sorry about this."

"No." Cookie stood up. "It's not your fault. I'll take care of this."

With a smile, I said, "Thanks, Cook."

I kissed Amber good-bye, then went back to the apartment. Reyes was gone. He'd left his knapsack there. That wasn't incriminating in the least. I threw on a black leather jacket and headed out to Misery. Garrett was back, sitting in his truck across the street. I paused, glanced around for Reyes, then opened my door and climbed in.

My cell rang as I turned the ignition.

"I need to speak with Charlotte."

I didn't recognize the male voice. "This is Charley."

"This is Donovan."

Nor the name. "Donovan?" I backed out and headed for the interstate. Garrett followed, naturally. How did he miss Reyes?

"From the mental asylum."

I was in a mental asylum? When the fuck did that happen?

"The abandoned mental asylum that you break into on a semi-regular basis?" he added when I didn't respond.

"Oh, right. The bikers."

"Right," he said. "I wanted to talk to you."

"Sure." I wondered if Rocket had finally taken down the building.

"Artemis," he started, then stopped.

I could hear the pain in his voice, and my heart seized. "Is she okay?"

"No. Apparently the poison did more damage than we'd thought, and when she was playing with you yesterday, she ruptured a kidney. She's at the animal hospital now."

A hand rose to my mouth before I could stop it. "Oh, my god, I'm so sorry."

"I'm not blaming you." His voice cracked and he had to catch his breath. "I want to hire you."

"What?"

"I want to know who did this," he said, a chilling resolve hardening his voice. "And either you can find out, or I can."

I assumed his methods would be a tad more brutal than my own. "No offense, but you can't afford me."

I was about to say I'd do it for free when he countered with, "I can afford ten of you."

"I'll find out. I'll try to get over in the next couple of days. Don't start without me."

"That's not soon enough."

Darn it. "Okay, let me think." I had to run out to Corona to be interrogated for murder. Other than that, my day was fairly open. "Barring an arrest, I can be there this afternoon. Are you going to be home?"

"I can come to you," he said, "right now."

"I'm headed out of town on a case. I'll come there. I need to look around the neighborhood and ask you about your neighbors anyway."

With a sigh of resignation, he agreed. "Okay. But if you're not here this afternoon, I'm looking into this myself. I only called you because Eric wanted me to. He thinks you'll have better luck."

I assumed Eric was one of his gang members. Obviously one of the smarter ones.

"I'll be there. I promise. Will you let me know if anything happens to her?"

"Sure." He hung up without further ado. Why would anyone do such a thing? My heart broke. I could almost feel the guy's pain through the phone connection, which would be a first.

I swung by for a mocha latte, then pointed Misery south when Garrett called. I almost didn't answer, but he'd only call back.

"Where we headed, Charles?" he asked, a grin in his voice.

"Nova Scotia."

"Looks like we're headed back out to Corona. You really liked that burger, didn't you?"

"Farley Scanlon was murdered last night."

"Damn, you get around."

"The sheriff's office wants to talk to us."

"Can a sheriff's office really talk?" he asked, stepping up his game. He'd have to if he wanted to keep up with the likes of me.

"Good-bye, Swopes."

"Wait, where were we?"

I made sure the sigh of annoyance I exhaled was blatant enough, even a child could understand. "Is that a trick question?

"Oh, right, number two. Ready?"

Of course, the list of things one should never say to a grim reaper. I blew out another breath for good measure. "Hit me."

"This relationship will be the death of me."

"Okeydokey," I said before hanging up. Freak.

I called Uncle Bob on the way to fill him in on the situation. "I have to be honest with you," I said when he answered, "I'm not sure you'll ever get a woman with that haircut you insist on sporting."

"Is that why you called?" he asked, only slightly miffed.

"Pretty much. And I might be charged with murder. Just wanted to let you know."

"You murdered someone?"

Why do people always assume the worst? "No, I might be accused of murder. Big difference, Ubie."

"Oh, how's the missing wife case?"

"It's there and yet nowhere. The guy won't leave his danged house."

"What can I do?"

"You can call Cookie. She's swamped, trying to get information. We need to know where all his property holdings are. He could have Teresa held hostage somewhere. Also, I'd like to know what happened to Xander Pope's daughter. Find out if she's okay."

"Xander Pope?"

"Yes. Yost could have hurt her."

"In what way?"

"No idea. That's why I have Cookie checking into it."

"I'll look into it and give Cookie a call. Does this murder rap have anything to do with an escaped convict named Reyes Farrow?"

"It does," I said after taking a big swig of the mocha latte. "I think Earl Walker did it. He's still alive, Uncle Bob, and he's tying up loose ends. He killed his girlfriend shortly after Reyes's trial, and now he's after everyone else who might know he's alive. Can you get someone over to Virgil Gibbs's apartment?" Gibbs was the other name on Reyes's list, the man I'd visited before I went to see Farley Scanlon in Corona. "He could be next, and while he's not the most productive member of society, he doesn't deserve to get his throat cut."

"Walker's going around cutting throats?" Ubie asked, alarmed. "Is Swopes still with you?"

I glanced in my rearview at the huge black truck behind me—Garrett was clearly overcompensating—and said "Yes" in the tersest voice I could muster, considering my lack of sleep.

"Good. Keep him close. I'll get a uniform over to Gibbs's apartment to check on him. You know what this means, don't you?"

I was busy dodging a flock of suicidal birds. I swerved and ducked behind the steering wheel, because that would help. "Not really. What?"

"It means I put an innocent man behind bars ten years ago." His voice had changed, become despondent.

"Uncle Bob, you thought he was guilty. I read the reports and the court transcripts. Anyone would have done the same."

"He didn't . . . I didn't listen to him, to what he was trying to tell me. He was just a kid."

My heart contracted at the image that popped into my mind. Reyes at twenty, accused of murder, all alone with no friends, no relatives, no one to turn to. He'd forbidden the only person in his life—his sister, Kim—from seeing him. And he sat there in jail, waiting to be put on trial for a murder he clearly didn't commit. Where was a time machine when I needed one? But now we could put this right. We had to. "We have a chance to redeem that mistake, Uncle Bob."

After a long silence, he said, "How do you pay back ten years, Charley?"

My heart broke at the guilt in his voice. I was actually surprised by it. He'd done his job. No one would deny that. Unless he knew more than he was letting on. Surely not. "Earl Walker is apparently really good at covering his tracks. No one will blame you for this."

He scoffed. "Reyes Farrow will."

Yes, I supposed he would. I could just imagine my uncle Bob drilling him for information in an interrogation room as he sat there cuffed, stewing in anger and confusion. "What was he like?" I asked Ubie before really thinking about the question, what it might do to him.

"I don't know, pumpkin. He was a kid. Dirty, unkempt, living on the streets."

Before I could stop it, a hand covered my mouth at the mental image. My left knee instinctively rose to steer Misery until I could lead my hand back to the wheel. I totally needed a hands-free phone accessory.

"He said he didn't do it. Once. And then never spoke to me again."

The sting in my eyes couldn't be helped. That was so like Reyes. Stubborn. Rebellious. And yet, maybe it meant more. Maybe he'd given up, like an animal that had been exposed to so much abuse, it figured, Why bother? Why fight back?

"But it was the way he said it," Uncle Bob continued, his mind clearly lost in another time. "He looked me in the eye, his stare so strong, so powerful, the weight of it was like a punch to the gut, and said simply, 'It wasn't me.' And then nothing. Not another word. No talk of lawyers, rights, food . . . He just shut down."

My lips pressed together hard as I drove. "We can fix this, Uncle Bob," I said, my voice shaking.

"No, we can't." He seemed resolved to the fact that Reyes would hate him until the day he died. And then he added, "I grabbed him."

Startled, I asked, "You what?"

"By the shirt collar. At one point in the interrogation, I was so frustrated, I lifted him from the chair and threw him back against the wall."

"Uncle Bob!" I said, not really sure what else to say and realizing he was lucky to be alive.

"He did nothing," Ubie continued, oblivious. "Just stared at me, his face blank, and yet I could feel the hatred simmering just beneath the surface. In all the years since, that look has haunted me. I've never forgotten him or the case."

"He's a powerful being, Uncle Bob."

"No, you don't understand."

My brows furrowed as I steered through a mountain range.

After a long moment that had me wondering if we'd lost connection, he said, "I knew, pumpkin."

I could almost picture Ubie's head in his hand as he spoke, his voice pregnant with such regret, such sorrow, it caused a cinch around my chest. "You knew what?"

"I knew he didn't do it."

I stopped breathing as I waited for an explanation.

"I'm not stupid. I knew he didn't do it, and I did nothing. All the evidence pointed directly at him, and because I didn't want to look like a fool, I didn't question it. Not for a minute. So you see," he said, resigned to his fate, "we can't fix this. He'll come after me."

I blinked in surprise. "No, he won't. He's not like that."

"They're all like that." He seemed to welcome the idea, as though he deserved to be punished.

I sat stunned to my toes, not sure what to say, how to proceed. "Can I see the interrogation tape?" I asked him, clueless as to why I'd want to see it.

"You won't find my outburst." His tone had changed again, hardened.

"I had friends in high places, and strangely that part of the tape was erased."

"It's not your outburst I want to see. It's him. I met him when I was in high school, remember? I know how powerful he is, how dangerous. But he won't come after you, Uncle Bob. I promise," I said, mentally adding my name to the roster of the Big Fat Liars Club. I had no way of knowing what Reyes would do. What he was capable of. And I was helping to free the one man who might want my uncle dead. Deep down inside, I wondered if that made me a bad niece.

18

There are very few personal problems that can't be solved with a suitable application of high explosives.

—T-SHIRT

When I got to the sheriff's department, I jumped out of Misery and hit the ground running. My plan worked. I was in an interrogation room before Garrett could get inside. I told the sheriff everything I knew. Farley Scanlon was a bad guy. He practically threatened me with a knife and then left when he saw Garrett, then he slashed my tires while we ate. It wasn't a difficult story for them to swallow, but I still had to account for every minute of the night, and they wanted to talk to Garrett to confirm.

So, while they interrogated him, I took off back out to Farley Scanlon's house, the weight of Uncle Bob's story still heavy on my chest. Or it could have been the fact that if Earl Walker was still at Farley Scanlon's place, or happened to stop back by the scene of the crime, I'd just ditched my best defense. That would suck.

My cell sang out. I answered it. "Hey, Cook. I just ditched Garrett."

"Good for you. You two weren't really right for each other anyway."

I grinned.

"So, here's the word off the street."

"I love it when you talk dirty."

"Yolanda Pope's niece almost died after having a routine tonsillectomy."

"No way."

"Way. Minutes after the good doctor showed up on the ward."

"Which is suspicious because?"

"He had no patients that day. He'd performed no surgeries and had no one to check in on, yet he checked onto the ward. Yolanda's niece went into cardiac arrest minutes after he checked out."

"Oh, my gosh. How old was she?"

"Twelve. They chalked it up to a reaction to the anesthetic, but she makes it through the entire surgery just fine, then has a reaction over an hour later?"

"Not likely. I can understand why Yolanda suspects him."

"Do you think he knew she was Yolanda's niece?"

"Positive. Poor Xander," I said, remembering her older brother with fondness. I couldn't imagine what Yost put him through. "How did you get this information so fast?" I asked her.

"I just happen to know the charge nurse who was on duty that morning."

"Sweet."

"Yeah, but none of it can be proved. The nurses just found the whole thing odd. Nothing was ever reported, but they believe Yolanda overheard the nurses talking about it, which is why she suspects him."

"Well, all this leads to one conclusion. Nathan Yost is more aggressive than I thought. I've never met anyone who could pull off such malice with such skill. The man is absolutely evil."

"I don't understand what he hoped to gain by it, though," Cookie said.

"Revenge. He's an opportunist, saw his chance. Yolanda left him. He was paying her back. Speaking of evil, I'm going out to get a look around Farley Scanlon's trailer. Obviously, Earl Walker was close, possibly even staying with him." The one time I'd seen him years ago, beating the fuck out of Reyes, was enough to last a lifetime. The mere thought of that man being close by made me lose consciousness a moment. Either that or the lack-of-sleep thing was catching up with me.

"And you're going out to his house because it's been days since someone has tried to kill you?"

With a weary grin, I said, "Of course. This everyday mundane stuff is getting old."

"Can you at least wait for Garrett?"

"Can't."

"Why?"

"Don't like him."

"Yes, you do."

"And I have to visit a biker gang this afternoon."

"If I had a nickel for every time you said that."

We hung up as I pulled into Farley's lot. The mobile home was little more than a tin can, and while I liked mobile homes as much as the next girl, this one left a lot to be desired. Like Spam. It should be ham, but it just ain't.

I picked the lock and ducked under the police tape just as a car slowed in front of the house. They didn't stop, thankfully, but they were probably calling the police at that very moment, or performing some other civic-minded duty. Then again, they could've just been checking out my ass. Which, who could blame them?

A huge, misshapen bloodstain sullied the olive green carpet and wood paneling that stood as a bold testament to the hideous décor choices of the seventies. Since I'd lacked the forethought to bring gloves, I found a set of oven mitts and quickly searched through stacks of papers and filthy trash cans, no easy feat in oven mitts. I realized Earl Walker was probably not using the alias Earl Walker anymore. There were a couple of bills with the name Harold Reynolds. Sounded like a fake name if ever I heard one. I stuffed the bills into my bag and continued rummaging through the insanity of it all.

I sat concentrating on a photo of a man in a hat with antlers when the doorknob jiggled. After a quick curse, I rushed down the narrow hall and ducked into the bedroom at the end of the house. The front door opened, skyrocketing my heart rate into near panic. If the cops caught me out here, it would probably look bad.

Hoping I wouldn't seize and make a ruckus, I peeked through the slit between the door and the wall. A man stood there with gun drawn, but I could only see part of his backside. The sun streaming in through a dirty window just past him made it impossible to see what kind of clothes he was wearing, but it didn't look like a police uniform. Then a hand covered my mouth from behind, and I struggled to keep that last cup of coffee from coming back up.

"Shhhh," the intruder whispered in my ear as his other hand slid over my stomach and down to the button on my jeans. The heat from his body left a white-hot trail wherever it tread, and I rolled my eyes, partly in relief and partly in annoyance.

I was going to kill him. Reyes Farrow. How the hell did he get out here? He eased me against him, his heat saturating my clothes and hair. He was scalding, and I couldn't help but let my head drop back against his shoulder and breathe him in. Then he started to unfasten the button on my pants, and I rushed back to attention, fighting him with both my mitted hands. He caught them and pressed into me, his steely arms wrapped tight.

"It's your boyfriend," he said into my ear. When I fought his attempts a second time, wrapping my hands awkwardly around his solid wrist as his fingers deftly unbuttoned my jeans, he shushed me again with a playful nip at my ear.

"Reyes," I whispered as softly as I possibly could as he slid the zipper down. Now was hardly the time.

"Are those oven mitts?" he asked as he placed hot kisses down my neck. Then his hand dived inside my panties. I couldn't stop the gasp that escaped when his fingers dipped between my legs, and footsteps sounded in the hall a moment later.

"Don't take this personally," he said with a disappointed sigh, and I felt a knife at my throat instantly.

My sudden voracity crashed and skidded across the ground like the bad landing of a hot air balloon. Again with the knife? Really?

Reyes walked back toward the far wall with me, his arms locked around my body like a straitjacket. Then Garrett walked in. He took one look at us and instinctively raised his gun, the tight quarters closing in on us fast.

I felt Reyes's head tilt to the side, as though questioning him. Garrett's silvery gaze darted between the two of us. He hesitated, pressed his jaw closed in anger, then lowered his gun, helpless to do anything else.

In my periphery, I saw Reyes grin. He lifted his hands in a gesture of mutual surrender, lowered his own weapon and dropped it on the ground. Then, with the gentlest of pushes, he eased me aside. I realized what he was doing the instant Garrett raised his gun again.

"Garrett, no," I said, but it was too late.

In the space of time it took a cobra to strike, Reyes relieved Garrett of the weapon and had it aimed at his head point-blank, an appreciative smile on his face.

Garrett blinked, realized what happened, then stumbled back with arms raised.

"Reyes, wait," I said, a harsh warning in my voice.

"Back," he said to Garrett, gesturing with the gun.

Garrett backed down the dark hall as Reyes pulled me into the threshold between us. He looked down at me, able to see both Garrett and me at the same time.

"I don't kill people, Dutch," he said, as though disappointed that I'd worried. "Unless I have to." He said the last while studying Garrett. Without taking his eyes off him, he took my chin into his hand and placed the softest kiss on my mouth.

Then he was gone. In a heartbeat, he was out a window about the size of a postage stamp, like an animal, a blur of sleek fur and muscle.

Garrett rushed past me to the window. "Son of a bitch," he said, biting back the anger that consumed him. He turned toward me. "Nice."

"Hey," I said to his back as he stalked out of the room and down the hall. "I didn't know he was here. And you didn't have to come in."

"I was worried about you," he said, an ice-cold contempt in his voice as he looked back and let his gaze wander to the front of my jeans.

I threw the oven mitts aside and refastened them quickly, but he scoffed, shaking his head, and started for the door again.

"Cookie called me," he continued. "I cannot believe you were stupid enough to come out here by yourself."

"Fuck you," I said. I didn't have to explain my actions to him.

He turned on me, anger sizzling around him. "And you're at the scene of a crime, fucking an escaped murderer."

"We weren't fucking, and Reyes didn't kill his father," I said, frustration sharpening my voice.

"Not his father. Farley Scanlon."

I blinked in surprise. "What? You think he killed Farley Scanlon?"

He laughed, the sound harsh as it echoed off the cheap wood paneling. "If the razor-sharp blade fits."

"Garrett, wait," I said, running after him as he stalked to his truck.

"We have to get the cops here before he gets too far." He took out his phone and dialed 911.

"No," I said, grabbing his phone before he could stop me. I closed it, hoping the call didn't make it through.

"What the fuck are you doing?" He reached for his phone.

I jerked it back. "Keeping it for a while." I hurried to Misery and started her up. He followed me and opened the driver's door before I could lock it.

"Give me the phone," he said from between clenched teeth. It was not a suggestion. The anger seething inside him had turned his aura to a smoky black. I'd never seen Garrett so furious before.

I held the phone away from him, hovering it over the passenger's seat, which was stupid, since his reach was almost double mine.

"Charles, I swear—"

Since he couldn't get past me and the steering wheel to the phone, he clutched on to my arm and literally dragged me out of Misery. I had no choice. I kicked his shin to divert his attention, then threw the phone as hard as I could. Garrett cursed and raised his leg, but oddly, the sound of a watery plop brought us both up short. We stilled and turned to the sound as a cold dread crept up my spine.

I stood there stunned and more than a little surprised by the fact that there was a pond beyond the tall grass and weeds. We both stared a long moment, then slowly, menacingly, Garrett turned to me, his expression hovering between shock and utter rage. Before he could do something we'd both regret, I jumped back into Misery and locked the door. A microsecond later, he pulled the handle hard enough to rock the Jeep. Considering the fact that my windows were made of plastic, I started Misery and tore out of Farley Scanlon's lot like I had a reason to live. In my rearview, I saw Garrett stand there glowering a good ten seconds before he sprinted to his truck.

I was so dead. I was so amazingly, inarguably dead.

I called Cookie. "Hey, Cook," I said, my voice light and airy.

"What's wrong?" she asked. Apparently I was a little too light and airy.

"Well, Reyes held me at knifepoint, but that was just a ruse to get Garrett's gun away from him, which he did and then proceeded to hold the gun to Garrett's head point-blank right before he kissed me, then jumped through a freaking window."

After a long moment, Cookie said, "So, it went well?"

"Damn straight. Garrett's a little hot under the collar right now, though. I'm giving him time to cool down. Oh, and I stole his phone and threw it into a pond, so don't bother calling him again." My voice turned accusative.

"I'm sorry," she said. "I was just so worried about you. How the heck did Reyes get out there?"

"Who the bloody hell knows? He probably ran. God, that man is fast."

"My goodness. Garrett on one end and Reyes on the other. It's like a really hot, melty s'more."

"Did I mention that Garrett is really pissed?"

"Oh! I just found out that Ingrid Yost's mother died one month before she did."

"No way. Who's Ingrid again?"

"Dr. Yost's first wife?"

"Right. I knew that. Wait, how did her mother die?"

"Same way she did. Heart attack."

"That was convenient." Nathan Yost was turning into quite the serial killer.

"And I talked to your uncle. Are you ready?"

"Is that a trick question?"

"Nathan Yost has property in Pecos."

"Really?" Score. "That's the best news I've had all day."

Since I had quite the drive ahead of me, I decided to call my BFF at the FBI.

"Agent Carson," she said, all sharp and professional sounding.

"Dude, you're so good at that."

"Thank you," she said, suddenly perky.

"Did you know that Dr. Yost might have tried to kill Yolanda Pope's niece as a way to get revenge on her?"

"No," she admitted.

"And that he killed Ingrid Yost's mother one month before he flew to the Cayman Islands and killed her?"

After a moment of thought, she asked, "Can you prove any of that?"

"Not even. But the bodies are racking up. This guy needs to be stopped. Have you found any evidence that Teresa Yost was planning on leaving him before she disappeared?"

"None. According to everyone on the planet, they were the perfect couple."

"Yeah, didn't everybody think the same thing about him and his first wife as well, until she fled the country and filed for divorce?"

"Pretty much."

"She knew she was in danger," I said. "That's why she went to the Cayman Islands. To get away from him. Apparently, he has abandonment issues."

I filled her in on everything Yolanda told me, including the part about her niece and what we'd found out since; then I told her about Yost's alter ego, his alias Keith Jacoby, before adding, "Again, I can't actually prove any of that. We should try to get ahold of that forger. He was doing business in Jackson, Mississippi, last we heard."

"So, this Keith Jacoby was in the Cayman Islands at the same time as the late Mrs. Yost?"

"Yep."

"Okay, I'll try to get someone in the Jackson office to have a talk with your forger."

"Yost also has land in Pecos."

"Yeah," she said absently, clicking away on a keyboard, "we had a team check it out. He has a cabin there, but we couldn't find anything."

"I'm on my way to interview a biker gang right now. I want to look the property over, just in case, but it may be tomorrow before I get to it."

"Knock yourself out," she said, then added, "Wait, you're joining a biker gang?"

19

I am an instrument God uses to
annoy people.
—T-SHIRT

With an extremely annoyed Garrett back on my ass, I took the Coal Street exit and steered Misery toward the Bandits' hangout. The sun hovered low over the horizon, preparing for a good night's rest, when I pulled to a stop in the front of their house. It sat beside the asylum itself, which was kind of cool, but I'd always wondered how a biker gang went about buying property. Whose name goes on the mortgage? A handful of leather-clad bikers sat on the front porch. A few more tinkered with their bikes in the dusky light. Loud music leached outside the cracks in the walls, of which there were many. Bikers were probably really hard on dwellings. Either that or this really was a crack house.

I'd never seen so many bikers there at one time before. Donovan must have called them in for the witch hunt.

"You're late," one of them said from a shadowy porch. I couldn't tell who was talking to me, but every man there stopped what he was doing and turned toward me.

I pulled my jacket tight and stepped closer until I spotted Donovan. He sat leaning back in a lawn chair on the porch, his booted foot on the railing, a beer in hand.

"How is she?" I asked, stepping past several unsavory-looking fellows, my very favorite kind. They were probably all sweethearts deep down inside.

The prince was there. He braced an arm on the railing as I tried to get past and spent a very long minute checking out the girls.

I faced him head-on, refusing to be intimidated, though I couldn't keep the wave of anxiety from rushing over my skin any more than I could keep the sun from rising the next day. Mafioso patted him on the shoulder and led him back so I could pass.

"Beer?" Donovan asked.

"No, thank you. Is she okay? Did something happen?"

"No," he said, taking a long swig. "She's still at the animal hospital. They wanted me to put her down. I said no."

I sank into a rickety chair beside him. "I'm so sorry, Donovan."

"Who's the tail?"

I glanced toward the big black truck parked down the block. "Just one of my many fans. He's harmless."

He put his feet down with a loud thud. "Well, we were just about to go find out who did this. Want to come?"

When he started to stand, I put a hand on the sleeve of his jacket. "I thought you were going to let me handle this?"

"I was. You didn't show." He pulled his arm away and stood.

I followed him. "I'm here now."

He paused and glared down at me. "I gave you until this afternoon."

"And it is after noon," I argued.

"It's evening."

"Which is most definitely after noon. You didn't give me a specific time."

When he started past me, I grabbed his jacket again, putting my meager life in danger if the glower he now wore was any indication. He glanced down at my hand as if unable to believe I'd touch him, then leveled a resolute stare on me. "Now, we do it my way." He pulled free again and started down the sidewalk with a veritable army at his side. The prince tipped an invisible hat, then took off after his comrades.

What were they going to do? Knock on every door in the neighborhood? Harass everyone in the general vicinity until they got themselves arrested? I could just see a SWAT team pouring into the area, blocking off the streets. Someone would get hurt. Possibly many someones.

"I know who did it," I called out in desperation, and they stopped. I hated to pull the reaper card, but he was leaving me no choice. If I called the police, I'd never get back in to see Rocket, and his information was invaluable.

No, this had to be done. I'd felt the guy's guilt the minute I walked up. It was one of their own, a brother, and if they got ahold of him, he probably wouldn't live through the night. Now I just had to figure out how to get the guy away from them and to the police before they killed him.

A sea of black leather turned toward me.

Donovan didn't hesitate. He strode back past his brothers and straight into my face, a peculiar kind of anger hardening his jaw. Because I was still on the steps, I could see the alarm on Garrett's face. He started to get out of his truck and I shook my head.

Both the prince and Mafioso followed Donovan and both seemed a tad worried. Well, the prince did. Mafioso seemed amused.

I stood my ground. We were standing eye to eye in a heartbeat, nose to nose the next.

"Don't even think about fucking with me," he said, his tone menacing.

"I'm not. I did some investigating this afternoon. I know who did it, but I need your word you'll stay calm."

His hands clutched my jacket in the next instant, and my breath caught when he pulled me closer. The prince shifted uneasily.

"You have three seconds," he said.

"Wait, I'll tell you, but I need you to promise you won't hurt anyone."

"Sure, okay," he said, lying through his teeth.

Garrett had started toward us and I waved him back. When everyone turned to look at him, including Donovan, I made another gesture. I pointed my index finger in the air and made a quick circle, which was Garrett-speak for *let's wrap this up*. If he picked up on my meaning, he'd get back in his truck and start it.

Donovan saw me gesture as well. He jerked me to attention as a couple of Bandits started toward Garrett.

"Wait," I said. "It's just a precaution. I don't want to die today, okay?"

They all turned back to me as Garrett got back in his truck—every move reluctant—and started it up.

"Let me closer to Garrett. I'll tell you, then I'll leave."

His eyes narrowed on me. "Do I look like a man who enjoys games?"

"Not at all, Donovan. I'm so sorry you're going through this, but you're angry and you'll take things too far. A girl's got a right to guarantee her own safety."

When he glanced back at Garrett, I looked over Donovan's shoulder to my left and leveled a cold hard stare on the guy who did it. He had stringy brown hair, a frizzy beard, and enough weight on him to make the run he was about to be forced into strenuous and most likely painful. The threat of imminent death should push him past the pain.

I wanted him to know that I knew, to worry. And he did. When his eyes widened a fraction of an inch in disbelief, I nodded so he would completely understand my meaning. Right as Donovan was turning back, I gestured to Garrett's truck with my eyes, letting him know what I wanted him to do.

"Fine," Donovan said, releasing my jacket with a soft shove. I stepped down and past the dog killer without trying to understand why he would do what he did. I flashed him a glare, then motioned toward the truck again. Slowly, so no one would notice, he backed that way.

When I was to the edge of the crowd, I turned back to them, trying to keep their attention locked on me. The biker was edging toward the truck, but I didn't know how long I could put Donovan off, so I decided to improvise.

I rolled onto my toes, wrapped my arms around Donovan's neck, and planted my mouth on his. He opened to me instantly. As angry as he was, he wasn't about to pass up a chance at true love. Or an easy lay. He tasted clean with a hint of beer, and behind me I heard footsteps running across the street.

"Hey!" one of the guys yelled.

I broke off the kiss and watched the guy lumber across the street and jump into the bed of Garrett's truck, but Garrett just sat there, waiting for me.

"Go!" I yelled.

He shook his head, and in that brief exchange, an army rushed toward the truck.

"Go!" I yelled again, rolling my eyes in frustration, and Garrett knew he had no choice. He threw his truck in reverse and peeled out to get away from the onslaught, then executed a wicked spin and tore down the street, rubber smoking a good fifty feet on the way.

They followed. A sea of leather ran down the street toward Garrett's truck as it disappeared into the distance. Some went for their bikes. Some came back for orders. All speared me with glowers of distrust.

"Get him," Donovan ordered before taking hold of my jacket a second time and dragging me, quite literally, into the house. Once again, the prince and Mafioso followed. We stumbled past broken furniture toward an office at the back. He slammed the door, but the two men following just opened it and let themselves in. I hoped I hadn't underestimated Donovan. He was a good guy, but even seemingly good guys could have an uncontrollable temper underneath. Damned testosterone.

He shoved me into a chair, then started pacing. "Blake?" he said from between clenched teeth. "It was Blake?" He was actually directing his question to his seconds in command. Then he turned back to me. With an agility I hadn't expected, he was in front of me at once, both hands on the arms of the chair around me, his face barely an inch from my own. "How did you know?"

"It's difficult to explain," I answered, my voice airy.

"You have one chance. Do you know him?"

"No. Please sit down."

He jostled the chair to get my attention. "Do you have any idea how much trouble you're in right now?"

I swallowed hard. Shaking in my Dolce & Gabbanas, I glanced over at the prince. He seemed to feel bad for me, but I doubted he would go against his leader. Mafioso might, though. He seemed a bit less reverent.

"Donovan, if you'll just sit down, I'll explain."

He crouched before me, keeping his hands locked on the chair. That was as good as I was going to get.

"I can feel things," I said, trying to take deep, calming breaths. "I . . . know things by assessing the emotions radiating off people and analyzing their auras."

"Don't give me that New Age shit."

"It's not New Age. It's old, actually. Very, very old."

His brows drew together, wondering how much he should believe.

"You know how I can talk to Rocket?" I glanced at all three of them for validation. Mafioso shrugged. "It's kind of like that. I sense things other people don't. Like right now." I looked back at him, a wrenching kind of sorrow making my heart heavy. "I can sense the pain that is completely consuming you. Those dogs were everything to you, and that guy, Blake, took that away." I put my palm on his jaw. "Your pain is so strong, I can barely breathe under the weight of it."

He leaned back a little, eyeing me warily, and I dropped my hand.

"It's like you're drowning in it, and I knew if you got ahold of the guy responsible for that kind of pain, you'd probably kill him."

He sat back on his heels and dropped one arm.

"You would go to prison for a very long time, and you're a good person, Donovan. I can feel that, too, sense it, just like when I sense Rocket's presence."

My phone rang then, and I waited for a nod of approval from Donovan before answering. I fished it out of my jacket pocket but didn't recognize the number. "This is Charley," I said as Donovan got up and started pacing again.

"What the fuck is going on?"

"Garrett? Where are you?"

"At a convenience store. Where the fuck are you?" he asked, clearly upset. "What the hell is going on?"

"Is that guy still with you?" I asked, glancing underneath my lashes at Donovan.

"Hell no."

Startled, I asked, "Where is he?"

Donovan stilled.

"He jumped out at a fucking stop sign. What the fuck was I supposed to do?"

Garrett seemed upset. He rarely used the word *fuck* that many times in a row. He usually staggered it more, used it sparingly. Surely he realized the act of incorporating the word into his speech that often lessened its impact, thereby systematically deteriorating its overall efficacy.

"Okay, you're right, I'm sorry. Just stay there. I'm fine."

"Are you still mingling with the *out* crowd?"

"Um, yes."

"Then fuck that. I'll be there in two."

"Swopes. I totally have this."

"You mean when they dragged you into the house by the collar?" he asked, clearly agitated. "Did you have that?"

"I'm telling you," I said, leveling out my voice, "I'm good."

"Damn it, Charles."

"Garrett, holy cow." Without waiting for another argument, I closed my phone.

"Where is he?" Donovan asked.

"He's on his way back." I knew my order would have done no good.

"With Blake?"

"No. He jumped out at a stop sign," I said reluctantly. I expected outrage, curses, flying chairs. What I got was a smile.

He glanced around at the gang. "He's ours."

Well, probably the only good I did was to prolong Blake's torture. Now they were angry *and* prepared. Wonderful. Maybe I was going to be indirectly responsible for his death. Maybe Blake the dog killer would be my guardian. I hoped not. I didn't particularly want a guardian who'd been a dog killer in his previous life. Why would anybody do something like that?

Then I realized Donovan was still smiling at me, a seductive patience shining in his eyes. "Now, about that kiss."

"Oh," I said, stumbling to my feet with an utterly inane giggle. I started to back out, but the prince blocked my path. The traitor.

Donovan closed the distance between us and placed his fingers under my chin. "That was a pretty brave thing you did. Ultimately a complete waste of everyone's time and energy, but brave." He ran his thumb from my bottom lip down my chin and back up again. "How do you do what you do?"

I decided impress them with brutal honesty. "I don't normally tell people this, but I'm the grim reaper."

Smiles snaked across all their faces, even the prince's. He looked around me from behind and winked.

Another emotion came over Donovan then, something startlingly similar to respect, admiration. He tensed as if fighting for resolve and studied me a long moment. "I'm so fucking in love with you," he said before dropping his gaze to Danger and Will. "You'd better go before I change my mind."

He didn't have to tell me twice. I ducked past a grinning prince and tore out of that place like a cat in a room full of pit bulls.

While I wanted to stop and chat with Rocket, now was clearly not the time. Those men were going to be out for blood. I just hoped Blake had a good pair of running shoes.

20

Some days you're the cat. Some days you're the brand-new, suede leather Barcalounger.

—T-SHIRT

Cookie had left the info on Yost's property in Pecos by the coffeepot in my apartment. I gave a shout out to Mr. Wong, then put on a pot of java before looking it over. According to the county tax assessor's report, Yost had a hunting cabin deep in a wooded area of the Santa Fe Mountains a short distance from the Pecos River. Shouldn't be too hard to find during the day. Since it was already dark, I'd have to wait and head out at first light.

In the meantime, I rummaged through my bag—a cross between a clutch and a suitcase—and fished out the mail I'd stolen from the crime scene of Farley Scanlon's mobile home. The girl with the knife looked on, slightly interested. I'd managed to abscond with two envelopes addressed to a Harold Reynolds and one addressed to Harold Zane Reynolds. Unfortunately, two were credit card offers, and one was a flyer inviting Harold to invest in gold.

After making a mega-sized cup of coffee, I sat at my computer to see what dirt I could dig up on the guy. The girl stood beside me, mesmerized by the computer screen, her knife clutched solidly in her hand.

It didn't take me long to find out Harold Zane Reynolds was fairly nonexistent. "Well, this sucks," I said to the girl. She ignored me.

I searched a bit more and found a previous address for a Harold Z. Reynolds, that looked promising. If nothing else, maybe a neighbor knew Harold and could tell me where he'd gone. If he hadn't killed them all.

I repacked my belongings, poured my coffee into a to-go cup, then headed out the door, leaving the girl in the incapable hands of Mr. Wong. She was too busy studying my screen saver to notice my absence anyway.

Garrett must have called it a day. Neither he nor his colleague was out front, which made me happy until I hopped in Misery and started toward the address. Something about it seemed familiar. And the closer I got, weaving my way through Albuquerque's south side, the colder the realization prickling my spine became.

I pulled to a stop in front of a condemned apartment building, the reality of where I was washing over me in stupefying waves. The last time I'd been at this particular building, I stood in the street with my sister Gemma and watched as a man beat a teenage boy unconscious. If I hadn't been sure Harold Reynolds was one of Earl's aliases before, I was now.

I looked up at the boarded window, the same window I'd thrown a brick through to get the man to stop. I looked to the side between the buildings where Gemma and I had run when the man came after us. I looked at the steps I'd taken the next day when I went back and found out from an angry landlady that the family in 2C had moved out during the night, stiffing her for two months' rent and a broken window.

Stepping out of Misery, I closed the door and stared for a very long time as memory after memory flooded my senses, tightened my chest. The crisp night kept me alert as several sets of eyes locked on to me. Most were homeless, hidden in the shadows of the apartment building and the abandoned school behind me. A couple others most likely belonged to gang members curious about my reason for being there. I offered none of them my attention. I just stared at the window. It had been so bright that night, illuminated with a sickly yellow as Earl Walker pummeled a boy named

Reyes. Counting back, Reyes had to have been about eighteen at the time. I was fifteen. Young. Impressionable. Ready to save the world with my super reaper powers. Yet the only thing I could do to save him was throw a brick from the abandoned school through the window.

It worked. Earl stopped hitting him and came after us.

If I had called the police that night, if Reyes had let me, I doubt I would've been standing here at this moment. I doubt Reyes would have gone to prison for killing Earl. Surely Children, Youth, and Family would've taken Reyes and Kim out of that situation. Surely they would have been safe.

With nothing to lose and hours before dawn, I grabbed a flashlight and a tire iron—partly for breaking and entering and partly for protection—and headed up the steps. The metal door had definitely seen better days, and it didn't take me long to gain access. I was certain the homeless people in the area had been entering the building the same way for months, possibly years. The entrance opened up to the second floor. The floor beneath sat half underground. And 2C was directly on my left. I stepped over trash, debris, and a couple sets of legs, careful not to shine the light directly in the faces of the people lining the walls, until I came to a door with half a *2* nailed to it and the unpainted remnants of a *C*.

"I wouldn't go in there, missy."

I turned to a voice echoing down the hall and raised the light. A woman sat wrapped in several layers of clothes, a shopping cart turned over beside her to protect her meager belongings. Or she needed driving lessons. She raised her hand to shield the light, and I immediately lowered it. I didn't need it anyway. Not for her.

"Sorry about that," I said, indicating the light as I aimed it to the side.

"Don't be sorry to me," she said, "it's just that's Miss Faye's place, and she don't take kindly to no visitors."

"Should I knock?" I asked, only half serious. The acrid smell that hit me when I'd entered snaked around me like a poisonous gas, and I couldn't decide which would be worse—breathing through my mouth or nose.

The woman chuckled. "Sure. Knock. Ain't gonna help, but you go right ahead."

"Have you ever heard of a Harold Reynolds?" I asked, again only half serious.

"Nope. Why you asking?"

"'Cause I'm looking for him. He used to live here." I lifted the lapel of my leather jacket and covered the lower half of my face, hoping it would help. It didn't.

"Oh, then you need to ask Miss Faye for sure. She used to run the place. Still thinks she does."

In a flash, I realized who Miss Faye had to be. The landlady's name all those years ago had been Faye. "I think I remember her."

"Yeah?"

"Bleached blond hair? Resembles death warmed over?"

She chuckled again. "That's her. You go on about your knocking, now. I could use me a good laugh."

That didn't sound promising, but the thought of actually talking to that landlady again had my pulse racing in anticipation. Maybe she knew where Earl Walker had moved off to after he left here. She hadn't been much help when I was fifteen, but the possibility was worth a shot. I raised my hand to the door, and the woman started cackling in excitement, apparently readying herself to be entertained. How bad could Miss Faye be? She'd had one foot in the grave the first time I'd spoken to her, and that was over ten years ago. Surely, with a little luck, I could take her.

About half a second after my knuckles made first contact, something crashed against the door, loud enough to startle the bejesus out of me. I ducked and stumbled back before raising the light first to the door, then back to the woman.

"What the hell was that?"

She laughed some more, holding on to her sides, then managed to say, "Soup, sounded like."

I frowned and glanced back at the door. "That didn't sound like soup to me, unless it was a few weeks old."

"In the can. You know, 'fore it's made."

"Oh, right, a can of soup. Wonderful," I said, complaining. "This place is like crazy on crackers."

The woman rolled onto her side with laughter. Normally, I liked making people laugh, but all I could seem to muster was a look of concern as I stepped back to the door and tried the knob.

"You still going in there?" she asked, her astonishment cutting the cackle-fest short.

"That's the plan." I turned back to her. "What do you think my chances are?"

She waved a hand. "She just likes to throw things. Her aim's wretched. Likely, she won't hit you if you run fast enough."

"Her aim sounded pretty good from here."

"Yeah, well, she gets lucky sometimes."

"Great."

Surprisingly, the door was unlocked. I raised one arm to cover my face, then cracked the door open. "Miss Faye?" I said through the opening.

Another can crashed against the door, slamming it shut, and the cackling started again. I'd have to make a run for it, possibly do a zigzag sprint until I found cover inside. I turned back to the woman and offered a sympathetic smile.

"What's your name?" I asked her.

"Tennessee," she said, pride brightening her aura.

"Okay." That was an odd name for a woman if ever I heard one. "Well, Tennessee, you can cross through me if you'd like."

A toothless grin flashed across her face. "I think I'll stay a bit. I'm waiting on Miss Faye. I reckon she won't be much longer."

"I understand. Wish me luck," I said.

She chortled. "You'll need it. I was lying about her aim."

"Thanks," I said with a final wave before bursting through the door. Something flew past my head. I stumbled over piles of junk and dived behind a decrepit couch just as another can was launched across the room. It crashed through the drywall and into the next room. "Miss Faye, damn it," I called out from behind the arms covering my head as I cowered behind the couch. "Don't make me call the police. I'm a friend. We met a few years ago."

The aerial assault stopped, and I peeked over my elbows. Then I heard a creaking sound along the floor as she drew closer and I suddenly felt like I'd landed in a horror movie, waiting to be pummeled to death by soup cans.

"I don't know you."

I jumped and raised both the flashlight and the tire iron to defend myself. Considering she only had a flyswatter, I figured my chances were pretty freaking good.

"How do you know my name?" Her voice was a cross between a bulldog and a cement mixer. She'd clearly led a rough life.

"Tennessee told me."

She frowned and studied me. I kept the light just close enough to her face to see her without blinding her. Since Miss Faye was still alive, I needed some kind of illumination to make out her features, unlike Tennessee.

"What's your name?" she asked, turning toward a kerosene lamp and lighting it.

I switched off my flashlight when a soft glow filled a room that smelled like dirty ashtrays and mold. "Charley," I said, glancing around at the piles and piles of magazines, old newspapers, books, and other nonessential paraphernalia. The place defined *use extreme caution when lighting a cigarette.*

"She never mentioned you," Faye said. She stepped to an aging recliner and crouched into it.

"I remember your hair." I searched for a place to sit and decided on a stable-looking stack of newspapers—thank god I didn't wear white—before turning back to her in all her bleached-blond glory. "I met you a few years ago."

"You don't look familiar," she said, lighting a cigarette.

I cringed. It was a wonder the place still stood at all. "I was here about ten years ago, looking for a family that had moved out during the night. They'd stiffed you for two months' rent and a broken window." I turned toward it. Its replacement now stood cracked, taped, and boarded.

"That was you?" she asked.

In shock, I refocused on her. "You remember me?"

"I remember the family. You, not so much, but I do remember a kid coming the next day. I had a migraine, and you wouldn't leave me alone."

Oops. "I'm sorry. I thought you had a hangover."

"I did have a hangover. Hence the migraine." Her tone softened as she thought back. "Did you ever find them?"

"No. Not back then."

She nodded, then turned her attention to the window. "I was hoping you would. I was hoping anyone would."

I sat my weapons on another stack of papers and asked, "Do you know what happened to them? Where they went?" When she took another draw off her cigarette and shook her head, I added, "I need to find the man, Earl Walker. It's terribly important."

The pleading tone of my voice must have convinced her to at least try to offer more. "I don't know where they went, but I remember those kids. Like it was yesterday. The girl so thin, I worried she'd break in a soft breeze. The boy so beaten, so hardened and fierce."

My chest tightened, and I shut my eyes a moment to get the image her words had instilled in my mind.

When I opened them again, she turned a passionate gaze to me. "That wasn't no man. That was a monster through and through."

I inched closer, sat on a stack of magazines a few feet from her. The low light cast hard shadows over her features, but the wetness shimmering in her eyes was unmistakable. Her empathy surprised me more than I would've liked to admit. I expected a stereotype. I did not get one.

"Miss Faye—"

"Nobody calls me Miss Faye but Tennessee," she said, interrupting, "so she must've sent you. That's the only reason you ain't bleeding to death from a head wound right now."

"Fair enough." I wiped my palms on my pants, wondering if she knew Tennessee had passed, and wondering how far to push her. "Ma'am, do you have anything at all that might help me find Earl Walker? I know this is asking a lot, but did they leave anything behind? A suitcase or possibly—"

"He left stuff in the walls."

I blinked in surprise. "Earl Walker?"

After an almost imperceptible nod, she said, "Harold, Earl, John . . . take your pick."

Earl had assumed several identities. She obviously knew a few. "What did he leave in the walls?"

She pressed her mouth together hard. Her breath caught in her chest. "Pictures."

I stilled. Kim had said that very thing, that Earl had left pictures in the walls. "Pictures of what?"

She shook her head, refusing to answer.

"Were they of Reyes? Were they of his boy?"

Her chin rose visibly, and I knew I'd nailed it. Why would Earl do that? What would he have to gain? The idea was utterly foreign to me, and I quickly scanned through the massive amounts of information I'd gleaned in college for an answer. Or at least, as much as I could recall offhand. Oftentimes criminals liked to keep trophies. Did the pictures represent trophies to Earl? And if they did, wouldn't he have kept them?

He was all about control. Maybe they were a way to control Reyes, to keep him under his thumb. Still, I just couldn't grasp why Earl would leave them. Kim had said there were pictures in the walls all over. Did she mean all the places they'd lived? They'd moved from place to place all over New Mexico, Texas, and Oklahoma, or so the police reports had said.

As bad as I hated to ask, I asked. "Faye, do you still have them?"

She wiped her eyes with the fingertips of one hand.

"They could have a clue. Something. Anything. I must find him." My mind conjured scenes from a murder mystery where something seemingly mundane in the background of a picture offered the clue that solved the case. Like I could get so lucky.

I felt heartbreak rush through Faye as she considered my request, and I realized she must still have them. After drawing in a deep breath, she stood and shuffled to a sideboard, barely recognizable under the weight of clutter.

"I only kept one," she said, her voice saturated with sadness. "I burned the others and kept the only one I could stomach to look at." She pulled a Polaroid out of a crippled drawer but kept her gaze averted. "Not that I look at it. It's just, the others were so much worse, I couldn't fathom having them in my house. I figured this way, if the police ever needed evidence as to what that man did to that boy, I'd have it."

Her words caused my heart to contract in dread and apprehension. She held out the picture, and I took it with a shaking hand, turned toward the light, braced myself, and glanced down.

Maybe it was my diet of coffee and more coffee. Maybe it was the fifteen days without sleep. Maybe it was the odor that hung like a heavy fog around me, making it difficult to breathe. Whatever it was, I took one look at that picture and the world slipped out from under me and disappeared.

21

I chose the road less traveled. Now I'm lost.

—T-SHIRT

I pulled Misery to a stop in front of my apartment building at half past three, my eyes so swollen, I could barely drive home. Faye had revived me and offered me some water after I blacked out. Blacked out! I'd actually fainted when I saw that picture. The same picture I now clutched to my chest. I couldn't look at it. Never again. Not that it mattered. The image had been emblazoned onto my corneas, and I knew I'd never be able to un-see what had been seen.

After stumbling up the stairs, I went straight to my dresser and stashed the picture facedown in my lingerie drawer without so much as another glance.

The ropes. The cuts and bruises. The shame. I almost felt like that was the worst part of it. How Earl seemed to purposely shame Reyes by taking that picture. He'd tied him up, the rope biting into his flesh, reopening wounds that appeared to have been healing. I recognized Reyes instantly despite the blindfold, his mussed dark hair, his smooth, fluidly mechanical tattoos along his shoulders and arms, his full mouth. He looked about sixteen in the picture, his face turned away, his lips pressed together in humiliation. Huge patches of black bruises marred his neck and ribs. Long garish cuts, some fresh, some half-healed, streaked along his arms and torso.

The mere thought of the picture made me cry, which was exactly what I did at Faye's place. I'd cried for over an hour. We talked. I cried some more. I wondered what the other pictures were like, the ones Faye had burned that were worse than the one I now had. Swallowing hard, I forced the image out of my mind and focused on my client, on finding Teresa Yost.

With a good three hours to dawn, I decided to take a shower and put some fresh clothes on along with a pair of hiking boots, since I was probably going to do some hiking. It would take me an hour and a half to get to Pecos. If I timed it right, I could arrive at sunrise and set out on my search for Teresa early.

"Left?"

"Right."

"Right?"

"No, you're right, turn left."

"Cookie, really?" I asked into the phone. Yost's property was proving much harder to find than I'd originally thought, even with Cookie on Google Maps back on her home computer pointing the way, since I kept losing the GPS signal on my phone.

When I'd left my apartment, Garrett's guy was there, and for once, he was awake. I had to sneak around to Cookie's silver Taurus and take it instead, a move that I informed her of when I called and woke her up at five thirty to let her know. Naturally I explained how I'd been forced to take her car as a ploy to sneak past my tail. Plus I was out of gas.

Thinking back, I realized I could've waited until I actually got to Pecos to tell her I'd committed a felony in the pursuit of justice, since I really hadn't needed her help until I actually arrived in Pecos over an hour later.

But waking her up was fun. And I needed to think about something other than the picture that had been scorched into my mind.

"Sorry," she said, still a bit groggy even after her shower. "No right, just left."

"Then I should be there, but I don't see a cabin." At this point, I was so tired, I was seeing two of everything *except* a cabin. I fought to stay focused with a hard blink. "These trees all look alike. I think they're twins or quadruplets or something."

"Is there a trail of any kind?" she asked.

I pulled her car into a small clearing just off a side road, rubbed my eyes, then looked around. "Well, yeah, it doesn't look like much, though. And I don't know if your car will make it through the brush."

She gasped. "Don't you dare take my car down a mountain trail."

"Really? Because it did great on the first one, aside from that rear axle thing."

"Charley Davidson!"

"Just kidding, for crying out loud." Geez, she was touchy about her car.

I wondered if I should tell her about the picture and decided absofreaking-lutely. If I had to be haunted for the rest of my days, then by golly, she did, too. No idea why. Misery loves company, I guess. The emotion, not the Jeep. I missed it dearly, but now was hardly the time to dwell on it.

"Maybe you should wait for Garrett," she said. "Where the hell is he?"

"He wasn't on duty when I left, remember? And since I ditched his phone, we have no way to get ahold of him that I know of."

"What about Angel?"

"I told him to stick to the doctor like green on guacamole. He won't be showing up anytime soon."

"Damn. You need to figure out a way to summon that kid."

"I know." I folded out of her Taurus's hard vinyl seat, still trying to shake off the layer of sorrow that'd enveloped me the instant I saw Reyes bound and blindfolded. "Maybe I shouldn't have thrown Garrett's phone in the pond."

"Ya think?"

I sighed. Nothing I could do about it now. "Okay, I'm heading that way. I'll call if I break a leg or get eaten by a bear."

"Play like a rock."

"Now?"

"No, if a bear starts eating you."

I thought a moment before replying. "Do they have screaming, sobbing rocks, 'cause that's probably what I'll be doing if a bear is gnawing my arm off."

"It would be difficult to just lay there and be eaten alive, huh?"

"Ya think?"

I stumbled up the trail and found a rustic hunting cabin with a carved sign that read YOST. After trying the door and finding it locked, naturally, I accidently broke a window. I had neither the time nor the inclination for locksmithing. A woman's life was at stake. Dr. Yost could bill me.

Finding nothing out of the ordinary inside, I walked the perimeter of the house, searching for a basement or other underground structure while the little girl with the kitchen knife followed me. She was a curious lot. I turned to her and knelt down, hoping I wouldn't inadvertently get stabbed in the eye.

"Wednesday . . . do you mind if I call you Wednesday?" Receiving no answer, I asked, "Do you see any kind of an underground structure?" Her arms hung rigid at her sides, one hand clutching on to the knife like her life depended on it, and she stared straight past me, her ashen face almost afraid. I decided to make physical contact, but when I went to touch her shoulder, she disappeared. Naturally. She reappeared on the hood of a four-wheeler, standing at attention, staring into nothing.

I stepped over to study it just as my phone rang. It was Nathan Yost.

"Hello, Ms. Davidson?" he asked when I answered.

"This is Charley."

The ATV looked pretty beat up, but most four-wheelers did. This one was a utility ATV with an electric winch and cable on the back.

"This is Nathan Yost. I was just wondering if you've had a chance to look over my wife's case."

While the winch looked relatively new, the part of the ATV it was attached to was broken, like the doctor had used it on something really heavy. Unless he was trying to pull trees out by the roots, I couldn't imagine what he'd need a winch for. But, admittedly, I wasn't a guy. Winching was apparently a guy thing. As was wenching.

"I'm looking into it right now, Doctor." I scanned the area again.

"So, you'll take the case?" he asked, trying really hard to sound excited.

"Absolutely."

Nothing else on the property seemed out of the ordinary. It was a nondescript cabin, and though it had electricity and running water, it was actually a little lower key than what I'd expected the billionaire doctor to have. Inside was a variety of camping paraphernalia, lanterns, sleeping bags, climbing equipment, rope.

"Thank you," he said, forcing relief into his voice. "Thank you so much."

"I'm happy to do it. I'll call you the minute I know something."

"Thank you again."

After hanging up, I trudged about the place for a solid hour and decided the whole trip had been a complete waste of time. My last cup of coffee was wearing thin as I stumbled back to the Taurus. I looked off in the distance and saw Wednesday again, her back to me, staring into the side of a mountain. With any luck, she'd stay there.

After digging the phone out of my pocket, I called Cookie.

"Any luck?" she asked.

"Does bad count?"

"Damn. I was really hoping we were on to something."

"Bear!" I screamed when I saw a real live bear lumbering through the trees.

"Oh, my god! Stop, drop, and roll!"

"What?" I asked, keeping my eyes locked on to it. I'd never seen one outside of a zoo. I suddenly felt sweet and salty. Maybe a little crunchy.

"Just do it!" she shouted.

"Stop, drop, and roll? That's your solution to a bear attack?" I asked as I unlocked her Taurus and climbed inside.

"No, wait, that's if you're on fire, huh?"

Just as I started to close the door before the bear made a U-turn and decided to brunch on my innards, I felt it. A heartbeat, faint. Fear, a little stronger. I quieted and stepped back out of the car.

"Cookie, wait, I feel something."

"Did he get you?" she asked, almost screaming in panic. We totally needed to get outdoors more.

"No, hon, just wait a sec." I stepped closer to the trees and scanned the area for Teresa, all the while keeping an eye out for the bear.

"What? Is it her?" she asked.

"I don't know. I felt a pulse of fear."

"Yell!" she yelled, scaring the bejesus out of me.

I struggled to keep hold of the phone, then placed it back at my ear. "Cookie, holy cow."

"Sorry, I got excited. Yell, maybe she can hear you."

"But won't the bear hear me, too?"

"Yes, but they can't understand English."

"Right. I'll try that," I said, stepping back to the car. "I'll call you if I find anything."

"Wait, I'm on my way."

"What?" I asked, completely taken off guard. "You're on your way here?"

"Yep."

"In what? The space shuttle?"

"I stole the extra set of keys off your fridge."

"Did you happen to notice the needle pointing to the really big *E*?"

"I got gas before I left."

Score.

"And you ditched Garrett again, remember? He doesn't have a phone, thanks to you. I just don't want you to almost get killed alone again. You always almost get killed alone. Though the bear thing will be new."

"That's not true. I almost got killed by a bear when I was twelve. Its name was Uncle Bob. There was a wasps' nest. He panicked. And you were with me the last time when that fake FBI agent chased us down the alley with a gun. We almost got killed then. The two of us. *Together.*"

"Oh, that's right. I never understood why he kept shooting that building across the alley from us."

"He was a bad shot," I said, keeping an eye on the horizon for an oversized ball of fur. It would be just like me to be mauled to death by a bear.

"Good thing he couldn't shoot. Then again, neither can you. Have you ever considered taking classes?"

"You know, I have," I said, checking Cookie's trunk. "I was thinking pottery or maybe basket weaving. Don't tell me you don't have a flashlight."

"I don't have a flashlight."

"A first aid kit?"

"Nope. Just wait for me," she said. "I'll be there in no time, and Misery has everything. She's like a sporting goods store."

"I don't want to lose Teresa. She can't be far. I've never felt someone's emotions over a long distance. Just call me when you get here."

"Fine. If anyone attacks and tries to kill you, including the bear, ask them to wait for me."

"You got it." I closed the phone and the trunk and, well, I yelled. "Teresa!" I called out. Nothing. I walked back up the trail, stopping every so often to call out to her. Admittedly, I didn't yell as loud as I probably could have. That bear thing freaked me out.

Wednesday was still staring at the side of the mountain, and that seemed to be as good a direction as any. Then I felt it again. A whisper of fear, feathering over me like a trickle of water.

"Teresa!" I screamed, this time with heart. And it hit me. Hard. A blast of fear and hope rolled into one.

I called Cookie again as I ran toward the sensation. "I think it's her," I said, breathless with excitement.

"Oh, my god, Charley, is she okay?"

"I have no idea. I haven't found her yet, but I can feel someone. Call Uncle Bob and Agent Carson and get them out here ay-sap. You were right. The cabin is up that trail. I'm heading to a hilly area just east of it, look around there."

"Okay, got it. I'll summon the cavalry, you just find her."

I closed the phone and called out Teresa's name again. The blast of fear I felt was quickly evaporating, being replaced entirely by a surge of hope that felt like a cool wind rushing over my skin. Then I remembered I had exactly zero survival gear. Hopefully, I wouldn't need any.

I ran past Wednesday, and asked, "You couldn't have mentioned this?"

She didn't respond, but I saw what she was looking at. A mine. An honest-to-goodness, boarded-up old mine. I had no idea there were any mines in this area. And, naturally, I didn't have a freaking flashlight. My lack of fore-thought when I'd left the apartment that morning, knowing I was going to be combing a mountainside, astounded me.

Not wanting to waste any time, I texted Cookie the location of the mine's entrance before winding my way toward it through the tree line. It was super dark inside, so I opened my phone. It shed just enough light to illuminate the uneven ground as I ducked inside, climbing through the partially boarded opening. For a mine, the opening was small. I thought they'd be bigger. Once inside, ancient support beams lined the walls and the skeletal remnants of a track led me deeper into the narrow tunnel. This was certainly a good place to dispose of a body. Is that what he'd done? Tried to kill her, then, believing she was dead, dumped her body here? Surely not. He was a doctor. He'd have known if she were dead.

I followed the railway tracks about five minutes before they stopped abruptly. The tunnel came to a dead end, a layer of rock and dirt blocking the way, and my heart sank. I turned in a circle, searching for another opening. Nothing. I was wrong. Teresa wasn't in here. Then I realized the fall was fresh, the earth and rocks hadn't settled as they would have over time.

"Teresa," I said, and a layer of dirt fell from overhead. The place was about as stable as a circus performer on a high wire. But I felt her again, closer this time. I climbed up the incline, stumbling and scraping my hands and knees.

At the very top was the faintest opening. I tried to look in, to no avail.

"Teresa, I can feel you," I said as loudly as I dared. "I'll get help."

Her fear resurfaced, and I realized she didn't want me to leave her alone. "I won't leave you, hon. Don't worry." I tried my phone, but we were too deep to get a signal. Looking back at the opening, I asked, "Where's your brother, Luther, when we need him? He's a big guy."

I heard a weak, breathless chuckle. She was so freaking close, I could almost touch her. Right there. Right past the opening, as though she'd climbed up it as well and tried to dig her way out.

"Are you hurt?" I asked, but received only a moan in response. "I'm going to take that as a yes."

Surely Cookie would bring the cavalry soon. I wanted to call her, have her get the flashlight out of Misery when she arrived, but I didn't want to leave Teresa. Since I had nothing better to do, I decided to move some of the rocks and try to climb to her. With meticulous care, I started taking rocks off the top and chucking them softly to the side. I lost my footing more than once and slid down, scraping my palms and legs on the jagged rocks even through my jeans. And each time, I held my breath, hoping the whole thing wouldn't come down on us.

After about fifteen minutes, I had cleared enough of an opening to reach my arm through. I felt around blindly and touched hair. Then a hand locked on to mine and I squeezed.

"My name is Charlotte," I said, relief flooding my body. "Did I already say that?"

She moaned, and I lay against the jagged incline for what seemed like hours, holding her hand, waiting for help to arrive. I whispered words of encouragement, told Teresa about my encounter with her brother. She laughed weakly when I mentioned that I'd called him an asshole.

Finally, after getting the pleasantries out of the way, I asked the million-dollar question. "Teresa, do you know how this happened?"

The emotion that spiked within her was the polar opposite of what I'd expected. It had me questioning everything I'd learned, everything I knew about the doctor. Because the sensation that radiated out of her with such force that my breath caught in my chest was not fear or anxiety, but guilt. Sorrowful, regret-filled guilt. I waited a moment, analyzed what she was feeling, until I heard a meek, "No. I don't know what happened."

Shame consumed her and shock consumed me. I didn't know what to say. If I were reading her right, she did this. It was somehow her fault. But that couldn't be. There was simply no way she'd done this to herself. Why would she?

And I had felt guilt so clearly on her husband, too. So deeply, he reeked of it.

I didn't ask her anything further, and let her rest as I mulled over the new chain of events in my mind. Was it a botched suicide attempt? What could she have had to gain by killing herself in such a way? Why not just take a bottle of pills? Her husband was a doctor, for heaven's sake. And even if she'd set the whole thing up, how did one go about causing a cave-in? Maybe she was feeling guilty because she'd accidently caused the collapse. But her guilt was much more than that. Her shame much stronger.

"Charley?"

I blinked to attention and saw Cookie stumbling along the tracks with her phone open to light the way. Clearly she hadn't taken advantage of Misery's sporting goods department.

"I'm right here. There's been a cave-in."

She stopped and looked up. "My goodness. Is she under that?"

"I think she's on it, but she's hurt. Did you get ahold of Uncle Bob?"

"Yes, and Agent Carson." She leaned against the mine wall, her breathing labored from her trek.

"What on planet Earth are you wearing?" I asked when I noticed the leg warmers around her ankles.

"Don't start with me. How did this happen?"

"I'm not sure yet."

"The mine just collapsed?"

"With Teresa in it." I thought that would get an emotional response from Teresa, but I got nothing, and I realized her hand had gone limp. "I think she passed out. We need to get her some water, and I need a flashlight."

With my eyes adjusted to the low light, I could just make out what Cookie was leaning against. A loose support beam. "Cookie, you might not want to do that," I said, just as the beam slipped and the world came crumbling down around us.

22

If all hell breaks loose, blame gremlins.

—T-SHIRT

A low rumbling echoed against the cavernous walls as rocks and dirt broke free from the ceiling. I reflexively covered my head with an arm and watched the landslide from underneath my elbow. The amount of earth that dropped straight away astonished me, as though it had been floating in a vacuum all this time, when fate decided to give gravity a kick start. My stomach lurched at the sight, and in an instant, time slowed until it barely crept forward, like a turtle struggling against a category 5 hurricane.

Rocks and debris hung in midair, almost glistening in the dark cavern. I reached out, ran my hands through a stream of dirt, sifted it through my fingers.

I could have run under the cascade of earth and debris and made it through unscathed. I could have run for help. Instead, I risked a glance around. Cookie was frozen midstumble, a massive boulder hovering over her head, inching toward her body, a body that would break like a matchstick house under its weight. She would be crushed.

I sprinted through the thick air, dived, and threw all my weight onto her, tackling her to the ground as time slingshot back with a roaring vengeance.

I managed to push her out from under the largest of the rocks as the explosion burst around us, but I didn't quite clear the boulder as it plummeted to earth, skimming the back of my head, its crushing weight scraping along my spine. A fire erupted down my back, and I clamped my jaw shut in preparation for the onslaught of pain as I covered Cookie's head with my arms. The rumbling continued for a few seconds more, then silence. Just as quickly as it had started, it stopped. As fine streams of dirt dwindled and the dust settled around us, Cookie let rip the most bloodcurdling shriek I'd ever heard. It reverberated against my bones and, surely, against the unstable ceiling.

"Really?" I said, my voice barely audible as I tried to crawl off her. "You're going to scream now?"

She stopped and looked around warily, blinking dirt from her eyes.

"Are you hurt?" I asked, spitting gunk from my mouth in a series of sputters.

"No, no. Oh, my god, are you?"

I stopped to think about it. "I don't think so. Not bad." My back was on fire, but I could move. Always a good sign. "You might not want to scream again. You know, with us being in an unstable cave and all."

"Sorry."

Then I remembered Teresa and scrambled over the new-fallen debris and back up the incline. I could still feel her. "Teresa, are you okay?" When I received no answer, I turned to Cookie. "I need you to get a flashlight, some water, and a blanket from Misery, if you can."

"Absolutely," she said, slowly rising to her feet.

"Are you sure nothing's hurt?"

"No, I just . . ." She looked at me a long time. "You saved my life."

"No, I didn't. Swear." Now was not the time.

"I've never seen it."

"Your life flashing before your eyes? Was it a bit disappointing? Because when that happens to me—"

"No, you. The way you moved. Your dad was talking about it, but . . . I've just never seen it."

She was all dazed and confused. "You need to lay off the sauce, hon. Flashlight?"

"Right. Flashlight, got it."

She stumbled toward me, and I tried really hard not to giggle. Well, not very hard. I pointed in the opposite direction. She opened her phone and followed the tracks out, walking past a departed miner. My breath caught as I gazed at him. He first watched Cookie walk past, then looked back at me. The lamp on his helmet kept his face dark, but my best educated guess put his death in or around the 1930s.

He tipped his hat toward me as I stared at him. I'd never seen a departed miner before. Minor, yes. Miner, no. His ragged clothes were covered in dirt. Considering the area, they'd probably been mining for copper, or possibly even silver.

He walked toward me, stopped at my feet, and tried to look past me, to see what I was looking at. The departed were a curious lot.

"My name is Charley," I said to him. He looked back at me, and since he was closer, I could just make out his face. He seemed to be in his late thirties, but mining was a hard life, so it was hard to tell for certain. He had crow's-feet around his eyes the dirt didn't quite make it into.

"Hardy." The hard line of his mouth thinned. "She's been in there awhile," he said, his voice strong. He gestured beyond the barricade with a tilt of his head.

I nodded. "She's been missing for several days. Do you know if she's hurt? I'm sure she's dehydrated."

"I'll check." He walked through the mound of dirt I lay on and clearly had every intention of walking straight through me, but was brought up short.

The departed could walk through me when they crossed to the other side. Otherwise, I was solid flesh and bone, even to them. His knee bumped against my rib cage, and he glanced at me in surprise.

"Sorry," I said, "you'll have to go around."

He studied me a long moment, then asked, "What are you?"

"I'm a grim reaper–type thing. But in a good way."

"Whatever you say, ma'am." He tipped his hat again and went around. In a matter of seconds, he drifted back through with his report. "Looks like she has a broken leg. She tried to splint it, but it looks bad."

"Damn. I'd be surprised if she doesn't have gangrene by now." I scanned the area for anything I might use to aid in my rather inadequate rescue attempt. His light helped, but the only thing available was dirt. And rocks. "Do you think I can make it through?" I asked him. "I need to get her out. I don't know how long that ceiling is going to hold."

"I think you better try, then, ma'am." He glanced around the cave. "Maybe you could brace that beam against it?"

"I'd probably just knock more loose."

"There is that."

I started digging again. "How's the other side look?"

"The ceiling is solid." He disappeared and reappeared again. "The beams on that side are sturdy."

Teresa was so weak. I could barely feel her now. Rocket said to hurry when he'd popped into Misery two days prior, and hurry I would. I scraped and dug until the opening was big enough for me to get through. With phone in hand, I crawled on my stomach over the jagged rocks. Dirt fell from the ceiling continuously, so my hair was pretty much a solid ball of muck.

Garrett would've come in handy about now. I shouldn't have ditched him. Or tossed his phone into a pond.

As I scaled the mountain of debris, I reached down for Teresa's hand. She moaned and tried to squeeze back.

"Hey, hon. I've got help coming, but we need to get you out of here if that is at all possible."

She squinted against the light coming from the phone, but it allowed me to check her pupils. They constricted perfectly. She had the same coloring as her brother and sister, dark hair and startlingly blue eyes. She was thin and pale, but that could be the circumstances as much as heredity.

I pushed through the opening and climbed over the top of her to turn around. After sliding down the incline, Hardy appeared behind me and cast his light toward a backpack that had apparently been full of supplies, water, basic medical aids, as well as a caving helmet and spelunking gear. She'd splinted her leg with the aluminum brace from the backpack and a rope. Smart girl. Apparently, she'd been exploring when the ceiling gave.

Now I was really confused. Dr. Yost was guilty—I'd felt it—but of what? Sabotaging the mine? And if he did that, then what the heck was Teresa so guilty of?

"Have you thrown up, Teresa?"

She shook her head. "No concussion," she said, her voice hoarse and whispery. She could barely lift her head. "Just a broken leg."

I felt her skin. Warm, but not overly so. Hopefully, the flow of blood to her foot hadn't been blocked and she didn't have gangrene.

"I don't know how much longer that ceiling is going to hold. Do you think you can make it through with my help?"

She nodded.

"I have more help on the way. We can wait."

"No, I just couldn't get through the opening alone. It wasn't big enough. How did you find me? Did my husband tell you where to look?" Just the thought of being rescued seemed to be giving her strength. I could feel adrenaline coursing through her veins, raising her heartbeat.

"I heard you," I said, lying as I combed through her backpack. "You have one more bottle of water." I took it and climbed back up to her.

"I was saving it."

"For a special occasion?" I asked, popping the seal on the cap. "I could shake it up and spray it all over you, if that would be more festive."

A thin smile spread across her face as she took a sip, then handed it back to me.

"Did your husband know you were here?"

She tried to shrug but gave up. "I explore this area all the time, but I didn't tell him I was checking out the mine again. I come here pretty often, though."

"So, he wasn't here with you at any time?"

She squinted her eyes, trying to figure out what I was getting at, then shook her head. "No. I left early Saturday morning, before he got up."

Then someone had to have done something to sabotage the mine before Teresa got here or while she was deep inside. But what? Those beams hadn't been cut. It literally looked like they'd slipped and shifted somehow.

Hardy knelt beside me, a grim expression on his face as though he knew exactly what I was trying to figure out. "She did it," he said, shaking his head.

Startled, I furrowed my brows in a question.

He nodded. "Loosened the beams herself." His gaze drifted about the walls. "Been working on it awhile now."

My heart fell. "Why?" I whispered.

With a shrug, he said, "Not quite sure, ma'am. But I don't think she was planning on being here when it gave."

I took a deep breath and forced the questions from my mind. "Are you ready, hon?" I asked Teresa.

"I think so."

"We'll take this slow." With infinite care, I wrapped one of her arms around my neck and hiked her farther up the incline. The miner did the same for me, boosting me inch by inch. After about two minutes of work, we were only about a foot farther. "Okay, not that slow."

She laughed softly, then grabbed her side.

"Are they broken?" I asked, gesturing toward her ribs with a nod.

"No, just bruised, I think."

With a little more effort, we were able to get her to the opening and scoot her through it. But Teresa paid a heavy price. She groaned through gritted teeth as she slid to the other side. Well, not *the* other side. Jagged rocks scraped and skinned along the way.

"Your friend's coming back," Hardy said.

Without hesitation, I chanced another cave-in and yelled through the opening. "Cookie, stay back!"

"What? No. What about the supplies?"

"I've almost got Teresa through the opening, but the ceiling is crumbling as we speak." As I looked out, I saw the beam of a flashlight bouncing off the ground. "Cookie, what the heck?"

"Don't *what the heck* me," she said, her voice winded. "I didn't walk all that way for nothing."

She put the flashlight on the incline and reached up to help Teresa. A steady stream of dirt fell a few feet from us and she looked back at me, her eyes wide. "Hurry."

The minute I got Teresa through, I scrambled back for the helmet, climbed over the mountain of debris with Hardy's help, then hustled down to assist Cookie. Together we eased Teresa toward us. She clutched on to me, moaning as pain pounded through her. So much so, I was worried she would pass out.

"Help is coming," Cookie said as I put the helmet on Teresa and wrapped my arms around her.

Teresa cringed as another wave of pain carpet-bombed her entire body. She cried out as Cookie and I started forward.

"I'm so sorry, Teresa," I said.

She shook her head, determined to make it. Adrenaline coursed through her as she hobbled and we dragged. Another avalanche of dirt plummeted onto our heads, almost knocking the helmet off Teresa's head. I repositioned it, and we started forward again.

Then, with a really inappropriate gasp, it hit me. "Aldrich-Mees!" I shouted.

When the ceiling started crumbling down around us, I realized how wrong of me that was.

23

Seemed like a good idea at the time.

—T-SHIRT

"You had to shout it?" Cookie asked, literally bitching all the way out of the stupid mine. "At the top of your freaking lungs?"

We were covered from head to toe in dirt and some kind of root system. "Now is not the time, Cook," I ground out as we struggled to get Teresa from the mine.

"This is where I get off," Hardy said. I started to protest, but he tipped his helmet and with a soft, "Ma'am," disappeared.

Then Uncle Bob rushed in, and a wave of relief washed over me. However, the look of shock on his face proved that either he had no faith in me whatsoever and was taken aback by my success in finding Teresa Yost, or I looked worse than I thought.

Agent Carson was there, too. Though I'd never seen her before, I recognized her instantly. Her looks matched her voice perfectly. Short dark bob, solid build, intelligent eyes. She hurried forward, and together with Uncle Bob took Teresa out of our arms. Before they'd gotten two feet, Luther Dean rushed in as well, ducking at the entrance and taking over for Agent Carson.

"Luther," Teresa said, surprised he was there.

The smile that warmed his face was simply charming. "You never call. You never write."

A soft laugh escaped her despite everything.

Carson turned back to me, and I tried to raise my hand to shake hers, but my muscles had completely given out. Though they did twitch occasionally. An officer helped Cookie outside while Agent Carson took my arm to help me, careful not to get too close. Dust still lingered in the air from the latest cave-in.

"I can't believe you did it," she said, shaking her head as daylight blanketed us.

"I get that a lot." My hair was so caked with dirt and rocks, it actually hurt. Then again, I did get pummeled by a boulder the size of Long Island.

"I left the flashlight inside," Cookie said over her shoulder, suddenly remembering.

"Well, you'd best go back and get it. It's not like I can get another one at pretty much any store between here and Albuquerque."

She snorted the likelihood of that happening. I couldn't wait to tell her about Hardy. I'd have to come back someday, get to know him better—another cave-in sounded down the shaft, sending a wave of dirt billowing out the opening—or not.

I saw Rescue hustling up the trail carrying an aluminum litter, bags of medical supplies, and a flashlight I was certain I could talk them out of. And Rescue was built. All three of them, in fact. Tall. Nice tone. Good overall posture.

"Who's the help?" I asked Carson.

"Your uncle brought them."

"Nice of him."

We stopped a moment to admire the view. "Sure was," she said. "By the way, I couldn't get a copy of the message the first Mrs. Yost left on the doctor's answering machine before she mysteriously died in the Cayman

Islands. Apparently, the investigator didn't actually hear it for himself. Just took Yost's word for it, since it wasn't a suspicious death."

"That's odd," I said, my eyes still glued to Search, Rescue, and Just Plain Hot. "I don't think he had any intention of killing his wife this go-around. Somewhere in their relationship, she caught on. I think he was trying to kill somebody else entirely."

"Mind if I ask who?"

"Can you give me half an hour to confirm my suspicions?"

She turned to me. "How about thirty minutes?"

I planted my best smile on her. "I'll take it."

Luther carefully helped Teresa onto the litter as his other sister, Monica, came running up the trail. My heart lurched at the sight of her. I wanted to run to her, explain what had been happening, but she was really busy.

"Teresa!" she shouted, tears streaming in rivulets down her face. "Oh, my god." She rushed up to them, threw her arms around her brother for a quick hug, then took her sister's hand as Rescue strapped Teresa in and started an IV drip. The emotion pouring out of Monica felt like cool water rushing over me, refreshing and pure.

Luther walked back to me then, amazed. My ego was taking quite the beating.

"You did it," he said.

I grinned as Agent Carson nodded and stepped away. "So I've heard."

He shook his head. "I owe you."

"You'll get a bill," I promised.

He laughed out loud, too happy to care about much of anything other than his sister.

I turned to Cookie and gave her a thumbs-up. "We can totally eat this month."

"Yes!" she said as Uncle Bob helped her onto a big boulder. "I've had my eye on a low-carb diet you're going to love."

"I said we could eat. I didn't say anything about eating healthy."

Uncle Bob walked up to me. "Well?"

"Well, what?"

"Did Yost do this?"

"In a roundabout way." Yost may not have used the ATV and winch to sabotage the mine as I'd originally suspected, but he drove Teresa to desperation, in ways I doubted she was even aware of. I led Uncle Bob a little farther into the trees as everyone worked around us. Talking quietly, I said, "You have to keep an open mind."

"My mind is always open," he said, slightly offended. "Twenty-four/seven." When I offered him my best glare of doubt, he waffled. "Okay, six/five, at the least. What's up?"

I leaned into him. "I think, and this is a big think, Nathan Yost is doing what he does. He's trying to control Teresa by controlling her environment." I put my arm on Ubie's, begging for an ounce of faith. "I think he's trying to kill Teresa's sister, Monica."

Uncle Bob frowned, looked back toward the crowd before refocusing on me. "That could be hard to prove."

After releasing the breath I'd been holding, I fought the urge to hug his neck. Displays of affection made him uncomfortable, which was exactly why I utilized them as often as I did. But I wanted him on my side on this.

"I have a plan, but we're going to have to work fast," I said as Dr. Nathan Yost hurried up the trail, still in his lab coat.

Angel was behind him, caught sight of me, offered a salute, then disappeared, his job apparently done. I could hardly blame him. He was a teenager, after all. Keeping confined to one place too long was tantamount to torture.

I glanced back at Yost. While the practiced look on his face was one of utter relief, the emotion in his heart was not happiness, nor was it disappointment, as might have been expected had he been responsible for the cave-in. It wasn't anger or resentment or fear. It was . . . a whole lot of nothing. No emotion that I could feel whatsoever. At least until he caught sight of Luther and Monica. Then emotion reared within him. And it was most decidedly resentment in the worst way possible. I realized in that instant how he saw them. As enemies. Barriers. Obstacles he had to get past.

Still, if my suspicions were right, Teresa did all this to leave him, which put her in mortal danger. The statement he'd made to Yolanda Pope all those years ago when they were in college rose to the surface of my dirt-covered brain. *One stick is all it will take.* "She's not out of the woods yet," I said to Uncle Bob. "Keep someone on her."

"Absolutely." He eyed the doctor with that hard gaze of his I knew and loved so well. Unless it was directed at me.

"Oh, and I need you to gather a few things and meet me at the hospital, including a bottle of flavored sparkling water."

He glanced back at me. "You doin' healthy now?"

I grunted. "Not likely. When all this is said and done, I'm heading straight for Margaritaville."

Since it took me over an hour to get back to Albuquerque, a little over half that to shower and change into clean clothes, then another forty-five minutes for Uncle Bob to get a warrant to search the Yosts' house, I had to call Agent Carson and give her the bad news. It took me longer to figure out how to prove the doctor's guilt than the thirty minutes we'd originally agreed upon, but considering travel time and the fact that cleanliness was next to godliness, she said we were still good. Which, whew.

Teresa Yost's leg didn't require surgery. They'd set it and wheeled her to a private room when she suddenly needed more tests, thanks to Uncle Bob and his wily ways with the women. Namely a nurse who looked at Ubie like he was a sugary morsel dipped in chocolate.

A couple of cops posing as orderlies wheeled Teresa into a labor and delivery room that contained some very interesting equipment. It made me only slightly less comfortable than that time I got to sit in an actual electric chair. You know, for giggles. As the men left, I stepped inside with a nod and closed the door. The lights had been turned low, and Teresa lay on the gurney half asleep as a result. She'd been covered in pale blue hospital gowns, and her leg, which had been propped up by pillows, had a temporary brace on it until the swelling went down enough for a cast.

"Teresa?" I said, inching toward her.

She blinked her eyes open and drew her brows together.

"I'm Charlotte Davidson. You might remember me from the mine?"

Her eyes registered recognition. "Yes. You found me."

I nodded and stepped closer. "I'm not sure how much you can recall. I'm a private investigator. Luther and Monica hired me. Kind of."

She smiled sleepily at the mention of their names.

I needed to hurry. Yost would know there was no reason for Teresa to be in a delivery room unless she was seriously holding out on him. Thankfully, he had rounds to make.

"We don't have much time, Teresa, so I'm going to sum up what I know happened and what I think happened and see where we stand. Is that okay?"

Her mouth thinned with worry, but she nodded.

"First, I know you sabotaged the mine." When she looked away without arguing, I continued. "You used the ATV and the winch to loosen the beams along the shaft. But I don't think you meant to be in it when it collapsed."

"I forgot to leave my cell phone," she said weakly, embarrassment wafting off her. "I went back in to leave it with my stuff so they'd think I was still in there."

"And that's when it collapsed."

With a hesitant nod, she confirmed what the miner had said. "The mines are so deep, they'd stop looking eventually."

"But before you did all this, you took out a life insurance policy on yourself for your sister, so she could get medical help."

She turned an astonished expression on me.

"Somehow," I continued, "you found out about Nathan's first wife. You found out he killed her when she tried to leave him."

Her expression didn't waver.

"He smothers you. Tries to control every aspect of your life."

A hint of shame flitted across her face.

"And you wonder how it could have come to this. How it could have gone so far."

"Yes," she whispered, the shame evident in her crinkled chin.

"Teresa, your husband is very good at what he does. He's a practiced surgeon in both the physical and the emotional realms. He knew what he was doing. He knew how to control you. That you wouldn't tell your brother what was going on, because you were afraid of what Luther would do."

A soft gasp echoed in the room, confirming everything I'd just said.

"Why should your brother have to pay for your mistakes, right? He would have hurt Nathan. Possibly killed him and then paid the price for the rest of his life."

Her nod was so slight, I almost missed it.

"So you took out the insurance policy, planned your escape, and tried to disappear. But you would never have left your siblings completely. You would have gotten them word that you were okay somehow, and Nathan would have figured it out, hon. He would have come after you. Or Luther would have ended up killing him when he found out why you'd left. Either way, it would have ended badly."

She pressed her mouth together and squeezed her eyes shut, trying to stop the tears that had gathered there.

"But what you did was so brave, Teresa. I admire you more than you will ever know."

"It was stupid."

"No." I put a hand over hers. "It was selfless."

She covered her mouth with the sheet and sobbed a full minute, and the sadness emanating from her was like a force field pushing against me. Taking deep breaths, I pushed back, fought to stay by her side.

"I was pregnant," she said, her breath hitching in her chest. "I think . . .

I think he gave me something. I got really sick one night and then lost the baby."

My teeth slammed together. I didn't know that part, and my heart ached for her loss. "I wouldn't be surprised if he did." Taking her hand into mine, I said, "Teresa, I have to tell you something, but you have to be very strong and know that I am working with the police and the FBI to stop it."

Without looking at me, she nodded, still lost in her grief.

I hated to tell her now, but she had a right to know. "I think he's been poisoning your sister."

Her attention flew to me again, aghast.

"The sparkling water that you bring her every day. He would have known you weren't drinking it. You weren't getting sick. Your sister was."

Both hands covered her mouth in horror.

"We had a warrant issued for your house," I said, rushing to assure her we were taking care of it. "We're having it tested now."

"How can you possibly—?"

"Her fingernails. She has what's called Aldrich-Mees' lines." When Teresa scanned the images in her memory and nodded absently, I continued. "Those are a symptom of heavy metal poisoning. It could be something like thallium or even arsenic."

Before Teresa could react, we heard the nurse outside. "Dr. Yost," she said, sounding surprised.

I hurried to the door and opened it a fraction of an inch.

"Have you seen my wife?" he said, looking around with a confused expression on his face. He frowned at the two orderlies who were standing around doing a whole lot of nothing.

One of them cleared his throat and pulled up his scrubs in discomfort.

"No," the nurse said, pulling the doctor's attention back to her. "Isn't she in her room?"

"She was, but . . . never mind. I'll check again."

"Nice to see you," she said with a smile. Then she turned to the door and rolled her eyes at me through the crack.

I waved her forward before rushing back to Teresa's side. "I have to get you back."

"How could I be so stupid?" she asked as the nurse unlocked the bed so the men could roll her out.

"Chin up, hon," I said, scanning the area before we snuck her through the delivery waiting area. "He won't ever do this again."

The fact that he'd gone after Yolanda's family summed it all up for me. Yost had done everything to keep Yolanda under his thumb. Same with his first wife, Ingrid. I had a sneaking suspicion he'd killed Ingrid's mother, and when Ingrid found out, she ran. In turn, Yost took the only recourse he had left. He killed her. He might have done the same to Yolanda if she hadn't been protected, insulated by a caring family.

Teresa had figured it out. What he'd done to his first wife. The consequences of her leaving. But she'd never dreamed he was trying to control her another way. He knew she was seeing her sister. He knew she was taking Monica the mineral water, so he laced it with just enough arsenic to make her sick, punishing Teresa for defying him and getting an obstacle out of the way at the same time. That was why the doctors couldn't pinpoint the problem. She was being slowly and methodically poisoned.

I left Teresa in the capable hands of two officers in scrubs and scrambled to make sure the scene had been set. Thanks to Uncle Bob, it had. Half an hour later, I stood in a quiet corner of the Presbyterian hospital with a magazine covering half my face, conspicuously trying to seem inconspicuous as the blond-haired, blue-eyed devil walked toward me. He stopped at the nurse's station to sign a chart, then continued my way.

"Ms. Davidson, I can't tell you how much you've done for me," Yost said.

I let a slow, calculating smile spread across my face. "Yeah, I bet. Can we talk?"

He frowned, then glanced around. "Is something—?"

"Look, Keith . . . ," I said, letting the name sink into him a moment before I slipped a manila envelope out of the magazine, held it up with raised brows, and waited. When his features smoothed from confusion to something akin to a used car salesman ready to bargain, I pointed to the supply closet and headed that way. "Coming?" I asked over my shoulder.

He followed.

After we stepped inside, he locked the door and glanced behind the shelves to make sure the room wasn't occupied. Then he stepped toward me, his façade, his charming demeanor, all but gone, completely replaced with the calculated actions of a criminal.

"What's this about?" he asked, clearly hoping I didn't know everything. A fruitless endeavor, as my knowledge was definitely the fruity type.

"It's about several things, Keith. Do you mind if I call you Keith?"

"Yes, actually, I do. What do you want?"

I let a lazy smile spread across my face. "Money."

After he sized me up a long moment, he said, "Figures. You bitches are all alike." He took hold of my jacket then and braced me against the metal shelves. I let him. I even placed my elbows on a shelf behind me while he felt me up.

He was nowhere near interested in me. His interests leaned toward self-preservation. But he opened my jacket and unbuttoned my shirt while keeping his eyes locked on to mine. When he got to the bottom button, he jerked the shirt out of my jeans and sent his hands behind me, feeling along the waistband of my jeans and the back of my bra. His hand brushed across the tender part of my back, and I bit back a gasp. He didn't notice. Luckily he was a doctor and saw half-naked chicks regularly. Otherwise, this whole thing could have been embarrassing.

Satisfied I wasn't wearing a wire, he took the manila envelope from my hand and opened it. It was all the research we'd done on him. Copies of the investigation on the man who'd forged papers for him with the name Keith Jacoby right beside his, a hotel receipt with the same name showing he was there on the day his first wife had died, a copy of a police report from this very hospital stating that several vials of a powerful muscle relaxant I couldn't pronounce had gone missing on the day Yolanda Pope's niece almost died. And so on, and so on.

I buttoned my shirt while he perused the papers. To say he was surprised would be an insult to the word. He was stunned, unable to believe I'd put it all together. Well, with the help of a lot of other people, but still.

He stuffed the contents back into the file, but his face showed no emotion, except of course those involuntary reflexes that poker players all over the world would pay big bucks to eliminate entirely.

"This has nothing to do with Teresa's disappearance."

"Oh, I think it does. It shows the lengths to which you're willing to go to be the homicidal control freak we all know and love."

He held up one of the printouts. It was a copy of the insurance policy Teresa had taken out. "I told Agent Carson. I didn't take out this ridiculous policy on Teresa. She did. She took one out on me and one on herself. I had nothing to do with it."

"Maybe you did," I said with an indifferent shrug, doing my best to protect Teresa, "maybe you didn't. But it sure looks bad, in my opinion." If he knew she'd been planning to leave him, there was no telling what he'd do to her.

"How much do you want?" he asked.

I maneuvered myself so that when he faced me, the hidden camera would pick him up. It was in the wall clock. An old trick, but a good one. I walked to the wall and leaned against it just underneath the clock.

"Well, Keith," I said—I couldn't help myself, "you seem to be doing very well in the net-worth department. How about an even mil?"

He scoffed, then leveled a really angry glower on me. "You've got to be kidding." He folded the envelope and stuffed it into the back of his pants. His light coloring made the emotion rushing through him turn his skin a ruddy shade of scarlet.

"I have another copy, don't worry."

A wave of anger and panic washed over him. "How can I get that one as well?"

"I told you," I said with a smile, "by giving me lots and lots of money."

He turned from me, his fury almost uncontrollable. Seems the charmer had a temper after all. "I don't have that kind of money," he said, dropping all pretense. "Why the fuck—?" He stopped before incriminating himself any further.

I needed to give him more incentive. Perhaps the threat of imminent death would do the trick. "Let me assure you," I said, offering him my own poker face, "I have one and only one copy of that file you're holding. I won't make another. It goes to the highest bidder."

Surprised, he stepped back, his gaze darting along the floor in thought before returning to me. "You're bluffing. The cops won't pay for this information." A triumphant smile slid across his face. "They'll arrest you for withholding evidence. It'll be useless in court."

With every ounce of my being, I wanted to snort. Useless? In his dreams. He was playing me, so I'd play him. "I have no intention of handing this information over to the police. I said the highest bidder, not the most desperate." Uncle Bob was going to kill me for that statement.

He fixed a suspicious frown on me. "Then who are you talking about?"

"I have someone in mind who'd be willing to pay lots of money for that information." I nodded, indicating the file he'd stashed. "A man with a vested interest in the health of your wife."

The moment realization dawned, a stupefying kind of dread fired his synapses and flooded his nervous system. I could feel it weigh him down like cement blocks on the feet of a drowning man. But he decided to keep up the pretense. "I have no idea who you're talking about."

"Okay." I shrugged and headed for the door, when he grabbed my arm none too gently and jerked me toward him.

"Who is it?" he asked, curious now, wondering if I really knew who'd pay good money for his life.

With a roll of my eyes, I said, "Luther, Dr. Yost. Luther Dean."

The emotion that swept over him was hard to put into words, but if I had to, I'd say it was one part astonishment and two parts paralyzing terror. I realized in that moment that he'd had a run-in with Luther at some point. He was too afraid not to have. I found the idea fascinating. Clearly Luther had been holding out on me.

Left with no other choice, he ran back to what he knew. A curtain fell over the second act, and the third stepped through it into the spotlight. He pressed his mouth together, regret and shame saddening his features as he amped up the lost-puppy expression he'd used so successfully over the years. I tried not to giggle.

"Charlotte," he said, his voice soft, hesitant, "I know you have no reason to trust me, but I felt a connection to you from the moment we met. I can explain everything, if you'll just give me a chance."

"Really?" With my best doe-eyed expression, I stepped closer. My breath quickened—mostly because I threw up a little in my mouth—and I bit my bottom lip in uncertainty before I said, "Because I'd have to be all kinds of stupid to trust you at this point, Keith."

He clamped his jaw together and turned away from me.

"How many have you killed now? Let's count," I said, holding up my thumb. "Okay, there's Ingrid, but that's a given."

"Shut up," he said, a sharp edge to his voice.

"But I've just started. Ingrid's mother," I continued, holding up my index finger. "Yolanda's niece." When the stillness of utter shock came over him, I said, "Oops, never mind. She lived, thank goodness. No thanks to you. I wonder what that little girl's father, Xander Pope, would pay for this information? Maybe he and Luther could go Dutch." He took a menacing step closer, so I brought out the big gun, the one thing that would send him running for the hills. "Oh, and let's not forget Teresa's sister, Monica."

He stopped, his eyes widening a split second before he caught himself.

"Arsenic in the sparkling water? Really, Nathan? That's the best you could do?"

His jaw dropped a solid two inches as he gazed at me.

"Yep. I know it all. Along with all those receipts and reports and things you stuffed down the back of your pants—not that I would touch them now—I figure you'll get a fairly long sentence if Luther doesn't get to you first."

He stood without moving, his mind racing a mile a minute.

"Now you've done harm to two of Luther's sisters. I doubt he'll see the bright side of any of this."

"I . . . I can try to scrape something up," he said at last.

"You'd best have a really sharp scraper, 'cause I ain't cheap, Keith."

He glanced around like a cornered animal before refocusing on me. "Will you meet me tonight? We can discuss this, make arrangements."

That time I did snort. "So you can kill me and bury my lifeless body in a shallow grave?"

He closed his eyes and shook his head. "I would never do that to you."

Oh, for the love of chocolate. I needed to throw a ticking bomb into the mix.

"Actually, I'm having dinner with Luther Dean tonight. Seems he was quite taken with me, or so his sister says."

With a frustrated sigh, he scrubbed his fingers over his face. I could imagine the walls closing in on him as his options dwindled down to nonexistent.

"I can get you a hundred grand right now," he said.

"Cash? Small, nonsequential bills?"

He nodded. "I can get you more later."

"And I'm just supposed to trust you're good for the rest? A man who kills wives for a living?"

He lowered his head. "If you had known my first wife. If you'd seen what kind of woman she was. Hateful and materialistic."

"Like you?"

Fury reared inside him, but he stayed calm on the outside. "You have no idea what she was like."

"You mean, besides alive?"

He turned from me for something like the tenth time, the melodramatic move losing its efficacy, but he had a decent-enough ass. "She was going to take everything from me. Everything I'd worked for. I couldn't let that happen."

Better. We were definitely getting there. "So, you killed her?" When he didn't answer, I added, "Wouldn't a good lawyer have sufficed?"

With a contemptuous sneer, he said, "So she could lie in court? Tell the judge I'd beat her or something?"

"Did you?"

He snarled, so I moved on.

"Fine," I said, drawing in a deep breath, "let's pretend for a moment I believe you, and you had no choice. What about Monica? What did she ever do to you?"

He visibly struggled to brace himself for what he was about to tell me. Either that or he had to go number two. "She was trying to steal Teresa away from me, telling her I wasn't good enough, that I didn't fit in."

I gasped. "Then by all means, let's poison her until her kidneys fail."

That coaxed a smile out of him. "That's going to be a bit tough to prove, don't you think?"

I couldn't argue with that. It would be hard to prove. With head bowed in defeat, I said, "You're probably right." Then I perked up. "Or I could just give the cops the bottles of sparkling water I found in your garage and watch you go up the river for thirty to life."

He didn't even try to defend himself. "Ever heard of the term *chain of custody*?"

"Ever heard of the term *Luther Dean don't give a shit*?"

Yost studied me a long moment, probably trying to figure out how best to kill me without raising undue suspicion. It was time to raise the stakes.

"The way I see it, this all boils down to three options."

"I told you, I can pay. You just have to give me time."

"One, I sell all this to Luther Dean."

"Are you even listening to me?"

"I'm listening," I said with an annoyed nod. "You're option two."

He frowned. "Then what's three?"

"I turn all this over to Agent Carson and see what she thinks."

He decided to call. "Fine. Turn it over to her. You can't prove anything."

Damn. Any lawyer worth his weight could explain away everything he'd said so far. I needed something solid. Something irrefutable. Maybe I'd gone about this wrong. Maybe I should have used my feminine wiles on him.

"I'll tell you what," I said, stepping around him to leave, "let me find out what Luther's highest bid is, then I'll get back with you."

He grabbed my arm again as I tried to walk past. "What will it take?"

Exasperated, I said, "I told you, a million clams." A spark of happiness jumped inside me. I'd always wanted to use the term *clams* in a real conversation. "But let me see what Luther is willing to pay before I commit to that."

He pulled me closer, fury sizzling around him. "Do you really think you're just going to walk out of here?"

"That was the general plan, yes." I wondered if it was too late to invoke my feminine wiles.

"Then you're stupider than you look," he said, wrapping one hand around my throat.

Yeah, it was probably too late.

He picked me up and slammed me against the shelves, guiding my head to a sharp corner, obviously hoping it would crack my head open and I'd bleed to death. Honestly, the man was an imbecile. Several people saw us come in together. What was he going to tell them? That I'd slipped and fell against the corner of a shelf that was actually taller than I was?

The guy would never learn. But before I could practice any of the fancy martial arts I'd learned in that two-week annex course, my head exploded with the fire of a thousand suns. An excruciating agony shot to the very core of my being. My eyes watered and I bit down to ride out the waves of pain. He let me drop to the ground but kept his hand around my throat and squeezed. Because bruises in the shape of his fingers wouldn't be incriminating at all.

Uncle Bob chose that moment to storm the place, and Yost stumbled back in surprise. I rolled over onto my side to catch my breath. Both hands locked on to my head as I curled into a cheese ball.

"Uncle Bob," I said in a super annoyed, *my head is killing me* voice, "you're too early."

I could see Yost out of the corner of my eye, the expression on his face priceless. He glanced at Ubie, then back at me, his mouth open in shock as an officer spouting the Miranda led his hands behind his back to be cuffed.

"I suppose I could've waited until he actually killed you," Ubie said, helping me up. "With the other evidence, we got plenty, pumpkin."

I grabbed for the stability of the shelf as Uncle Bob clutched me.

He brushed the hair out of my eyes. "You okay?"

After bringing my other hand forward to gloat about all the gushing blood I'd accumulated, I said, "There's not a drop." I turned my hand over in case I missed any. "There's no blood whatsoever. How am I not bleeding to death right now? 'Cause that freaking hurt." I said the last through gritted teeth while glaring at Yost.

In a fit of anger—or epilepsy, it was hard to tell—he ripped his yet-to-be-cuffed hand from the officer and lunged at me. I had no idea what he'd hoped to gain. Half a second before he was slammed onto the concrete floor, he'd grabbed a handful of shirt. The experienced officers took him down fast, and I went with him with a squeak of surprise, my shirt ripping all the way. I prayed to God the hidden-camera recording would never leave the evidence room. Ubie helped me up a second time, and I tried to give the girls their privacy, but with only half a shirt, it was difficult.

I collected myself the best that I could, then looked down at Yost. "This is so going on my bill."

He growled under the officers' weight as they cuffed him before dragging him to his feet and escorting him out of the hospital. The accumulation of dropped jaws as every head turned to watch in disbelief would have been humorous if my head didn't hurt so bad.

Uncle Bob stayed behind with me. "So," he said, watching them walk away, "are you going to call Agent Carson with the good news, or shall I?"

"You can do it," I said, suddenly despondent. Was Yost just being mean, or did I really look stupid? "Just make sure Luther Dean isn't anywhere nearby when you call her."

"Why?"

"For one thing, he's big."

"And two?"

"His name is Luther, if that tells you anything."

"Got it."

24

If life hands you lemons, keep them.
Because, hey, free lemons.
—T-SHIRT

By the time we finished everything up with Dr. Death, it was late, I was tired, and my head was throbbing. All things considered, Luther took the news that he almost lost both his sisters pretty well. Either that or his sisters had sedated him. I envied him that as I trudged up the stairs to my humble abode with the realization that I needed sleep. Period. Reyes or no Reyes, I had to catch some *Z*'s. So when I opened my door and found my TV on, a sleeping Amber on the sofa, and a large man sitting on the back of it, holding a gun at her head and watching me with seemingly infinite patience, the fact that I almost blacked out was completely understandable.

I took in the scene as the man raised a meaty hand and put a finger over his mouth to shush me. Then he gestured toward Amber with a nod. The gun was literally touching her temple, and I could only pray the cold metal wouldn't wake her. I eased my bag and keys onto the counter, then raised my hands to show compliance. He smiled and summoned me over with another nod.

He'd aged since the last time I saw him. But his build, the oily gray of his hair, the thickness of his stubby hands, were all unchanged from the time I threw a brick through his kitchen window to stop him from beating a boy to death. His image had been scorched into my memory.

"I hear you're looking for me," he whispered, and my gaze darted to Amber's sleeping form. "She's out," he assured me. "I been here for hours, and she hasn't moved an inch."

My breath shook the next words from my mouth. "Did you do anything to her?"

"No." He offered me a chastising frown. "Little girls aren't really my thing."

And I remembered what his thing was. I had proof sitting in the next room, nestled beneath my lingerie. Thinking about what he'd done to Reyes growing up, I could honestly say I'd never hated anyone more in my life.

"Let me take her home," I whispered, "then I'm all yours."

"Do I look stupid?" he asked.

"Hardly," I said quickly, placating him. "That's why I made the suggestion. You're supposed to be dead. You certainly wouldn't want anyone to see you here. If they find your fingerprints, this game that you've been playing for over a decade will end. Where's the fun in that?"

His scrutinized me from head to toe, sizing me up, before saying, "Fingerprints aren't usually a problem when I burn the place down."

"That makes you a smart man."

"Don't patronize me," he said, the warning in his tone unmistakable. He leaned in, his hot breath fanning over my face. "We're going to wake her up and walk her to the door. If either she or her mother comes back, they're both dead. I'll kill the first one through the door, then go after the next. Do you understand?"

I swallowed hard. "Completely."

He moved the gun just enough so I could raise her up. If it were just my ass on the line, I could've made a run for it the moment I saw him, but not with Amber. I would never have risked her life like that.

"Amber, honey," I said, shaking her softly. "You better get to bed, munchkin."

She blinked and tried to focus her sleepy eyes on me.

"Your mother's going to wonder where you are."

"Okay," she said, her voice groggy and spent. "I'm sorry. I fell asleep."

I smiled. "That's okay, hon. I just don't want your mom to worry."

I helped her to her feet and led her as she padded to the door, thanking all things holy she didn't even notice the monster with the snub-nosed .38 in the room. After one attempt for the closet and one for the pantry, she finally made it out the right door. Walker grabbed my arm then, not allowing me past the threshold. Thankfully, her door was unlocked. She opened it and went inside without another thought.

In the second I had to think about it, I contemplated running. Would he really go after Amber and Cookie? Of course not. He'd come after me. But what if he caught me? What if I didn't make it? In that case, I had no doubt whatsoever he'd come back to fulfill his promise. And I would be dead in the parking lot or the alley, unable to stop him.

About one-point-five seconds after Amber closed the door, I felt a sharp pain explode in my head for approximately the third time that day, and I knew the decision had been made for me.

"Dutch."

I heard Reyes's voice from a distance. I tried to reach out and take his hand but found that my own was like smoke, a swirling white mass. "Reyes."

"Shhhh," Earl Walker said as I jerked to consciousness, not that he was actually trying to keep me from screaming. He hadn't taped my mouth, hadn't gagged me in any way. He'd just warned me.

After he'd dragged my limp body to a chair and fastened my arms and legs to it with cable ties, it occurred to me that I could be in trouble.

"Have I mentioned how much I hate torture?" I asked, fighting for every consonant.

He put the gun on the end table to his left and scrunched my face in his thick hand. Which really wasn't so much torturous as annoying. "Here's how this is going to go," he said, speaking softly, slowly, so I would understand. "I cut, you bleed. You can scream if you think it'll help, but the first person through that door will die. Your pretty little receptionist's throat will be slit before she even knows I'm here." He leaned closer, his hot breath sour against my face. "And who will come running in next?"

Amber. He didn't have to say it.

"Amber."

Or maybe he did.

"And let me make something very clear." He leaned in farther so he could whisper in my ear. "Hurting children makes me happy."

He'd probably had a really bad experience as a child.

Twenty minutes later, he was proving how skilled he was with the scalpel, one slice at a time. I couldn't help but wonder why he didn't become a surgeon.

A sharp burn shot straight to my core as he cut me again, this time on the inside of my thigh. Jeans. No jeans. He didn't care. I welded my teeth together, my eyes rolling back in my head as I felt the nick he'd placed along a tendon. The cut was deep that time and very near my femoral artery. Or right on it. I could no longer see. Blood from the wound on my scalp was streaming into my eyes and clinging to my lashes.

"One more time," he said, seeming a little annoyed.

Well, join the club, buddy.

"Why were you looking for me? How did you know I was still alive?"

I wanted to answer him—I really, really did—but I couldn't seem to push my voice past the crushing pain. I knew if I opened my mouth to answer, I would scream. Cookie would come. Amber would follow. And my world would cease to exist.

Once again, I had placed the people I loved most in mortal danger.

Maybe my father was right. Maybe I needed to give it up, become an accountant or a dog walker. How much trouble could I get in then?

Reyes was always here for me, but I'd bound him. I'd kept him from killing himself and killed myself instead. It was a sad testament to my ineptitude that I could hardly go two weeks without needing him to save my ass.

"Your choice," he said, a microsecond before I felt a fiery slash on the underside my left arm.

I felt tendons snap apart that time, and my head fell back as I bit my tongue to keep from screaming. But the pain overwhelmed me. My eyes rolled heavenward as I tumbled back to Reyes.

"Dutch," he said from somewhere in the darkness. "Where are you?"

"Home," I muttered, fighting to stay with him.

"Unbind me," he commanded breathlessly, and I had the distinct feeling he was running. "I won't get to you in time. Charley, damn it."

"I don't know h—"

"Say it!" he ordered through gritted teeth. "Just say the words."

"I'm sorry." Helplessness washed over me as I felt myself leaving him again. For the first time in my life, I believed I was going to die and there was nothing he or I could do about it.

The scalpel sent another shock wave skirting over my nerve endings. I blinked past the blood pooling in my lashes as a jolt of the most unimaginable pain I'd ever felt brought me skyrocketing to the surface again. I breathed in deep, as if coming up for air from the bottom of the ocean.

Walker had sliced up my rib cage, the scalpel running along the bones like a kid with a stick and a white picket fence. Shaking so hard I wondered if I was seizing, I clutched the chair and forced my teeth to stay locked. But trying so desperately to stay in control of certain bodily functions had me losing control of others, and I felt the warmth of urine seep between my legs and pool underneath me, mingling with the blood already there.

He bent over me and was poking around the cut on my thigh. Then he turned, looked right into my eyes. I could barely focus, but he was frowning, studying. "Reyes," he said, and I blinked back to him. "You're like him. You heal like he did." He pressed the scalpel against my cheek, readying for his next strike. "What are you?"

He didn't wait long for an answer before blood was streaming into my mouth and down my throat. I tried to spit it out, but that would require the unclenching of my jaw, a risk I wasn't willing to take.

"I wonder what would happen," he said, prying my hand off the arm of the chair, "if I took a finger."

Just as he started to do that very thing—the sharp sting of metal slicing through flesh becoming mind shattering when it hit bone—we both heard someone running up the stairs in the hall.

"Finally," I heard the monster say. He smiled and turned back to me. "It's our little escaped convict, isn't it?"

Half a heartbeat later, the door crashed open and the silhouette of a large man stood framed in the doorway.

Reyes. No.

Before I could say anything, before I could think, the gun went off. Walker had been waiting for him, knowing he would come. And I closed my eyes and stopped the spin of the Earth on its axis.

When I opened them, the bullet was inching through the air halfway between Walker and Reyes. It crawled forward, and I struggled with every ounce of my being to keep my grip on time, but it slipped through my fingers like smoke in a summer breeze.

I could only watch as it crept forward, its target still unaware of its existence, and the words came to me in a flash.

"Rey'aziel," I said, forcing my teeth apart. *"Te libero."*

In an instant, Reyes materialized beside me as time crashed through my barrier with a vengeance. I heard another gunshot a microsecond before I heard the *shiiiiing* of Reyes's sword.

His robe, thick and undulating like an ocean wave, swallowed half the room as his blade sliced through Walker with the grace of a seasoned golfer.

Walker froze, his eyes wide with disbelief as he glanced down, wondering what was wrong, because Reyes sliced from the inside out. No external trauma. Nothing distasteful like gaping wounds or gushing blood. So the fact that he had been drenched in pain and could no longer move boggled him. I wished he could see Reyes, the massive presence of his robe and what lay beneath it. Since he couldn't, he'd have no idea what was now picking him up and throwing him across the room. The walls shook when Walker hit, and I realized I could no longer see Reyes's corporeal self. I could only hope the bullets were less strategically placed than Reyes's blade. It would take more than a couple of bullets to bring him down.

Then he turned toward me and lowered the hood of his robe, revealing the most beautiful face I'd ever seen. He kneeled and took mine into his hands. "Dutch, I'm so sorry."

"Sorry?" I tried to say, but I realized my mouth and throat were too full of blood to say anything. Then I tumbled back into oblivion and slept at last.

25

An integral part of any best friend's job is to
immediately clear your computer history
if you die.
—T-SHIRT

"I think you're right. Should we get a doctor?"

I tried to focus on the voice by my side, male and distinctly Uncle Bob–ish, but I couldn't quite place the source. Then another one chimed in, so I tried to focus on it instead.

"Definitely, yes, go get someone."

Cookie was on my left. She had my hand in hers, which was silly. We rarely held hands in public. Before I could comment, I realized someone had superglued my eyelids shut. Damn it. I tried to protest, but my mouth seemed to have suffered the same fate. After someone stuffed cotton into it.

I frowned, and an unattractive moan escaped me.

"Sweetheart, it's Cookie. You're in the hospital."

"Mm-mm," I said. And I meant every word. This was ridiculous. I'd never actually been admitted into a hospital before, like in a room with a view—or without a view, since I couldn't be sure, but I felt the distinct presence of a bed beneath me.

"Is she awake?" I heard a bustle of people entering the room and my sister's voice. "Charley?" she asked, and I had so many comebacks, it was unreal. Damn the inventor of superglue.

"What do you think?" Gemma asked, and I wanted to tell her exactly what I thought about this whole freaking situation, but a nurse interrupted before I got the chance.

"Her sutures look good. The surgery went well. She should have the full use of her arm back with therapy."

My arm? What the fuck happened to my arm?

Someone walked out and Gemma followed, asking questions.

"Hey, pumpkin head," the Uncle Bob voice said. I totally could not put a face to it. "Can you hear me?"

"Mm-mm."

He chuckled. "I'll take that as a yes."

I lifted my free hand and tried to feel my face. It was gone! Then Cookie led my hand a little farther left.

"Here you go," she said.

Oh, thank God. I had some kind of headband on, which was slightly mortifying as those went out in the eighties, and half my face was covered with a huge bandage. That couldn't look good.

What the hell happened to me? Then I remembered. "Oh, my god!" I mumbled, and tried to sit up.

"Oh, no, you don't," that voice said, and I was beginning to think it might have been Uncle Bob.

"Walker," I said, though it sounded more like *muffler.*

"Did you get that?" Ubie must have asked Cookie. "Me neither." He leaned closer and talked really loudly, enunciating each syllable. "Do you want some water?"

After a strong wince, I took my hand and felt for his face.

"I'm right here," he nigh yelled.

When my hand came into contact with his face, I covered his mouth and said, "Shhh."

Cookie giggled.

"I'm sorry," he said, taking my hand into his.

"I can't see."

"Here, I have a warm cloth." Cookie wiped my eyes and face, at least the part that wasn't bandaged, and I was finally able to pry my lids apart.

I blinked and tried to focus. Uncle Bob was on my right, and I reached up and felt his face again, his dark mustache tickling my palm. Cookie was on my left and had my other hand, but I couldn't squeeze.

"Reyes," I said, and she glanced at Uncle Bob.

"He's fine, honey. Don't worry about him."

So I didn't. I drifted off again, in and out for hours. People were there one minute only to be replaced by other people the next. When I finally awoke without feeling like a house had fallen on me—well, no, I still felt like a house had fallen on me, but I was able to stay awake for more than ten seconds—the room was dark with only a soft light glowing from the instrument panel beside me. And empty, save one. Reyes.

I felt him, his heat and energy. I pried open my eyes and spotted him instantly, balancing on the back of a chair in the corner, his robe sliding along the floor like a black fog, creeping up the walls and around the instruments. His hood was back as he watched me, his powerful gaze unwavering.

"Are you okay?" I asked, the cotton still in my mouth.

He jumped down, his robe swallowing in on itself. When it settled around him, he turned to look out the window at the lights of the city. Or the Dumpsters out back. Who knew?

"This is my fault."

My brows slid together. "This wasn't your fault."

He glanced over a wide shoulder. "You really need to figure out what you're capable of," he said, scanning me from head to toe.

I was suddenly self-conscious. I had a huge gash in my face and an arm in dire need of therapy. Walker had actually cut the tendons in my arm and partially cut them in my leg. Speaking of Walker . . . "Where is he?" I asked.

"Walker?"

I nodded.

"He's in this very hospital."

Alarm leapt within me. I'd never been afraid of anyone in my life—well, besides Reyes—but I recoiled at the mere mention of Walker's name. And because of it, I felt as though he had taken something very valuable away from me. An innocence. Or possibly an arrogance. Either way.

"He won't be going anywhere or hurting anyone ever again."

I was certain he was right, but for some reason, that didn't help much. He stepped to me and ran his fingertips over the arm that I could feel healing already, my fingers moving ever so slightly.

"I'm so sorry."

"Reyes—"

"I had no idea he would go to such lengths when he came after you."

My thoughts screeched to a halt, and I took a mental step back. That was an odd thing to say. "What do you mean?"

"I knew he would try something," he said, closing his eyes in regret, "but this. I just had no idea. And since I was bound—"

"What do you mean, when he came after me?" He lowered his gaze and like a baseball bat hitting me upside the head, realization dawned. "Oh, my god, I'm so slow sometimes, I astound myself."

"Dutch, if I had known . . ."

"You set me up."

He bowed his head, pulled away from me.

"I was bait. How amazingly slow can one person be?" I tried to sit up, but pain shot through my arm. And rib cage. And leg. And, oddly enough, my face. It was still too early, even for me.

"I didn't know where he was or how to find him. You had bound me, remember? But I knew if we rattled enough cages, he'd come running. I planned on being with you when that happened. I followed you everywhere. Then I lost track of you."

"Reyes, he threatened Cookie and Amber. He would have killed them."

"Dutch—"

"This wasn't just about me. Or you, for that matter."

"Had I known . . . had I thought for a moment—"

"You didn't think. That's the problem."

Anger spiked within him. "You bound me," he argued.

"I bound you two weeks ago," I said, the side of my face throbbing with the workout. "Why didn't you go after him before that?"

"I didn't know." He raked his fingers through his hair in frustration. "I thought he was dead, just like the rest of the world."

"Then how did you find out otherwise?"

He seemed embarrassed. "The fact that I'd spent ten years of my human life behind bars for something I didn't do was a source of great entertainment for the demons when they were torturing me. Until they told me, I had no idea. Then you bound me, and I couldn't go after him."

"So you set me up?"

"I set us up, Dutch. I was going to be with you every step, but your boyfriend was on your ass everywhere you went. If I'd just hung out with you, I would have been arrested."

The irony of the situation was not lost on me. First my father, then Reyes. When would I learn? What would it take for me to see the true nature of a man? Me. The one person on the planet who could see into men's souls. Who could feel their deepest fears and see the color of their worth.

"I just have one more question."

"Okay."

"Why didn't you just tell me? Honestly, you're as bad as my dad. What is it with men and their inability to just be open and tell the damned truth?"

He pressed his lips together before answering. "I didn't trust you."

"What?"

"You bound me, Dutch. And quite frankly, if you had the slightest inkling of what you are capable of, you could do a lot more than that. Which, by the way, you need to figure out." He pierced me with a cold stare. "This war isn't going anywhere."

"What war?" I asked, appalled. "Your war? The one your old pals from the underworld started?" I shook my head as much as I dared. "I don't want anything to do with that. I'm done. With you. With all of it."

"Dutch, you're all they want. They want the portal, and you're it. And they've found a way to detect you. They have a way to find you." He leaned over me, his brows drawn together in what could have been anger or pain. Or both. "You have to figure out what you're capable of, really capable of, and you have to do it now. No more screwing around with these humans. You need to concentrate on your real job."

"These humans are my real job."

"Not for much longer," he said, about half a second before he looked over me toward the door and disappeared. Just like a man. Utterly unable to stand up to a fight.

I scanned to the door as well to see a police officer standing there. Not really in the mood to give a statement, I closed my eyes and pretended to be asleep.

"You're awake," the officer said.

"No, I'm not." I opened my eyes and looked at him, but the light at his back made his features too dark to recognize. He stepped into the room, and the glow from the instrument panel illuminated the face of Owen Vaughn, my archenemy. He was most likely there because kicking a girl when she's down was fun.

He picked up my chart. "You keep coming back," he said, surprise evident in his voice. "You get knocked down again and again, and you keep coming back."

"Are you here to finish me off?"

He leveled a startled expression on me, one that turned to resolve. "I guess I can see why you'd think that."

After the day I'd had, making nice with the guy who tried to kill and/

or horribly maim me in high school was super close to the bottom of my things-I'd-most-like-to-do list. In fact, he was right under *shove bamboo shoots under my fingernails* and right above *get betrayed by someone I love. Again.* Cleary, it was a long list.

I studied him a moment, my curiosity burning despite his position on the list. "What did I do to you in high school?" I asked, barely moving my mouth.

He shook his head. "Nothing. That was a long time ago. It doesn't matter now."

The dam broke at last, and emotion of every shape and size poured out of me. "Just tell me," I said, not above begging. "Just tell me what I did wrong so I won't do it again. What I keep doing wrong, over and over and over." My breath caught in my chest, putting a stop to the *overs*.

"Charley—"

"Owen—," I covered my face with the one hand I could lift and bit down hard to keep from crying. "—just please tell me."

He exhaled slowly. "You took my pants."

I lowered my hand just enough to see him over my fingertips. "What?"

"About a month before I tried to run your ass down until you died a prolonged and painful death, I'd spilled orange juice all over my pants. When I went to the restroom, I took them off to rinse them in the sink, and one of the guys grabbed them from me, joking around. He ran out and threw them into the girl's restroom. And you took them."

"I don't even . . . Wait, that's right. Larry Vigil opened the bathroom door and threw in a pair of guy's pants. So—" I leveled an apologetic gaze on him. "—I took them. I just thought they were from the locker room. And the next day," I added, hating to say it aloud, "I wore them. As a joke. Owen, I had no idea they were yours. I figured they'd taken them out of someone's locker and whoever they'd belonged to had sweats or something else to wear."

"They weren't and I didn't. They left me there, and later when you wore them, I thought you knew they were mine." He glanced down, embarrassed. "You looked right at me and laughed the next day as you walked past."

I ran a hand through my hair and winced when my fingers brushed over stitches. "Owen, I wasn't laughing at you. I was just, I don't know, laughing. Probably at something Jessica said." Jessica had been my best friend growing up before I made the mistake of telling her too much about me.

"Well, I know that now," he said. He stood and stalked to the window that overlooked the college campus.

"But there's more to that story, isn't there?"

He nodded and turned away. "I couldn't leave the restroom. It was the end of the day and everyone went home, and I was just there, stuck in the restroom with no pants. So, I waited for all the buses to run, tied my jacket around my waist, and started walking home."

I cringed. The embarrassment he must have felt. "Oh, my god," I said, as the memory of that time rushed back, "you were the kid. The South Nines beat you up."

After a long moment, he nodded. "They caught me in an alley and basically kicked my ass for not wearing pants."

"But you were at school the next day."

He shrugged. "I didn't tell anyone. I told my mom I crashed my bike. If the Nines had kept their mouths shut, no one would ever have known. Then when I saw you wearing my pants the next day and everyone laughing . . ."

My hand covered my eyes, trying to block the memory. "Talk about adding insult to injury."

"I just couldn't forgive you. The Nines never left me alone after that. I had to face them every day."

"Owen, I'm so sorry. That's why you withdrew. Neil Gossett said you just kind of drifted away from them."

"Being harassed on a daily basis has that effect. Still doesn't change the fact that you're a bitch."

"That's true."

He turned back to me. "But you just take this shit and take it and keep coming back for more. The guys in my division can't figure out if you're really good or really stupid."

I peeked out from between my fingers. "It's a fine line."

He lowered his gaze. "I wanted you dead."

"Yeah, I got that when you came after me in your dad's SUV."

"I wanted to drag your lifeless body down the street, dropping limbs along the way."

"Okay, but you're over that, right?"

"Not really. But you're all fucked up, so I can't give you a hard time. We can pick this back up when you're better."

"Sounds like a plan."

The next day, I woke in the late afternoon, a soft sun filtering through the window. Uncle Bob was there as well as Cookie, her eyes rimmed with a redness that hadn't been there before.

"Are you getting enough sleep?" I asked her.

"You're one to talk," she said with a sad grin. "Everyone's been here. And it's all over the news. About the man who'd been in prison for a murder he didn't commit. I think Reyes is going to be famous."

"So he doesn't have to go back to prison?"

"I talked to your friend Neil Gossett," Uncle Bob said. "They're going to keep him in minimum security until all the paperwork goes through."

"But why don't they just let him out now?" I asked, alarmed. "The man he went to prison for killing isn't even dead."

"For one thing, they have to prove that really is Earl Walker. Then papers have to be filed and a judge has to review the case. It's not like in the movies, hon."

"So how is he?" I asked.

"Farrow is fine," Ubie said. "He'd called the police before he ever got to your place and was there when we got there. He surrendered with no complications. And that is really the man he went to prison for killing?" he asked at the last.

I knew he would take it hard. Sending a man to prison for a murder he didn't commit would wreak havoc on the heightened moral codes of a good cop. "There was no way for you to know, Uncle Bob. Wait." My brows slid together. "What do you mean he surrendered? He didn't really have much of a choice, did he?"

"Actually, the first officers on the scene were a little busy. They had no idea who he was. He identified himself and told them the guy lying in a heap of broken limbs was Earl Walker."

"He told them? With the gunshot wounds?"

Ubie and Cookie exchanged glances. "He wasn't shot, sweetheart," Cookie said.

"Oh, my gosh, he's faster than I thought. I could have sworn he was shot. I mean, I saw Walker pull the trigger. I saw the bullets head straight for his heart."

Again with the glances. Cookie took my hand. "Hon, that wasn't Reyes." She bit her lower lip, then said, "That was Garrett Swopes."

I blinked in confusion, closed my eyes, and replayed the memory. A tall man came bursting through the door, and Reyes had been on his way. I'd just assumed.

"Swopes?" I finally muttered. "Garrett came through the door?"

"Yes," Uncle Bob said.

"Garrett Swopes was shot?" I simply couldn't wrap my mind around it. "No, that was Reyes. It had to be. He crashed through the door and . . . the gun went off."

"Sweetheart, why don't you get some rest."

"You must be mistaken." Shock and denial fought for a front seat in my convertible to la-la land. They had to be mistaken. Garrett was shot? Because of me? I struggled to get out of bed. "Is he here? I have to see him."

Uncle Bob lowered me back onto the mountain of pillows. "Charley—"

"I can't believe I got him shot. Again. I need to see him. He's going to be so pissed."

"You can't, hon." Uncle Bob lowered his head, sorrow and regret coming at me in white-hot waves.

I glanced at Cookie, at her red-rimmed eyes, and the dread that crawled up my spine was so cold, so crushing, it swallowed me where I lay. I forced myself to look at Uncle Bob. And waited.

He visibly struggled with what to say, how to word it; then he raised his lashes and whispered, "He didn't make it, hon."

And everything else slipped away.

26

Sometimes that light at the end of the tunnel
is a train.
—T-SHIRT

Slowly, and with a sharp pain that echoed off the hollow walls of my heart, the realization that I'd actually gotten a man killed, a friend, sank in. There comes a time in every woman's life when she has to reevaluate her priorities. Did I really want to kill off all my friends one by one?

Another thought surfaced, one that centered on the fact that the men in my life found me incapable of walking and chewing gum at the same time. True, my track record didn't instill a lot of confidence, but I'd solved case after case, I'd weathered ridiculous odds, and damn it, I'd looked good doing it.

A momentary sense of pride swelled inside me until I once again remembered I'd gotten a man killed. Not just a man. Garrett Swopes. My Garrett Swopes. A bond enforcement agent with more talent in his little finger than I had in my whole body. I replayed the scene in my mind, the bullets heading toward him, too fast for him to react. And I'd watched, like a voyeur. Thinking it was Reyes, I figured he could react, he could defend himself against those odds. Had I known it was Garrett, would I have done more? Would I have tried harder? Could I have?

If Reyes had just trusted me. That was another thought that played itself over and over in my mind. If he had just trusted me. If he had just filled me in on the freaking plan. Quite frankly, Reyes Farrow could bite my ass.

When I started pulling needles and tubes out of every available surface of my body, Uncle Bob jumped up from a chair in the corner.

"What are you doing?" he asked, trying to stop me. And succeeding with minimal effort.

"I need to go home."

"You need to lie back."

"Uncle Bob, you know how fast I heal. And I'll heal even faster at home. I just want out of here. I've been here for two weeks."

"Hon, you've been here for two days."

"Are you serious?" I asked, more than a little appalled. "It seems like forever. And then some."

"Charley, let's just talk to the doctor first, okay? He'll make his rounds again in about an hour."

With a heavy sigh, I fell back, opened my mouth in a silent scream at the pain shooting through every molecule in my body, then clamped my jaw shut because silent screaming hurt, too. Holy crap, I hated being tortured. I hated that Reyes didn't trust me. And more than anything, I hated getting my friends killed.

"I killed him, Uncle Bob." I plastered a hand over my eyes so he wouldn't see the evidence of how pathetic I could be.

"Charley," he said, his voice soft, "that wasn't your fault."

"It was entirely my fault. Maybe Dad was right. Maybe I need to be a plumber."

"Your dad wants you to be a plumber?"

"No," I said, my breath catching between sobs, "he just wants me out of this business."

"I know. But since he essentially got you into this business, I'm having a difficult time with it." A hardness seeped into his voice, and I blinked past the tears to look at him.

"I don't want you to be mad at him."

He smiled. "I'm not, honey. It's just, he gets you into this, gets you to solve all his cases for him, then when it comes time to hang up his badge, he decides it's suddenly too dangerous for you? I have to wonder if that's not why he retired when he did."

I hiccuped a sob. "What do you mean?"

"He retired earlier than we thought he would. I think he felt guilty about using you like that. Whatever the case may be, I'll talk to him, pumpkin. Don't you worry."

The doctor came a while later and argued for a good half hour, but Uncle Bob and I won. They were releasing me on my own recognizance.

"Where are you going?"

I looked up as Dad walked in. Uncle Bob was helping me with a pair of slippers as Cookie retrieved a robe out of the closet.

"Hey, Dad, they're letting me walk. It's crazy. They apparently have no idea how dangerous I am." I realized about mid-*crazy* that Dad seemed upset. "What's wrong?" I asked when he frowned at Uncle Bob and me.

Uncle Bob stood. "Leland, she wants to go home."

"You just keep encouraging her, and now a man is dead and she is in the hospital after having been tortured almost to death, yet again."

"Now is not the time for this conversation."

"Now is precisely the time. She refuses to listen to anyone, even her own doctor." Dad's aura crackled with anger. "This," he said, gesturing to the equipment surrounding me as I sat on the side of the bed, fighting the pain throbbing in my arm and leg, "this is what I'm talking about."

I didn't have the energy to argue with him. The pain leached it out of me as fast as my body could produce it.

Gemma walked in then, her eyes wide with worry, and I realized there was more going on than just Dad's anger. "I tried to talk him out of this, Charley."

"Why?" He turned on her, his jaw set in anger. I'd never seen my dad like this. He was always the calm one, the stable one. "So she can end up in the hospital every other week? You want this for her?"

"Dad, I want her to be happy. She likes her job and she's good at it and it's not up to us."

He turned from her as though disgusted. I wondered where Denise was, the stepmother from hell; then I saw her standing down the hall, worry lining her face. She looked up as two officers walked past and stepped into the room. And lo and behold, one was Owen Vaughn, naturally, and I knew this was about to get much, much worse.

"Charlotte Davidson?" the officer that I didn't know and who had never tried to kill me asked.

"Dad," Gemma said, "please think about what you're doing."

"That's her," Vaughn said, as though he hated to do it.

Uncle Bob spoke up then, suspicion thickening in his voice. "What are you doing, Leland?"

"What I should have done a long time ago."

"Ms. Davidson," the officer said, "we're here to place you under arrest for aiding and abetting an escaped convict and obstruction of justice in the apprehension and arrest of said convict."

My jaw fell to the floor. I looked from them to Dad and back.

"Dad, please," Gemma said.

"Due to your physical condition, we're going to ask that you come in voluntarily within the next week to be formally arrested. Your rights and privileges as a licensed private investigator have been suspended until an investigation can determine the extent of your involvement in Reyes Farrow's escape and continued evasion."

With the wind knocked completely out of me, I sat in stunned silence as he spoke. My father did this. The one person I could always count on growing up. My rock.

Somewhere between the drips of a leaky water faucet nearby, I slipped into a surreal state of consciousness. I heard Dad and Uncle Bob arguing violently, nurses rush in and out, Gemma and Cookie talking to me in soft, soothing tones. But the world had been dipped in red. My dad. Reyes. Nathan Yost. Earl Walker. It was enough to bring out the anger in a girl.

My sudden spike in annoyance must have summoned Reyes. He was there at once, enshrouded in his undulating robe. He looked from the arguing crowd to me, then back again. And he was not a person I wanted to see. In fact, he was more a person I wanted to punish. Because I saw betrayal. Unconscionable behavior. Murder.

"Rey'aziel," I whispered under my breath with every intention of sending him back to his body for good, but he was in front of me at once.

"Don't you dare," he said, his voice a low growl.

I glowered at him. "You don't get to order me around."

He pushed his hood back, his face startlingly beautiful, inches from mine. "So you're going to punish me? Unbind me when you need me, then bind me again when you don't?" He leaned so close, I could smell the lightning storm roiling inside him, the earthy dampness of morning dew evaporating under the heat of the sun. "Fuck you, then."

I shook to my core, the anger sparking within me, catching fire and flooding the area with the energy pouring out of me. In a word, I threw a fit.

"What is that?" I heard someone ask.

I looked up, a curious slant to my gaze as I watched everyone around me grab for furniture, the doorjamb, each other . . . anything to stabilize themselves. Uncle Bob stumbled, then rushed toward me. He knew. Somehow he knew.

He took my chin into his hand. "Charley . . ."

The lights flickered overhead. Sparks cascaded around us and screams filtered toward me from the hall.

"Charley, honey, you have to stop."

Cookie came into my line of sight, her eyes wide with fear as she clutched an equipment cart.

"Charley," Uncle Bob said again, his voice soft, soothing, and in an instant I blinked back to reality. He was in front of me, and I was back in my body, grounded in flesh and bone. I forced myself to calm, to take deep, cleansing breaths, to control the arcs of energy surging out of me.

Screams and shouts echoed down the hall. People were struggling to their feet. Equipment had toppled over and light fixtures hung from the ceiling by wires.

And my father looked at me. And he knew.

Then Reyes was in front of me again, an expression that was part anger and part satisfaction lit his beautiful, traitorous features. "Finally," he said, right before he disappeared.

Then it was silent and Uncle Bob was leading me out of the hospital, carrying me up the stairs to my apartment, onto the sofa where Cookie had built a bed with sheets and my Bugs Bunny comforter and set a soda on the end table she'd scooted within easy reach. I was back at my apartment, stitches, arm sling, leg brace, and all.

"They're calling it an earthquake," Cookie said, the relief in her voice evident. Like they would ever suspect that undulating force had come from a person, especially one unable to walk and chew gum at the same time. She needn't have worried. "And Neil Gossett from the prison called. He has information on Reyes's status, and he wants to know how you are." Oddly enough, I didn't care. "I gave him the usual. But if you want to call him later, I'll leave your phone right here." She put it on the table beside the soft drink.

"I'll take care of this, hon," Uncle Bob said, hovering almost as much as Cook. "Don't worry about what your father did. I'll get everything dropped." He left worried and angry, and I wanted to warn him about the dangers of driving in his condition, but I was so numb, even the thought of being a smart-ass didn't appeal to me.

So, I sat in shock and wallowed in self-pity for a good long while before drifting off, Cookie at my side. At least I could sleep now, and suddenly sleep was all I wanted to do.

A knock sounded at the door. I didn't quite have the energy to invite a visitor in. I'd used it all hobbling over to the snack bar and climbing up it with my one good leg. I raised the other knee and sat on the hard tile surface with my back against the wall, the coolness biting into my injuries. I didn't deserve to be comfortable, spread out on a sofa watching soaps all day, even if I was decades behind.

Wednesday sat cross-legged on the opposite end of the countertop, the knife in her lap, and I wondered if it was there to protect her, to keep her from being betrayed by almost every man in her life. Probably not.

The drugs had kicked in and lessened the throbbing in my leg and arm. Clearly, my judgment had been clouded when I decided to make the hazardous journey to the snack bar and summit it like a rookie climbing Everest. I had no idea how I was going to get down.

I could feel Reyes hovering, sticking to the shadows but looking on, watching, waiting. I was just about to tell him to beat it when the door opened and my biker guy, Donovan, walked in like he owned the place. Mafioso and the prince were right behind him. I looked away in embarrassment. Face sutures couldn't possibly be appealing. Thank goodness I had a huge white bandage covering half my face. Maybe he wouldn't notice. I'd hate for him to fall out of love with me so soon after falling in.

He fixed a curious gaze on me, then sucked in a soft hiss of breath.

I covered my face with one hand, the other still impossible to raise without screaming.

"What the fuck happened to you?" he asked. He moved a barstool aside for a better look. "Did Blake do this?"

"Who?" I asked, peeking between my fingers.

The prince was studying my leg brace. I had changed into shorts with

Cookie's help and she reattached the leg brace to keep me from bending my leg. Apparently, the tendons had to heal first. The bandages around the knife wound were visible from between the straps on the brace. He put a hand on them then glanced up at me, worry in his eyes.

Mafioso stood against the wall at my feet, hands in his pockets, a decidedly uncomfortable expression lining his features.

"Blake, the guy whose life you saved the other night."

"Oh, no." I closed my fingers again. "This is my own doing."

"Kind of hard on yourself, aren't you?"

"How's Artemis?" I asked, but I knew the answer instantly. The same regret suffusing the air. The same pain as when Cookie told me about Garrett.

"She's gone."

My mouth pressed together. I'd had enough death for a while. I breathed deeply before saying, "I'm so sorry."

"Me, too, darlin'."

"Did you find your guy?"

"Who, Blake? He wised up and went to the police."

"I would have, too, if you had been looking for me."

"Somehow, I doubt that." I felt his fingers slide along my forearm and rest on my wrist. With the greatest ease, he tugged my hand away from my face. From where I was sitting on the bar, my head was actually a little higher than his, and I looked down. He was quite handsome for a scruffy biker sort. Of course, scruffy biker sorts were exactly my type.

"What are you doing here?" I asked.

He'd kept the fingers of one hand laced within mine while the other fished something out of his pocket. "I brought you a key."

I blinked in surprise when he placed it in my palm. "A key to what?"

The prince spoke up, a bitterness in his voice. "To the asylum."

"Whenever you need to visit Rocket," Donovan said, glowering at his cohort, "you can go in through the front doors. No more scaling fences and climbing in through windows."

"You're ruining everything," the prince said.

Clearly he didn't want me visiting, and I thought we were friends. "I'm sorry. I wouldn't go in there if Rocket's information weren't so invaluable."

"You misunderstand his annoyance," Donovan said.

"Our annoyance." Mafioso seemed just as perturbed.

Donovan grinned. "They don't want you to have a key, because watching you get on your stomach and crawl through that itty-bitty window is one of our favorite pastimes." He held up a gloved thumb and index finger to emphasize the small size of the opening.

The prince smiled. "I especially like it when the window closes about halfway in and you get your ass stuck."

He high-fived Mafioso.

"I'm completely appalled," I said, completely appalled. "You guys have known all this time? You watch me?"

"Mostly just your ass," the prince said with a wink. Charmer.

"What happened, sweetheart?"

I glanced back at Donovan, at the sympathetic gaze in his eyes, and it all came rushing back with hurricane force. A lump swelled in my throat, and my eyes blurred instantly with wetness. "I got one of my best friends killed." A telling moisture pushed past my lashes as I studied Donovan. At least with a biker, you knew where you stood, which was usually ten feet away from his bike. There were no illusions that you would come first. No promises or guarantees or sweet nothings whispered in your ear.

My breath hitched in my chest, and he stepped within my reach.

So reach, I did.

I wound my fingers into his shirt and pulled him closer. I should have been thinking about how bad I looked. My face had nearly been sliced off, but all I wanted was the taste of him on my tongue. I eased over and pressed my mouth to his. He leaned forward and let me kiss him. The kiss was gentle and patient and a little hungry.

I led my hand inside his jacket and pulled him closer. He deepened the kiss, just barely, trying desperately not to hurt me.

"Is this for me, Dutch?" Reyes growled—so close, I could feel the heat layer over me like a warmed blanket. I offered him a mental *fuck you,* and he disappeared. But the pain that exuded out of him just before he did so stole my breath and I gasped.

Donovan broke the kiss instantly.

When I raised my lashes, the prince had his hand on Donovan's shoulder, as if coaxing him to stop. Donovan nodded in acknowledgment, and the prince dropped his hand.

"Sweetheart," Donovan said, appreciation glittering in his eyes, "I don't know where to touch you without hurting you, and the last thing you need right now is to be hurt." He brushed his fingertips along my good cheek. "But I'd be a liar if I said I wasn't tempted beyond comprehension."

"I'm sorry. I shouldn't have done that," I said, suddenly embarrassed. The little girl sat wide eyed, the NC-17 rating way above her pay grade. I was seriously going to have to get rid of her.

With the help of his two bodyguards, Donovan lifted me into his arms.

"What are your names?" I asked Mafioso and the prince as they carried me to my bed, which made no sense, since all my bedding was on the sofa. But they threw a couple of blankets down, moved my supplies to my nightstand, and called it good.

The prince spoke up first. "I'm Eric," he said, offering another wink. "And the ape at your feet is Michael."

"Ape, huh?" Michael asked. "That's the best you can do?"

I had to admit, Michael exuded a Brando-esque kind of coolness that I'd have bet my sutures made him quite the chick magnet.

Prince Eric laughed. "I'm working with a limited education here."

"It shows."

Once they had me all tucked in and Eric and Michael had stepped out of the room, Donovan kneeled down beside me. "I'm Donovan."

I smiled even though it hurt. "I know."

"I like you."

I placed a hand on my chest as though I were insulted. "Last I heard, you were fucking in love with me."

"Yeah, well, that's how rumors get started," he said with a sheepish shrug. "Nobody wants a fool in love for a leader. There'll be rebellion, chaos, matching biker-gang shirts." He kissed the back of my hand. "Get some rest."

He'd barely left before the pain set in again, the emptiness and betrayal swirling inside me. Reyes could bite my ass. My dad could bite my ass. Uncle Bob could . . . Well, no, I still liked Uncle Bob. I was in serious wallow mode when my lids drifted shut again. Depression really did make a person want to sleep all the time. Who knew?

27

Sorry about what happens later.
—T-SHIRT

Right in the middle of an unsettling scene where a girl with an eye patch kept trying to convince me I owed her twelve dollars for picking up my teeth off the sidewalk and putting them in a Dixie cup, I heard another voice. One so familiar, so close to my heart, it swelled in response.

"You gonna sleep all day?"

I rushed toward consciousness and threw an arm over my eyes in protest. Maybe this time it would work. Maybe this time it would block out reality and I wouldn't have to face it, 'cause reality was sucking of late.

"I'll take that as a yes."

After a long exhalation, I opened my eyes. Or, well, one eye. One was superglued shut again. I started to rub it, but I forgot and tried to use my left arm. A scalding pain shot up the underside of it. Clearly, pain meds were overrated. But my fingers were moving better. Grim reaperism definitely had its advantages.

I took a deep breath, clamped my teeth together, and focused through my bedroom doorway on the man sitting on my snack bar just as I had been earlier. He was wearing the same shirt from several days before, loosely fitted jeans, and work boots. With one leg up, an arm resting on the knee, he sat studying me, his silvery eyes taking me in, and he seemed almost disturbed by what he saw.

"Is it my new look?" I asked him when he said nothing.

"You weren't kidding," he said. "You're bright, like a beacon, shimmering and warm. You're like the flame that draws the moth."

A lump swelled in my chest as he spoke. I had taken everything from him. He had so much more to do, so much life left to live. "I'm so sorry, Garrett," I said, unable to stop the sting of my eyes. This crying bit was becoming a tad ridiculous, but I couldn't stop it. Any more than I could stop the rains from heaven.

I covered my eyes with a hand and tried to get a grip on my emotions.

"Charles, how on earth is this your fault? I was doing my job."

"And your job was me." I looked back at him. "I did this. I got you killed."

"You didn't get me killed. And I should have ducked."

A small chuckle escaped. Oddly enough, there'd been two people in that room who could've avoided a gunshot wound by ducking. Garrett was not one of them. "You should have called for backup. I figured the military would have prepared you better."

"They should've prepared me better for the likes of you." His turned away from me. "I have to tell you, now that I can actually see Mr. Wong, he freaks me out even more."

"And I love knowing that more than you can possibly imagine. It's too bad you have to go through eternity needing a shave."

He smiled. "Actually, I don't. But it is too bad you have to go through life with those chicken drumsticks." He gestured toward my legs.

I gasped, seriously appalled. "I beg your pardon. These are great legs." I tried to lift my good one, but doing so hurt the bad one. Maybe it was jealous of the attention its sibling was getting. "These legs are legendary. Just ask the chess team from high school. And whatever you do, do not let the words *chess team* fool you."

Then a realization dawned, and I fixed an astonished gaze on Garrett.

"I was indirectly responsible for your death. You're my guardian. The one Sister Mary Elizabeth told me about. This is fantastic. I so didn't want a dog killer as a guardian, or a big fat liar."

He let a lazy smile slide across his face. "I'm not your guardian."

"Are you sure?"

"Pretty darned."

"Damn it. How many people am I going to be indirectly responsible for killing this week?"

"I don't know, but I'm not one of them."

My phone chose that moment to ring and I chose that moment to ignore it. It was Cookie's ringtone. She'd understand.

"You might want to get that," Garrett said.

After casting him a look of suspicion, I reached over and grabbed the phone off my nightstand. How could such a simple act be so painful? "That really hurt," I said into the phone.

"Charley, Charley, oh, my god."

"I've heard that from men in the past, but I had no idea you felt that way about me."

"He's back. They brought him back."

"Oh, good. I was worried. Who are we talking about?"

"I'm at the hospital. Garrett. The resuscitated him. He died on the table, but they brought him back and no one told us. They've been in surgery."

I bolted upright, steeled myself against the pain as I eased back down, then glanced over at Garrett. He was grinning. "But, he's here."

"Exactly, he's here. He's not gone. Oh, my gosh, the doctor's coming. I'll call you right back."

I closed my phone and stared wide-eyed at Garrett.

His grin widened.

"I don't— How are you—? How is this—?"

He pointed up and shrugged. "They said it wasn't my time."

"They? You mean—?" I stopped to catch my breath, unable to believe it. Things hadn't really been going my way lately. Surely there was a catch. No. This was a good thing. I couldn't question it. My eyes landed on him. "Wait, if you're alive, how are you here?"

"This is your world, Charles, I just live in it."

"Would you come in here so we don't have to yell across my apartment?"

"First, your apartment is the size of one of those balls that hamsters roll around in."

"Is not."

"Second, I can't. Your guardian takes her job very seriously."

"What? Where?" I glanced around. "He's a she?"

After trying unsuccessfully to sit up again, I managed to scoot a couple of inches and brace myself against the headboard, when a low rumble filled the room. A coolness settled in the air, causing my breath to fog, and I scanned the room from corner to corner but saw nothing. I held out my hand, palm up, in an invitation to whoever was suddenly haunting me, and a loud, guttural bark exploded beside me, shook the walls, and echoed around the room. My bed dipped as Artemis jumped on.

"Artemis!" I said, pulling her into a hug. She wanted to play but seemed to sense my inability to do so. She lay beside me and nudged me with her nose, her stubby tail wagging a mile a minute.

"I tried to come into the room earlier," Garrett said. "Just a warning, she goes for the jugular."

"Artemis? A dog? Oh, my god, that's right. I was indirectly responsible for her death when we wrestled behind the asylum. I just never imagined a dog. I've never seen a dog left behind. That movie wasn't kidding when it said all dogs go to heaven." I scratched her ears and hugged her to me. Suddenly the pain seemed minor. "I wonder if I should tell Donovan."

"Is that your new boyfriend?"

Oh, geez, not that crap again. "Look, I get enough of that from Reyes about you."

"He thinks I'm your boyfriend?"

"That's what he calls you."

He frowned. "So am I?"

"A pain in the ass?"

"You're one to talk. We ever gonna hit it?"

"Ew. Not if you were the last skiptracer in the known universe."

"What the fuck?" he asked, all offended-like. "You almost killed me."

"*Almost* being the operative word."

"And you practically raped that biker guy, which, by the way, what the fuck was that about? Scraping the bottom of the barrel there, Charles."

"And that barrel is hot." I looked down at Artemis. "And Donovan's genuine. He would sell me to the highest bidder for a carburetor, and we both know it. So when it happens, when he lies and cheats and uses me as bait, I won't be totally blindsided like I am when all the other men in my life lie and cheat and use me as bait. It's called self-preservation."

"It's called self-loathing."

"Whatever," I said. Then I remembered we had unfinished business. "You never finished your list."

"Oh, yeah." He leaned his head back against the wall and asked, "Where was I?"

"You're asking me? I wasn't really paying attention."

"Okay, let me think." He counted off with his fingers. "The top five things you never want to say to a grim reaper: I'm dead tired. You're killing me. I'm dying to try that. This relationship will be the death of me."

"So, we're at number one," I said, trying not to laugh.

He grinned and fixed a steady gaze on me. "The number one thing you don't want to say to the grim reaper is . . . Are you ready?"

"Would you just say it?"

"You're going to love this."

"Swopes."

"Till death do us part."

I stilled, reality slapping across my face like a physical blow, thanking god it didn't come to that.

"I thought you'd like that," he said, his mannerisms jovial, "you being almost indirectly responsible for my death and all."

"I thought you said I wasn't almost indirectly responsible for your death."

"I lied."

"See, blindside."

"I'm planning on cheating later, too. Possibly using you as bait." He smiled and locked his arms behind his head, seeming to bask in all the possibilities.

"You know, I feel a lot better about almost being indirectly responsible for your death."

"I'm so glad. Who's the dead chick?"

I looked over at Wednesday as she stood beside my bed. She had completely changed with the entrance of Artemis. She still held the knife as though her life depended upon it, but she smiled and ran her hand down the Rottweiler's sleek back before looking up at me. Right at me. Like into my eyes. It caught me off guard, as did her crossing. Before I could even ask for a name, she stepped forward and crossed through me.

"Wow," I heard Garrett say, but I'd closed my eyes and riffled through her memories for information. Her name was Mary. She died when she was six of the fever. She had no idea what year it was, but from the clothes and décor of her memories, I guessed it to be somewhere in the very late 1800s. She'd wanted a pony for her birthday, but her family couldn't afford one. Instead, her father made her a doll and she threw it in the river behind her house in anger. Regretting it, she instantly jumped into the icy water to retrieve it and died three days later as a result.

Her family had tucked the doll in her coffin with her, never knowing what she'd done. But when she heard the angels talking about me, she exchanged the doll for a knife and decided to be my guardian until the real one showed up. I didn't have the heart to tell her she wasn't very good. After all, it's the thought that counts.

"That was the most amazing thing I've ever seen," Garrett said, his face a picture of awe when I refocused on him. "It was like a thousand sparklers followed by a sunburst. Absolutely beautiful."

I dragged in a deep, cleansing breath then planted my face in Artemis's neck and said, "Shouldn't you be getting back to your body?" When he didn't answer, I looked up at him.

He was watching me, gauging my emotions. "Is that what you want?"

"It's where you belong."

His head tilted and he was at my doorway before I could blink. "You need to figure out what you're capable of."

I frowned. "That's getting really old."

"I heard Farrow. He wants you to figure that shit out because of some war. I thought he was exaggerating. I've heard things, and I was wrong."

"I'm working on it," I said, getting tired. I wanted nothing more than to bury myself against Artemis and sleep.

"Hon, if this war is half as bad as Farrow thinks it will be, you really need to figure these things out."

Great. Another Riddler. Just what I needed. "So, what do you know about it?"

"I know that they're coming. And Charles—" He planted a warning gaze on me. "—they're mad."

Before I could ask for a little elaboration, he disappeared into thin air. Hopefully he'd stay in his body this time.

I scooted closer to Artemis. The coolness wafting off her felt good. She wagged her little tail and burrowed her nose under my neck. I glanced one last time at the door where Garrett had been before I let sleep overtake me.

Men.

Turn the page for a sneak peek at
Darynda Jones's new novel

Fourth Grave Beneath My Feet

Available November 2012

1

There are only two things in life that are certain.
Guess which one I am.
—CHARLEY DAVIDSON, GRIM REAPER

I sat watching the Buy from Home Channel with my dead aunt Lillian and wondered what my life would've been like had I not just eaten an entire carton of Ben & Jerry's Chocolate Therapy with a mocha latte chaser. Probably about the same, but it was something to think about.

A mid-morning sun filtered through the blinds, cutting hard streaks of light across my body and casting me in an ultra-cool film-noir glow. Since my life had definitely taken a turn toward the dark side, film noir fit. It would have fit even better if I weren't wearing *Star Wars* pajama bottoms and a sparkly tank top that said EARTH GIRLS ARE EASY. But I just didn't have the energy that morning to change into something less inappropriate. I'd been having lethargy issues for a few weeks now. Ever since a man named Earl tortured me. It sucked. The torture. Not his name.

My name, on the other hand, was Charlotte Davidson, but most people called me Charley.

"Can I talk to you, pumpkin cheeks?"

Or pumpkin cheeks, one of the many pet names involving the fall fruit that Aunt Lillian insisted on calling me. Aunt Lil had died some time in the sixties, and I could see her because I'd been born the grim reaper, which basically meant three things. One, I could interact with dead people—those departed who didn't cross over when they died—and usually did on a daily basis. Two, I was super-duper bright to those in the spiritual realm, and the aforementioned dead people could see me from anywhere in the world. When they were ready to cross, they could cross through me. Which brought me to three: I was a portal between the earthly plane and what many refer to as heaven.

There was a tad more to it than that—including things I had yet to learn myself—but that was the basic gist of my day job. The one I didn't actually get paid to do. I was also a PI, but that wasn't really paying lately either.

I rolled my head along the back of the sofa toward Aunt Lil, who was actually more like a great, great aunt on my father's side. A thin elderly woman with soft gray eyes and pale blue hair, she was wearing her usual attire as dead people rarely changed clothes: a floral muumuu and love beads, a testament to her demise in the sixties. She also had a loving smile that sometimes tilted a bit south of kilter. But that only made me adore her all the more. I had a soft spot for crazy people. I wasn't sure how the muumuu came into play with her being so tiny and all—she looked like a pole with a collapsed tent gathered about her fragile hips—but who was I to judge?

"You can absolutely talk to me, Aunt Lil." I tried to straighten, but couldn't get past the realization that movement of any kind would take effort. I'd been sitting on one sofa or another for two months, recovering from the torture thing. Then I remembered that the cookware I'd been waiting for all morning was up next. Surely Aunt Lil would understand. Before she could say anything, I raised a finger to put her in pause mode. "But can our talk wait until the stone-coated cookware segment is over? I've been eyeing this cookware for a while now. And it's coated. With stone."

"You don't cook."

She had a point. "So what's up?" I propped my bunny-slippered feet on the cluttered coffee table and crossed my legs at the ankles.

"I'm not sure how to tell you this." Her breath hitched and she bowed her blue head.

I straightened in alarm despite the expended energy it took. "Aunt Lil?"

She tucked her chin in sadness. "I-I think I'm dead."

I blinked. Stared at her a moment. Then blinked again.

"I know." She sniffled into the massive sleeve of her muumuu, and the love beads shifted soundlessly with the movement. Inanimate objects in death carried an eerie silence. Like mimes. Or that scream Al Pacino made in *The Godfather: Part III* when his daughter died on those steps. "I know, I know." She patted my shoulder in consolation. "It's a lot to absorb."

Aunt Lillian had been dead since long before I was born, but I had never been sure if she knew. Many departed didn't. Because of this doubt, I'd never mentioned it. For years, I'd let her make me invisible coffee in the mornings or cook me invisible eggs, then she'd go off on another adventure. Aunt Lil was still sowing her wild oats. A world traveler, that one. And she rarely stayed in one place very long. Which was good. Otherwise I'd never get real coffee in the mornings. Or the twelve other times during the day I needed a java fix. If she were around more often, I'd go through caffeine withdrawal on a regular basis. And get really bad headaches.

But maybe now that she knew, I could explain the whole coffee thing.

I was curious enough about her death to ask her, "Do you know how you died? What happened?"

According to my family, she'd died in a hippie commune in Madrid at the height of the flower power revolution. Before that, she really had been a world traveler, spending her summers in South America and Europe and her winters in Africa and Australia. And she'd continued that tradition even after her death, traveling far and wide. Passport no longer needed. But no one could really tell me how she died exactly. Or what she did for a living. How she could afford to do all that traveling when she was alive?

I knew she'd been married for a while, but my family didn't know much about her husband. My uncle thought he might've been an oil tycoon from Texas, but the family had lost contact and nobody knew for certain.

"I'm just not sure," she said, shaking her head. "I remember we were sitting around a campfire singing songs and dropping acid—"

I used every ounce of strength I had to keep the horror I felt from manifesting in my expression.

"—and Bernie asked me what was wrong, but since Bernie had just done a hit of acid himself, I didn't take him seriously."

I could understand that.

She looked up at me, her eyes watering with sorrow. "Maybe I should have listened."

I put an arm around her slight shoulders. "I'm so sorry, Aunt Lil."

"I know, pumpkin head." She patted my cheek, her hand cool in the absence of flesh and blood. She smiled that lopsided smile, and I suddenly wondered if she'd perhaps dropped one hit of acid too many. "I remember the day you were born."

I blinked in surprise. "Really? You were there?"

"I was. I'm so sorry about your mother."

A surprisingly sharp pang of regret cut off my oxygen supply. I wasn't expecting it and it took me a moment to shake it off. After recovering, I said, "I'm sorry, too." The memory of my mother's passing right after I'd been born was not my favorite. And I remembered it so clearly, so precisely. The moment she parted from her physical body, a pop like a rubber band snapping into place ricocheted through my body, and I knew our connection had been severed. I loved her so much.

"You were so special even then," Aunt Lil said, shaking her head with the memory. "But now that you know I'm a goner, I have to ask, why in tarnation are you so bright?"

Crap. I couldn't tell her the truth, that I was the grim reaper and the floodlights came with the gig. It just sounded so bad when I said it out loud. I decided to deflect. "Well, that's kind of a long story, Aunt Lil, but if you want, you can pass through me. You can cross to the other side and be with your family." I lowered my head, hoping she wouldn't take me up on my offer. I liked having her around, as selfish as that made me.

"What?" She snapped to attention and slapped a knee. "And miss all the crap you get yourself into? Never." After a disturbing cackle that brought to mind the last horror movie I'd seen, she turned back to the TV. "Now, what's so groovy about this cookware?"

I settled in next to her and we watched a whole segment on pans that could take all kinds of abuse, including a bevy of rocks sliding around the nonstick bottom, but since people didn't actually cook rocks, I wasn't sure what the point was. Still, the pans were pretty. And I could make low monthly payments. I totally needed them.

I was on the phone with a healthy-sounding customer service representative named Herman when Cookie walked in. She did that a lot. Walked in. Like she owned the place. Of course, I was in her apartment. Mine was cluttered and depressing, so I'd resorted to loitering in hers.

Cookie was a large woman with black hair spiked in every direction and no sense of fashion whatsoever, if the yellow ensemble she was wearing was any indication. She was also my best friend and receptionist when we had work.

I waved to her then spoke into the phone. "Declined? What do you mean declined? I have at least twelve dollars left on that puppy and you said I could make low monthly payments."

Cookie bent over the sofa, grabbed the phone, and pushed the end-call button while completely ignoring the indignant expression I was throwing at her.

"It's not so much declined," she said, handing the phone back to me, "as canceled. I've put a stop to any new charges on your Home Shopaholic store card."

"What?" I thought about acting all flustered and bent out of shape, but I was out of shape enough without purposely adding to the condition. In reality, I was a little in awe of her. "You can do that?"

She took hold of my wrist and hefted me off her sofa. "I can do that," she said as she nudged me toward the door.

"How?"

"Simple. I called and pretended to be you."

"And they fell for it?" Now I was officially appalled. "Who did you talk to? Did you talk to Herman, because he sounds super cute. Wait." I screeched to a halt before her. "Are you kicking me out of your apartment?"

"Not so much kicking you out as putting my foot down. It's time."

"Time?" I asked a little hesitantly.

"Time."

Well, crap. This day was going to suck, I could already tell. "Love the yellow," I said, becoming petty as she herded me out of her apartment and into mine. "You don't look like a giant banana at all. And why did you cancel my favorite shopping channel in-store credit card? I only have three."

"And they've all been canceled. I have to make sure I get paid every week. I've also funneled all of your remaining funds out of your bank account and into a secret account in the Cayman Islands."

"You can funnel money?"

"Apparently."

"Isn't that like embezzling?"

"It's exactly like embezzling." After practically shoving me over my threshold, she closed the door behind us and pointed. "I want you to take a look at all this stuff."

Admittedly, my apartment was a mess, but I still didn't know what that had to do with my card. That card was a tool. In the right hands—like, say, mine—it could make dreams come true. I looked around at all the boxes of super cool stuff I'd ordered. Everything from magical scrubbing sponges for the everyday housewife to two-way radios for when the apocalypse hit and cell phones became obsolete. A wall of boxes cut my apartment in half. Since my apartment was about the size of a LEGO, the half that was left was like a broken LEGO. A disfigured one that didn't survive the invasion of little LEGO space aliens.

And there were more boxes behind the walls of boxes we could actually see. I'd completely lost Mr. Wong, the dead guy who perpetually hovered in a corner of my living room, his back to the world. Never moving. Never speaking. And now he was lost to the ecology of commerce. Poor guy. His life couldn't have been exciting.

Of course, it didn't help that I'd also moved out of my offices and brought all of my files and office equipment to my apartment. It was a necessary move, as my dad had betrayed me in the worst way possible and my offices had been above his bar. Sadly, the bar was only about fifty feet north of my apartment building, so I would have to avoid him when coming and going from my new work digs, but since I hadn't actually left the apartment building in over two months, that part hadn't been difficult. The last time I left was to clear out my offices, and I'd made sure he was out of town when I did so.

I surveyed all the boxes and decided to turn the tables on Cookie. To play the victim. To blame the whole thing on her. I pointed to the boxes and gaped at her. "Who the hell left me unsupervised? This has to be your fault."

"Nice try," she said, completely unmoved. "We are going to sort through all of this stuff and send back everything except what you'll actually use. Which is not a lot. Again, I would like to continue collecting a paycheck if that's not too much to ask."

"Do you take American Express?"

"Oh, I canceled that, too."

I gasped, pretending to be appalled. She led me to my own sofa, took boxes off it, piled them on top of other boxes, then sank down beside me. Her eyes shimmered with warmth and understanding, and I became instantly uncomfortable. "Are we going to have the talk again?"

"I'm afraid so."

"Cook"—I tried to rise and storm off, but she put a hand on my shoulder to stop me—"I'm not sure how else to say that I'm fine."

She looked down at Margaret.

"What?" I asked, a defensive edge coming into my voice. "Lots of PIs wear guns."

"With their pajamas?"

I snorted. "Yes. Especially if they're *Star Wars* pajamas and your gun just happens to resemble a blaster."

Margaret was my new best friend. And she'd never funneled money out of my bank account like some *other* best friends who shall not be named.

"Charley, all I'm asking is that you talk to your sister."

"I talk to her every day." I crossed my arms. Suddenly everyone was insisting that I seek counseling when I was fine. So what if I didn't want to step out of my apartment building? Lots of people liked to stay in. For months at a time.

"Yes, she calls and tries to talk to you about what happened, about how you're doing, but you shut her down."

"I don't shut her down. I just change the subject."

Cookie got up and made us both a cup of coffee. Her coffee was so much better than Aunt Lil's. I took a sip as she sat next to me again.

"Gemma thinks that maybe you need a hobby." She looked around at the boxes. "A healthy hobby. Like Pilates. Or alligator wrestling."

"I know." I leaned back and threw an arm over my eyes. "I thought about writing my memoirs, but I can't figure out how to put seventies porn music into prose."

"See," she said, elbowing me. "Writing. That's a great start. You could try poetry." She stood and rummaged through my box-covered desk. "Here," she said, tossing some paper at me. "Write me a poem about how your day is going and I'll get started on these boxes."

I put the coffee cup aside and sat up. "For real? Couldn't I just write a poem about my ultimate world domination or the ecstasy of eating guacamole?"

She peered at me from behind one of my more impressive walls. "You bought two electric pressure cookers? Two?"

"They were on sale."

"Charley," she said, her tone admonishing. "Wait." She dipped down then popped back up. "These are awesome." I knew it. "Can I have one?"

"Abso-freaking-lutely. I'll just take it out of your pay."

This could work. I could pay her through my Buy from Home purchases, though that might not help her keep her lights on or continue to have running water. But she'd be happy, and wasn't happiness the most important thing in life?

"You do realize that to use a lot of this stuff, you have to actually go to the grocery store."

Her words shoved me deeper into the pit of despair often referred to as buyer's regret. "Isn't that what Macho Taco express delivery is for?"

"You'll still have to buy other food."

"I hate going to the grocery store."

"And cook."

"Fine," I said, letting a defeated breath slip through my lips. I had a fantastic flair for the dramatics when needed. "Send it all back."

"Even the Jackie Kennedy commemorative bracelet?"

"Do I have to cook it?"

"Nope."

"Then it stays." I lifted my wrist and twirled the bracelet. "Look how sparkly it is."

"And it goes so well with Margaret."

"Totally."

"Pumpkin butt."

I looked up from my Jackie Kennedy commemorative bracelet toward Aunt Lil. Now that she knew she was dead, I would never have to go through that surge of panic at the prospect of her insisting on cooking for me for two weeks straight. I almost starved to death once. "Do you think this is too much?"

"Jackie goes with anything, dear. But I wanted to talk to you about Cookie."

I looked at the boxes and shook my head in disappointment. "What has she done now?"

Aunt Lil sank down beside me and patted my arm. "I think she should know the truth."

"About Jackie Kennedy?"

"About me."

"Oh, right."

"What in the world does this monstrous machine do?" Cookie asked from somewhere near the kitchen. A box appeared out of nowhere, hovering unsteadily over a mountain of other boxes.

I smiled in excitement. "You know how sometimes we order coffee and it comes with that incredible foam on top?"

"Yeah."

"Well, that machine does the magic foam trick."

Her dark head popped up. "No."

"Yes."

She looked at the box lovingly. "Okay, we can keep this. I'll just have to carve some time out of my schedule to read the instructions."

"Don't you think she should know?"

I nodded at Aunt Lil. She had a point. Or she would have if Cookie didn't already know. "Cook, can you come here a sec?"

"Okay, but I'm working out a system. It's in my head. If I lose it on the way over, I won't be held accountable."

"I can't make any promises."

She sauntered over shaking another box at me, a disturbing kind of joy in her eyes. "Do you know how long I've wanted a salad spinner?"

"People actually want those?"

"You don't?"

"I think that was one of those four A.M. purchases where I'd lost all sense of reality. I don't even know why anyone would want to spin a salad."

"Well, I do."

"Okay, so, I have some bad news."

She sat in a chair that catty-cornered the sofa, a wary expression on her face. "You got bad news since you've been sitting here?"

"Kind of." I tilted my head discreetly to my side, indicating a *presence*.

Cookie frowned.

I did it again.

She shrugged in confusion.

With a sigh, I said, "I have news about Aunt Lillian."

"Oh. Oh!" She looked around and questioned me with a quirk of her brows.

I gave a quick shake of my head. Normally, Cookie would play along, pretending she could see Aunt Lil as well, but with Aunt Lil's recent change in awareness, I didn't think that would be appropriate. I put a hand on hers and said, "Aunt Lil has passed away."

Cookie frowned.

"She's gone."

She shrugged in confusion. Again.

"I knew she'd take it hard," Aunt Lil said by my side. She sniffled into her sleeve again.

I wanted so badly to roll my eyes at Cookie. She was not getting my hints. I'd have to try harder. "But you know how I can *see the departed*?"

A dawning emerged on Cook's face as she realized Aunt Lil had caught on at long last.

I patted her hand. Really hard. "She's here with us now, just not as you will remember her."

"You mean—"

"Yes," I said, interrupting before she could give anything away. "She has passed."

Cookie finally caught on. She put her hand over her mouth. A tiny squeak slipped through her fingers. "Not Aunt Lil." She doubled over and let sobs wrack her shoulders.

Subtle.

"I didn't think she'd take it this hard," Aunt Lil said.

"Neither did I." I looked on in horror as Cookie acted out that scene from *The Godfather.* It was even more eerie from this close proximity. "It's okay," I said, patting her head. Really hard. She glared through her fingers. "Aunt Lil is with us incorporeally. She sends her love."

"Oh, yes," Aunt Lil said with a delirious nod. "Send her my love."

"Aunt Lil," Cookie said, straightening and looking beside me. Only on the wrong side.

I nodded in Aunt Lil's direction again, and Cookie corrected her line of sight.

"Aunt Lil, I'm so sorry. We'll miss you so much."

"Aw, isn't she the sweetest thing? I always liked her."

With a smile, I took Aunt Lil's hand into mine. "I always liked her, too."

I decided a shower was not out of the question and hopped in as Cookie continued taking inventory and Aunt Lil decided to see what Africa looked like from her "new" perspective. I wondered if she'd ever figure out how long she'd been dead. I certainly wasn't going to tell her.

After drying my hair and pulling it into something that resembled a ponytail, I dressed in jeans and a white pullover with a zippered collar, then inspected myself in the mirror. No idea why. I'd only change back into my pajamas in a couple of hours anyway. Why did I get dressed? Why did I bother? Why did I shower for that matter?

The nasty scar on my cheek was almost gone. On anyone else, it would have remained as a constant reminder of events better left forgotten. But being the grim reaper had its benefits. Namely, quick healing and minimal scarring. Nary a shred of visible evidence to support the reasoning behind my sudden case of mild agoraphobia. I was so stupid.

I took the lotion I was rubbing into my hands and smeared it across my mirror image. White streaks distorted my face. A definite improvement.

As I did every morning, I strolled to the window to see if my traitorous father was at work yet. He seemed to be coming in later and later. Not that I cared. Any man who would have his own daughter arrested while she lay dying in a hospital bed after being tortured almost to death didn't deserve my concern. I was just curious, and curious was way on the other side of concern. But instead of seeing his tan SUV, I caught sight of one Mr. Reyes Farrow, and my breath stilled in my chest. He was leaning against the back of Dad's bar, arms folded at his chest, one booted foot leveraged against the building.

And he was out.

I knew he would be, but I had yet to see him. He'd been in prison for ten years for a crime he didn't commit. The cops figured that out when the guy he supposedly killed tied me up and tortured me. I was glad he'd been freed, but to get there, Reyes'd used me as bait, so we were once again at an impasse. I was mad at him for using me as bait. He was mad at me for being mad at him for using me as bait. Our relationship seemed to hinge on these impasses, but that's what I got for falling in lust with the son of Satan. If only he weren't so deliciously and dangerously hot. I had such a thing for bad boys.

And this particular bad boy had been dipped in a lake of beauty when he was born. His arms corded with muscles across a wide chest. His dark hair was forever in need of a trim. It curled at his neck and tumbled over his forehead. And I could have sworn I could see his thick lashes fan across his cheeks from where I stood.

After a moment, he looked up. His angry gaze locked on to mine and it took every ounce of strength to tear mine away from him and jerk the curtains shut. What the hell was he doing out there? And why was he so angry? It was my turn to be angry. He had no reason to be. And I would have told him that very thing if I felt like leaving my apartment. But it was cozy inside, and I couldn't imagine leaving for any reason, let alone just to get in a fight with the son of evil incarnate.